SOME
MEN
JUST
NEED
KILLING

SOME
MEN
JUST
NEED
KILLING

ROD BEEMER

PRAIRIE STORM
PUBLISHING
MINNEAPOLIS · KANSAS

Prairie Storm Publishing
Minneapolis, Kansas
prairiestormpublishing.com

1.1.1

Produced in the United States of America

ISBN-13: 978-0-9818617-3-9

Designed by Chuck Beemer

— for —
My sons Chuck, Nathan, and David

Prologue

IN THE YEAR OF OUR LORD 1861 the Battle of Fort Sumter lured a defiant South and a resolute North deep into the valley of the shadow of death. This shadow became reality for more than six hundred thousand mortals who ventured into that valley.

Four long years later at Appomattox a war-weary people struggled to grope their way out of that valley and to stand at last on the sun-swept plains of peace.

But for some souls that valley and its shadows stretched on ahead, seemingly forever. The way of escape unclear, the path uncertain, and the memories of this Armageddon an unwelcome, haunting companion.

Listen.

"The contest touches everything and leaves nothing as it found it, great right, great interests, great systems of habit and of thought disappear during its progress. It leaves us a different people in everything."
— NEW YORK TIMES editorial

"He is at rest and we who are left are the ones to suffer."
— GENERAL ROBERT E. LEE at the death of A.P. Hill

The war's shadow was especially ominous and the valley endless for those who were keepers of the sick, the wounded, and the dying. Medicine had scarcely emerged from the dark ages; sanitation was neglected and causes of disease greatly misunderstood. Doctors, nurses, and facilities proved pitifully inadequate.

Amputations ruled when medical knowledge failed. An arm or leg severed with a surgeon's knife and saw, in as little as forty seconds and all too often without the comfort of anesthesia.

Listen.

"I saw 200 six-mule army wagons in a line, ranged down the street to headquarters, and reaching so far out on the Wilderness Road that I never found the end of it; every wagon crowded with wounded men, stopped, standing in the rain and mud, wrenched back and forth by the restless, hungry animals all night – The dark spot in the mud under many a wagon told all too plainly where some poor fellow's life had dripped out in those dreadful hours."

— CLARA BARTON

"This place [hospital] *seems to have got the better of me. I have bad nights and bad days, too. Some of the spells are pretty bad . . . The doctors have told me for a fortnight I must leave. I think I shall come home for a short time."*

— WALT WHITMAN

"Oh! It is awful, it does not seem as though I could take a knife in my hand to-day, yet there are a hundred cases of amputation waiting for me. Poor fellows come and beg almost on their knees for the first chance to have an arm taken off. It is a scene of horror such as I never saw. God forbid that I should see another. They look to me for help, and I have to turn away heartsick at my want of ability to relieve their sufferings."

— SURGEON GEORGE STEVENS

"I have seen too much. Two questions haunt me day and night, ever begging an answer: Who am I now, and how am I to live?"

— DR. BENJAMIN FREDRICK KELLEY

Over the sound of weeping and mourning, the nation heard once again the sound of marching masses, the rumble of wagons, and occasionally the clash of arms.

Moving not to war, but west.

Manifest destiny and, perhaps, peace; leave the old and start anew.

Ah, was this the answer? The path out of that dreadful valley?

Ben Kelley gambled it was.

Listen.

PART I

— 1 —

Death and destruction were not new to Ben Kelley, but this was different. This was close to hearth and heart.

"Damn, Darkie, everything's gone."

Ben spoke to the black he was riding as he reined in at the edge of the timber along Kinchafoonee Creek. He looked toward the knoll above a bend in the creek where Welsh Hall once stood proud and elegant. The mansion had been built by planter Daniel Welsh and was home to his wife and family for many happy years before the Civil War destroyed most of his family and all of his fortune. Daniel's wife had died from some unknown malady, and three of his sons were killed in the war and one son was still missing. The youngest son, Alec, survived the war.

The Welsh family were neighbors to the Kelleys and the families intermingled business and pleasure as far back as Ben could remember. He had played and worked with the Welsh boys from childhood to adulthood. Then, about a year before the war, it finally registered on Ben's mind that they had a sister named Adeline. After that day she wasn't far from his thoughts, and was close by his side whenever possible.

Ben set staring at the desolation and wishing Adeline still had the black mare that was a perfect match to the stallion he was riding now. But, there were no horses, no mules, no cattle – not even a dog visible anywhere.

Before the war, Welsh Hall plantation kept some four hundred of the finest slaves available. As with other large operations, they had accounted for half of the Welshes' considerable fortune. Now they were as gone as the plantation's buildings. Now, where the mansion once stood, a pile of rubble with six blackened chimneys pushing skyward reminded Ben of a dead beetle on its back.

Amidst the scene of destruction Ben recognized a Confederate hospital tent with a fly stretched in front over a stove, table, and other items either salvaged or scrounged. On the right side of the hospital tent stood a large wall tent and on the other side stood what looked to Ben like a csa copy of the Union's Sibley tent. The tents were dirty, stained with Georgia's red soil, and patched where wear had frayed the canvas. Ben guessed they'd been abandoned after a Union rout or perhaps stolen from a captured supply train.

A half mile northeast of the remains of the Big House Ben saw the rows and clusters of dark rubble stretching northeast; the remains of the slave quarters and outbuildings. The cotton and corn fields visible beyond the ruins hadn't been cultivated for years and were choked with stubble and weeds. He also noticed the pink azaleas lining the lane and the colorful flower beds that had once graced the plantation were especially rich this year, Ben thought, and wondered if the earth was trying to apologize for the insanity of war.

Ben spoke to the horse, "Darkie, let's go see Adeline. It's been a long, long time." He turned onto the lane where live oaks arched gracefully over the grand lane that now led only to dirty tents. The stately trees had suffered from bummers, the homeless, and from both armies that used them for firewood, wagon repair, and railroad ties.

Minutes later he drew rein in front of the large tent. "Hello, it's Ben Kelley."

"I've been expecting you," Daniel Welsh answered as he pushed back the tent flap with a double-barreled shotgun and stepped outside.

Now, mere weeks after Appomattox, Daniel had finally made a very difficult decision regarding his only daughter, Adeline. It could help solve the family's desperate situation if he allowed Adeline to marry Ben Kelley. The young Kelley's rumored wealth was immense and would be even greater when his father, William, passed. Daniel wondered if Adeline's love for Ben was great enough to overcome what had happened to him physically and mentally during the war. And, if he could live with a son-in-law that some were saying had turned yellow.

Daniel hated all things Yankee, and his son Alec had taken the hate even further by vowing to shoot on sight any Union soldier or sympathizer. Together, with their hate and hope, the remaining Welshes clung stubbornly to the desolate plantation.

"I've waited a long time for this moment," Ben said as he dismounted, grabbed his cane, and limped toward the tent explaining, "My father has been very ill and the job of keeping him comfortable and alive has delayed my visit to see Adeline."

"Well, you may have to wait a bit longer," the old man said. "Alec, come on out."

Adeline's brother, also carrying a shotgun, stepped outside followed by Adeline and a stranger.

"Hello, Adeline," Ben said as he touched the brim of his hat.

Hello, Ben," she answered. "I must look a fright to you in this old dress but it's the only one that didn't get burned with the house."

"You look as lovely as I remember."

She blushed, "You're very kind."

"Adeline, I do remember the dress from a picnic we had yonder at the river."

Ben continued, "I'd heard about the destruction of Welsh Hall, but it is worse than I'd imagined. I'm sorry about your misfortune. I know it doesn't help, but I can assure you that you're not alone."

Ben turned toward the stranger and offered his hand. "I'm Dr. Ben Kelley from Oak Grove, but I imagine they've already told you who I am."

"They have." He didn't take the offered hand.

"I was with Forrest's Cavalry, and I see you were with an artillery company," Ben said.

Alec nodded toward the young man wearing a butternut frock coat with red cuffs, red collar, and the chevrons of a corporal. "This is Corporal Charles Squires. He was in General Longstreet's artillery. And he's the man that just might marry Adeline."

Ben turned to Adeline. "Is this a joke? You promised before I left that—"

Adeline's father interrupted, "Corporal Squires has asked me for Adeline's hand in marriage. I know Adeline was betrothed to you before the war, but since there has been so much talk about your ability to father a child and perhaps your unwillingness to protect my daughter, unfortunately I've been forced to reconsider the marriage. Adeline, however, has convinced me to give you a chance to prove you're not a Yankee lover or the coward people say you are."

"Obviously you've been listening to rumors, so you should know I fought with Forrest at—"

Mr. Welsh cut him short. "Alec, go fetch that case."

Alec emerged from the tent with a mahogany case, faced Ben, and opened the lid. "I know these," Ben said looking at Mr. Welsh. "I never forget firearms, and my father restored these dueling pistols for someone about five years ago. But what does that have to do with Adeline and me?"

"The pistols are from my family," Corporal Squires answered stepping forward to confront Ben. "I challenge you to a duel for the hand of Adeline."

Ben looked at the man who had just challenged him and saw a soldier's soldier. It was weeks after Lee surrendered at Appomattox, yet Corporal Squires was still wearing an impeccable uniform, blacked boots, and a kepi set squarely on his black hair that ran down into a neatly trimmed beard. Ben recognized in his eyes the familiar, faraway look of someone who'd seen death up close and personal.

"You can't be serious," Ben said as he tried to decide if he'd heard the man correctly. "Has this family not told you anything about me?"

"Yes, your reputation precedes you. You served in Bedford Forrest's Cavalry as a member of his special forces until you were wounded at the Battle of Shiloh. I know about your skill with firearms and about the man you killed in a duel. But, people are also saying you've lost your nerve and nerve is far more important than skill. I'll take my chances, because I never lost my nerve during twenty-seven engagements with the damn Yanks. And, just so you know, I've also defended my honor in a duel."

"And if I kill you," Ben replied, "what will it prove – what has all the death and dying proved?" He was aware that Adeline was watching him intently, almost holding her breath. The wind teased her hair that was as black as a crow's wing and the sun danced on the highlights when she tossed her head. He remembered the fragrance of her when he'd held her close. Pleasant, desirable memories, but now he had to focus.

"Adeline, if he kills me do you want that on your conscience? Or, if I kill him can you live with that? Either way what will it prove?"

"It will prove to this family," Daniel answered, "that Adeline will be properly cared for and protected. You know there are still gangs of bummers roaming the countryside looting, burning, and sometimes ravishing our womenfolk. From the rumors I've heard, it sounds as if you would be opposed to defending my daughter if it meant fighting and killing. And, I see you're unarmed now."

"Adeline, you know I'll always protect you. Don't you?"

"Ben, I never feared anything or anyone when I was with you. But, now I'm uncertain. It's the first time I've seen you unarmed. Grant said officers could keep their sidearms, and I understand that your father escaped the looting and burning so I'm sure there are weapons at Oak Grove. And look at you. You could be mistaken for one of the despicable bummers that burned us out."

"I would die before I'd let anyone harm you, Ben said. I promise I'll protect you."

Adeline walked over and looked up at Ben and then took his hands in hers. "I need more than a promise. How, without fighting, and perhaps killing, would you protect me if the worst should befall us?"

"There is always a way if we just look for it and don't react out of fear or hate."

Adeline gazed into Ben's eyes. "I will gladly honor my pledge to marry you if you prove that you'll protect me." She removed her hands from his and stepped back.

Alec shoved the dueling pistol case toward Ben. "If you weren't a cripple, you'd have the right to select weapons, but we've decided firearms would remove any complaints that it wasn't a fair fight. I'll be Colonel Squires's second, and Father will be yours. You know he'll be fair and honorable. Now, select your piece."

THE WARM SPRING WIND, tired of whispering among the new leaves of the giant trees, began caressing Oak Grove's Big House like a gentle lover. It slid over its peeling white paint to inspect the carved capitals atop four fluted columns. Suddenly the wind paused in its journey to peek into random holes about the front door, then whistling softly, as if surprised, when it found them to be bullet holes.

The stately mansion welcomed the breeze that carried the scent of spring and fresh flowers. The house feared neither the summer storm nor the winter blizzard; it asked only for a bit of careful repair to again be the crowning jewel of Oak Grove plantation. The proud edifice had indulged and rebuffed the seasonal winds for thirty-five years, only lately, grudgingly, letting it slip through the cracked siding and broken windows to sometimes discomfort owner and builder, William Stratford Kelley.

After his wife's passing, William had never again set foot in the opulent master bedroom at the back of the house. Now he lay in a plain iron bed, which he knew would be his deathbed, in a plain room that overlooked the road, the barn, and the slave quarters that sprawled north from the house. He couldn't leave the bed now, but he knew the sun was three hours up in an overcast sky.

It was almost nine o'clock, Ben should have been back by now, he thought, and then prayed: Ben is all I've got left now, God. Don't let anything more happen to that boy until we've made our peace. He prayed again: God, give me the words to show him why his new ways won't work in this world. Lord, it may be noble, even godly, but it just can't be done among mortal men.

He coughed until the tears ran, then rolled over and spit into the brass spittoon. The coughing left him fighting for breath so he lay back, and as old men are wont to do, recalled the days of his youth. He measured all his sixty-eight years of living and had only two regrets. First, his only true love had died so many years ago, and he had never found anyone to take her place. But, he'd see her soon.

Second, he regretted that he wouldn't live to see his only surviving son marry and sire his grandchildren, flesh-and-blood heirs to carry his name. But he could see it in his mind's eye. He was ready. Again he checked the clock; where the hell was his son?

Ben had awakened early that morning, rousted from sleep by a recurring nightmare. It was always the same: exploding melons, dying soldiers, and eternal vultures.

By the age of twelve Ben was a remarkable shot with any firearm he could get into his hands, and his father's hobby of repairing and building firearms provided plenty of them for Ben to shoot. William's favorite show for prospective customers featured Ben galloping along a fence row and shooting melons which had been placed atop each post. It became a spectacle that brought neighbors to watch and cheer as a carefully placed ball exploded each melon. Ben never missed.

Colored servants loaded the weapons and tossed them to Ben as he rode by. It became such a popular event that Oak Grove plantation planted acres of melons. At harvest the slaves would dig pits, line them with hay, and store the melons for winter shooting.

Then one chilly November night following the Battle of Franklin, Tennessee, Dr. Ben Kelley had been treating the wounded for forty hours straight. The plantation's big house was serving as a hospital, but now could not find room for one more wounded soldier so Dr. Kelley was treating the wounded on the front porch. There were four dead CSA officers lying dead near where he was working on a belly wound that would probably prove fatal but he had to try to save the youth who didn't look over fourteen years old. Dr. Kelley cleaned the injury as best he could, sutured it up, and let the lady of the house bandage the boy's wound.

Fatigue finally overpowered the physician and he slumped down against the house wall and fell into a fitful sleep while his mind distorted memories of home and shooting exhibitions into a gruesome nightmare where the melons became the heads and faces of soldiers he'd tried to save but couldn't. In his dream he was riding down the line of fence posts, trying to miss the ghostly faces, but no matter where he aimed, the faces always exploded like ripe melons. Then vultures would glide down and feast on the remains. No matter how carefully he aimed, he never hit the vultures, not once. Horrified and enraged he would fix bayonet and charge the ugly birds that rose into the sky and faded away before he could reach them.

After that night the dream was a frequent visitor and he would awaken exhausted and drenched with sweat as bouts of depression spilled through his first conscious moments following the nightmare's visits. Experience taught him that occupying his mind with physical action helped banish the nightmare for a time.

Now, Ben realized he was home and shoved the memories back in the recesses of his mind. He'd lost a lot of weight since riding off to war, and his clothes hung loose on his six-foot frame. He ran his fingers through his hair and rubbed his jaw. He needed a haircut and a shave but decided it wasn't worth the effort. Before leaving the house Ben walked down the hall to check on his father who was still sleeping so he left a note saying he'd be back by nine o'clock.

— ❧ —

Ben looked down at the brace of dueling pistols, and then up at Squires's forehead where he envisioned a hole left by a .50 caliber ball. He knew he could kill him, but he didn't know if he could live with another death at his own hand.

Alec shoved the pistols toward Ben again, "Here's your chance to prove ya ain't got no yellow streak."

Ben turned, mounted Darkie, and rode back toward Oak Grove. He never looked back and rode with his mind searching for words that would change Adeline's mind if he could just talk with her alone. Maybe the old man had snapped under the pressure of losing everything during the war. Maybe Adeline was refusing to see him just to please her father in the same way he was remaining at Oak Grove just to please his father. Maybe they were jealous because the Kelleys had come through the war so much better than they did. Maybe she'd change her mind once her father died. Or, maybe Adeline really didn't want to see him, maybe she couldn't accept him as a cripple.

Maybe she really believed he had become a coward. Ben's thoughts turned to despair and he explored, as he did from time to time, that perhaps those countless souls who had died on the battlefield were the lucky ones.

The thought of death eventually led Ben's mind to his father's sickness which was terminal unless he could convince him to move. Hell, it may be terminal anyway. How could he encourage his father to move? He'd considered just moving him but, even if his father lived, it would alienate Ben from his only living relative. Maybe it'd be best just to let the sickness run its course and let his father find some peace in a better life.

Darkie knew the way home and they had just left the road beside Kinchafoonee Creek and topped the rise that was once the boundary between Oak Grove and Welsh Hall. Ben was so lost in thought and worry that he didn't notice the approaching riders until the stallion threw up its head and quickened its stride. Instantly Ben knew they were bummers, and instinct made him reach for the cavalry carbine that he'd carried during the war. He got his cane instead. He hesitated a second and then returned the cane to the boot.

His mind flashed back to the little volume that had helped change his life: Sun Tzu's *The Art of War*. What would Sun Tzu do? The ancient Chinese warrior said the ultimate art of war was to defeat the enemy without violence. Ben didn't want to defeat or fight anyone, but he suspected these were violent men.

What happened in the next few minutes proved him right, and when Ben regained consciousness, he was alone; Darkie and the bummers long gone. He sat up, wiped the blood and dirt from the gash on his forehead, found his cane in the grass beside the road, and started walking toward Oak Grove.

He sure had a lot to learn about Sun Tzu's art of war he told himself as he walked. He hadn't subdued his enemy, but he hadn't given in to violence, and he was still alive. He guessed that was half a victory because his father needed him even if no one else did.

– 3 –

WILLIAM KELLEY WAS WRESTED from his memories by uneven footsteps and the thump of a cane on the staircase. Ben was back. William thought his twenty-five-year-old son looked fifty when he entered the bedroom. No words were exchanged as William watched his son cross the room to the dresser where he opened a drawer and removed bandages and medicine.

The sight of a bloody gash on his son's forehead and his bloodstained shirt fired William's anger. He forgot his recent plea to the deities for well-chosen words, "What the hell happened this time?"

"Ran into some rebs that don't know the war's over or care whose side I was on."

William struggled to sit up, "Tell me you didn't—"

Ben wheeled and held up his hand, "Dad, don't start." He turned back to the medicine on the dresser and measured out a portion of heroin and prepared a tea of horehound leaves and honey. When he finished, he faced the bed. "Sorry I'm late, but I had to hoof it two miles, and now it's past the time for your medication. Here, drink this."

William took the cup while desperately wishing he could mend the rift between him and his son. They had been close before the war but now there was a distance he was unable to bridge. He didn't even know the details about his son's injured leg, only that it had happened at the Battle of Shiloh in 1862 while serving with General Forrest's cavalry.

William occasionally still saw the old fire that smoldered in his son's steel-gray eyes, but now it was clouded by a sadness that seldom left, only changed from day to day, event to event. Today his son's shoulders sagged beneath an invisible burden. Many times, like now, Ben's eyes looked right through him into another world.

"I can't seem to get warm anymore. Hell, I feel like I'll freeze to death before this blessed consumption takes me." William shivered and tugged at the red and gray quilt. Ben tucked the quilt around his father's thin shoulders and then went back to the mirror and wiped away the blood running down his cheek.

"Did you fight back?" William again forgot his prayer for well-chosen words.

"No."

"Son, folks are calling you a coward."

"I know and don't care."

Quiet. Only the measured heartbeat of the clock for long seconds.

William fixed his pale blue eyes on the figure in front of the dresser. "Who was it?"

"Don't know."

"What'd they take this time?"

"Darkie."

"Damn, Son, if you don't do something, they'll figure we're easy picking." The old man sighed. "Well, guess the whole South is easy picking now," he said, then added, "You ought to have someone look at that cut."

"Dad, I'm a doctor. Remember?"

Silently William watched as Ben laid out needle and catgut, removed the temporary bandage, and deftly pulled the gash together with quick, neat sutures.

His condition is getting worse fast, Ben thought as he strained to hear his father's voice. "Doesn't it bother you none what the folks are saying about you?"

Ben limped to the bedside chair. "No more than being stubborn and pigheaded ever bothered you."

The coughing lasted a long time, but finally his dad quieted, removed his glasses, and wiped his watering eyes. "I've never been ashamed of anything I did."

"I know that, but remember how they talked when you sold most of the business holdings, all the slaves, and didn't even try to join the army?"

A smile lit up the old gentleman's face. "By god, they did carry on, didn't they? You know why I didn't try to join up. And didn't it prove to be a mighty good decision?"

Ben picked up his black medical bag and found the thermometer. "Dad, I killed a man because of that decision."

The old man shoved away the thermometer. "Hell, that damn slave trader needed killing. Anyway you're doing what you dreamed about: being a doctor. Your mother would be proud."

"I know."

"Right or wrong, it left us in a damn sight better position than the rest of the South."

Ben only nodded.

"You've got enough gold to buy back the land, improve your horse herd, and keep Oak Grove from those goddamn carpetbaggers."

Ben nodded again, wondering how he could tell his father he didn't want the property, didn't want to stay here.

His father ran a hand through his silver beard. "Some things I want to get settled before I die. First, the next sunny day we have I want you to take me out to see the place once more."

Ben tried the thermometer again. His father stopped stroking his beard and shoved it away. "Damn, boy, I don't want you poking nothing more in me. You say there's not much you can do, so let me die in peace."

Ben laid the instrument on the table. "If we took you to a warmer, drier climate, you might recover."

"I know you've said that, but I ain't leaving Oak Grove. I built this house and this plantation, your mother and sister are buried here, and you'll bury me here beside them."

Ben went to the dresser where he wet a towel in the water basin and dabbed at his swollen eye. "Even old Doc Jacobson told you a change in climate might help. I think it's worth a try."

"No, damn it." Softening a little he repeated, "No, Son, and that's final."

Ben walked to the window and watched the low, gray clouds scurry across the Georgia sky, momentarily letting the sun drag its yellow rays across the bleak countryside. "Looks like the weather may break soon. Maybe tomorrow you can go out."

He listened to his father's labored breathing as he watched another ragged band of travelers struggling along the road below the house. They were part of Georgia's countless army of poor and homeless, but these were proud enough not to stop and beg like so many.

"Son, when you going to marry Adeline?"

Ben finished his thoughts, wondering what would become of the poor people down there on the road. He finally answered, "Dad, I don't think she will ever accept what's happened to me."

William waved a frail hand at his son, "Nonsense, boy, I'm told that family lost every blessed thing they ever had. She'd come running to you just for a pretty dress and a chance to live at Oak Grove."

Ben started to tell his father about his confrontation at the Welsh place but thought better of it. "Look, Dad, I don't want to buy her. I want her to accept me despite what's happened."

The old man removed his glasses and rubbed his eyes. "I don't guess I understand things anymore. Damn war's ruined everything just like I knew it would."

"Dad, you really should rest. We'll talk later."

"No, I want to finish what I've got on my mind, before it's too late." He hooked his glasses behind his ears and fixed Ben with unblinking eyes. "I want you to promise me you'll not leave

Oak Grove after I'm gone. I don't want to go to my grave thinking some damn Yankee will be living in this house that I built for
your mother."

"Is that all?"

"No, promise me you'll not take any more abuse from those
damn bummers and thieves. I know because of that leg you can't
fight like you used to, but there ain't a man living that can shoot
like you. Knock a few of the bastards out of the saddle and they'll
ride wide of this place. At least defend yourself."

"Dad, we've been over this a hundred times before. I can't
promise either one."

— 4 —

BEN WAS ASLEEP IN THE STUDY at Oak Grove where he'd remained sequestered since his father's funeral two days prior. He was slumped over the walnut desk, his arms folded across a black journal, his head on his arms. A pen and inkwell sat next to the lamp on his right, along with a dirty linen napkin and half-eaten biscuit that were strewn on top of the desk along with reports and maps of the Santa Fe Trail, the Oregon Trail, and the Smoky Hill Trail.

The house was cold and the stiffness in his body woke him to a blurry world until he rubbed the matter from his swollen eye. He stretched his frame back in the leather desk chair and began working his neck from side to side, then opening and closing his hands until the circulation returned.

His white shirt was open at the collar, his vest unbuttoned, and the gray suit he'd worn to the funeral was badly rumpled. Sometime since the funeral the fires had gone out in the house and he'd put on a topcoat against the chill. Out of respect for his father, he had forced himself to shave and trim his mustache before the funeral. Now a rough stubble gave his face a dirty shadow, and disheveled black hair hung over the bandage on his head.

He lifted his bad leg and propped it on an open desk drawer, carefully rubbing and kneading with his fingers until the ache subsided somewhat. Satisfied, he gathered his cane and slowly stood up and began working the sleep from his mind. He was home, the war was over, his father was dead.

Ben stepped into the parlor and saw the grandfather clock's brass pendulum winking in the morning sun as it swung rhythmically back and forth in the cherry wood case. He considered the familiar sight and sound and realized he had not started the clock since his return home.

His looked around the room where the furniture, the pictures, the rug, and the curtains were all the same. But the fireplace was clean of ashes with kindling and logs laid on the grate ready for lighting. He had not put them there. The lines softened around his mouth and eyes, for he knew it was either Elmo and Jenny Niemechek or Mule Anderson.

Freshly baked bread along with grits and two eggs waited on the table in the kitchen. The coffee pot sat ready on the stove. These deeds of caring touched him for he knew he had a few loyal friends. But, he wondered, for how long? How would they react when he told them he'd finally promised his father he wouldn't leave Oak Grove?

He lit the fireplace and the stove before walking to the north window where he could see the row of slave quarters. Smoke came from the chimneys of several of the small shacks. There were no blacks there now, but this morning he wished they were empty of all people. Shifting his gaze to the east window he saw two freight wagons parked in front of the blacksmith shop. Elmo must have bought more wagons for their journey west.

After eating the welcome breakfast, Ben returned to the study where he sat down in the desk chair and opened the large black journal that he'd begun during the war. The journal was his way of ensuring that no humans he attended departed this life without a record of their having lived. The last entry recorded his father's death.

Loud knocking at the front door interrupted his gloomy thoughts. He ignored the pounding, hoping whoever it was would go away. The knocking was insistent, and finally, reluctantly, he answered the door.

A rotund man with spectacles and gray muttonchops removed his hat with a flourish. The man eyed Ben's bandaged head and cane before holding out a smooth, plump hand. "Dr. Benjamin Kelley, I take it?"

"Yes."

"Silas Wompler at your service. May I come in?" The hand the man held out was limp and moist and there was no warmth in his eyes to match his smile.

Ben looked past the man to the expensive rig and sleek horses in the circle drive. Carpetbagger, he thought, but the man's speech was Southern. Ben didn't move. "I'm busy."

"My condolences on your father's death. We were acquaintances."

Ben stood rooted in the doorway. "I don't recall him ever mentioning your name."

"Rumor has it that you are planning to depart Georgia. What I have to say will be of great interest to you. Perhaps we could talk inside."

Ben pushed the door open and stepped aside. Wompler waddled past him and made straight for the study. "I represent a group of investors who have authorized me to offer—"

"I'm not selling."

Proceeding to the study, Wompler lowered his obese frame into a red leather wing chair. "I'm afraid you've misunderstood. I want to sell you land, not buy yours."

Ben followed him into the study and stood behind his desk.

The pudgy little man squirmed forward to the edge of the chair. "Our group believes that you have the ready capital to purchase back all of your family property. Of course it's available at a fraction of what your dad sold it for."

"Tell your group I'm not ready to sell or wanting to buy."

Wompler scooted the bundle of papers onto the corner of the desk and stood at attention, snapping a thumb-back salute at Ben. "These are gloomy times," he said.

Ben only stared. Wompler held the salute and with his left hand pulled a red-and-white string from his coat pocket and displayed it before his protruding girth.

Ben's eyes narrowed and his jaw muscles corded. He pointed his cane toward the door, then at Wompler. "If you're suggesting I'm a damn Red String, you can get out now," Ben said as he stepped around the desk.

Wompler involuntarily took a step back and sat down hard into the chair, a cold smile playing on his pudgy face. "Not implying that at all. Just making sure. You see we have to be very careful, and in your case especially so, considering your father."

"What about my father?" Ben snapped at the man.

"Certain actions during the war, how shall we say, cast doubt on his position."

"Are you saying my father was a Red String?"

"Dr. Kelley, even though it may be true, we prefer to overlook the possibility. It is you we are concerned with now."

Ben fought down the impulse to hit the man. Instead, he returned to the desk and sat down. "What's your concern with me?"

"We've had you watched. We know you served as an exceptionally able and honorable cavalry officer until you were wounded. But more than your military ability, we are interested in your medical expertise. We don't even care that you won't fight anymore."

"Who are you people and why are you interested in my medical skills?"

"A group of loyal and prominent Southerners are planning a retreat to Mexico. There we will set up a government in exile and return to liberate the South."

A smile touched the corners of Ben's mouth. "God knows we've had plenty of experience retreating." When Wompler didn't respond, Ben continued, "That would be one foolish move if you ask me. We've been beat six ways from Sunday and every soldier, North and South, is sick of war. I wouldn't be interested."

"I think you will recognize some of these names," Wompler said, sliding several papers toward Ben.

Ben slid them back without looking. Throw the fat bastard out, he thought. But instead he opened a drawer and extended a cigar across the desk, then selected one for himself. When the room was awash in blue velvet smoke he asked, "How much will the property cost me?"

Wompler exhaled and held the cigar under close scrutiny. "Damn good Southern leaf. Yes sir, some of us still can appreciate the good things God intended." He paused and savored the cigar before continuing. "We've been buying large parcels of choice Southern property. Already Northern interests are buying property that rightly belongs to the South. This, of course, will drive up the land prices. We sell after a year to finance our army. Our sources up north assure us it will bring a nice profit."

Ben asked, "Who would hold control of this property?"

"You do cut right to the quick. I told 'em you were smart."

Wompler fidgeted. Ben repeated the question.

"Those most qualified to lead. You, providing you join us, would be included in the leadership – small risk for big rewards."

Ben laid his cane aside and adjusted the bandage around his head as he spoke. "If we didn't win a second time?"

"If, in a year, the venture appears unwise, we sell the property and take our gains at that time. As you can see, we can hardly lose either way," Wompler said.

Ben took the cigar from between his clenched teeth. "I wouldn't be interested in your scheme. But I'm damn interested in what you're saying about my father. There's no way in hell my father was a traitor."

"You, of all people," Wompler said, "should be asking yourself some pretty obvious questions."

Ben stood. "Like what?"

Wompler rose. "How do you think Oak Grove survived? There's not a house between here and Atlanta that hasn't been burned or looted." He pointed at the racked guns on the wall. "How come these weapons weren't confiscated? Or your horses? How do you think your father moved so freely between North and South?"

Ben started around the desk. Wompler grabbed his papers and backed toward the door. "How many patients have you seen since the war? Doesn't it strike you as strange that people aren't coming to you for medical service?"

"Get out," Ben said, waving his cane in the retreating man's face. "You should thank God that I don't fight anymore or I'd kill you where you stand."

Wompler's hand came out of his jacket pocket with a derringer. "And I believe you would. I saw you kill that slave trader. You're as cool a fighting man as I've ever seen. Or you were."

Ben stalked after the man, his eyes trained on the gun. The pudgy hand was steady and the gun never wavered.

A shadow fell across the room as a man stepped into the doorway behind Wompler. Nobody filled a doorway like Elmo Niemechek. Elmo was a blacksmith of exceptional skill and awesome stature. He stood six feet eight and tipped the scales at three hundred and twenty pounds – all muscles and hair. Black hair, black beard, and body hair so heavy it appeared that a black bear from yonder Blue Ridge Mountains had come calling in homespun clothing. Wompler turned and Elmo knocked the small gun from his hand as easily as brushing a fly from a biscuit, then grabbed the astonished man and slammed him against the wall. Holding him with his left hand, he drew back his right fist.

"Elmo, don't!" Ben hollered. "Just throw him out and make sure he keeps going."

The big blacksmith glanced over his shoulder. "You sure, Ben? His kind ain't no use to nobody around here."

"I'm sure. You bust him open and I'll just have to put him back together. Lord knows I've done too much of that."

Elmo jerked Wompler away from the wall, set him out the door, and shoved him toward the buggy. Ben picked up the derringer and then pointed to the papers scattered underfoot. "Gather his papers and burn them just as soon as he's gone."

Ben studied the weapon as he turned the small piece in his hand. It was one of Remington's new Double Derringers which, at close range, could be extremely deadly but extremely inaccurate. He released the breech and extracted the two .41 caliber rimfire cartridges and dropped them into his pocket. Then he went out onto the porch and saw Wompler, under Elmo's watchful eye, heave his bulk into the buggy, gather the lines, and shout, "You'll live to regret this."

"Elmo, bring him back here."

Grinning, Elmo shucked the man off the buggy seat and set him in front of Ben.

Ben leaned close to the flushed, sweating face, "Just let my father rest in peace. If I hear you spreading lies about my family, I'll—"

"And what would you do except hide behind your big blacksmith?" Wompler interrupted, grinning back in Ben's face.

Elmo tensed. Ben slowly stepped back. Wompler straightened his jacket, turned, and walked quickly back to the buggy.

Ben and Elmo watched the rig bounce and clatter down the drive and disappear behind the roadside trees. Ben heaved the derringer after the buggy. "Vultures," he shouted. "Men like you are nothing but vultures, and I hate vultures."

BEN TOOK ONE LAST LOOK down the road before returning to the house where he sat down in the study and began brooding on the implication that his dad was a traitor; and the news that he was being watched. Later that afternoon he began pacing from room to room, his uneven footsteps echoing off the high ceiling.

He stopped in front of the parlor fireplace and studied the painting above the mantel. When his mother died in 1844, she had seemed old to Ben. Now she looked younger. Raven-black hair, piercing green eyes, a firm jaw and full, wide mouth. The artist had captured perfectly her strength and her gentleness. She would have looked stern if not for the smile lines at her eyes.

Now he was a physician, and he still wanted to save a mother's life so a child wouldn't have to grieve. Reaching up, he touched her hands where the artist's oil had worn through almost to the canvas. Stepping back, he looked around the room. The stool was gone. He remembered that a slave had made the stool shortly after his mother's death so that whenever doubts and fears crept into his young life, he would climb onto that stool and touch her hands.

Ben wondered if the reason he was so attracted to Adeline Welsh was because she looked so much like his mother. God, how he longed for Adeline. And he hated to lose Darkie because he was a perfect match to the black mare that Adeline always rode.

Looking out the window at the gathering darkness he moved deliberately through the kitchen and down the back steps toward the slave quarters. What remained of the old plantation was deathly quiet now but he remembered the times before the war when the plantation had hummed with industry: slaves in the fields early; black children playing in the road between the living quarters; horses, wagons, and men hustling to tend the crops and keep Oak Grove productive and profitable.

The yard was frequently filled with fancy carriages and fine horses during his youth and on those festive social evenings the big house sparkled with lamplight and overflowed with music and laughter. Of late there had been little laughter and he'd not heard chamber music for years.

He had a very unpleasant job to do. Steeling himself, he walked toward the shack where Elmo and his wife Jenny had lived since the war. Many other couples who had also pledged to go west with him now lived in these shacks.

Elmo, Mule Anderson, and the rest of the men cared for the stock and spent the days preparing for the journey. In the evenings they talked about a new beginning somewhere in the West.

Elmo looked up from his supper as Ben entered the small cabin. "Jenny, set another plate for Ben. I imagine he could use a proper meal."

The aroma of corn bread, coffee, and lye soap helped hide the pungent odor of years of wood smoke and fried foods.

Ben shook his head. "Thanks, but I didn't come to eat. Elmo, I need to talk."

Elmo got up from the table and motioned to one of two chairs by the crude fireplace. "You look mighty low which is understandable seeing how your kin's all gone now. But you're free to move on with your life. I got a lead on some more wagons over in Summerville."

Ben sat staring at the dirt floor. I've never run from the truth, he thought, but this is one time I wish I could lie.

Elmo stopped talking about the wagons and studied his friend. He filled a briar pipe and pointed the stem at Ben. "You okay, Ben?"

"Ever hear any bad rumors about my father?" Ben asked as he leaned back in his chair.

Elmo's eyes flicked to Jenny who was clearing the dishes off the table. "Such as?"

"That man implied my father was a Red String. One of those anti-war Southerners who helped the North." Ben said it like a question.

Elmo shifted his bulk in the oversized rocker. "Nothing most of us who knew him ever paid any mind to," he said.

"Ever wonder how come this place survived better than most?" Ben voiced the words that had rung in his ears since Wompler had used them to taunt him.

"Hell, your dad was a tough businessman, a shrewd negotiator, and a stubborn fighter."

"I guess," Ben said doubtfully, lost in thought while Jenny fixed coffee and Elmo tamped the bowl of his pipe with the head of a horseshoe nail.

Satisfied with his pipe, Elmo wiped the nail on his trousers and dropped it in his shirt pocket. "Ain't sure what that feller said to you, but if you're afraid we're all going to change our minds about you, or your father, you can forget that."

"Thanks, but it will take a long time for me to forget." Ben had not missed the glances between Elmo and his wife.

"We're grateful for what you and your father done for us. We've all got a good future ahead of us out west," Jenny said and laid a kind hand on Ben's shoulder as she handed him a cup of steaming coffee.

"Elmo, I promised my father that I wouldn't leave Oak Grove." Jenny removed her hand from Ben's shoulder and looked at her husband who had paused with his pipe halfway to his mouth. A burning log popped and snapped in the fireplace, the only sound to break the deathly quiet.

Finally, Ben stood and paced to the other side of the room, then turned to face his friends. "He died hard. That promise made it some easier for him."

Elmo looked at Ben until both were uneasy. "I ain't knowing how to say this, but is it something you aim to stick by?"

Ben glanced out the cabin's one small, dirty window at Oak Grove nestled against the leafless oaks. "We've known each other since we were kids," he said. "Have you ever known me to go back on a promise?"

"Never," Elmo said flatly, then added, "but we've all had our minds set on this chance for a new start." Jenny moved to Elmo's rocker and stood close beside the big man. They both studied Ben's silent form.

Elmo finally stood, walked to the door, and stepped out into the darkness. A wave of cold air rolled through the cabin making the lantern flame flicker and dance. Jenny shivered and pulled her shawl tight around her shoulders.

Ben followed Elmo outside leaving Jenny standing alone in the shack.

Outside, Elmo's frustration and disappointment were almost tangible. Ben considered many ways to justify his promise, many words to ease his own feelings. "Let's sleep on it," he finally said and walked toward his dark, lonely home.

Elmo stopped at the back steps of Oak Grove at five o'clock the next morning. He could hear Ben thumping around the kitchen, the smell of coffee wafted through a broken windowpane, and lamplight shone from every window.

The big man stepped through the kitchen's back door and closed it behind him. "Ben, have you gone daft?"

Ben was cutting thick slices of ham on the butcher block. He paused only long enough to flash a smile at Elmo. "You hungry?"

Elmo just stared at the table that was set with fine china, polished silverware, and clean linen napkins. A skillet full of grits sat on the back burner of the cook stove.

"You hungry?" Ben repeated.

Ben's hair was neatly combed, he was clean shaven with a fresh bandage on his forehead. He had on clean riding breeches, a ruffled white shirt with diamond studs, a tie, and a dark brown jacket. His black riding boots were scuffed but clean. Over it all was a white bib apron. The deep-set gray eyes flashed like those of the young Ben Kelley Elmo had known in their youth.

Ben grinned. "I sure can't eat all this myself. I may not be the best cook in the world but I did learn to do some of my own cooking during the war."

"I was going to start the forge fire – saw all the lights – what's happening?" Elmo stammered.

Ben set another skillet on the stove and filled it with sliced ham. "What's happening is a mighty fine morning. If you're not going to eat, reckon you could drag Mule up here?"

Elmo eyed the stove and table. "I'm eating soon as I go get Mule."

Mule's reaction was equal to that of the blacksmith. Mule was a slight, wiry man who was seldom without a cud of Mule Skinner tobacco in his cheek – a habit that had earned him his nickname. They ate in silence and by the time they were into their last cup of coffee the sun was up bright and warm.

Ben pushed back his chair before speaking. "Before he died, I promised my father that I wouldn't leave Oak Grove. He didn't want Yanks living in this house. Anyhow, I've figured a way to keep my promise and still head west."

Mule stood up and moved to the stove. He lifted a lid and arched a stream of tobacco into the coals, "Going to burn the place down? Only ways I can figure to do both."

"No, we've all seen enough burning buildings to last us a lifetime," Ben replied.

What ya got in mind?" Elmo asked.

"We're going to take the house with us," Ben grinned.

"Ben, I'm sure looking for a way to go west but this ain't no time for funning," Elmo said.

Ben grabbed his cane and began pacing the kitchen. "I'm not joking. Elmo, how many wagons you reckon Sherman had when he marched through Georgia?"

"Heard tell it was most near twenty-five hundred."

Ben stopped and faced Elmo. "And what all did he have in those wagons?"

A light went on in Elmo's eyes and he jabbed his pipe stem toward Ben. "Everything for a long campaign, damn near a whole army post."

"Exactly," Ben said and began to pace again. "If he can haul an army post, we can haul one house. Thankfully Dad didn't build a huge house like some of the planters."

Elmo jumped up. "It'd take a bunch of wagons and teams, but by god just maybe it could be done."

Mule spat and wiped his mouth with his shirtsleeve. "Have you forgot it's a fer piece to where we want to be going. There's Injuns, mountains, desert, and only God hisself knows what else is between here and yonder."

"That's all true, but I'd rather face the unknown than stay here. Any place is better than living with these memories," Ben answered.

Elmo grinned down at Ben. "How soon we leaving?"

Ben cleared the dishes from off the table before grabbing a map and spreading it on the table. He stabbed a finger at their location in Georgia and then pointed to Kansas City, Missouri. "I'd like to be in Westport before the rivers freeze next winter, and if we work like hell, we should be able to reach that goal. Once we get there, we'll worry about the next part of the trip. Now, let's get to work."

$- 6 -$

Isaiah Benteen forded Elk Creek after a five-days' ride north out of the prairie settlement called Elk Springs. Here he stopped under a cottonwood tree, its new leaves the size of squirrels' ears. Just upstream a wild plum bush showed tender buds, promising many scented, white blossoms to cheer those who passed its way. The rider noticed all this and drank in the familiar sights and smells of the earth.

Slipping from his horse, he ripped off his store-bought clothes and threw them aside. He untied his bedroll and spread it on the ground, then selected breechclout and moccasins.

He patted the bay mustang's neck and spoke to it in Crow. "Ho, it is time for us to be Indian again. I can't believe my mother was a white. If all white eyes are like Captain Keeferly and Jake Smith I know I want to be Indian. Those two need killing – maybe someday after I've kept my promise to Mother." Then he added, "And Sheriff Barton was about as much help as a busted leg."

Sitting down, he built a smoke in his long-stemmed pipe. He offered it to the earth, the sky, and the four winds, then smoked in silence. When the pipe was finished, Isaiah spoke to his pony grazing nearby on the new grass. "This is Sioux country, good place to find scalps, or lose them. You still willing to go on to our homeland?"

Lifting its head, the horse pointed its ears to the west. Isaiah followed the animal's gaze across the rolling grassland to the darkening horizon. The sun still shone on the morning side of the sky, but in the west a spring storm was being birthed.

"I know, we'll get soaked unless we move out and ride hard. But a good rain might wash the white stink off us," he said, cleaning the ashes from his pipe and gathering his bedroll. Before mounting he hesitated, then retrieved his store clothes and tied them behind the old white man's saddle he'd decorated with beads and feathers.

He followed the creek north, watching his back trail and the storm to the north and west. He rode slowly, enjoying the wind on his skin and Mother Earth's spring ritual of new life awakening around him.

Sun Boy was directly above when his pony threw up its head and stopped. Immediately Isaiah reined into the trees and reached for his bow and quiver. "You catching Sioux on the wind?" he asked the pony. The rider checked the four directions and then focused to the northwest where his pony's black ears pointed.

Riding in the shadows of the few trees along the creek bank they moved upstream to a small rise where he dismounted. He studied the animal intently. "You're telling me it's not Sioux," he said stroking the pony's nose. "Let's see what's got your attention."

Isaiah mounted and rode along the ridge until he saw the wagons. "Ho, a wagon train traveling on the old cutoff. Must be in a hell of a hurry or plumb stupid," he said out loud. But, he thought, whites weren't very smart most of the time.

Lightning flashed and thunder cracked to the west and for a moment thunderheads blocked out the sun. Isaiah watched a rider on a big sorrel stop on a rise and look back at the following wagons. About to dismiss the train and resume his journey, Isaiah looked again at the wagons. "By damn," he said to his mount. "Those are freighters and those are horses in harness, a six-horse hitch on every wagon." Now what kind of fool would use horses, he asked himself. He looked again. The teams were all matched and it was the biggest train he'd ever seen.

The wind died and his pony swung his head south and snorted as a small herd of antelope dashed by. Looking south Isaiah saw a faint orange glow on the horizon. Ho, he thought, there's a prairie fire coming and those fools are right in its path. The whites I don't care about, but I'd sure as hell hate to see all that fine horseflesh get roasted. And, besides that, I wouldn't be surprised if we get a flash flood from all that rain up in the hills.

Ben Kelley reined in and watched the storm which had been building in the northwest. He had never outgrown his childhood excitement in the raw power of a wild storm. This was his first prairie thunderstorm and he watched it with delight. He spoke to his mount. "Ol' Jeb, this promises to be a fine storm. One worth watching and comparing to some we've had back home." For long moments he surveyed the land and sky. He let his eyes walk unfettered across the trackless grassland, thinking that he hadn't known one could see so far. Wildlife seemed to be more abundant today than he had noticed. If, he thought, I ever had reason to spend time here, I might learn to like this land.

The wind died down to a whisper and an eerie calm was on the vast prairie. "Spooky isn't it?" Ben said. Ol' Jeb rolled his eyes and jerked nervously at the bit. The crack and rumble of distant thunder brought his attention back west to the gathering storm. An angry black wall cloud boiled along the horizon. Lighter gray clouds scurried back and forth atop the black ribbon. Above, snowy-white towers stretched upwards where the afternoon sun played tag among the cottony peaks. Lightning stabbed and booming thunder strolled with heavy footfalls across the waiting earth.

Wagon guide Sam Hoffman rode in from the north and joined Ben on the knoll. "A real son of a bitch brewing, looks like."

"We will get wet it appears." Ben liked the small, leather-tough scout and the hard-bitten mustang he rode. Sam was borderline uncouth and his horse was the most miserable-looking animal Ben had ever laid eyes upon – but both had proved reliable.

The wagons were less than a quarter mile back. The rough voices of teamsters and the crack of their whips could be heard when the wind died down and the thunder rested.

"Rider coming and it looks like he wants to kill his horse." Sam pointed south. Both men watched the approaching figure against the backdrop of a darkening horizon. Sam tensed, spit a stream of tobacco juice and jerked his Henry from the saddle boot. "Damn Indian," he declared.

"Where do you think he's going in such a hurry?"

"Can't never tell with those bastards, but if he keeps coming I can drop him before he gets close and it won't make no difference."

"No," Ben said sharply. "There's only one and surely he can't cause us trouble."

"Ben, you may be educated and you may be rich but you sure as hell got a lot to learn about Indians." As the figure drew closer, Ben could see the rider's long black hair and saw that his mount could have been a twin to Sam's horse.

The wagons were beginning to arrive at the knoll where Mule Anderson drew rein next to Sam. "That looks like an Indian," he said seeing the horseman approaching. "You want I should shoot him?" he asked as he shouldered his Sharps.

"Put it down, Mule," Ben said. "He hasn't done us any harm."

The six-horse teams were becoming harder to control as the storm clouds boiled closer. To the south it seemed that the dark clouds were touched with a tint of scarlet. A hundred yards from the knoll the Indian cupped his hands to his mouth and hollered, "Fire!"

A vicious south wind slammed into tense men and plunging horses. On the wind rode the unmistakable smell of smoke as a wall of flames burst over the crest of a distant rise stretching a wall of fire across their path.

Isaiah rode straight to Ben and Sam. Ben shot him a question. "Can we outrun it?"

"No way in hell," Sam answered before the Indian had a chance to respond.

Ben's mind raced, his memory reaching back. "Will a back-fire work here like in a forest?"

"It just might work," Sam said. Any feeling of animosity between the two was overcome by the present danger.

Isaiah added, "It's the only way to save your wagons."

"Follow me," Ben said, turning and riding toward his Conestoga. The driver had his hands full managing the teams so Ben rode to the tailgate, and half climbed, half fell inside and handed Sam a can of lamp oil and some sulfur matches.

Isaiah hollered, "You got a loose blanket or extra clothing in there?"

Ben threw him a blanket and then watched as he rolled it into a ball and tied it with a leather thong before dousing it with the lamp oil. "Anybody got a rope?" Isaiah asked.

Sam handed him a rope which the Indian tied to the soaked blanket and then asked for the matches. "I'll ride down wind and start the backfire."

"I'll help with the teams," Ben shouted. "They're going to be a handful."

Mounted again, Ben rode quickly to each wagon, explained the backfire, and told the men to spread out in a line and wait for Sam's signal to run for it.

The teams fought the lines, testing the skill of even the most experienced teamsters. A yell brought his attention down the line of wagons where a wagon had broken away from the others and was headed directly for the rushing flames. Giving Ol' Jeb his head, Ben urged the big stallion toward the wagon.

The driver, young Niles Jackson, feet braced and body arched back over the seat, was sawing with all his strength on the lines. Ben put Ol' Jeb in close to the nearside leader, grabbed the line, and kneed Ol' Jeb against the terrified animal. Slowly the lead team gave ground, slackened pace, and soon were headed back away from the flames.

Niles's face showed a mixture of relief and guilt. Ben let go of the line and fell back beside the wagon. He pointed toward the backfire that was burning to the north. Niles nodded, and Ben managed a smile and a wave before he reined around to check the rest of the wagons.

Ben could hear the flames now and the smell of smoke was overpowering. Seeing Sam riding among the wagons he galloped over and slid to a halt beside the guide. "We can't wait much longer. Set them running when you think it's time."

Soot, ash, and cinders rode the wind like a black and orange lace curtain. The strip of prairie was under a spell of ghostly light, howling wind, and growing terror. The Indian galloped up. "You'd best go now. The flames are flanking us on the left."

"Let's go!" Sam yelled. The three mounted riders spurred up and down the line of wagons urging them toward the smoldering black carpet behind the retreating backfire. The line of riders and wagons was chasing one wall of flame and being chased by another.

"Looks like we may make it," Sam said as he drew alongside Ben.

Niles's team and wagon again careened out of control and locked wheels with Mule Anderson's rig when they were still two hundred yards from the backfire. Mule reacted to the impact without looking back, hauled hard on the off-team lines and for a moment kept his wagon upright. Then the front wheel on Nile's rig collapsed and both wagons went over in a tangle of flying cargo and frantic horses. Young Niles was thrown hard amidst thrashing horseflesh. Mule jumped clear, rolled several times, and was back on his feet as the flames surged toward downed horses and drivers.

"Cut those horses loose," Ben screamed at Sam as they slid to a halt beside Nile's wagon and team. Sam quit the saddle as Ben grabbed the bridle of his horse. Knife flashing, Sam hacked frantically at the harness. Ben could feel the fire crawling closer.

Finally Sam slashed the last restraining leather and the horses bolted free. Mule finished cutting a horse loose, grabbed the horse's collar, and vaulted astride as it plunged toward safety.

"Let's get out of here," Sam gasped.

"Sam, Niles is down there somewhere," Ben shouted. Sam's horse, terrified of the onrushing flames, broke free and bolted.

Ben swung out of the saddle and grabbed Ol' Jeb's bridle, spoke quick words and dropped the reins. He hopped and crawled to Niles, pulled him to his knees, and slapped him across the face. The youth's eyes snapped open. "On your feet!" Ben shouted.

"My rifle. I can't go without my rifle." He pushed Ben away and stumbled to the wagon.

Sam helped Ben to his feet. "We've got to get out of here now," he yelled.

Isaiah saw their danger and guided his mount straight toward Niles who had found his rifle and was standing paralyzed by the coming wall of fire. Ben and Sam watched as the Indian leaned over the side of his small pony, and on a dead run grabbed Niles and hauled him over the pony's withers.

Ol' Jeb stood wide-eyed where Ben had ground tied him. Ben and Sam reached the big stallion, and not taking time to mount, they clung to each side of the saddle as Ben's words released the horse from the iron discipline. In two strides he was racing at full speed for the safety of the backfire.

A good half mile passed before the drivers could fight the teams to a halt and saw with relief that the flames died at the edge of backfire and raced around the edges to come together again leaving the wagons on an island of smoldering black. Ben watched the fire as it raced over the low hills where they had been moments before. He realized their wild scramble for life had left them in a small valley between the hills. They had little time to celebrate before thunder, lightning, and rain bore in with relentless fury. They were engulfed in a deluge that transformed the burned prairie into a sea of mud.

Sam rode hard among wagons. "Circle 'em, now. Get a move on!" He shouted at the teamsters. "Come on, Charley, get that son of a bitch in line."

"Why make them circle the wagons in this storm? Let 'em get out of the weather wherever they can," Ben hollered.

Sam barked back, "Ben, in a minute we're going to be bogged down in this mud and may not be able to move. At least this will give us some protection in case Indians stumble upon us."

Finally the wagons were circled and Ben caught up with Sam who was racked with coughing spells and could barely talk. "Sam, if the Indian is still with us, tell him to come to my wagon," Ben said. "And, Sam, you come by the wagon when you get things like you want them out here."

Ben had lost his hat and his hair was matted down and his soaked clothes clung to his body. He lowered his head against the driving rain and rode between two wagons into the inner circle looking for the covered wagon that was his home.

The mud sucked at the sorrel's hooves. "Sam was right," he said to Ol' Jeb. "This is a damn mess." At the wagon, he dropped the reins and crawled inside expecting to see the driver but he wasn't there. The interior of the wagon had been wrecked by the wild ride but he found the big trunk and was soon in dry clothes.

As he was putting the wagon back in order, the Indian stuck his head inside. "You wanted to see me?"

"Yes, yes. Come in out of that god-awful rain." Isaiah ducked his head and entered.

"I wanted to thank you for your help." Ben measured the man as he spoke. He was about the same height as Ben, and built with a bit heavier frame.

"You're welcome," Isaiah said.

"My name is Dr. Benjamin Kelley. I'd be proud to know yours."

"My Crow name or my white name?"

"Are you Indian or white?"

"I am both," he said. "My mother was white and my father Indian, so I'm a breed. My white name is Isaiah Benteen."

"And your Indian name?"

Just then, dripping wet and coughing, Sam ducked through the wagon cover opening. "Jeez, ain't seen it rain like this for a spell." He sank wearily onto the floor of the wagon, removed his hat, and fished for his tobacco. "Ben, got some more bad news," he said.

"Whatever it is it will have to wait until I have a look at you," Ben said, opening his medical bag.

"Hell, I just got a snout full of that damn smoke. I'll be okay." His answer was followed by a coughing spasm.

Ben found some medicine in his bag and held it out to Sam. "Mix this powder with a cup of water and drink it all. And do it right away. Come back and see me if the coughing doesn't stop."

"You are a medicine man?" Isaiah asked.

"Yes. Now, Sam, what was that bad news about?"

"One of the horses broke a leg when the wagons wrecked."

Ben groaned. "Are you sure it's broken?"

"I know a broken leg when I see one. And, besides that, there are six or seven others that don't act right. A couple of drivers said they had to go through some really heavy smoke to get into the backfire burn."

"When it quits raining, I will look at your horses if you will allow it, but right now we've something else to worry about," Isaiah interjected.

"What could be worse than this?" Ben questioned the Indian who was staring out the back of the covered wagon.

Isaiah pointed out through the falling rain, "Too bad you ended up down here in the flat because the way it's been raining up in the hills I wouldn't be surprised if we got a flood coming down on us."

"The man's right," Sam offered. "The little draw that runs down this valley is dry unless there's a big rain in them hills and then it can become a river."

"Should we try to get to the hills? At least get all the men out of harm's way?" Ben queried, then added, "The rain is letting up now so maybe we don't have to worry."

Isaiah went to the front of the wagon and said, "We may get flooded but it won't get high enough to wash the wagons away."

"How so?" Sam asked once his coughing lessened.

"I can see some drift wood at the foot of that hill a little to the east that was left by the last flash flood and it tells me the water won't rise high enough to get into the wagons," Isaiah told them.

"I guess we can only pray you're right," Ben said. Then he continued, "There aren't many trees around here so where'd all that driftwood come from?"

"There are lots of cedars and other trees growing in some of the canyons up in those hills."

The rain soon stopped falling but an hour later the dry streambed began to run water and in minutes a churning brown wall came tearing down the valley.

Isaiah's prediction proved correct and the level of water only reached to the hubs of the wagons and their biggest worry was keeping the horses calm while praying that no big driftwood pieces would slam into the wagons.

Ben sat in his wagon and watched the men on their wagons trying to dry their clothes and thought that things can certainly change in a hurry out here, change from a sea of grass to a sea of flames to a sea of water in just minutes.

"How long will the water stay up?" Ben asked Isaiah. The men were wet, cold, and hungry, and that would have to be dealt with before long.

"Water will be gone by sunup but the mud will be here a long time. It's going to be a while before you can move the heavy wagons."

7

THE NEXT MORNING THE SUN ROSE bright and warm and the floodwaters were gone just as Isaiah had predicted. The men welcomed the day of bright sunshine, but the sun did little to fill their bellies. Ben mounted Ol' Jeb and rode around the circle of wagons talking to the men and looking at the horses. On the north side of the circle Niles's teams were still tied to a wagon. "Ben, we're going to have to put this one down. You want I should do it?" Sam stepped back and pointed to the horse's foreleg. The guide was right but Lord, Ben hated the idea of destroying the beautiful animal.

"Okay, Sam. Do it."

Ben reached his Conestoga where Elmo and Niles were leaning against a rear wheel and talking about the lost wagons. "Son, don't think it was anything you did. Don't worry about it none. Any recollection what was in your wagon?" Elmo asked.

"Got no idea, I was going to walk back and see."

"It was the extra medical supplies. I was just on my way to see how bad the damage is," Ben said. "But first, I want to have a look at you in the wagon." Niles's face was cut and bruised and he held his left arm across his stomach with his right arm. "Hell, Ben, I'm plumb able to help without no fuss over me."

"Get yourself up in my wagon."

A rifle shot shocked the silence and turned all eyes to the north and most hands reaching for weapons. "What was that?" Niles asked.

"Sam had to put down one of the horses. Broken leg," Ben explained.

Niles looked sick. "One of my team?"

"Yes, now let's have a look at you." Ben dressed Niles's facial cuts and set his broken arm while he talked to Sam about the Indian. "I wondered if he's still around. What do you think of him?"

"I don't trust redskins, but he did warn us of the fire," Elmo offered. "But he sure seems to be interested in your horses. He's been over there looking at and talking to that sick team. If it wasn't the sick team, I'd bet he was looking to steal some horseflesh."

Sam was coughing almost continually when he returned to Ben's wagon. "I think I'd better have another look at you," Ben said.

At noon, with a bright gold orb hanging in a clear, innocent prairie sky, a grimy and hungry group of teamsters gathered by Ben's wagon. "Sam's down sick, got too much smoke," Ben told the group from the wagon seat. "Elmo, you're in charge of things until Sam gets back on his feet," Ben said.

"What the hell we supposed to eat?" a driver asked.

"How about some horse steaks from that dead horse?" another answered.

"You'll have to eat it raw," someone said. "There ain't nothing dry left to burn around here."

"Eat anything you want to except for that horse," Ben said.

"Going to let that Indian roam around camp after dark?" a teamster questioned.

"He's my guest in this camp if he chooses to stay. And there will be no arguments. Understood?" Ben turned to Mule. "Mule, find Isaiah and send him to my wagon."

"Who's Isaiah?"

"That's the Indian's name."

Ben checked on his sick guide. "Come on, Sam, this outfit's still got a ways to go before we settle down." Ben talked to Sam as he made the guide as comfortable as possible. "Our deal was to get us to the forks of the Platte River and I'll be damned if I pay you the balance of your wages if you ride the rest of the way in my wagon." Tired and hungry, Ben used his unheard words to beat back the despair that had overtaken him.

The following day they buried Sam just before sundown. After the last shovelful of mud had been heaped on Sam's final resting place, Ben told Mule to find Sam's horse and gear, hoping that the scout's possessions would have papers with names of kin so at the next town they could send news of his death and forward his gear.

The next day dawned bright and promised to be warm and dry with a light southerly wind, as if repentant, caressing the scarred prairie. Vultures wheeled in lazy circles above the dead horses a hundred yards or more outside the circled wagons. Ben had ordered two more of Niles's team put down when he realized there was nothing he could do to lessen their suffering.

The sun wasn't far above the horizon when Mule realized the Indian was gone and so was Sam's horse and the outfit. No one had seen the horse since last night when it was tied at Ben's wagon. Mule trudged through the mud and manure to Ben's wagon.

"Ben, I reckon that breed stole Sam's horse and outfit." Mule spit and gestured northward. "Two sets of tracks heading north. One shoed and one ain't."

Ben was unable to offer an explanation to the evidence there in the mud. He stared silently along the two sets of hoof prints that disappeared over a knoll on the horizon.

"It's plain as fresh horse turds in new snow," Mule continued. "He'll be back with his friends so I'd better get the boys ready. You want I should fetch you a gun?"

"No. Maybe he just wanted Sam's horse and gear."

"Don't bank on it. I don't know much about Injuns, but I hear they love to steal horses."

Ben probed the mud with his cane. "How soon do you think we can move?"

"If no more rain or floods, a couple of days at best." Mule was still staring northward, anger smoldering in his eyes. "If he hadn't stole Sam's horse I'd ride out and see how far this burn goes and maybe get us some game. Everyone's hungry as hell."

"I want to check the wagons we lost," Ben said. "I'll ride out and take a look and then you can take Ol' Jeb and scout around."

Ben could see that one of the wrecked wagons lay on its side, the other upside down with the wheels motionless against the sky. The fire had blackened them but they were far enough up the side of the hill that they escaped the floodwaters. Ben thought they were like more dead carcasses on the land. He almost expected to see vultures overheard. He hated vultures.

Ben knew the sun and wind would eventually dry the ground and they could be on their way. But on their way where? His guide was dead and none of the others had ever been this far west. Unlike the well-traveled main trail, there were few wagon tracks to mark this route. Yesterday Sam had said there was a small town ahead about four or five-days' travel. Hopefully he could hire a guide there.

He rode out to the wrecked wagons where he dismounted and poked around among the broken bottles of medication and scattered medical instruments that identified the contents of one wagon as his apothecary supplies. The other wagon had carried their food staples. He guessed that at least half or more of both wagons' contents was destroyed. Even though he hated to lose the medical supplies, his immediate concern was the loss of their food. The men were already hungry, and hungry men are hard to manage.

Ben mounted and rode back to the circled wagons. Elmo and Mule were standing by his wagon smoking and talking. They asked about the wrecked wagons' contents. "My medical supplies and our food staples," he answered.

"That's damn bad," Elmo said. "The boys are already hungry and short tempered. They want to put down another of the injured horses and take some steaks to eat. I told them I'd shoot the man that did. They also don't want no part of the rest of this trip unless you can come up with a reliable guide."

"We aren't going anywhere for awhile. We'll worry about that when we can travel," Ben said as he dismounted and checked the cinch before handing the reins to Mule. "Best go see the lay of the land. We need to get the teams to some grazing before long and our fresh water isn't going to last forever. I suppose the fire drove the game out, but if you see anything we can eat, don't miss."

Mule mounted, fussed with Ben's special fender and stirrup until it suited him, reached out and took his Sharps from the wagon seat before riding north. Ben climbed into the wagon and fished a cigar from his gear, bit off the end and fired it, then leaned back, thinking about all the adjustments that would have to be made if they were to continue their trip west. He finished the cigar and then walked through the mud to a large group of men gathered at one of the wagons.

Ben heard the crack of a rifle and saw a half-dozen vultures flapping up from the dead horses. The rifleman had missed and the remarks of the teamsters were not kind. "Let's see one of you bastards do any better with a busted arm." It was young Niles.

Ben looked out and saw the big birds gliding back down to continue their feast. He pushed through the group and stood by Niles. "May I have a look at your rifle?"

Niles hesitated before handing the gun to Ben. "I guess it's okay."

Ben saw it was a Ballard sporting rifle in excellent shape. "You have some cartridges?"

Niles held out a single round.

"You mind if I try my luck? I'll need five more rounds if you have 'em."

The young man fished in his pocket and held out more cartridges. "Go ahead, but you'll only get one shot."

The gathering spectators looked at one another anticipating a good laugh at their leader's expense. All, that is, except Elmo who took dollar wagers that Ben would get five of the six. They figured Elmo was as dumb as Ben. Elmo just grinned and took their bets.

Ben worked his boots into the mud until his bad leg was braced just right and then jammed his cane into the mud and accepted the .46 caliber rimfire cartridges from Niles. "What do you reckon, 125 yards?"

A couple of voices agreed, and Ben asked, "How does she hold? Dead on?"

"Dead on," Niles answered. "My daddy made sure of that."

Ben worked the action once, adjusted the sights, and chambered a cartridge. Next, he stuck a round between the little finger and ring finger, ring finger and middle finger, and middle finger and index finger of his left hand. He placed the last two rounds between his teeth. Shouldering the gun he drew a deep breath, paused, and squeezed off the first shot. Moving with familiar rhythm, Ben threw the action, grabbed a round from between his teeth, slipped it in the breech, and locked the breech – all so smooth and quick that the second big bird was knocked down before it was airborne. Again and again in less than half a minute the rifle barked and six vultures flopped on the ground around the dead horses. Ben exhaled, lowered the rifle, and extracted the last spent cartridge case.

"I hate vultures. Thanks, Niles, that's a very nice piece. I can see why you didn't want to leave it behind." He handed the gun back to a speechless Niles, grabbed his cane, and headed inside the circle of wagons.

8

THAT SHOULD GIVE THEM SOMETHING to take their minds off their bellies, he thought. And to help keep them occupied, I'll have them unload one of the wagons so I can retrieve the supplies from those wrecked wagons.

Ben was hardly around the first wagon when the men recovered. "Damned if I don't believe that's impossible. I wouldn't have believed it if I hadn't seen it," somebody said.

"I thought Elmo said he didn't have no use for guns?" another asked.

"Don't know about that, but he sure as hell knows how to use one. I swear that's the best shooting I ever seen," Niles said. "I'm going to give him this here gun to use until my arm heals. If we get attacked by Injuns I want to see him kill a bunch of them devils."

Niles charged around the wagon after Ben, soon followed by the others. The group caught up with Ben as he checked under the tarp of one of the wagons. Niles held out the Ballard to Ben. "This is the only thing my daddy ever left me and he said I weren't never to let nobody else use it, but I want you to use it until my arm heals. I'm sure my daddy wouldn't mind if he saw the way you shoot."

Ben jerked hard on the tarp and tied off the rope, then turned to face Niles and the gathering men. "I think you do just fine with the gun and I wouldn't want to go against your daddy's wishes again," Ben said.

Niles persisted, "I know daddy wouldn't care none. He'd be plumb proud to have you kill some Injuns with it."

"We haven't had any Indians bother us, and I'm betting we won't even see any," Ben said while thinking of Isaiah's abrupt disappearance.

Several men shoved their way to the front of the crowd just behind Niles. "You seem to forget that half-breed that stole Sam's horse and outfit," one said. "Rumor has it that underneath all your highfalutin ideals and beliefs you're just plain yeller when it comes to shooting anything except birds."

"Who and what I choose to shoot at is my business. It was when you hired on and it still is. You were all real anxious for a way to get out west and I'm providing that way and I still believe if we work together we can still get there. Since we've lost Sam and run into some trouble, I'll pay extra wages to those that see this trip through."

Elmo shouldered his way forward. "Ben, you know I'll stick with you, and I ain't needing no extra money. And, since I'm in charge, so will the lot of you. Those that don't agree can strike out on their own right now." He waited. No one left.

"I want that wagon unloaded," Ben said pointing with his cane to the third one down the line. "When it's empty, look me up and some of us will go back to the wrecked wagons and salvage what we can." He turned to Niles, "You'll have a hard time cleaning your rifle with a broken arm. Bring it by my wagon later and I'll clean it for you."

A driver hollered as they began to unload the wagon, "Damn, Ben, we're most near starved. When do we get something to eat?"

"Mule is out scouting right now and, if we're lucky, he'll get some game," Ben hollered back.

"You want us to off load the stuff right in the mud?"

"Take the canvas off and put it on the ground and stack the load on top."

Ben turned to another driver. "You get your team in harness and hooked up to the wagon. The rest of you start unloading."

The morning was warm and the ever-restless wind, tugging at anything in its path, blew south to north across the camp. The soaked, raw earth was yielding to the sun and wind, turning it to the consistency of glue. It stuck to the men's boots and trousers, the horses had mud balls hanging from their fetlocks and tails, and any horses that had rolled in the mud would take a lot of hard work to clean up before harnessing.

By mid-morning the wagon was unloaded and the team hitched just as Mule rode in from the northeast. Everyone crowded forward to hear his report. "The burn stops just over that yonder rise. Grass for the horses and about a mile to the east is a small stream with good water," Mule said.

"See any game?" someone asked. Mule answered that the only thing he'd seen were a couple of burned carcasses already fly infested and bloated.

"Mule," Ben asked, "do you think it would be safe to drive the horses to grass and water?"

"I didn't see no sign at all of any trouble." Mule replied. "But we best leave about half the men here to guard camp and take the rest to help herd the horses. We can load the water barrels in the wagon and some of the men can ride shotgun."

Elmo picked six armed men to ride in the wagon before climbing up onto the seat. As soon as Ben mounted Ol' Jeb they moved out. Ben noticed that even the empty wagon was difficult to drag through the sticky mud. It's going to be at least a couple more days before we can move the loaded wagons, he realized. He also wondered how and where they would get food. If the men didn't get something to eat by nightfall, most likely they would have to resort to horseflesh. Besides his aversion to eating something he was so fond of, they were already one team short and they would need every horse in harness when they were able to move out.

The men stomped through the mud and after plenty of cussing the horses moved out of the wagon enclosure and followed behind Elmo's wagon. Once over the knoll and into the prairie grass the herd put their heads down and grazed allowing the men to gather in small groups, talk, smoke, and envy the feeding animals.

Ben waved Mule over to the wagon. "They're going to graze for a while, but soon they will want water more than grass. If they get a smell of the water we won't be able to stop 'em. You best go around and tell the boys that if they start for the water to let 'em go."

9

ISAIAH BENTEEN CUT THE TRAIL of a dozen horses about ten miles upstream from Ben's wagon train. He quickly kneed his mount deep enough into the trees lining the creek to be hidden before he dismounted and tied Sam's horse to a tree. He pulled Sam's Henry from the scabbard and checked the chamber. After a moment of listening and watching, he walked back to study the tracks in the damp earth. He didn't have to spend much time deciding they were either a small hunting party or a raiding party headed downstream. No doubt Sioux or Cheyenne and because they were coming in from the north, they would have killed all the game they needed since the fire would have driven hundreds of deer, antelope, and other game right into their path. So it would no longer be a hunting party, but rather a raiding party looking for the likes of Ben Kelley's stranded wagon train with many horses, many coup, and many scalps.

Isaiah selected a big cottonwood tree close enough to the edge of the timber to give him a view of the rolling countryside, squatted down, and leaned back against the tree trunk. He was making an honest effort to be white. Hell, he was doing good. Didn't he have a big elk and some firewood lashed on Sam's horse? Wasn't he taking it back to the wagons?

The struggle was back with him, the endless conflict to be red or to be white. He was neither, and neither Indians nor whites accepted him. He could almost feel the thoughts and emotions of the Sioux or Cheyenne when they discovered the wagon train.

The warrior blood would run hot and the prospect of blood on a scalping knife would bring them alive as nothing else could.

He could see in his mind's eye the victorious warriors telling of the battle and the singing of the victory song before the council with the firelight sparkling off the eyes of the young maidens. His tribe, the Crow, were bitter enemies of the Sioux, but for a minute he wished he were riding with them.

Isaiah closed his eyes and sought to speak with the spirit of his mother. His mother's memory, never far from his consciousness, came forward strong and vivid as if only yesterday he'd ridden away from the Crow camp. It was the last time he'd seen his mother.

He'd learned that his mother was eighteen when she was captured from a wagon train. She had endured the hardships of a slave until eventually earning the respect of the tribe. His father had taken her as a wife in the third year of her captivity, and even now Isaiah could still hear, in his mind, the arguments between his parents about her teaching their son the white man's language and ways. His mother persisted and eventually prevailed. Her one sustaining passion was to educate Isaiah to white ways and to prepare him for an eventual life in the white man's world.

Wise beyond her years, she foresaw the time when the Indians would have to yield before the onrush of the white man's westward migration. In secret she would tell him that the Crow's way of life was doomed. He would have to learn to be white to survive. He should choose to be white. She extracted a promise from him that he would live three winters among the whites and then choose, for he would have to choose. He could not be both Indian and white.

The memory faded and Isaiah opened his eyes, remained motionless against the cottonwood, and scanned the prairie before him. Why couldn't he be both? In reality he was both. With growing excitement he realized here was an opportunity to be both. He could return to the wagon train with the food as he had planned and he could fight the old enemy – the Sioux – at the same time.

Blood pounded through his veins as he rose and walked to the horses. He untied his roll from behind the saddle and spread it on the ground at his feet. He picked up his medicine bundle and hung it around his neck thinking of the vision he had sought and the items the Great Spirit said should make up his sacred medicine. Last, he picked up a small deerskin pouch, opened the leather drawstring, and painted his face and body.

He was lashing the roll behind the saddle when the horses lifted their heads and looked downstream. Isaiah knew his mount wouldn't give them away but he wasn't sure about Sam's sorrel. Quickly he was beside the horse talking to it in low, soothing Crow, ready to put his hand over its nostrils if necessary. I'll bet it's a Sioux warrior headed to the main camp, he thought. Following the direction of the horse's gaze, he watched downstream while he slipped a quiver of arrows onto his back and shoved a tomahawk into his belt.

He considered Sam's Henry for only a second – besides the noise, he wanted to meet this Sioux, if that's what had the horse's attention, warrior to warrior as a Crow brave.

There would not be time to circle around and warn the men at the wagons. The best way to help Ben was to intercept the scout so reinforcements would be delayed. He could tell by the horses that whatever had their attention was coming close. Probably the band would send a young brave, one less worthy of battle, to carry the message back to the main camp.

He had guessed right. A young brave was riding hard across the open prairie headed northwest. Isaiah let the rider pass before swinging up on his own mount. He was just at the edge of the timber when Sam's horse whinnied long and loud. The young Sioux pulled up his mount and looked over his shoulder.

The Sioux rode warily toward the creek while scanning the countryside and peering into the shadows of the trees. Sam's horse called another greeting. The Sioux drew an arrow and fitted it on the bowstring before continuing slowly forward. Isaiah was leaning over his pony's neck talking softly about the scalp he would take and the part he expected his mount to do. He was thankful his mount was trained for war and could be guided by the shift of his weight and the press of his knees. When the oncoming rider was fifty yards from the tree line, Isaiah rode into the open slightly downstream to cut off retreat to the war party in case the Sioux decided to run instead of fight.

The young Sioux was a fighter. With a wild war cry, he charged straight toward Isaiah who held his ground until the distance shrank to a dozen horse lengths and the Sioux had drawn his bow, ready to release the shaft. Isaiah grunted to the pony and slid down on the far side of the animal as the feathered shaft leapt from the bowstring through the space where his body had been. Isaiah swung upright in the saddle, drew his tomahawk and kneed his horse on a collision course with the charging Sioux. The young warrior frantically tried to notch another arrow when Isaiah swung the tomahawk and buried it in the Sioux's chest. Instantly Isaiah was on the ground running toward the young brave who had slid from his horse. The Sioux tried to stand and draw his own knife but sank into the grass just as Isaiah reached him.

"I am Two Suns, born on a day that lived twice, son of a Crow chief. Your scalp will hang in my lodge and I will tell my children not to fear the Sioux for they fight like a toothless old woman," Isaiah boasted as he watched blank eyes roll back in the youth's face. He grabbed the raven-black braids and scalped him even as the last convulsions of death made his limbs quiver and twitch.

He gathered up the horses, tied the wet scalp to his saddle, retrieved his weapons and the spoils of victory from the dead enemy, mounted and, leading the Sioux's pony, rode back to get Sam's outfit.

Leading the two animals, he crossed the small stream and headed south. His mother would frown at the scalp but be pleased with his decision to help the people of her own race. His father would be proud of the scalp but frown at his decision to help a train of whites who wanted to drive the Crow from their sacred ground. It was hard as hell being a breed for even now, flushed with the heady wine of victory, he couldn't escape what he was.

He rode downstream in the cover of the tree line along the meandering creek, feeling at home in the wild setting and feeling pure Crow brave, but a brave with no lodge pole to hang the Sioux scalp from and no council of warriors to hear his deeds of war. He stopped along the stream to slake his thirst and, bending over the water, he saw his reflection. A yellow circle on each cheek and a black line down the bridge of his nose was the facial war paint of Two Suns. After he and the horses had their fill of water, he washed the paint from his face. It wouldn't do to be mistaken for a hostile and shot by one of the whites he thought. He changed his bow and quiver for Sam's Henry, his breechclout for worn trousers and faded shirt, then rode toward the wagons.

10

THE HORSES GRAZED WHILE BEN, realizing he was also hungry, could only listen to his stomach growl. The sun in a cloudless sky had warmed the morning and the south wind blew clean and fresh. It was a peaceful scene, but the events of the last twenty-four hours overrode the tranquility of the moment in Ben's mind. He reined over and spoke to Mule. "I'd like to get the horses back to the wagons as soon as possible. I don't know quite how to describe it, but somehow I feel naked out here. I think we should push them to water now."

"You too? The hair's been up on my neck most ever since we left yonder camp. I'll feel better once the whole shebang is done and we're back amongst the wagons. Let's move 'em along. Maybe we can let them graze a bit more on the way back."

The men in the wagon held their weapons at the ready, and their eyes flicked nervously over the empty countryside. They were unshaven, muddy, tainted with soot and smoke from the fire, and mighty gaunt. They would make good rebs, Ben thought and wondered how they'd stand up in a fight.

Ben rode around the grazing horses and soon the men had them moving toward the distant tree line that Mule said flanked a small, fresh, running stream. Before long the lead horses scented the water ahead and broke into a trot and then a gallop. When they were within a hundred yards from the trees, a heavy-caliber rifle report slapped the prairie awake and the trees belched a line of painted warriors.

At the rifle shot and war cries, Elmo bellowed, "Let's get them damn horses back to the wagons!" Then he whipped the team savagely and raced to get between the charging Indians and the herd. "Men," he hollered over his shoulder to those in the wagon. "That son of a bitching breed has done brung his friends. Let's show 'em some powder and shot."

As the wagon careened across the grass, empty water barrels rolled from side to side in the wagon box, slamming into the riflemen, causing the first volley to go wild. One of the men threw the barrels overboard where they bounced and rolled aimlessly on the grass like living beasts. Elmo pulled the wagon to a halt in the path of the Indians and the men hunkered down and poured an effective fire into the charging warriors.

The horses milled in confusion for a second, then turned and stampeded through the line of dismounted teamsters. Ben swung in on the north side of the fleeing herd, knowing that if the horses were lost they could never move the wagons or get any further west and they might all perish out here on foot. He didn't want to believe it, but it looked like the men were right about Isaiah. He heard the gunfire behind him as he urged Ol' Jeb on to overtake the herd and turn it back toward the wagons. An arrow impaled itself in the sod ahead and quivered there, its feathered shaft like a bright, deadly prairie flower.

A gun barked and he heard the angry hum of a bullet. That unforgettable sound pulled him back to the battlefield where the cry of wounded and dying men and horses was woven together between the snap and whine of Union bullets. He remembered the cavalry charge, the crash of artillery, the searing pain, and then blackness.

Willing himself back to the present, he urged Ol' Jeb up beside the lead horse and used his cane to turn it toward the wagons. He had to spur his mind hard to outride the memories and fight down the panic that seized him. He'd survived the insanity of the war, but now he wondered if he was going to die before he'd had a chance at his new life.

Glancing over his shoulder, he saw a half-dozen Indians cutting out horses and driving them north as two other warriors dogged his tracks. He was sure he could outrun them but he couldn't leave the rest of the horse herd. Damn. He rode low hoping for a miracle, praying he could somehow drive the herd into the circled wagons. They pounded over the rise that marked the end of the green grass and were in the mud of the backfire when he again looked back. The two warriors still dogged him. He could see that Elmo and the teamsters had driven back the rest of the Indians, but his men were too far away to offer any help.

Three shots in rapid succession made Ben look back again. One of the Indians pitched forward over his horse's neck. The second reined up and fired an ancient smoothbore musket at someone Ben couldn't see at the moment. Then, through the flying mud and charging horses he caught a glimpse of a saddled horse standing beside a kneeling rifleman who was taking deliberate aim at the warrior who gave up the fight and fled.

Whoever it was saved my life, Ben thought. Then he recognized the horse beside the rifleman. A bay mustang, Isaiah's horse. The breed sent one more round after the fleeing rider and then swung up on his mount. The Indians broke off the attack, retrieved their fallen comrades, and raced after the stolen horses. Mule's big Sharps spoke one last time and then the battlefield was quiet.

Ben pulled up the lathered and mud-splattered Ol' Jeb and slumped in the saddle. He absentmindedly picked mud from his clothes and wiped it from his face as he watched some of his horses disappear. Maybe his dad had been right. Maybe you can't survive out here without fighting and killing to protect yourself and yours.

He was tired and his bum leg hurt like hell. He reached down and began rubbing it as Isaiah rode up. "You hit?"

"No," Ben looked up. "I'm okay. I don't know much about Indians, but since you seem to be on our side, I don't believe you brought them here. But, I'd like to hear you tell me that, and why you stole Sam's horse and outfit."

"You think that I brought the Sioux? I am Crow; they are my enemy. He flung the wet scalp at Ben. "There is how I treat the Sioux. I didn't steal Sam's horse. I borrowed it to carry food and firewood back to your camp."

Ben caught the bloody scalp and looked at it with curiosity and revulsion.

"Where did you get this?"

"From a young Sioux riding back to bring more warriors," Isaiah said and held out his hand for the scalp. "But, if you don't believe me, I will go and leave you and the others to die out here from your own folly. But, before I go, I will bring back the guide's horse and outfit and the elk that I killed."

"I believe you," Ben said, knowing he owed this man his life. "But it will be a different story with them." He pointed to the wagons and men.

"I know your men don't like me so it'd be best if you talked to them while I ride back and pick up Sam's horse. When I return, if they still won't accept me, I'll move on."

"I'll talk to the men. You will always be welcome at my camp. I'll see to that."

Isaiah rode north in a wide circle and soon dropped from sight behind a distant rise. Ben trotted toward the men and wagon where Elmo walked out to meet him. "Wasn't that the breed?

"It was, but he didn't bring the Indians," Ben said. "In fact, he saved my life and killed at least two of 'em. I saw one of the scalps myself."

"In a pig's arse. You ain't believing no stinking redskin are you?" someone shouted.

Ben waved Elmo up front. "Yes, I am. Isaiah's coming back with Sam's outfit, food, and dry firewood, which was his purpose all along. Elmo, you see that he's not mistreated."

"I'll believe that when I see it," a driver said. "You'd best take a look at Smith. He took an arrow in the leg."

Ben reined Ol' Jeb toward the rear of the wagon. Smith was stretched out on the ground, his trouser leg cut off exposing a nasty wound to the upper thigh. Ben dismounted and limped toward the group. As he entered the circle of men, Mule stood with his back to Ben directing a stream of dark yellow urine onto the wound.

"What the – Mule?" Ben demanded.

"He just got stuck with a damn ol' arrow. I done pulled it out. Didn't know if you were going to live long enough to doctor him so I done fixed him up. Hell, everybody knows you spit on a wound above the gut and piss on anything below." A couple of the men nodded agreement. "I done did both. Slapped on a good, fresh chaw of tobacco after I pulled out the arrow and she's done been pissed on real good," Mule said, buttoning his trousers.

"I'd sure like some water," Smith said.

"Mule, you take Ol' Jeb and get the rest of the horses inside the wagons," Ben said handing him the reins. "You men on foot give him what help you can. Elmo, you take the wagon and some men and fill the water barrels at the creek. Stop by here on the way back and pick us up. I'll look at Smith while you're gone."

"Did you say the breed was bringing food?" Elmo asked.

"That's right, a fresh killed elk and some dry firewood."

The mention of food turned everyone's head. "How do we know it ain't some trick?" someone asked.

"You don't," Ben answered. "But at least if the Indians come back, you can fight on a full belly. Now let's get cracking. If there is a Sioux camp not far from here as Isaiah believes, I'd like to be inside our wagons before they return."

Thoughts of food and Indians galvanized the men into action. Ben knelt beside Smith and began cleaning the wound. He finished cleaning the tobacco away before taking Smith's bandanna and tying it around the leg above the wound.

"Sure could use a drink of whisky," Smith said.

"I certainly agree with that. As soon as we get you back to camp I'll treat the wound properly.

"I don't have any whisky, but I can give you something to hold down the pain when we get back to the wagons," Ben replied and thought that at the moment it wasn't a life threatening wound but getting it clean and avoiding gangrene was critical.

"Ben, do you think the Indians will come back?"

"I don't know. I'm hoping Isaiah will return because he's the only one who knows this country and the Sioux."

"We're in kind of bad shape, ain't we?" Smith asked. "How many horses did they get?"

"I'd guess about a hundred head. Haven't had a chance to get a count."

"Sure could use some water," Smith said licking his dry lips and closing his eyes.

"They'll be along with the wagon soon. You best rest quiet 'til then," Ben said, hauling himself to his feet with the help of his cane and retrieving Smith's hat which he took back and put over the man's eyes. Then he sat down in the grass beside Smith and took a mental tally of their situation. He guessed they were at least fifteen six-horse hitches short. Which wagons would he have to leave behind? Could, and would, Isaiah guide them to the next settlement? What if he didn't come back? They would have to eat at least one horse; they couldn't do without food forever. And if the Sioux did come back? He didn't know; he didn't want to think about that now.

This country is sure big, he thought as he looked around at the waving grass and the cloudless sky. The south wind surged and ebbed like the inhaling and exhaling of a giant, mournful, living thing. The feeling of loneliness was almost overpowering, and he felt a new respect for anyone who could traverse these trackless expanses. He checked Smith's leg and noticed that even out here the flies wasted little time in visiting a fresh wound. He poked at the grass with his cane and saw the new shoots of green among the brown, dry clumps and stalks. Other plants, too, were beginning to push their way upward toward the warm spring sun. He was surprised to discover tiny, delicate purple flowers

already in bloom. Here at his feet was a renaissance of life unaware of insane wars, prairie fires, and war-painted savages. He
was glad when the wagon drew rein beside them. They loaded
Smith in the back and Ben struggled up to the seat next to Elmo.

"Couple of the water barrels got busted up. If I can find the
blacksmith tools, I can fix 'em," Elmo said, holding the lines
loosely in his big hands.

Ben could hear the sloshing of the water in the barrels and
realized how thirsty he was, which reminded him that the horses
hadn't made it to water and that would have to be done soon.
Once back inside the circled wagons, the teamsters crowded
around with tin cups, water skins, and any container that would
hold water. After they all had their fill of the sweet, cool water,
they moved Smith to Ben's covered wagon and made him as
comfortable as possible. Ben was intrigued by the wound, which
seemed to be much larger than a mere arrow would warrant. It
also resisted his efforts to stop the bleeding. Ben was just applying the finishing touches on the dressing when a shout of "Rider
coming!" made its way around the camp.

Isaiah stopped on the rise north of the camp and squinted
across the black, muddy plain to the circled wagons. At least one
of the white eyes is a damn good shot, he thought when he saw
the dead vultures near the horses' remains. He rode toward the
wagons thinking of his mother and wondered how she would
feel if she could ride down to the camp and rejoin her own kind.
Isaiah decided his mother would be disappointed in the whites
with maybe the exception of Ben. Somehow, Ben was different
and Isaiah found himself drawn to the cripple. He thought his
mother would like him too.

He could see the teamsters gathered behind the wagons
watching his approach. He caught the glint of sun on steel and
bet the ungrateful bastards had at least a dozen rifles trained on
him. He rode straight toward the group.

"It's the breed, just like Ben said," Mule drawled, sighting
down the barrel of his Sharps.

"By god, you're right. Got a critter lashed on Sam's outfit and some firewood. Let him in," Elmo hollered.

Empty bellies overcame hostilities as Isaiah rode through the group toward Ben. Stopping, he said loud enough for all to hear, "Here is Sam's horse, firewood, and food just as I said." He tossed the reins to Ben. After a brief hesitation he handed Sam's Henry to Ben.

"You keep it," Ben said handing it back. "You've more than earned it. I'm much obliged to you for saving my life and I apologize for doubting you." Ben held out his hand. "I'd be proud to have you join us. We could sure use your knowledge of this land."

The men crowded around as Isaiah leaned over and shook hands with Ben. Their eyes roamed over the breed and his captured Sioux mount and the fresh scalp tied to his saddle. "Mule, you and the men get this animal skinned and a fire going," Ben said.

Knives slashed at the binding that held elk and firewood. Someone tied a raised wagon tongue to the front of the wagon and soon the critter was hanging there ready for butchering. Two teamsters skinned it with dispatch and by the time the carcass was hanging naked, a fire was roaring. Men appeared with various utensils to hold a hunk of meat over the fire. Some had pulled the end-gate rods from the wagon boxes, some simply stuck a chunk on the end of a knife and waved it over the fire a few times before wolfing it down.

Elmo produced a Confederate officer's sword and impaled his small portion on the tip while crowding his way between the men grouped around the fire. He squatted by the blazing fire and turned the blade as the hunk of meat sizzled and the tantalizing aroma of roasting meat filled the air. A hunk of meat slid off a knife blade into the fire. The owner stabbed it, held it up, pronounced it just right, and proceeded to eat it with obvious relish.

Niles pushed through the group with a coffeepot in his good arm. A pair of helping hands grabbed the pot and set it onto the coals and soon the smell of brewing coffee added to the aroma.

Frenchie, a tall, thin Frenchman who somehow managed to maintain an air of dignity despite the circumstances, approached the fire with a chunk of meat in one hand and an ancient smoothbore in the crook of his arm. At the fire he set the gun on its stock, affixed a long bayonet, and skewered the meat. Then with solemn dignity he bowed his head and said grace in French. That done, he knelt on one knee and held the roast over the fire.

"Frenchie, is that son of a bitch loaded?" Elmo asked, looking across the fire directly into the gaping bore of the rifle.

"Oui," Frenchie replied, and then slipped into English. "For the Indians I have loaded it with double powder and shot."

"Frenchie," Elmo said as he moved to a less threatening spot, "I wonder if I might not be safer with the Indians than with you."

Somebody laughed, tin cups clanked against the coffee pot, and someone belched loud and long. More laughter. Ben and Isaiah stood together by Ben's wagon. "A little food sure can brighten one's outlook."

"Yes," Isaiah answered, running his hands over the Sioux pony. "But they will soon enough be hungry again. And if you are serious about me working as your guide, we have much that needs to be done."

"I'm dead serious," Ben replied. "I'll pay guide's wages until we get to the next town and then we can decide what to do."

Elmo walked over where Isaiah and Ben were talking in the shade of his wagon.

"Brought you a bit of meat," Elmo said, holding out the sword. "One elk doesn't go all that far feeding this bunch of hungry men."

"Thanks," Ben replied, taking the offering. "Get someone to boil a chunk of this. It'll make good broth for Smith."

"You said Mule was to help me run things. I thought you ought to know that he's been acting a might queer since the Indians done made off with the horses," Elmo said.

Ben nodded. "I suspect that has made all of us do some right hard thinking. I'll talk with him the first chance I get. Thanks."

Elmo stood with his hand shoved in his pockets toeing the mud with his boot. Finally he looked up at Isaiah. "Guess I had you figured wrong. Can't rightly say how the others feel, but I'm plumb grateful for your help." He turned and left before Isaiah could respond.

11

BEN SAVORED THE MEAT and when he finished, for lack of a better option, he wiped his mouth on his shirtsleeves and his hands on his trousers. He felt grubby. Hell, they were all grubby. He climbed into the wagon and checked Smith's wound. The bleeding had slowed some but hadn't stopped completely. That worried him, but thankfully the morphine had allowed Smith some relief and even some fitful sleep.

The wagon shifted as someone climbed aboard. "That you, Isaiah?"

"Yes. There is much that must be done before nightfall," Isaiah said.

"I'll get word to the men that you're the new guide. But first, two questions. My medical curiosity is aroused by that leg wound. Is there any way you could come up with an arrow like the one Mule pulled out of Smith?"

"Sure, got a quiver full of 'em on that Sioux's horse." He ducked out of the canvas and returned with the quiver and handed it to Ben.

"Thanks," Ben said, looking briefly at the quiver and then setting it aside. "You mentioned a need to take care of some things before dark; you're thinking Sioux, right?"

"Sioux, thirsty horses, more food, and whether or not the men will accept me."

"Let's get this thing with the men settled right now," Ben said picking up a tin plate from among the wagon utensils and hammering on it with the head of his cane until the men stopped what they were doing and looked his direction. He waved them to the wagon. Word was spread and soon the entire group had gathered.

"I have just hired Isaiah as guide, and he will have that position until we reach the next settlement. Are there any questions?" Ben noticed that Mule and three of the men stood together at the side of the group, but they offered no objections or comment.

"How about the Injuns that jumped us. They coming back?" a man asked.

"Isaiah knows the Sioux better than any of us. I'll let him answer."

"I am sure the Sioux will be back," Isaiah began. "With how many warriors I don't know. That is why I am going to ride out and scout the Sioux camp."

He addressed the group with an ease and confidence that surprised Ben. After Isaiah finished speaking, the men exchanged excited talk among themselves until Isaiah lifted the Henry above his head for quiet. "If you don't trust me, I'll accept a volunteer to scout the Indian camp and their movements."

Quiet prevailed. Watching the men, Ben thought that Isaiah knew more about handling men than most officers he'd seen. Isaiah let the quiet stretch thin. He stood impassive and immovable staring at the men. The point was unmistakable; Isaiah would be the train's new guide.

"I will go," Isaiah reiterated. "There are other things that must be done before sundown. The horses need water, the water barrels need refilled, the wagons need to be tightened up, and more camp meat must be killed. Any volunteers?"

Elmo came forward and Isaiah asked, "Can you get the horses to water and refill the water barrels?"

"You can count on it," Elmo replied.

"Thanks," Ben said, then added, "Elmo, get a good tally on the horses." Ben swept his cane toward the horses and wagons. "I've got to figure out what to leave behind." Elmo nodded.

Mule approached Ben and Isaiah. "If you want, I'll try for some camp meat if you can tell me which'd be the best direction to hunt."

The breed grinned, "Why not ride along with me? We can hunt on the way out, and if we're lucky, you can get back to camp with fresh meat before dark."

While Isaiah and Mule were getting the two Indian ponies ready to leave camp, Ben looked in on Smith. He was still resting quietly on the pallet of blankets, the dressing on the leg soaked red. Ben searched through the wagon but was unable to find the supplies he wanted. Got to get back to that wagon and salvage what I can, he told himself. Soon as the men get back with the horses and wagon, I've got to remember to send someone to get those supplies. He decided to let Smith rest since he didn't have a clean change of dressing anyway.

Mounting up to ride out of camp, Isaiah grabbed the Sioux scalp and held it out toward Mule, "Aren't you afraid I'll scalp you once we get over that rise?"

The big Sharps moved almost imperceptibly yet it trained without waver on Isaiah's chest. "I don't think it'd be worth your trouble," Mule said, sweeping off his hat and revealing his gleaming bald head.

Isaiah dropped the scalp back on the saddle pommel and held out his hand. "We may be riding into trouble and I just wanted to make sure you had some sand in your craw."

Ben came up just as the two shook hands. Ben watched the pair ride off and thought, good and brave men whom I'm lucky to have with me. He eyed the sun and figured at least three hours until sundown. Soon as the men get back from water, we've got to get cracking and close up those gaps between the wagons. He didn't really expect an Indian attack, but one thing he had learned during the war was to listen to battle-hardened veterans. Out here, Isaiah was the only Indian fighter in their group.

He walked a ways outside the wagons and checked the ground. The horses and men had the earth inside the circled wagons tromped down, so he couldn't really tell if it was drying or not. The sun and wind had worked on the black earth. Most of the surface water was gone and his boots and cane told him it was much firmer. If they could get the wagons sorted out, maybe they could move day after tomorrow. That is, if no more trouble overtook them.

– 12 –

AFTER CRAWLING BACK INTO HIS WAGON, Ben put his stethoscope on Smith's chest and heard the rhythmic beat of a strong heart. Good, he thought, as he dropped the instrument into his black leather bag. Then he sat down on the wagon floor and stretched his leg to ease the pain. Like Mule, he had mostly learned to ignore the physical discomfort. It was the mental agony that he sometimes couldn't shake.

Minutes later the wind rattled the canvas against the bows and whistled mournfully through the wagon. Fighting back the depression, he crawled outside as Elmo walked up.

"Did you get a count?" Ben asked.

"It may be a bit worse than we thought."

"Damn," Ben said. "We're going to have to lighten some loads."

Elmo was silent for a moment and then asked, "If it's okay by you, some of the men would like to take the team and wagon and gather up a load of firewood. Fire sure would be welcome come sundown."

"I agree," Ben answered. "I don't expect any trouble, but Isaiah said we should close up the gaps between the wagons. Harness as many teams as you need to drag the wagons tight together so a rider can't get through – wheel to wheel."

"That's going to be a lot of hard work," Elmo said, taking off his hat and scratching the back of his head.

"I know, but let's get it done before dark. And, make sure those men are back from the creek before sundown."

Elmo left and Ben tried to recall as much as he could of Sun Tzu's *The Art of War*. He searched his mind for anything that would help them if the Sioux returned. Experience had taught him that time to think could be his best ally or his worst enemy. His old adversary was here now, wanting to pull him down into despair and depression, focusing on the injustice of it all. The war, his injury, being left with only half his manhood, and being rejected by Adeline. Ah, dear sweet Adeline. Before he rode off to war, she had accepted his proposal of marriage when he was tall, strong, and proud in his officer's uniform. Now she had refused to see him, and worse, maybe believed he was a coward.

With great effort he drew his mind from his once betrothed to the muddy prairie, halfway to nowhere, and in the middle of hell. Smith's wound still refused to stop seeping. He saw Elmo and crew headed for the creek with the team and wagon, and once more he made a mental note of the urgent need to salvage the apothecary supplies, but for now it would have to wait.

Ben seated himself in the wagon bed and picked up the Sioux quiver. His examination of the arrows was interrupted when the men hitched four teams to his wagon and hauled it forward to lock wheels with the wagon in front. Shadows were growing longer, reminding him that it wouldn't be long before sundown. He knew Isaiah could take care of himself, but he hoped like hell Mule made it back before dark. Slowly, his head dropped to his chest and his eyes closed.

He slept while the sun slid behind the horizon, painting the prairie sky with a thousand hues of scarlet, and the wind died down to a peaceful calm. Mule, after hollering to the camp from the knoll, rode through the break in the wagons. In the fading twilight he appeared as a mythical creature: part horse, part bird, ridden by one of the ancients. The scarlet of the sunset clung like dew to Mule's drooping, white mustache and reflected like glowing coals from the eyes of his mount. The shiny old Sharps rested like a sword of fire across the saddle. When he pulled up at the campfire, the Pegasus wings dropped to the ground as Mule untied a dozen turkeys from the saddle pommel.

"Sorry, boys, but you're all going to have to eat fowl, or go hungry," Mule said to the men.

"See any Injuns?" someone asked.

"Nary a one, but Isaiah said if they didn't want to be seen, I'd not spot 'em until it was too late."

"How about Isaiah, you think he'll be back?" a teamster asked.

"Reckon you can stake your life on it," Mule answered.

A full, blood-red moon paused momentarily on the eastern horizon as if to garner strength before its climb to join the countless stars overhead. A large campfire blazed and the camp waited, each man with his own thoughts. All hoping one half-breed Indian would appear and reassure them they were safe, but fearing instead that many Indians would sweep down upon them with the morning dawn.

Ben slept sitting in the wagon, Sioux quiver and arrow in his lap until Smith's stirring awoke him. Moonlight streamed through the canvas and the cool night air crept into every joint in Ben's body. He shivered and reached for his watch and tilted it to the moonlight. It was almost two in the morning.

"Edward, Ed Smith, can you hear me? It's Dr. Kelley," he said rubbing the circulation into his leg before trying to get up. No answer. He struck a match to look for the bull's-eye lantern that he always carried. In the brief illumination of the match he could see the sheen of sweat on Smith's face.

The wagon shifted. Glancing over his shoulder, Ben froze as a naked, painted torso appeared at the canvas opening. "Ben, you in here? It's Isaiah."

"Jeez, you trying to scare me to death?" Ben asked. "Or, get shot?"

Isaiah crawled the rest of the way in the wagon. "Didn't have time to change to white clothes. I've had company. If I didn't make it back, I wanted to die as a Crow warrior."

"What do you mean you had company?" Ben asked as he adjusted the lantern's wick. Pulling aside the canvas Isaiah pointed north where three riders were silhouetted against the horizon.

"Sioux?"

"Yes?"

"How many?"

"Only those now. Ho, they will not brag around the council fire tonight. Three Sioux braves couldn't catch one Crow."

"Are more on the way?" Ben questioned as he watched the riders' silhouettes.

A hint of excitement tinged Isaiah's voice as he answered, "Many more, many lodges, many warriors. I hope the men with you are brave."

"How soon will they be here?"

"The main party will probably be here sometime tomorrow afternoon," Isaiah replied.

"We better alert the rest of the men," Ben said.

"No need to worry them until just before dawn."

"That's fortunate," Ben said. "Obviously our sentries aren't worth a damn. But you better get out of those clothes before someone does notice."

Ed Smith's feverish eyes opened to focus on Isaiah's breech-clout, war paint, and braided black hair. Ed's screams awoke the camp, and Ben had his hands full trying to calm Smith while letting the men know that Isaiah, not a Sioux, was the warrior among them.

Eventually the camp settled down so Ben could find the last of his supply of morphine. He gave it to Smith, waiting for it to bring the man relief while the camp buzzed like a hive of angry hornets.

After Smith calmed, Ben tromped through the mud to the campfire where Elmo and the rest were watching the Sioux on the distant rise. Isaiah had changed into his white clothes but a smear of paint was still at the edges of his face when he joined Ben. Armed men stood around the circle of wagons, peering into the night, checking and re-checking their weapons.

"When do you think they'll attack?"

"How many?"

"Can we make a run for it?"

Isaiah answered all their questions patiently, assuring them that they wouldn't be bothered until dawn. Maybe not even then. The group fell silent. Mule and two of the teamsters approached Ben and Isaiah. "I allow there ain't no doubts about the situation now," Mule said.

"Guess not," Ben answered, trying to read Mule's face in the flickering firelight.

Mule shifted the Sharps from one hand to the other, rubbed his face with a dirty hand, tugged at his hat, let fly with a stream of tobacco juice, cleared his throat, and then looked at Ben and Isaiah. "Don't rightly know how's to say this but me and a couple of the boys here would like to shove on ahead of our own self."

"I'll be damned," Ben said. "You're the last one I'd have figured to break our deal."

"Now I reckon it looks like we're running yeller on you, but it ain't like that no how."

Isaiah walked over and began checking the two Indian ponies he would trust with his life in the hours ahead. As he rubbed down the horses and checked the gear he thought how complicated the whites made their lives. All a man really needed was a good horse and gun. He didn't believe he could ever understand them.

Ben waited until Isaiah was out of earshot. "If it isn't as it appears, would you mind telling me how it is?"

"I'm not yeller. I done my share of fighting and I got nothing against killing Injuns." Mule retrieved a folded letter from inside his jacket and offered it to Ben. "Remember the little settlement we come through at the railhead a couple weeks back and there was mail for some of us?"

Ben nodded, remembering how he'd secretly hoped against hope for a letter from Adeline.

Mule continued, "Well, there ain't many that would rightly understand, so I didn't make no mention of it, but I reckon I'm a granddaddy."

"Congratulations," Ben said, noticing a flicker of pride in the man's eyes. "But what does that have to do with us?"

"I thought surely you would understand. You know the war took all my family."

Ben did understand and he cursed the war silently – he cursed killing and dying; he cursed guns and swords; he cursed men who couldn't work out their differences without violence; he cursed the memories that followed a man a thousand miles and made him live it all over again in the middle of a bright day as well as the dark of night.

The two men were drawn together in a brotherhood of remembrance and suffering that blocked out the rest of the world. After reading the pain and hurt in his eyes, Ben spoke. "Mule, I'm not wanting to pry, but you spoke of a grandchild?"

"You remember how the loss of the boys was too much for Ma. She just pined away and died. She just lost the will to live. Especially after Ruben come home."

"I remember."

"Reckon I don't blame her none because I about gived up myself except Ruben needed caring for. There's some sure enough good people in this world. Ruben's wife accepted him back and helped care for him without a whimper. He didn't never get much better, but she loved him. As you recall, we buried him about half a year ago. I didn't think he could make no baby but his wife said in this letter that I got a grandson to carry on my name."

"You can send for them to join you when we get to wherever it is we stop. And I'm betting it won't be too long before the rails run clear to the Pacific," Ben said.

"I ain't got much religion left after the war. I ain't even sure there is a God if he'd let man do those things to other men. I ain't asked for nothing from him since the war until I got that letter and then I been asking every day that I get to see that little feller before I cash in."

"You appear to be a long way from cashing in, but when we reach the next settlement, if you want to catch a party going back, I won't hold you to our deal."

Mule spit, "I'm beholden that you would do that, but you see I'm needing to leave here right soon."

"Why not wait 'til Isaiah has a chance to scout the Sioux? I'm betting that they were so glad to get all those horses that they are not going to cause us any more trouble."

"Listen, early in the war I took a Union ball and still carry it lodged up near my shoulder blade. Most of the time, since it healed, I just pay it no never mind. When I went back to the front lines, it always started hurting to beat hell just before those blue bellies would jump us. Every mother's son in my old outfit will tell you it never failed. Right now it's paining me something fierce. There's going to be hell popping around here before long and I'd like to be plumb on my way to see that young'n before that happens."

Ben reached out and placed a hand on Mule's shoulder. "I really think it would be best if you stayed."

Mule hefted the Sharps to his left hand and held out his right. "I know you had a rough time of the war too. Thanks for listening, but I've got to see that young'n."

The reason my leg hurt like hell was from tromping through this damn mud, Ben thought. Hell, it would make a good leg ache. No, he didn't believe a bad shoulder or a bum leg could predict anything. Not really. There was no medical basis for such a belief. But he took Mule's hand and wished him luck.

Ben hollered for Isaiah to join them and when he walked up, Ben said, "Mule has talked to me about moving on before any more Sioux arrive. Do you think these three could reach the next settlement on their own?"

"It would be a foolish thing to try," Isaiah said.

"You said yourself that when the main party arrives we'll be outnumbered at least five to one, maybe more," Mule replied.

"Yes, but out there you'll be outnumbered a hundred to one and you don't know the lay of the land. Those Sioux live here."

"Ben, we're going. I'm sorry, but I can't just sit here and wait to die without seeing that young'n," Mule said. "If we forfeited our pay could we take three horses?"

"I wish you would reconsider," Ben said. "I know I told you that I wouldn't hold you to our deal, given the circumstances. There may be a way out of this if we all stay together."

"How about the horses?" Mule's question answered Ben.

"You can take three of the horses, but I don't think the harness horses will be much good. You know they're not broke to ride," Ben answered as Isaiah turned and walked away.

Mule and his two companions were giving Ben their personal papers to be sent to next of kin if anything happened to them when Isaiah returned leading Sam's sorrel and the Sioux pony.

"I don't think you should leave, but sometimes the heart leads us where we must follow regardless of the danger." He held out the reins to Mule. "At least two of you will have a better chance on these, if it's all right with Ben."

Ben caught the grateful look on Mule's face, turned and whispered something to Isaiah, who then quietly slipped away. War bags and bedrolls were soon lashed in place while Ben questioned them about their ammunition supplies.

A swell of voices drew their attention to the men standing guard behind the wagons. They looked to the north ridge where seven riders were silhouetted against the skyline.

Isaiah returned with another horse and handed the reins to Ben who reached up and stroked the big stallion's nose and spoke a few soft words to the animal before offering Mule the reins.

"For your grandson, take Ol' Jeb. He should get you through if any horse can. Leave him at the next settlement when you get there." Ben held up his hand to stop any objections or words of thanks. He shook hands with the three and told Isaiah to give them good directions to their destination.

DAMN, BEN THOUGHT AS HE STARED at the ridge where the Sioux had been, but now there was nothing. I like it better when I can see them. He'd just started back to his wagon when shouting and cussing erupted at the south side of the circled wagons.

"Ain't nobody running yeller. Don't give a Yankee goddamn if Ben agrees, I'll shoot any cowardly mother's son that deserts." Ben hurried toward the voices.

"Mule, you're a good man, but by damn I'd rather shoot you than let you run when we're facing long odds."

"If you pull your head out of your arse and think on it a mite, you'd know we ain't running yeller," Mule said, looking down on the group.

"What'd you mean?" This time it was Elmo. The big man stood at the small gap between the wagons, his back against the two wagon tongues that served as a gate.

"I'll explain it," Ben said, pausing to catch his breath.

"I ain't needing no one to do my talking," Mule said. "This here outfit is in trouble. Me and these two have volunteered to ride for help. If any of you would like to take over the chore you can hop to it."

No one moved.

"At least one of us should get through to bring help. Isaiah said there's a small town three, four days ride about due south. Reckon you all just hunker down and we'll be back with the cavalry. Keep your head down and your powder dry."

Satisfied with Mule's explanation, everyone agreed to let the trio ride for help and by the time the wagon tongues were slid out of place, the men were wishing them good luck.

Ben stepped into the opening before the men could ride through, "Best dismount," he said grabbing the bridle of Ol' Jeb.

"What the hell for?"

"I'm thinking there's something we should do before you ride out," Ben said scooping up a handful of mud. "This damn stuff caused us a bunch of trouble, maybe we can get some good use out of it." Ben began rubbing the mud into the white blaze of Ol' Jeb's face. After the white was darkened he knelt in the mud and began the same treatment on the stocking feet.

"Ben, you would make a good Crow, but this will work better," Isaiah held the big camp coffeepot in which was a mixture of campfire ashes, his black war paint, and coffee grounds. He applied it to the white of the Sioux horse and soon every light colored patch of hair, clothing, and skin was blackened. Ben scooped up another handful of mud and squeezed it into the bit's curb chain to deaden the rattle of the chain against the bit.

"Let's see the Sharps," Ben held out his hand to Mule.

Ben rubbed the shiny barrel with mud before handing it back. They led the horses outside the circle and wagon tongues were slid back across the opening, the sound not unlike the closing of a door. An almost tangible feeling of isolation and loneliness enveloped the small group. They stood together for a moment and looked through the moonlight at the barren scene stretching out before them, silent and threatening.

"Not meaning to tell you your business, but I'd think it best to lead the horses away from camp a good long ways before mounting up. Reckon you know not to get separated and to keep off the high ground," Ben offered. Then he added, "Godspeed."

"For damn certain," Mule said and then they walked away, headed south. Ben and Isaiah watched as men and horses melted into the night. "I believe Ben Kelley has done some night fighting in his time."

"More than I like to think about."

"You are a strange man. You show no fear, yet you don't talk of war deeds. Have you counted coup?"

"Isaiah, I don't count coup. I've been to war and I don't like it, and as far as I'm concerned fighting never solved a damn thing."

"You walk like you do because of your war?"

"Yes." Usually a question about his leg was considered an intrusion, a probing into his private life that no one could enter unless by special permission. With Isaiah it was like a child seeking an explanation for the world around him. Simply a gathering of facts, not in the least offensive.

"Among my people," Isaiah explained, "I have seen a bad wound to the body make the heart weak, like the body. Those that live may grow strong again if they are a true warrior. Even stronger than before. Perhaps it will be that way with you. What did you whites fight about?"

"I'm not sure I know what it was about anymore. I was in the cavalry during the war."

"Ho, Ben Kelley was a pony soldier."

A horse snorted, then snorted again. Isaiah turned back toward the wagons and stood rock still, his senses straining to glean information from the night air. Like an animal checking the wind, Ben thought.

"The Sioux are on the far side of the camp. At least some of them."

The camp was quiet, fire burning, and men watching anxiously past the wagons into the night.

"You said they wouldn't attack at night. Still true?" Ben asked, starting for the far side of the circled wagons.

"Not to worry about attack tonight. They're just looking over the lay of the land."

"How did you know they had moved to the other side of the camp?"

Isaiah stopped and pointed to his small war pony that stood apart from the other horses, head up and ears pointed south.

"He doesn't like the Sioux any more than I do. He's worth a dozen warriors. Ben, if I'm to make a Crow of you, you have got to learn to listen to the spirits that are all around you."

"I might like being a Crow if fighting wasn't necessary. I noticed you are good with horses; maybe I can make a white man out of you."

"I promised my mother I would stay three snows with the whites, but to become a white man I think is impossible for me."

They reached the south side of the circle, leaned against a wagon, and peered across the dark of the land until it melted into the night sky. Ben looked back at Isaiah's horse and tried to fix the direction of its eyes and ears. Glancing at Isaiah he saw that he was looking and listening in the same direction as the horse. Ben strained both senses. "I don't see a thing. You sure they're out there?"

"At night a warrior's ears see much more than his eyes. Put the camp noise into a very small bag, tie it tight, and then listen to what the wind spirits whisper to you."

"I don't see or hear anything. I'll take your word Sioux are on this side of the camp and we're all taking your word that they won't bother us until morning which isn't too far away. Why won't they fight at night?"

"They will if they are attacked, but since we aren't attacking them and we'll damn sure still be here in the morning, they won't take the chance of being killed at night and losing their way to the next life. My mother called it superstition. Listen."

Ben strained to shut out the camp noise and listen outside the camp. "I can't hear a thing. You best go and make sure sentries are awake. And first thing in the morning we need to send some men out to the wrecked wagons. If the Sioux attack, I'll probably need those medical supplies."

Ben walked back to his wagon where he found Smith's wound had stopped bleeding. He was lighting a cigar when Elmo poked his head in the back of the wagon. "Hey, Ben, something's up. You better should come have a look."

"Attack?"

"Don't rightly know. There's a fire out south of the wagons."

Grabbing his cane, Ben blew out the lantern and went with Elmo. Before they were halfway across the circle, Ben could see a faint glow on the horizon and knew instantly what it was. Had the night spirits whispered it to him, as Isaiah had said they would?

"There go my medical supplies and our staples."

A group of men had gathered and were peering across the dark landscape toward the fire. Ben, tired and angry at himself for neglecting to salvage the supplies, lashed out. "All right, it's a fire. Now get back around to your posts. What if it's a diversion tactic and you're all bunched up like a covey of quail. They could pot shoot the whole lot of you. Where's Isaiah?"

The same man who had threatened Mule answered, "Don't know where your damn breed is and don't give a damn. We're thinking Mule was right. Let's unload a couple more wagons and make a run for it before the rest of the bloody bastards get here.

"Why sit here? There's only a few of 'em now. We can out-gun them and be long gone before the rest get here. If you want to stay with your damn wagons, that's your business. I say let's get the hell out of here."

Ben knew waiting for a battle was worse than the fight and he'd even seen it unnerve seasoned troops. He understood the men's anger and need for action. Elmo went to the man who was doing the talking. He stood over him and said something that Ben couldn't hear. The man dropped his eyes and moved through the crowd toward the far wagons. Elmo went from man to man and soon all were standing guard around the circle of wagons.

Ben said a prayer of thanks that Elmo was his friend. He turned to look back at the burning wagon and could make out four figures scurrying about. A cold chill ran up Ben's back as the figures danced in and out of the flickering firelight.

A teamster stepped to his side. "I got me a spyglass. Thought you might could use it."

Without looking, Ben took the glass. "Thanks. I haven't held one of those since the war. CSA officer's issue, right?"

"You've got some damn good eyes," the man said, then added, "I best be getting back to my post."

Ben's hand slipped the glass from the leather case and telescoped the sections with practiced ease. How did I know it was an officer's glass, he asked himself. He couldn't explain it but he had known, or guessed, or thought he had known. Hell, next thing you know I'll be believing in Isaiah's spirits. Wonder where he is.

He focused the glass on the burning medical wagon and groaned. The Sioux had pulled the unburned wagon parts into a pile and fired them. They were sifting through the pile of medical supplies and food. What didn't interest them they pitched into the flames.

Ben watched as the Sioux discovered his surgical instruments and held them up for inspection, the fire and moonlight gleaming and flickering on the polished steel. A brave held up the long amputating knife. When another saw the knife, it looked like an argument arose over it. Then, his surgeon's saws were picked up and examined closely. The original discoverer claimed the knife and stuck it in his belt while two others divided the saws and bone nippers.

Ben swore. Those instruments were the latest and best money could buy. God only knows how long it will take to replace them. It would take months to get more of their quality – if they ever got to a town with a telegraph where he could place an order.

Isaiah was at his side, silently appearing as if an apparition. How long he had been there Ben didn't know, but he was naked from the waist up and even in the cool night air his skin glistened with a sheen of sweat.

"Damn, now they're burning things, and what they're not burning they're stealing." Ben slid the glass back into its leather case before asking Isaiah, "Any idea what we can expect next?"

"I made a wide circle of the camp to check on our friends."

Ben glanced at the horses. Isaiah's war pony was still there, still focused on the fire. "You went out on foot?"

"Only way to be unseen, close to Mother Earth where her spirits could help hide me."

"Anything new out there; any more Sioux arrived?"

"I went out as far as the big cottonwood where you got water and then around. Nothing different; no more Sioux."

"Jeez, you were out that far? Must have been three or four miles. You weren't gone that long. You must be damn fast afoot."

"Maybe for a white that would be a long run, but for Two Suns it is nothing. You seem troubled about the wagon out there. Was it important to you?"

"It was all my medical supplies. I'd planned to open a hospital when I decided where I wanted to live. It is only important now if a lot of us are wounded. The lost food is only important if you can't keep bringing us game. Right now, those of us with military experience are meeting at the campfire. I need your Crow mind on Sioux warfare."

At the fire Elmo had placed some stools and nail kegs around for seating. The man who had given the spyglass to Ben approached. "Know you are mostly rebs and I may not be too welcome since I was Union. In fact I got that there glass off one of your officers. I understand if you'd rather not have me here."

"Sit," Ben said, indicating a keg with his cane. "War's over and I don't think the Sioux give a damn if we wore blue or gray. Another mind can't hurt."

"Ben, I ain't council-in' with no damn Yankee. I lost a lot of family and friends to those bastards."

"Both sides lost a lot. Now that war's over and we've got another one to think about. As I'm remembering, they whipped us, so maybe we need some of their thinking to get out of this fix. Damn it, I don't want to hear anything more on the matter. Now, do we run or do we stay?"

The group consisted of Ben, Isaiah, Elmo, Davis of the Union, and Morris who had served with Stonewall Jackson. Probably not the best military minds in the world, Ben thought as he looked in turn at each man.

"How many guns, what kind, and how much ammunition do you have among you?" Isaiah asked the first question.

Everyone looked at Ben. "I guess a lot of the men are armed but I don't know for sure. Elmo, get one of the men to take a very careful count."

Elmo sent a man to take the arms count, then he asked, "Does anyone know just exactly how far we are from any kind of town or settlement? Either in miles or riding time?"

Everyone turned to Isaiah. "On foot or horseback I could make it straight through in one day and a night. With the wagons it would take a good four or five days, or longer."

"Any good places to fort up between here and there that's close to a well-traveled trail?" Davis asked.

"You're on a shortcut off the Platte River Road. Not likely to be many parties traveling this route. Between here and Elk Springs the lay of the land is about what you have right here."

"That's between here and Elk Springs. What if we went another direction?" Ben asked.

"North are the Sioux, Northern Cheyenne, and Blackfoot; south there are the Southern Cheyenne, Arapaho, and Kiowa."

Someone handed Elmo a paper with the arms tally. He studied it a moment before asking Isaiah, "You still got Sam's Henry?"

"The rifle, a full box of cartridges, plus eighteen rounds," Isaiah answered.

The men in the little council gave Elmo information on their guns and ammo as he noted it on the paper with a stub of pencil fished from a dirty shirt pocket. They waited while he added up the list.

"Ben, ask your guide how the Sioux will be armed if you think he'll tell us straight." It was Morris, talking toward the fire and looking at neither Ben nor Isaiah.

Isaiah stood. "I will tell you and I will tell you straight, but I don't know why I should. I have risked my life for you. I have brought you food and still you treat me as a lowly prairie skunk. My mother was white like you and she told me many stories of how great the white eyes are, but you are not like the men in her stories. Why should I stay and fight with you? You know by now that I could escape, then I could come back after the Sioux are finished and howl over your bones like the prairie wolves."

"Why didn't your mother escape?" It was Morris again.

"She did try many times but was caught and beaten for her efforts. Few white men are a match for an Indian out here, and there's no chance for a young woman from the East. After the children came, she no longer tried to leave. Will your women not endure hardship for their children? Who wants a woman who wouldn't?"

Ben had purposely let the confrontation continue knowing that sooner or later it was bound to be an issue. He thought it best to get it resolved now before they faced the Sioux. Somehow, Ben felt this intriguing half white, half Indian held the answer to their deliverance. Right now he didn't have a clue to what it was.

Three rapid gunshots brought them all to their feet. "Elmo, go check out those shots, on the double," Ben snapped. "Isaiah, could it be the Sioux attacking?"

Isaiah had remained seated, "No. I think your young man with the broken arm is trying to hit a long shot at the burning wagon."

Ben looked south to the fire which had died down to a small glow in the night. Remembering the glass, he fixed it on the wrecked wagons. Nothing, no Sioux, just a pile of rubble and a dying fire.

He didn't relish the task of walking the muddy circle but picked up his cane and steeled himself, "Let's take a walk and settle the men down and see what Niles was wasting his ammo on."

"I don't like Morris. You think he is good white man?" Isaiah asked as they moved around the circle telling the men to save their powder and shot.

"Don't really know. I hired him to drive a team and wagon. You are angry because he doubted you?"

"Everyone doubts a breed. 'Goddamn stinking breed' is almost like my name. I can't believe my mother was white."

"You heard those two at the fire. It's just natural when people don't understand each other. People are people, doesn't much make any difference what color uniforms they wear or what color skin they have. Mostly they are afraid."

"You are not afraid like them?"

"Afraid, but not of the same things they are," Ben answered.

They reached the wagon where Elmo was giving Niles a good tongue lashing. Niles looked about to cry.

Ben interrupted, "Elmo, get the men back together at the fire. We'll be along shortly."

Elmo pointed to the east where pre-dawn shades of light were struggling with the night. "Won't be long before daybreak, what ya reckon about the Sioux?"

Isaiah answered, "Not enough warriors for an attack. Just tell the men not to doze off close to the wagons. Their braves could crawl to the wagons and cut your throat without a sound. Other than that, no worry."

"You shooting at ghosts with your daddy's Ballard?" Ben asked Niles.

"No sir, Ben. I know'd I wrecked your wagons and that those supplies are important should we have to fight. I watched real close when you shot those vultures and I thought I could hit those Injuns out there. Reckon I didn't hit a damn thing and wasted three rounds. Boy, my daddy would wear all the hide off my ass if he knew I done a stupid one like that."

"Son, you can't blame yourself. Believe me it just does no good." Ben reached down and patted his leg. "After this injury I blamed and cussed everybody from God himself to my mother for giving me birth, but it just doesn't solve a thing. So let it go. No harm done, but I do think you ought to save the cartridges until it gets a bit more serious."

"Okay, but when we get out of here, will you teach me how to shoot like you done with the vultures?"

"Ho, Ben Kelley shot the vultures? Damn good to have a marksman like that when the Sioux come."

"Maybe sometime I'll show you what I can about shooting a rifle," Ben told Niles. "Now, back to night watch."

They made their way over to the fire where someone handed Ben a cup of coffee just before he sat down and stretched his aching leg.

"Now, where were we?" he asked the group as he watched a sleek black mare walk into the firelight. He had wondered if the Indians had gotten the black. Ever since that day when he was fifteen he had kept at least two blacks in his herd. Silly, he supposed, but it was a tie to Adeline he couldn't bring himself to sever.

The old memories flooded over him and he was back home. Plenty of money to spend, plenty of blooded horseflesh, and more than enough willing Southern belles.

He and Adeline had ridden off one fine summer day of his youth for a picnic at their favorite secluded spot hidden beneath the Spanish moss on a giant oak. Their hideaway lay close to a clear stream whose soft murmuring serenaded the couple.

She rode sidesaddle on a black that was as sure-footed and graceful as a cat, and her jet black hair matched the silky, blue black of the mare's coat. Adeline had dark, haunting eyes that could either dance with laughter or smolder and pout if she didn't get her way. A flawless white complexion accented the dark hair and eyes. Her nose had the slightest bit of upturn that gave here an aloof manner which she could magnify by the tilt of her head.

They had spread a blanket and eaten the lunch a house servant had packed for them. During the meal he'd tried to muster enough nerve to kiss her. Each time he moved close she kept avoiding him. Later he realized it was just a coy little game she played. All too soon she announced she had to get home. He was almost wild with desire to kiss her and moved to her side and knelt down. She turned her head away and started to stand up, but caught her heel in her skirt. The sound of tearing material violated the moment for him. She sat down and went into convulsions of laughter. He didn't know what to do. His moment had slipped away.

"I don't know why they make us wear these silly things," she had said and proceeded to lift up her skirt and inspect the tear. Looking up, she broke out in more laughter at the expression on his face.

"What? Haven't you seen all the stuff they say young ladies should wear? Here, let me show you."

Dumbstruck, he watched as she disrobed, laying aside each piece and telling him the name and how uncomfortable it could be. She reached behind and after some difficulty undid the last garment and dropped it among the others.

14

"HEY, YOU FALL ASLEEP?" Elmo hollered as he prodded Ben.

Ben flinched as he regained the present, asking, "Isaiah, what kind of weapons will we be up against?"

"Bows and arrows, lances, and hand-to-hand weapons. Most Indians aren't great shots with firearms, but they do have a few repeating rifles. Don't be fooled by their weapons; they're deadly in the hands of a warrior."

"How many warriors you reckon they'll have?" Davis asked.

"About four hundred or more now, and if they join up with another band before getting here – anybody's guess."

"What's the chances of that?" Ben wanted to know.

"Can't say, but since the Blue Water incident they're moving around a lot, looking to even the score."

"Could we offer them gold for safe passage?" Ben asked.

"They figure they'll get everything you have anyway. What they really want is for whites to get off their land."

"How about giving them the horses?"

"Same as the gold, they figure they'll get them anyway. After Blue Water they're in no bargaining mood."

Ben leaned toward the fire and rubbed his hands in the warmth. "Elmo, recap our arms and ammo count?"

"Got three repeating rifles: Sam's Henry and two Spencers. Nineteen breechloaders, twenty-seven cap and ball, four shotguns and thirty-one side arms. Nearest we can figure, got near about eight, nine hundred rounds of ammunition including powder and ball."

By degrees the early morning light pushed the darkness westward across the prairie. Usual morning sounds, especially the songs of birds, were noticeably absent. Even the camp was subdued and men talked in hushed tones as if trying not to be noticed by the new day.

If Ol' Jeb were here, Ben thought, I'd ride out and have a look. Thinking back, he wished he had not been so quick to offer Mule the big stallion. But then, maybe Mule and the other two would be the only ones to escape death.

He mentally ticked off the attributes of each gun Elmo mentioned and thought that here would be a situation to fire William Kelley's blood. His dad had loved good firearms and a good fight.

About 1855, William had given the day-to-day operations of the plantations to his foreman. That freed his time to serve the wealthy customers who wanted a sporting gun of uncompromising quality.

As a youth, Ben hadn't had the patience to do the detailed work required of a handmade gun, but he'd displayed remarkable skill at shooting any weapon. His dad soon began to have him test all the guns and give shooting demonstrations for prospective customers.

An endless stream of guns found their way to the bustling shop for repair and conversion. By the time Ben was fourteen, he had handled hundreds of various makes and styles. Firearms to him were like horses: once handled and conquered, never forgotten. Even though he didn't do any of the actual work, he understood the craft and recognized all the various methods employed in gunsmithing. After handling and shooting a piece, he often made excellent suggestions for design modifications.

When the rumors of war had washed across the land in the late 1850s, William Kelley's gunsmith business employed twenty-two skilled craftsmen. Anytime Ben wanted a diversion from his horses, parties, or young ladies, he would go by the shop and test fire the guns. It was a source of tension between him and his father that he wouldn't adhere to a schedule, but Ben always got the pieces fired within a day or two of his dad's request, so he couldn't understand his dad's worries. The one exception to his loose schedule was an appointment to shoot a demonstration for wealthy gentlemen and their ladies. If they happened to have a daughter or two along, the shooting was breathtaking. He had spent many hours thinking of ways to expose his ability to hit any target under any circumstance. His ability to handle the arms never wavered, but his ability to cope with living, breathing men frozen in his mind's eye atop those gun sights destroyed his love of guns and shooting.

Now looking around the wagons at the bare earth stretching hundreds of yards without any obstruction, he wondered: If I could get some height to have a clear field of fire and had men load for me, just how effective could I be? He didn't like the thought, and, using Isaiah's example, he put the thoughts of killing men into a small bag and tied it tightly.

It was full light when the decision to stay instead of run was reached. "Elmo," Ben instructed, "divide up the perimeter into quarters. Give one man the responsibility for directing the defense of that section. No firing unless I give the command."

15

THE FACES AROUND THE COUNCIL FIRE belied the excitement that coursed through the Sioux village. Reverent, unhurried hands offered the pipe to the earth, the sky, and the four winds before passing it around the circle of elders.

The council fire burned in the lodge's center; the tribe's leaders were seated on buffalo robes. Behind them other warriors crowded inside. The lodge's inner lining of skins was painted with the extraordinary deeds of its owner, Talking Lance, and behind him hung his ceremonial weapons of war and sacred medicine bundle.

After the pipe ceremony was finished, Talking Lance opened the council. "It is good to see our brothers, the Cheyenne. The moon of starving is past and the Great Spirit has again sent us the buffalo. Has the Great Spirit also sent the buffalo to our brothers?"

Limping Bear, the Cheyenne chief, was long of limb, with pinched cheeks, and a hawk nose which gave him the countenance of one raised on foul water and rancid meat. He chafed under the need for protocol. "The Great Spirit has sent us buffalo, and our scouts tell us that he has sent us something better – the white eyes that are bogged in the prairie mud. More horses and scalps than we have been given in many moons. Let us go and avenge the wrongs to our people."

Talking Lance didn't like the Cheyenne leader, but he respected his reputation as a warrior. "Our medicine men fast and seek a vision, but my lance has not spoken to me concerning the whites. The Great Spirit is silent."

"My brother, has the Great Spirit not delivered them to us by the Thunderbird? He has seen the terrible wrongs done to his children and shed many tears that trapped the white eyes in Mother Earth. We should accept the Great Spirit's gift and go kill the whites."

Back and forth the council talk continued: war, sacred land, scalps, horses, coup. Only Talking Lance and a few of the old Sioux warriors insisted on a more positive vision from the spirits.

Finally, Talking Lance invited both camps to a feast and gave many of the stolen horses as placating gifts until he could purify himself and seek a vision. His lance must talk to him if any war efforts were to succeed. He hated the whites. He wanted as much as any of the warriors to ride down and kill these whites for their kind's atrocities to his people. But he had learned to be more responsive to his gods than to his passions.

He ended the council and went to his sweat lodge. There, intense heat cleansing his body, he wanted to believe that the whites had been given to them as a gift by the spirits. But sitting naked he ran his finger over the old battle scars. He'd gotten them the only time he had led a war party without a confirming vision spoken to him through his lance. He'd failed, the war party had failed, and many warriors didn't return. From that day forward he listened carefully to the spirits. When the stones in the fire pit grew cold, he left the lodge and walked out onto the prairie to be alone with his guiding spirits and his sacred lance.

16

"UNLOAD THE WAGONS," BEN TOLD ELMO AT SUNUP. "We'll leave the foundation stones behind." The sun promised a warm day which would be welcomed after the cool, nerve-racking night.

Elmo frowned and scratched at his beard. "Going to be a helluva job 'cause there's some stones in every wagon, but I do reckon we've got to lighten the wagons somehow."

"I figure without those stones we can get by with a four-horse hitch on some wagons," Ben said.

Elmo and the men headed for the tough job of unloading and Ben headed for his wagon, and his neglected, but not forgotten, patient, Ed Smith, whom he found thrashing around on the wagon floor. The morphine was wearing off, pain and fever rising. Ben hollered for someone to bring water. While he waited to clean the wound, he once again picked up the Sioux quiver. Made of a cougar pelt with leg, claws, and head still on the pelt, it was decorated with bright red trade cloth and dyed porcupine quills. Very handsome, Ben thought as he withdrew the feathered shafts and placed them on the wagon floor. He noticed that the arrowheads were of two designs. Of the dozen arrows, about half had arrowheads rounded on the back, the other half flared to points.

A teamster handed a wooden bucket of water over the wagon tailgate. "Here ya be, Ben. How's Ed a doing?"

"He's hurting, but I'm sure he'll recover. If you see Isaiah, tell him I'd like to talk with him."

"I'll tell him, but if you ask me, he ain't much help. He jist sits there most neart naked on a dang blanket."

Ben listened, then said, "I want him to come to my wagon. Tell him it's very important."

Holding a Sioux arrow he twirled it in his fingers. Damn wicked, he thought. Could do more damage than a lead ball. He laid it down and cleaned Smith's wound, talking soothingly to his patient. As he probed the wound, he realized what could be responsible for the continued bleeding. "That damn arrowhead must still be in Smith's leg," he said half aloud. He brushed the flies away and laid his last clean shirt over the wound.

He shoved himself to his feet, opened the rear canvas, and looked outside. The contents of his wagon train squatted dejectedly in the mud as if ashamed to be seen in such primitive surroundings. The foundation stones were beginning to rise in imposing piles as the men sweated and cussed while the horses milled amid the activity, inspecting the piled objects with a curiosity caused by boredom.

Isaiah, clad in nothing but his breechclout, was sitting on a blanket watching the teamsters unload the wagons. When he saw Ben wave, he gathered his war bag, rolled the blanket, and walked toward the wagon. He made his way among the stacks of items looking at each, but not stopping until he came to a large music box sitting in the mud. He walked around it and studied it for a few minutes before continuing to the wagon.

Ben, somewhat impatient, started talking to him before he reached the wagon. "Come around to the back. I want you to tell me about arrows."

Isaiah pulled himself inside and sat on a trunk. "What do you need to know?"

"Here," Ben said, handing him two arrows. "Why the different arrowheads? And, have you ever seen other wounds inflicted by these types of arrows?"

"Ho, Ben forgets I am a warrior? I have seen many wounds."

"Would you look at Smith's leg?"

Reaching down, Isaiah lifted the shirt that was already spotted with blood. Smith groaned and flung his arms around and
tried to roll over. Isaiah put a hand on his chest and held him,
all the while talking to him softly. After Ed calmed down, Isaiah
picked up the arrow with the pointed ends. "Your patient was
shot with this type arrow, a war arrow. This one," he said, pointing to the other, "is a hunting arrow."

"Is there a chance the arrowhead is still in the leg?"

"War arrows are built to do that," Isaiah said leaning over
and looking closely at the leg. "A hunting arrow can be pulled
out and used again. Can't pull a war arrow out. Shaft comes
off and leaves the arrowhead. Usually kills sooner or later." He
dropped the shirt back over the wound. "I think this man has an
iron arrowhead next to, or in, his leg bone."

"I was afraid of that."

Isaiah held an arrow in the stream of sunlight that poured
through the canvas opening. "It could be worse, they could be
using poison arrows. You're lucky these are not."

"You mean they use poison?" Ben asked, picking up one
of the arrows and looking at it closely in the sunlight. "Is the
poison effective?"

"Yes, they use a paste of dried rattlesnake venom mixed with
certain berries. When it's smeared on the arrowheads and is
dried, it kills without fail. Even if the wound is very slight."

The worry line in Ben's face deepened and his shoulders
sagged. He imagined what rumors of poison arrows would do to
the men. "Isaiah, best we don't mention anything about the possibility of poison arrows. The men have enough to think about."

"The main body of Sioux will be here just before sundown,"
Isaiah said, gazing at the northern horizon. "Then it won't make
much difference what they have in their quivers."

"How do you know when they'll get here?" Ben asked.

"It is what I would do, and it is what the spirits have told me."

Watching the men unload the wagons, Ben thought about
spirits and poison. It's as if man's one obsession, regardless of

race or religion, is to devise more effective means of killing one another.

Elmo had the men cussing less and working more than Ben thought possible. The pile of foundation stones in the center of the circle was taking on impressive proportions and he thought it would make a hell of a shooting platform. It angered him that his thoughts kept returning to shooting, killing, and war. It was not to be a part of his life anymore.

Ben picked up his medical bag, assessed the contents, and knew it was going to be a tedious operation to remove the arrowhead from Smith's leg. He'd need more light and he'd either have to move the patient or remove the wagon's canvas. Unless, he thought, the operating table was already unloaded. He grabbed his cane and left the wagon. The sun was directly overhead and the men had taken a break to eat what food they could find and to drink a rationed cup of coffee.

He made his way around the wagons, noticing the familiar items that spoke to him of another lifetime. The mahogany bed and dresser from his parents' bedroom. The four fluted Corinthian columns which had been his mother's pride and joy. They had stood like sentinels in front of Oak Grove. He had hated to do it, but they had to be sawn in half to fit into the wagons.

There was the harpsichord that he had loathed as a child of six. "It isn't sissified for boys to play a musical instrument," his mother had said a thousand times over as he sat on the stool and dreamt of horses, hunting, and his friends. Despite his objection to music lessons, he had learned more than he realized, and actually had retained enough skill to bang out a few tunes to entertain the recovering soldiers at the Murphy house.

Stopping beside the sentry at the north perimeter he asked, "Any sign of our anxiously awaited guests?"

"Nary a damn thing. Isaiah says some of 'em are sure enough out there watching. Kind of spooky ain't it?"

"Yes. We'd all feel better if we could see what we're up against. Keep a sharp eye."

Ben moved on, leaving the man to his thoughts. Which were probably of a wife back home, family, and dreams of a new start on free or cheap land that had enticed most of them on this journey.

There in the mud and manure were the carpenter and black-smith tools. Sitting clustered together like frightened animals were the nail kegs that Ben had filled and secured himself. It was a job he could do while the house was being dismantled. He'd sat hour after hour straightening the cut nails that the workers brought him. Then, when the men had gone for the night, he would retrieve either a bag of gold coins or a bar of gold and put it in the middle of the keg, finish filling the keg with nails, hinges, door knobs, or other hardware before closing the keg. There was a fortune in gold hidden in those kegs, Ben thought, but it was worthless in the middle of a burned, muddy prairie.

He walked past pile after pile of lumber from rough-cut framing stock to finished interior trim stacked next to several beautiful raised-panel doors. Amazingly, the French doors had only one broken glass. Two wagons farther along, he passed crate after crate of books. He had almost completed the circle when he came to the examination table that he sought. Calling two workers to him, he instructed them to carry it over and set it up at the rear of his wagon.

"TURN THE TABLE A LITTLE TO THE LEFT so I've got the sun over my left shoulder," Ben told Elmo as he removed his jacket and rolled up his sleeves. He put on his half-rim glasses and picked up a scalpel he always kept in his medical bag. He had a fleeting thought of seeing his medical instruments being destroyed by the Indians. He forced himself to let go of his hate and focus on saving Smith – if that were possible.

As Ben made the first cut with the scalpel, Smith fought and almost broke loose. Isaiah ran over from his inspection of the wagon contents to help the men restrain Smith. One of the men left abruptly and made it only a few steps before he vomited.

Isaiah wasn't fazed by the sight of the scalpel biting into the flesh, exclaiming, "Ho!" when the arrowhead was exposed. Ben worked quickly and carefully, knowing the arrowhead lay dangerously close to the artery.

"Elmo," Ben commanded, "get over here!"

The big blacksmith looked over Ben's shoulder, his skin white beneath his heavy beard.

"I'm going to need more bandages, see what you can find."

Smith was strong and Ben was afraid to remove the arrowhead until he could be quieted. Elmo returned with an armful of bedding that was soon ripped into strips.

"Tie Smith to the table. I've got to have him immobile when I go after that arrowhead."

When they had lashed Smith to the exam table, Isaiah asked, "How you going to stop the bleeding?"

"Normally I'd sew up the wound, but all my catgut was in the burned wagon. First I'll try some ashes. If that doesn't work, I'll have to cauterize it. Don't like to do that without any sedative for the patient."

"Could you use something else?" Isaiah questioned as Ben lifted out the arrowhead. He dabbed at the wound with clean rags until he was sure the artery wasn't harmed. "Maybe. What'd you have in mind?"

Isaiah left and was back in a moment with a small pouch. From it he took the contents and held them out to Ben, "Could you use this sinew? It is what we use to sew many things."

Ben wiped his hands and the bloody scalpel on some bedding and took the small bundle from Isaiah. "Too stiff," he said.

Isaiah took it from Ben's hand and placed several lengths into his mouth while Ben dabbed at the bleeding wound. "Somebody get a couple of handfuls of cold ashes from the campfire," he said.

Isaiah reached out and tapped Ben on the shoulder while he pulled a single strand of sinew from his mouth and held it out.

"By god, this will work," Ben said, then asked, "Any of you have a needle?

"I've got one," a fellow said. "I'll be right back."

The man ran to his wagon and returned with a needle which he handed to Ben, who threaded it and then with quick, sure movements, closed the wound. Finished, he wiped his hands and checked Smith's pulse. Weaker than he would like, but steady and consistent. He bound up the leg with clean strips of bedding and told the men to put Smith back into the wagon.

A teamster approached Ben. "That was some fine work. Sorry I didn't help, but just can't take the sight of blood and a knife no more. I was drafted into the medical corps and did my job, but I swore I'd never do it again. That's about the best damn job of field surgery I ever saw."

"Thanks, I can understand your decision never to do something again. Let's both hope we can keep the promises we've made to ourselves."

The tall, blond man in front of Ben could have been anywhere from twenty-five to forty-five years old. Once, Ben knew, he'd been a proud, handsome young man, but now his eyes were dull and sad, his shoulders sagged.

The man rubbed a hand over a three-days' growth of beard, "You got any morphine or such for Smith? Him and I was from the same town back home."

"No, there's nothing left of the medical supplies and what medication I kept in my bag is gone. Ed's going to have to tough it out."

The man looked long at the blood-soaked exam table, shuddered then turned away and shuffled through the mud.

Ben cleaned up his instruments and was closing his medical bag when the same man returned carrying a gallon crock jug. He set it down carefully on the wagon tailgate. "Ever since the war I kind of drown the nightmares in this here 'shine. Only ways I could keep from going crazy. I imagine Ed needs it more than me." He caressed the jug with his eyes, ran his tongue over dry lips, then left.

"Thanks," Ben called after him, thankful for the liquor and touched by the man's sacrifice. He poured enough corn whisky down Smith to quiet him, then set out to find Isaiah.

Isaiah, still in his breechclout, was inspecting the contents of the wagons. Some items he passed over as if they were familiar to him, others he examined with a childlike awe. Ben wondered how much was ignorance and how much was Indian.

The large crystal chandelier had been packed between several big goose-down quilts for the journey. Now the top quilts were half off, exposing the sparkling cut lead glass to the bright sunlight. Isaiah studied it from several angles before finally squatting down and touching the glass. After a bit he arose and walked to the music box, raised and lowered the lid a couple of times, and looked at Ben. "You have been watching me. Is it against your wishes for me to look at your things?"

"No, not at all. I was just thinking."

"I have been thinking too. Ben Kelley has strong medicine."

Isaiah saw that Ben felt somewhat embarrassed by the compliment. Isaiah didn't understand his new friend. Someone as good as Ben Kelley should boast of his deeds. He wondered if this was the detestable thing his mother spoke of as humility. Another day he would ask the crippled medicine man to explain. Now he had other things on his mind.

He asked, "Do you have any tobacco?"

"Yes, I've a few cigars left."

Isaiah pointed to Ben's wagon. "Let's sit and smoke before the coming battle. I have some questions to ask you."

Ben retrieved two cigars while Isaiah spread a blanket and laid out his war bag. Ben handed him a cigar and sat down on the blanket. Isaiah broke the cigar in half, ground it between his palms, and filled his long-stemmed pipe. He offered the lit pipe to the earth, the sky, and the four winds before handing it to Ben.

"You do not yet understand why we offer the pipe to the spirits. Someday I will teach you. Now, smoke with your Crow brother."

Ben smoked in silence before passing the pipe back to Isaiah. "You're right, but I too believe there are things that you, my friend, don't understand. The spirits told me you would like to know about the lidded box over there and the glass teardrops." Ben's eyes hinted at humor.

Isaiah grinned. "I told you I'd make a Crow of you. The spirits have told you right. Some of this I have seen before. Those things I have not. And that," he said pointing to the harpsichord.

"Come on. I'll show you some things that will help make you a white man."

"I want to finish the pipe. It is good to smoke and talk with someone who doesn't keep calling me breed."

It was a bright sunny afternoon with a few cotton clouds adrift in a blue sky. A gusty south wind sucked the moisture from the soggy earth, promising dry, solid ground soon.

Ben fired a cigar as Isaiah spoke. "You are ready for the fight?"

"No, I'll never be ready for another fight. You think there is any possible way around it?"

"You speak straight for a white. Most would tell you they are ready to kill a hundred Indians," Isaiah said.

Looking around at the working men, Ben answered, "If most would 'speak straight' as you say, they would tell you they're about to piss in both boots."

Isaiah smiled and interrupted Ben, "Maybe white eyes should fight naked and not ruin their clothes and boots."

Ben had to smile at the ludicrous picture. He guessed he'd never thought of Indians laughing. "Do you think we did best to stay instead of run?"

"Should never doubt yourself. Good military decision because if I were out there like the Sioux, I would want you to run. We'd lose fewer warriors and get it over with quicker."

Ben exhaled the pungent cigar smoke while they watched the men wrestle the last of the big stones out of a wagon and onto the pile. "How about you? Are you ready?"

"My people teach us as youth that it is better to die in battle while you are young and strong than to grow old and become a burden to the tribe. Since you spoke straight, I will too. I will fight, but I am not ready to die until I find out whether I fit in the red man's world or the white man's world."

Ben picked up the pipe bag and examined the beaded design. "Do you think there is a way to avoid fighting?"

"You like my pipe bag? You may have it and the pipe. Be a good thing for becoming a Crow."

"I couldn't do that. It is very beautiful and took someone many hours to craft. You need it."

Isaiah knocked the ashes out of the pipe bowl, took the bag and inserted the pipe, closed the flap and tied it. Then he held it out to Ben on the palms of both hands. "Indians are not like most whites think. To give a gift is a good thing here," he said, touching his chest. "Besides, you gave me the Henry rifle. This is my gift to you and I will give you an Indian name – 'Little Knife' for the small knife you use so well as a medicine man."

Ben accepted the pipe. Even though the man was a 'breed' and they had met far from royal palaces, the presentation was fit for a king's court.

"I am honored. I will treasure it always."

Isaiah measured every inch of Ben with steel blue eyes as if weighing the possible reaction to his next words. "I said I had a question. We have smoked the pipe, you are a good brother. If you should survive and I don't, will you try to get word to my mother that I died bravely trying to help the white eyes?"

"I would do it gladly, but how?"

Isaiah told him where his tribe's winter camp would be, where he might leave word that would eventually get to his mother. Ben got his journal from the wagon and recorded the details. Satisfied, Isaiah gathered his war bag and stood. "You will tell me about the white man things now?"

Moving around the circle, Ben explained items Isaiah pointed out. The chandelier with its hundreds of crystals sparkling blue fire in the sun fascinated the man, but it wasn't until Ben wound up the big music box and the lilting melody of "Dixie" filled the air that Isaiah was truly awed by the spirits that inhabited Ben Kelley's world. Isaiah found the harpsichord almost as impressive. Ben banged out a couple of melodies, and if he hadn't insisted on checking Smith's leg, Isaiah would have kept him pounding the keys much longer.

Smith was resting quietly, so Ben and Isaiah went to climb to the top of the foundation stones in the center of the wagon circle. Isaiah pointed north. "The wait is almost over. Probably more warriors than I thought coming."

"You see them?" Ben said straining his eyes while uncasing the glass.

"See a little haze in the sky and discolor on the grass. Over there," Isaiah said pointing a bit west of due north.

Even with the glass, Ben couldn't see what Isaiah described. It was not until he stood behind him and aimed the glass along Isaiah's outstretched arm that he found the approaching Sioux. He readjusted the glass. When the images jumped into focus, he exclaimed, "My gosh, it looks like an entire army on the move!"

Elmo called from below, "Thank God them damn wagons is finally empty." He scrambled up beside Ben. "You see any sign of Injuns from up here?"

"They're on their way." Ben handed him the glass and pointed.

The big man didn't see them until Isaiah helped. Then he drew in his breath and swallowed hard. "By the patron saint of mercy there's a mess of 'em."

"Elmo, do you trust Isaiah?"

"Reckon he proved hisself by me."

"I want you to deal with the men, but always listen to Isaiah if it comes to fighting. I can't move in this damn mud fast enough to get everywhere someone might need help. I can probably do the most good from up here."

Elmo and Isaiah climbed down from the stone pile while Ben sat and stretched his leg. Something was tugging at the back of his mind, but he couldn't understand what it was. It was as if he could see a dim figure shouting from a distance, but the wind snatched away the message before his ears could grab it.

Isaiah had given him a small peek into the red man's mind, but not enough for Ben to think like one of them. The desire for revenge he understood. Perhaps he could offer himself in exchange for the lives of the men. He would have to ask Isaiah about that. Maybe if they had one white to torture and kill, it would pacify their need for revenge. He tried to peel away all emotions, all dreams, and all hopes from his soul to ask himself whether he could do it if it meant the lives of the men. He knew the story of one man who made the same sacrifice centuries ago but he was far, far from the equal of that man.

"Ben, don't mean to butt in, but could I ask a favor?" Ben was so engrossed in his thoughts that he hadn't heard Niles climb up beside him. He thought he could read fear in the youth's eyes but his voice was strong and steady.

"If the present circumstances will allow, I'll be more than happy to do a favor for you," Ben replied.

Niles strained his eyes north trying to see the Indians. "If I don't make it, would you try to get word back to my family?"

Ben tried to sound confident. "I think we'll all make it, but I'll do it if you'll go fetch that big journal, ink, and pen from the back of my wagon."

It was late afternoon when Ben had recorded the last family and next of kin information in the journal. Word had spread among the men, and one by one they climbed the rock pile to tell Ben their next of kin and to see for themselves the approaching Indians.

Elmo and Isaiah had briefed the men, but all their words didn't prepare them for the drama that unfolded as the sun dipped to kiss the horizon and paint the sky many shades of red and pink.

The first warriors crested the north knoll and set their mounts motionless in the light of the dying day. They blended into and became a part of the vast prairie, part of the natural order like the grass and trees, earth and sky. Their numbers swelled and soon the large body of warriors began to send out riders like tentacles that encircled the wagons. It was not a noisy or threatening demonstration, more like a statement of fact.

Within a few minutes the rest of the tribes arrived, and soon tipis blossomed on the prairie, campfires blazed, dogs barked, and all the sounds of a settlement on Saturday night flooded the countryside.

Ben watched through the glass. It was almost more fascinating than frightening. In a matter of minutes, a travois would be unloaded and a tipi set up. Naked children scurried about and youth ran to the knoll to get a glimpse of the whites that Mother Earth had clutched to her bosom.

He saw many things that he didn't understand and made a mental note to ask Isaiah about. He believed the more he understood of how the Indians thought, the better were their own chances of staying alive. One thing gradually became clear to him: with their lodges set up and the warriors' families in camp close by, the Indians seemed confident of killing them with ease.

Nightfall was almost upon them when Isaiah and Elmo joined Ben atop the rock pile. "Isaiah, I'm assuming that we don't have to worry about an attack tonight. Right?"

"Not tonight."

Elmo, something akin to awe in his voice, spoke while peering through the spy glass, "Lord almighty, got to be pretty near a thousand fighting men out there."

"You are right, plenty of Sioux for any Crow," Isaiah said.

"Elmo, put someone up here in two-hour watches," Ben said as they climbed down. "Isaiah, come with me. And, Elmo, I want a report every hour." He took out his watch. "The first one due at eight o'clock."

Back at Ben's wagon, they poured more corn liquor down Smith. "Where's your blanket? Let's sit and talk," Ben said to Isaiah. "I want to know everything you can tell me about those people out there."

Ben listened mostly, only occasionally asking a question as Isaiah told him of the Plains Indian. Frequently Ben felt a thought tugging at his mind. Something from his deepest subconscious was struggling for recognition.

At eight o'clock Elmo reported no change. The eternal prairie wind had died with the day and a full moon bathed the night with quicksilver. In the distance a coyote cast its nocturnal lullaby onto the gentle night breezes. Soon, from another direction, it was cast back. At every animal sound, Isaiah would listen intently, his senses strained to read the night spirits.

Elmo hadn't made his ten o'clock report when the drums started. Chants of dancing warriors and throbbing drums came relentlessly across the muddy prairie. Isaiah gathered his medicine bundle, stood up, and told Ben, "I'd better let the men know about the drums. They may as well get used to it because it will last most of the night."

Alone, Ben mentally went over the fighting attributes of the Sioux, but he didn't find a single weakness that he could use to his advantage. Even if he forgot his vow and decided to fight, it was going to be a long, bloody siege. Eventually the Sioux would win. They could win by simply pinning the men and wagons here until ammo and water ran out, or they could win with an overwhelming charge.

He recalled all he could about the writings of Sun Tzu. How could they be applied here? The nine varieties of ground. The five methods of attacking with fire. The rules for marches. Assessing weaknesses and strengths. The chapter on dispositions where the ancient warrior said the skillful fighters first make themselves invincible and await the enemy's moment of vulnerability. He saw no way to make their position invincible and he saw no vulnerability in the Sioux.

Tired as he was, Ben tried, until his head ached, to analyze every angle, to think like the enemy leaders, to maximize their own defenses and arms. Mixed among the tumbling thoughts was the vivid memory of the vow he had made never to take another human life. Finally, mentally and physically exhausted, he fell into a fitful sleep.

– 18 –

BEN AWOKE WITH A START. The plan for deliverance was there in his mind, complete and stunning. Which of the gods had put it there Ben didn't know. Was it the God of his youth who supposedly resided in the Baptist church on Main Street in Americus, Georgia, or was it some strange god that roamed the vast prairies and communed with hapless travelers?

He didn't care. Now he understood the message his mind had been trying to tell him: use their superstition. It is their one weakness. He recognized the messenger as old Doc Jacobson standing in his mind's eye with a copy of *The Art of War* held toward him.

Ben recalled Isaiah's words about superstition as he rubbed the sleep from his eyes. Isaiah had explained that to the Indian everything has a spirit – animals, trees, water, night, day, everything. What they don't understand they view as works of the spirits. To all spirits they give a measure of reverence believing the spirits are stronger than the individual. When the spirits choose to help a certain person, then that person is held in great respect.

Ben looked up at the stars and judged it was already an hour past midnight. They would have to hurry. He stumbled through the piles of freight and scrambled up the rocks where Isaiah and Elmo stood watch. He told the two of his plan and waited for their reply.

After a moment Isaiah answered, "It's a good plan, worth a try, and if your men are brave enough, it could work. If it doesn't, we can always die fighting."

"Elmo, what do you think?"

The big man didn't look away from the Indian camp, where tipis glowed like candles in the darkness. "I kinda like the first part, but I ain't thinking much of the last part. Ain't sure it's necessary."

Isaiah convinced Elmo that the plan must be carried out in its entirety. Then he woke the camp and assembled the men at the rock pile. Ben outlined his plan and then Isaiah explained why it could work on the Sioux. The sheer numbers of Indians had convinced the men that unless help came, they would all die. Ben's plan offered hope and they soon agreed.

"Let's get to work because we've got to be ready by sunup," Ben said.

The pile of rocks began to be refashioned into a platform. Eight men stumbled through the night lugging the harpsichord to the rock pile. The chandelier arrived next followed by more men toting the music box and someone laid a fiddle on the harpsichord.

Elmo drove the men hard. During a brief lull in the activity, Ben realized the Sioux camp was silent. Getting ready to go to war, he thought.

Elmo interrupted his thoughts. "Ain't yet got it figured out how to get that chandelier up above the rocks. First I figure to use wagon tongues, but don't think that will get it high enough."

"Use two tongues lashed together. Make three sets," Ben answered, envisioning a tripod supporting the chandelier atop the rocks.

"Ain't got time to forge irons to hold 'em."

"Get the wagon tongues and meet me by the fire," Isaiah said. Then he located a horse, put a rope around its neck, and plunged his knife deep into its jugular. When the horse reared, Isaiah threw it to the ground. After a couple of minutes of thrashing, the horse lay still. With skilled hands Isaiah skinned out one side and took the bloody hide to the fire. Most of the men had stopped what they were doing, watched, and made a mental note never to get on the wrong side of that flashing knife.

Isaiah slashed the hide into narrow lengths while four men held each of the corners. Taking two of the wagon tongues, he lashed them together with the rawhide. He threw a couple of pieces of firewood on the fire and told them to hold the spliced tongues over the fire. As the hide dried, it shrank, making bands almost as strong as steel. The men fell to work and soon another set of rawhide-wrapped wagon tongues was drying over the fire.

When the rock platform was complete, the last few stones were laid on the north side for steps, but Isaiah had them move the steps to the east side, explaining that the east was special to the Indian.

Ben and Isaiah walked to Ben's wagon to pour more whisky down Smith and to get some lamp oil. Hurrying back with the oil, they came upon Frenchie kneeling and praying softly, a Bible spread before him. Isaiah addressed him in flawless French, "Truly we are in the valley of the shadow of death. If we don't make this work, I doubt we have enough 'rod and staff' to save our butts. Let's go."

"Where did you learn French?" Ben asked.

"From my mother and the French traders. Mother said I have a gift of tongues."

This wild land held many surprises. A half-breed Indian in the middle of nowhere, speaking better French than I can after years of study, Ben thought.

Finally, everything was in place atop the rocks except attaching the chandelier. Elmo lashed the three spliced wagon tongues together at one end, tipi fashion. He passed a rope over the top and tied it to the chandelier. They pulled it upwards as Ben climbed the rock steps and it worked just as Ben had envisioned. Lighted, it would be spectacular and clearly visible in the Indian camp.

Ben divided the oil among the lamps. All was in order except for the hardest part. He checked the eastern sky. There was little time before the first, pale light of dawn, which according to Isaiah, was the Sioux's favorite time of attack.

19

TALKING LANCE MAINTAINED HIS LONE QUEST sitting on the prairie outside the Indian camp. He had waited, but his lance, unsheathed from the beaded bag, had not spoken. The drums and dances had stopped, allowing the warriors to sleep and then prepare themselves and their horses for war. Talking Lance looked across the plains to the wagon train. The night was quiet. Perhaps the Great Spirit was teaching him to be patient. He would wait a little longer.

The night was pristine. Uncountable stars winked in the velvet night sky. The four old men who controlled the wind were at rest tonight. Talking Lance felt the presence of someone before he heard the soft footsteps behind him. The footsteps stopped and waited.

"Come, Quiet Flower," he said. She was the wife of his youth. No longer as beautiful as his younger wives, but still his favorite. She was food for his soul, satisfying and nurturing. Like the deep, shaded pools of a clear, cool stream that refreshed and invigorated the body and mind after a long ride under the burning sun.

She sat beside him, the two in perfect harmony with each other and with Mother Earth. She knew the lance had not spoken to her husband which meant he had a hard decision to make. To fight would be inviting the wrath of disapproving spirits. On the other hand, not to fight could split the band, weaken their alliance with the Cheyenne, and their tipi would be looked upon as the lodge of a warrior with a woman's heart.

"I will stay in your lodge no matter what they say. I am not young and beautiful, but I will cook your meat, sew your moccasins, and warm your sleeping robes."

He smiled. It always amazed him that she could read his mind. He didn't care what they said. His concern was what would be best for the tribe.

They sat in silence until he knew it was time to lead his braves into battle or leave, either by himself or with what few followers would still believe in his medicine.

As he reached to pick up his lance, Quiet Flower laid her hand on his arm and pointed to the wagons.

Ben checked that he had a couple of cigars and matches before he climbed halfway up the rock stairs and turned to face the men.

"We are about to be tested. I won't try to tell you that our situation isn't perilous. Our one chance is to prove to those Indians that we're crazy, possessed of strange spirits which they don't understand and thus fear. It will take more courage to do this than anything you've ever done before. Nobody can show the slightest fear or concern. You all know what to do in the beginning. After that we may have to improvise. If any of you believe in God, now would be a good time to start praying."

He climbed the rest of the way to the top, laid the cigar and matches on the harpsichord, unbuttoned his jacket and laid it aside. His hands trembled a little as he removed his shirt, dropped it onto his coat, and then struggled out of his trousers and undergarments. He shivered in the cool air and willed himself to focus on the chandelier. Isaiah appeared by the big music box, naked as the day he was born. Big Elmo, body covered with black body hair, picked up the fiddle and bow.

Elmo spoke to Isaiah, "Is it true what's been said about the Indians' treatment of captives, and do ya reckon we best tell the men to save the last round for themselves?"

"I've already told them," Isaiah said. Then added, "Some will not be able to do it, so those of us up here should make sure none are taken alive."

It took a moment to register with Ben. "You mean shoot our own men?"

Isaiah pointed to Ben's leg, marked with a wide, jagged scar from ankle to groin. "A thousand times worse than that. If you have any compassion for these men, you will not miss when the time comes."

He wanted to protest, to scream, but with great effort he accepted Isaiah's wisdom and simply said, "Elmo, you load for me and, Isaiah, direct my field of fire – if that time comes."

They nodded their understanding.

Ben struck a match and fired the cigar, then one by one lit the chandelier lamps and told the men to haul it up. It rose and cast a warm, golden light over the naked men. He moved the harpsichord bench back and sat down, flinching at the cool bench on his bare backside.

"Elmo, do you know 'Dixie'?"

Elmo raised the fiddle and tucked it under his chin with a dignity befitting the best concert performer. He set the bow and soon notes, imperfect but recognizable, greeted the rising sun.

A tiny flicker of light appeared above the center of the wagons. It was joined one after another by others until a ring of twelve stood suspended in the white-eyes' camp. The lights grew stronger, becoming an orb of sparkling fire. Talking Lance and Quiet Flower caught their breath as it rose upward in the night sky, then stopped and hovered above the camp.

A low, mournful sound reached them and was soon joined by another sound, mixed together hauntingly. It set dogs barking and howling behind them in the Indian camp. In minutes, most of the Sioux and Cheyenne were gathered, spellbound, on the rise overlooking the wagons. After a few minutes the noise stopped and then abruptly started again, this time joined with the sound of voices.

Limping Bear sought out Talking Lance. "Your lance has spoken of these things?"

"It has kept its silence. It needs not speak for me to know that the white eyes have strange and powerful medicine."

"Yes, but they are few and we are many. We have our medicine that is also strong. We are ready. Come, put on your paint, for Sun Boy is about to start his journey."

Talking Lance looked at the east where the glow of pre-dawn tinted the sky. He slowly picked up his sacred lance and the beaded cover. Without a word he walked toward their camp. Quickly, he painted his war pony and himself, then dressed in his finest war garments. Quiet Flower watched as he unsheathed the lance. He mounted his horse and led his warriors toward the wagons.

Ben picked up the melody and they felt their way through three stanzas. He shouted to the men to sing and struck up "The Battle Hymn of the Republic." The fiddle caught the tune and men's voices soon rose in accompaniment. At the last note of the song, Ben nodded to Isaiah who cranked the handle and the music box plucked out a slow waltz.

The men stood on the wagon seats like statues, all facing the rising sun, naked before God and the Sioux. The music box wound down and Ben said, "Isaiah, walk 'em around one time."

Isaiah leapt off the platform and walked across the enclosure to the easternmost wagon. The teamsters dropped to the ground, and in single file they circled just outside the wagons, each driver joining in as the column passed. The circle was about completed when one of the men ran forward to Isaiah. "I can't, I ain't getting back up there no ways. I feel like a damn fool, and besides, we're just plain easy targets."

"Guess it's working because we're supposed to look like fools." Isaiah touched his knife that was now dangling around his neck. "No time to change mind now. You not get on wagon, Two Suns cut off your branch. Or, as you white eyes would say, get your ass back on that wagon seat or I'll cut off your nuts and slit your belly from your dick to your throat." He said it loud enough for all to hear.

Once the circle was complete, the men climbed back onto the wagon seats. Elmo began playing "When Johnny Comes Marching Home." Ben yelled at the men to sing as a ring of mounted warriors surrounded the wagons. Hundreds emerged into existence as the night faded away, as if they were formed out of the substance of waning darkness. Warrior and war horse materialized resplendent in ceremonial war dress. Majestic war bonnets, brightly decorated coup sticks, feathered lances, and painted bodies all hauntingly beautiful and savage, poised across the half mile of barren prairie that stood between the wagons and the warriors.

The night unwrapped itself and the naked men became exposed to the Indians, an absurd scene of naked, singing men on wagon seats, naked men on a rock pile coaxing wailing spirits from unknown habitats. The Indians waited and watched.

The song ended and the quiet was like a physical blow, as though even the insects were walking on tiptoes. Isaiah bounded up the rock steps and pointed toward the east. "By god, Ben, we've got 'em thinking. Couple of their chiefs are having a hell of an argument."

"Let's give 'em something else crazy. Anybody got an idea?" He started another song trying to think of something more to do. Halfway through the song Elmo stopped playing and laid the fiddle under the harpsichord next to the Ballard and the Henry. "Got me an idea," he said.

"You need help?" Ben asked as he played.

"No, this is a one-man show."

Elmo stopped at the bottom of the stairs, bent down and picked up one of the foundation stones. Huge muscles rippling, he hefted it to his shoulder and headed for the nearest wagon. His mouth a thin hard line as the stone bit into his flesh. By damn, he thought, everyone said I was the strongest man in Georgia. I wonder if I can impress these feathered bastards. I hope so 'cause right now, more than anything else, I'd like to see my Jenny again. I don't want'a see no more prairie, no more dirty, naked men, and damn sure no more Indians. He came to the first wagon, turned, and yelled for Ben to stop the music.

In the silence Elmo hollered across the distance toward the Indians, "You Sioux ever read your Bible? Story about a mean son of a bitch that kilt a whole bunch of heathens. Well, by god, some people call me Samson." Satisfied he had their attention, he half squatted and then exploded upwards launching the huge stone in an arch over the wagon. He quickly vaulted into the wagon box and out again next to the stone.

"Ben," he hollered. "Let's have some dancing music."

As the music began, Elmo heaved the huge stone to his shoulder once more and settled it in place before doing a lively little jig as he started dancing around the wagons.

"I'd not believe it if I didn't just see it," Isaiah was talking partly to himself and partly to Ben. "But, he can't make it all the way around – can he?"

The men were clapping in rhythm, the Indians momentarily forgotten as they watched Elmo. Halfway around he stumbled, bringing a gasp from the men as he fought to keep his feet. A teamster shouted encouragement and the naked blacksmith resumed his balance. When Elmo finally reached the spot he had started from, he set the stone on end and kneeled as if in prayer. He then stood and again started around the circle stopping at each wagon to reach up and shake hands with the man on the wagon seat. Early morning sun glistened on bulging muscles and sweating body as he walked back and picked up the violin.

"Damn impressive," Ben said, his fingers picking out a Negro spiritual. "They're still out there, but they haven't attacked. Let's just keep doing what we're doing."

The sun climbed slowly, perhaps distracted by the drama unfolding below. The naked men became less self-conscious, singing lustily with the piano and violin. Every half hour, Isaiah would lead them around the wagons, stopping to touch the big stone Elmo had placed there.

By mid-afternoon the men were beginning to notice the hot sun on parts of their body that had never felt its rays for more than fleeting moments. Throats that had never before sung more than a few minutes in church services cried out for water.

"Elmo," Ben said, "you've got to solo awhile, play anything you like."

He got up and stretched an aching body that had been eight hours at the keyboard. He immediately regretted his invitation to "play anything" as Elmo struck up "The Girl I Left Behind" and past memories overpowered Ben.

When Adeline had refused to see him after he returned home from Appomattox he became so angry and hurt that he whipped his team all the way to Americus where he limped into the nearest tavern. Soon, he was awash in bourbon and self-pity, repeating to himself that he was still a potent man. Hell, he was a physician. He had studied these things, and besides, his knowledge of animals assured him he could perform with only one seed. But he had to know. Maybe, if he was certain in his mind, he could argue more forcefully with Adeline.

He had staggered unsteadily out of the tavern and secured a hack, telling the driver to find him a good whore.

"Why certainly, sir," the driver answered. "That would be Madam Simpson's establishment."

Ben fumbled with his wallet and laid several bills onto the seat beside the driver. "Madame Simpson's it is," he said.

The old house had lace-curtained windows open to the warm night air. Laughter and music spilled softly with the lamplight onto the gathering night. The song was "The Girl I Left Behind" and it plunged him deeper into the blackness of his pity and anger. Inside, he paid the money and accompanied a buxom blond down the hall to a small room. Drunk as he was at the time, he remembered it in bitter detail. She was very young and luscious in the lamp's glow but she kept staring at his leg and looking at the clock on the wall. Try as he might, he couldn't prove what his medical knowledge told him was fact.

He gave up in disgust, self-consciously pulling on his clothes while she sat on the bed, twirling her blond hair around her fingers, watching him struggle to get his bad leg into his trousers. Why couldn't she have just kept quiet? Instead she invited him back for another try, saying she always felt sorry for the wounded boys.

Ben wheeled on her, screaming about honor, duty, war, death, and what she could do with her pity. He smashed the lamp and clock with his heavy cane, lurched into the hall, and raked an oil sconce off the wall. It burst into flames. Doors flew open, a woman screamed, and a male customer stormed, half naked, out of a room. Ben hit him a glancing blow on the head and then hobbled on down the hall. House security intercepted him in the lobby and he spent the night in jail.

For the next two months he wallowed in alcohol, pity, and anger until only his father's worsening illness shocked him into sobriety. The demands of caring for his father kept his mind off himself part of the time. The other part was spent wondering what would happen if he tried to prove his manhood again.

He ventured back to the soiled dove district when he could no longer live with the doubt. Of course Madame Simpson's was out of the question, so he picked a small, well-kept house several doors down. He almost lost his nerve but the brunette at the end of the settee caught his eye. He could sense an understanding spirit. Her eyes told of a life that had not turned out like her childhood dreams. Her brown eyes were sad beyond her years, a sadness that threatened to extinguish a very small flicker of hope.

Once in her room he simply talked, unable to try for fear of another failure, unable to leave without knowing. At last he was comfortable with her quiet ways and asked if he could keep her company for the rest of the night. She took the extra money, undressed, and pulled the ribbons from her hair letting her long dark mane spill over her bare shoulders.

That night his scarred body proved what his mind had already known. He never again returned to that part of town, but many times regretted that he had not somehow made an effort to help the girl that was so kind and so gentle and so sad.

When Elmo stopped playing the song, it released its grip on Ben's mind and the memories faded. Sitting back down at the harpsichord he made his hands pick out a melody as he watched the charging warriors rolling toward them like a colorful wave, first firing a volley of screams and yells, then of rifle balls and arrows. Ben yelled for everyone to hold steady and again began to play "The Battle Hymn of the Republic." Isaiah leapt off the rock platform and Ben caught a glimpse of his naked form strolling casually from wagon to wagon talking to the men.

A rifle ball smashed through the chandelier, raining broken crystal and burning oil into the harpsichord. Several keys went flat and for a heartbeat Ben figured he was done. He slung his cane at the lid support; the lid crashed down and he prayed it would smother the flames. Thick smoke rolled out around the lid as he pounded the keys. Elmo stayed with him, never missing a note, his eyes wide, trying to see all directions at once.

The Indians came within a hundred yards of the wagons, circled, and fired a second volley. Ben stole a glance around him. Miraculously, the men were still on the wagon seats unhurt. Some singing, some frozen with terror, and a few bolder ones taunting the circling Indians. Ben pounded out "I Wish I Was in Dixie" and another key or two went flat, but the melody was unmistakable.

A horse screamed, then another as arrows rained down on the herd. Ben tore his eyes from the warriors and looked to the horses. Two were down. Isaiah came up the steps, a bright light burning in his blue eyes, "Ho, my brother's medicine is strong. They will not charge again, for they are unsure, afraid of our spirit."

"I can't play this thing much longer," Ben said. "Suppose we should circle the men once more?"

"Once more," Isaiah said, winding the music box.

It wasn't necessary. The circling warriors began a slow retreat to their camp and soon the tipis were coming down and within an hour the tribe was on the move north.

Ben and Isaiah held the men to their positions until the last vestige of the Indian caravan faded from view. Ben felt like he'd just proved to the world that you didn't have to resort to violence and killing to solve problems. He would give anything if his father and all those who had scorned his declaration of non-violence could know what had just happened. For the first time since the war, he prayed a sincere prayer of thanksgiving.

Wisps of smoke still drifted from under the harpsichord lid, but Ben found enough notes to begin playing "Amazing Grace." Elmo put the fiddle back under his chin and, with closed eyes, joined Ben in a heartfelt duet. From one of the wagon seats a clear, resonate tenor added the words. The sun paused on the horizon, as if to gaze one last time on such strange behavior and to catch the last moving words of the song, then yielded the cloudless sky to the first evening star.

PART II

20

TODD KEEFERLY SWUNG HIS LEGS over the edge of his bed and sat for a moment rubbing the sleep from his eyes. Like every morning, sweltering summer heat or bitter winter blizzard, the seventeen-year-old savored this time of day. He never really thought of it in well-defined terms, but it was like stealing a little bit of his life back from his father.

Todd dressed, picked up his boots, and walked barefoot down the hall, through the living room and into the kitchen. Long-time house servant Angelo set a cup of steaming coffee on the table while Todd pulled on his boots. A tin plate of kitchen scraps was already on the table as it had been every morning for the past two years. Since Todd's mother's death, old Angelo and the animals that Todd nursed back to health had been the only comfort in the youth's life.

He finished his coffee, stood up, and stretched. Outwardly, the boy was a slightly smaller version of his father, Captain Simon Keeferly. Todd was just over six feet tall with broad shoulders that tapered to a slim waist. Inwardly, he was his mother's son – quiet, kind, and compassionate.

Angelo, perpetual twinkle in his eyes and kindness in his voice, spoke to Todd from the maple butcher block where he was slicing bacon. "I looked in on the new fawn last evening. You did a good job on the leg but we're going to have to find another cow for milk. I'll do that after the crew is gone for the day."

"Thanks, Angelo. The little one needs the milk, but don't let Dad catch you."

The old gentleman grinned and waved his hand toward the door. "Go take care of the animals and don't worry about the captain. He doesn't know everything that happens while he's gone."

Todd walked to the lean-to he had built against the south side of the large barn where he lit a lantern and tended his small menagerie: the new fawn, a raccoon, a coyote pup, and a great horned owl. The owl was strong enough to leave, but even though the cage door was always open, the owl returned each morning for its free food.

Todd carefully inspected each animal before looking up toward the house. No light in his father's bedroom meant he still had a few minutes. He carried the lantern into the far corner. A cur dog, one stub of a front leg bandaged and bloody, lay on a bed of hay. The dog's tail thumped at Todd's approach and then eagerly took the table scraps that Todd offered.

Captain Keeferly awoke, got up from his bed, and walked to the window to see lantern light spilling from the lean-to. Todd was with those goddamn crippled animals again, he thought. Why couldn't the boy learn that this land was no place for cripples? Best thing you could do was knock 'em in the head and spend your time on the healthy ones.

Every time he looked at the boy, he saw himself as a strong, virile youth and that made him proud. But, all the boy's actions reminded him of his wife. Hadn't her death proved this land was for the strong? What good was a woman if it wasn't to give a man many sons? By the time he'd dressed and rethought the events around his third wife's death he went to breakfast with the same festering belligerence that had hallmarked the past six months.

"Angelo," he said as he lowered himself into a chair, "get Jake up here to eat this morning."

"Jake didn't come back last night," Angelo replied, pouring steaming coffee.

"How the hell you know that? You been to the bunkhouse and cook shack?"

"Old men don't sleep as good or as much as they did when young. Besides, someone has to keep an eye on things around here."

Todd came in and sat at the big table as his dad replied to Angelo, "You're damn right there. Right now it looks like you're about the only one who understands what it means to work a ranch. Son of a bitch Jake must be holed up in that damn whorehouse again."

Todd knew the remark about ranch work was aimed at him but he ignored the barb and said, "We shoved that bunch of yearlings up to the Vine River area like you said. Ain't much grass up there – won't keep 'em more than three or four weeks."

The captain studied his son over the coffee cup. "See anyone up that way?"

"No, but I still think someone should ride line up there. Those critters will be drifted all over that range in a few days."

The captain assured Todd they would send a hand up there soon. He thought, however, that drifting cattle was what he was planning on. He hoped every one of those son of a bitches ended up on the McGregor claims.

"Todd, I want you to ride over and check the horses at Wild Horse Flats." There was a hint of pride in his voice. His son had a natural gift when it came to working with horses, and in fact the only reason he tolerated Todd's sick animals was because the boy had nursed a prize horse colt back to life three years ago.

Todd's eyes brightened. "You're wanting to know if that two-year-old is ready to bring in?"

The captain nodded.

"I should be back tomorrow night," Todd said.

Breakfast finished, the captain shoved away from the table and stood up; six feet four of solid, cagey, frontier-hardened man. "If that stallion looks as good as I think he will, I wouldn't want anything to happen to him. I'd go myself if I didn't have to go drag Jake's ass out of town. You know he won't listen to anyone but me."

Todd saddled his favorite chestnut mare, stopped by the kitchen for food, and swung out of the ranch yard headed almost due west, the early sun pushing and his long shadow pulling horse and rider across the rolling grassland.

He loved anything to do with horses and the opportunity to go to Wild Horse Flats was a treat. The wild horses that roamed the flats fascinated Todd. They were a hardy lot but not as flashy as his dad wanted for his own use or to be associated with the Guidon K brand. That's why three years ago his dad had brought in a blooded stallion to turn loose with the wild mustangs. Most folks thought him crazy, didn't figure the big bay would last the first winter, but it had proved them wrong. The mares were throwing some mighty good-looking colts, and Todd could hardly wait until spring roundup. He wanted to break the bay stallion if his dad would let him. He figured that horse was about the best horseflesh within a thousand miles.

The smell of the prairie and the beauty of the rolling countryside were not lost on the young rider. He loved the land. His body fairly itched to work with the horses and cattle that were the lifeblood of the Guidon K. The only cloud in his young life was his father. Always stern and reserved, but lately he had become obsessively strict, not only with Todd, but with the hands as well. The captain had withdrawn into a world of anger and hostility where even the talk of Indian uprisings didn't bring its usual reaction. As much as he loved the land and the life here, he wasn't sure he could stay with his father unless something changed and changed in a hurry.

Besides that, he didn't like the crew his father was hiring these days. He didn't even like some of the old crew. Especially Jake and Shorty. Jake was big, strong, dull, slow, crass, and with a mean streak a yard wide. It had always been a puzzle to Todd why his dad kept Jake around.

Shorty, the ranch foreman, reminded Todd of a cross between a badger and a weasel. Short, compact muscular body topped by a long-nosed, pinch-faced head much too small for the thick body. But Todd had to admit he knew ranch work. Shorty smarted like a whipped pup when Jake gave him orders, but the two ran the ranching operation exactly like the captain wanted – very military. If it hadn't been for the extremely high wages at the Guidon K, no self-respecting ranch hand would ride for the brand.

Todd reined in atop a knoll and looked around. It was all part of his father's empire, one day to be his. The exhilarating thought of that was dulled by the relationship with his father. He pushed on toward Wild Horse Flats, diverting his thoughts toward the coming roundup.

The captain took his cup of coffee into the study where the sun sliced through the window and highlighted his collection of books lined military straight on the bookshelves. He sat down at his cylinder-front desk and finished addressing a letter to the territorial capital, looking up as he heard the crew ride out, followed shortly by hoof beats of a lone rider. That would be Todd. For a moment he wished he had ridden with his son or asked him to accompany him to town. The boy needed to begin to see the real world, get a few calluses on his mind, learn how to deal with both weak men and strong men. Given the right knowledge, people could be broke just like a horse to do whatever you wanted. He made a mental note to start taking Todd into some of the ranch decisions, especially when it came to dealing with people.

He stuck the envelope into his vest pocket and leaned back. The ranch was quiet. He was alone except for Angelo. He wondered if the big house would ever again hear the sounds of a busy woman and playing children. Hell, he may be getting old, but that didn't mean he couldn't have another wife. Women still stirred his blood and he'd like to have more sons.

Right now he had to ride into town and find Jake, pound some sense into his damn hard, simple head. He also needed to see the sheriff so it wouldn't be a wasted trip. A half hour later he stepped up on a big, leggy dapple gray and spurred out of the ranch yard toward the high rock bluff that sheltered the ranch buildings from the howling north winds of winter. It was out of his way to town, but he spent a lot of time there when he was troubled in mind. A well-worn trail wound around the back side of the rise and through a grove of cottonwoods. He reined in at the edge of the timber and rode at a walk through the big trees as the bright morning sun was seeking and devouring shadows that tried to hide in the underbrush. He emerged from the grove and dismounted. From here the headquarters of the ranch lay below and to the south. A quarter mile to the east ran meandering Elk Creek.

He wasn't sure why he was here this morning. Over the years he had come up to sit and gaze out over his holdings, letting pride and ambition wash through his body like a belt of good whisky. Lately, it seemed, he always went away more disturbed than ever.

The ranch held little challenge for growth since it already encompassed all the good grazing within miles and now he was having to fight off the homesteaders just to keep what he considered his. Maybe it was time to move on to other territory, namely political territory, and he believed becoming the next governor was possible if he played his cards right. If Todd would just take hold of things here at the ranch, he could move to Elk Springs and then on to Omaha. Along with running the biggest ranch in the new state, he'd run the whole damn state itself. His mind licked at that thought like a kid licking at rock candy.

He took off his hat and nodded to the graves, only for a second, then ran his hand through his silver hair, jammed his hat on, and mounted. He wondered why he couldn't or wouldn't feel very much about his dead family members. He always told himself a man couldn't afford those emotions out here. One had to be tough, hardened, unfeeling to deal with life on the frontier. His mind forgot his ambitions for a moment and nibbled at a troubling question. If he could put aside the willed and practiced hardness that he needed to survive, what were his true feelings toward those buried here? And to the living that surrounded him?

His mind preferred to focus on adding "governor" to his name so after a moment he swung his horse northeast out of the grove and urged the gray into an easy lope. Then, on a whim, he changed directions and veered to the west.

It was past high noon when he hit the Vine River, what he figured to be three or four miles above the single homestead he'd been told about. Surely the sheriff had informed the poor, misguided sodbuster that this was Guidon K land and it would be best to settle elsewhere. Sheriff Barton had most persuasive ways with squatters. The few times the old badge-toter had been unsuccessful within the law, Jake had handled the job with relish.

He forded the river and rode downstream for half a mile before reining up in disbelief. There was a large cabin, a barn, a corral, and a passel of kids and armed men in the yard. They calmly watched him ride in and some walked out to meet him in front of the cabin.

"A good day to you, sir. If you've a mind, you be welcome to climb down for a spell." The spokesman for the group was medium height, with dark hair and a beard with silver streaks at his chin. His dark eyes seemed to sparkle, and laugh lines at their corners appeared to have enjoyed little rest during his lifetime. The man turned to a wide-eyed boy of about eight. "Go tell Mother to heat up the coffee."

Captain Keeferly sized up the group. My god, they're all from the same litter he thought. The old boy that sired these nine bastards must have been one hell of a stud.

"I'm Will McGregor," the man said offering his hand up to the captain. "And these are my brothers. Most folks have trouble telling us apart," he said reeling off their names. They all smiled, showing even white teeth behind black beards.

"Climb on down, mister. Ain't nothing to be feared of. Only reason we're all carrying guns is because of the Indians."

The captain hadn't said anything. He didn't want to climb down. He wanted to shoot the stupid bastards who just stood there and grinned at him, but the mention of Indians got his attention.

He leaned over and took Will's hand that was still offered. It was like trying to squeeze a rock. "I'm Captain Keeferly," he said curtly, gladly releasing the handshake and dismounting. "What about these Indians?"

Will motioned to another boy, "Take the captain's horse, give it a bit of water, rub him down, and tie him in the shade. If that's okay?" He looked at the big man in front of him for approval. The captain nodded.

These were not the run-of-the-mill squatters, and he imagined the sheriff and Jake would earn their money with this lot. Everywhere he looked there were kids – behind the corral fence, looking out of barn doors, and peeking from cabin windows. All these people must do is breed, he thought. He looked up as the cabin door opened and understood why. A redheaded woman was stepping off the porch carrying a big porcelain coffee pot. Several small girls carrying tin cups followed shyly behind.

Will, still smiling, touched the woman's arm as she passed, "Captain, this is my wife Anna. Fairest lass ever born in Scotland."

The captain touched his hat brim, "Pleasure, ma'am."

Anna smiled and brushed back a strand of fiery hair that had fallen across her face. "Will," she said in a husky voice. "Don't be embarrassing me in front of strangers."

Will and his brothers chuckled while she poured coffee for everyone. He sucked at the steaming coffee and gestured to the parade of womenfolk who emerged from the cabin and stood on the porch. Will was rattling off their names and who they belonged to, but the captain heard nothing of the names. He tugged his hat down lower and studied Anna from under the brim. Green eyes, a few freckles across the bridge of her nose.

His eyes slipped to her full bosom, then down to her flat stomach under a frilly apron.

He forced himself to speak. "When did you see Indians, where, and how many?"

He listened for Will's answer while his mind undressed Anna.

Will called up one of his brothers who described the Indian camp and the trail that led west from the river about ten miles upstream.

"You actually see 'em?" the captain asked as he finished caressing Anna with his eyes and then dressed her again in the latest fashions of his imagination. She would turn heads in any company.

"No, I didn't stick around long. Had to be Indians though, hundreds of 'em. Left a trail even the blind could read."

Captain Keeferly looked past Anna's red hair, past the cabin and fought to keep control as he saw a strip of freshly turned sod violating the rich, lush prairie grass. Goddamn, he thought with silent rage, the Almighty surely wouldn't fault a man for killing someone who plowed under good grassland. He wanted to kill them now, but prudence, and Anna, made him play the part of a gentleman which he could do so well. Looking at the man who had seen the Indian trail he asked, "Trail lead straight west?"

From behind a black beard an answer rumbled, "Mostly west but some north. Mean anything?"

"Maybe," the captain said, suddenly wanting to put some distance between the grinning men and the hypnotic redheaded woman. He asked for his horse and handed the empty coffee cup to one of the small girls who hovered among the legs of the parents. Now that he had finished with Anna, he noticed the other womenfolk, realizing there wasn't a bad looker among the lot.

Will rattled on, each word an irritant to the captain. "Don't know much about Indians. Reckon it wouldn't be good to get caught out alone. You're welcome to stay until we decide if they mean us harm."

The men all nodded agreement. Will's words continued like the drip of a leaky roof. "We all got cabins and claims down the river. Figure best to hold up at one place. We're armed good. Even the young'ns and womenfolk are tolerable good shots."

More claims and cabins down the river? What's with these bastards, the captain thought. Don't they know who I am? The old hatred mixed with the new, almost uncontrollable rage of late, made his hand tremble as he took the reins from the boy who brought his horse.

Mounted, he almost gave in to the emotion, but Anna standing there checked one emotion and replaced it with another. He touched his hat brim with his hand while his eyes once more touched the fiery redhead. "Thanks for the coffee, ma'am." His gaze moved to the other women, "Perhaps I'll have the pleasure again. Right now I'd best get on to Elk Springs."

$$- 21 -$$

CAPTAIN KEEFERLY WAS BARELY PAST the last corral post when the McGregor homestead erupted with animated talk. "I tell you, Will, he sure didn't act like the Captain Keeferly we'd been warned about."

Will stared down river after the departing rider. "He's a tough one, don't any of you forget that. Just because he drank a cup of coffee, nothing's changed."

The men drifted toward the barn. "Maybe he checked the land office and knows we've legal right to the land?"

Will shook his head at his younger brother's remark. "He's made his own law for too long to worry about a few words on a piece of paper. Besides, we got to prove up before it's actually ours."

"Sure wishing he'd said more about them Indians. Acted like they didn't worry him a bit," the youngest brother said.

As the men walked to the barn, the women returned indoors. "That's the one they all said would shoot us on sight. He really seemed like a gentleman to me," a willowy brunette said as she returned to kneading bread dough.

Anna set the coffee pot on the stove and shooed the wide-eyed children from the cabin. "He was very polite, but he is a mean man deep down. I don't trust him."

"That's just because he kept staring at you."

"All the men stare at Anna," a doe-eyed blonde said as she tied an apron around her waist. "I wish sometime one would stare at me like that. Maybe I could trust him to do something."

The women giggled and busied themselves with domestic chores. Anna was solemn as she peeled potatoes at the big plank table that dominated the rough cabin interior. She had felt many a man's eyes. Most were just wishful, but occasionally a Captain Keeferly came along and that always led to trouble.

Downriver and out of sight of the McGregors, the captain pulled up and looked west over the rolling prairie. He didn't doubt that Indians had been seen because he'd heard of several sightings lately. If they were headed west and north, that would take them close to Wild Horse Flats. After a moment he reined the dapple gray downstream and raked hard with his spurs.

A half-mile brought him to another cabin and corral, not as large as the first but well built, neat, and very permanent in appearance. The rich grass had again been violated by the damnable plow. He spurred his mount again and a half mile further downstream was another cabin, corral, barn, and busted sod.

His first thought was that Sheriff Barton had missed the settlers, however now he guessed that the McGregors were workers. Together they had built the homesteads quickly. No ordinary dirt grubbers this bunch, but he anticipated the thrill of running the grinning bastards out of the country after he got what he wanted from the redhead.

The McGregor claims seemed to stretch forever down the river. Nine cabins, nine barns, nine corrals. Nine times the captain cursed and raged in the empty yards. By the time he arrived at the last cabin the dapple gray was lathered, sides heaving, and nostrils flared. Unlike the others, the occupants of this claim had left abruptly. Two milch cows, a calf, and several oxen were still in the pole corral.

A handmade stool, washboard, and wooden tub stood just outside the cabin door. On the other side of the door a cornhusk doll sat dwarfed and lonely in a big handmade rocking chair.

He dismounted, kicked open the door, and stalked into the cabin. The smell of fresh-worked wood mingled with that of a dead fire in a stone fireplace. Sunlight sneaked through the simple curtains on a single south window and formed a yellow square on the hard-packed earth floor. The two rooms and loft were sparsely furnished, but clean and neat with the undeniable presence of a woman's touch.

It had been in a cabin much like this that he had started ranching. He didn't know why he had wanted to see the inside of the cabin because he knew he wouldn't like the memories it brought. Turning on his heel he stepped through the door, leaving it standing open. In frustration he picked up the big rocker and flung it into the yard. Once mounted, he rode to the corral, roped the gate post, and pulled it down.

The docile critters were content to remain in the corral, either way, gate open or closed. They watched the mounted rider with keen interest and Captain Keeferly thought how like the owners they looked, content and stupid, not recognizing danger when it stared them in the face. He herded them through the open cabin door and leaned over and pulled the door closed. He rode back to the barn where a plow rested against the side, dropped a rope over the handle, dallied around his saddle horn, and dragged the plow around the yard, wiping out his mount's tracks. He was about to start for the river, but spotted the rocker in the yard. The dragging plow bounced over the rocker, crushing it and the cornhusk doll that lay small and vulnerable in the dirt.

Satisfied at last, he rode to the river and dragged the plow into deep water. Shaking the rope loose and recoiling it, he hoped to god the damn plow would rust beyond use. With a little luck the Indians would get the blame. It would be better if he burned the buildings, but ever since the Sioux had burned his ranch, killing his first wife and child, he couldn't bear the sight of a blazing building.

An hour later he reached the edge of Elk Springs where he stopped in a grove of mossy cup oaks. He dismounted, took a folded burlap from his saddle bags, and rubbed down the gray. Then he replaced the burlap with a flannel rag and brushed the dust from his cavalry-style boots and the new saddle he'd had shipped all the way from a custom maker in El Paso. All his personal effects received attention until he felt ready to be seen by the citizens of town.

Lights were beginning to wink on in the little town that lay below the oaks, much as the Guidon K headquarters lay below the stand of cottonwoods. He wished to hell Todd would buck up and take over the ranch so he could build a house among the oaks here at the edge of his town that one day soon just might be a governor's home.

I'll find that damn Jake and knock him between the horns and then stay the night, he thought as he rode down the main street, and tomorrow see that money-grubbing land agent. If the son of a bitch doesn't accept my offer soon, I'll have Jake help him see the wisdom of doing business with an old pillar of the community.

– 22 –

SHERIFF BARTON STOOD IN THE SHADOWS of the livery watching Captain Keeferly ride down the main street and rein up at the Bear Skin saloon. No secret why he's in town, the sheriff thought, both angry and amused at the charade he would have to endure.

The sheriff had arrived at Elk Springs like most of those who stayed – trail weary and broke. That had been four years ago and about four hundred bottles of Dr. Seeley's Body Liniment, sure cure for both man and beast. It hadn't been a cure, but it did relieve the pain somewhat. Why couldn't it have been his left arm instead of his right? Didn't make no difference, he guessed. If he could just hang on for another year, he'd be set for life.

The liniment was soaking fire down into his shoulder, temporarily overcoming the pain and stiffness. He flexed his right arm carefully. A sigh and a smile later he was ready for dinner and then his evening rounds. He'd have to lie again about the smell of the liniment. Most of the folks considered it a noble gesture on his part to nurse that old stoved-up horse. He wondered what they would think if they knew he paid a hundred dollars for the damn crowbait and then purposely lamed it just to give him an excuse for the ever-present odor of liniment.

He watched the town from the deepening shadows. More people than usual on a weekday due to the fact that the Indians were scaring the hell out of folks. But all in all, except for Captain Keeferly and Jake, it promised to be a quiet evening. A buckboard pulled up at the hotel bringing another outlying rancher or nester and his family into town because of real or imagined Indians. He'd drop by the saloons later to catch up on the grapevine that provided most of the area news long before the struggling *Elk Springs Advocate* printed anything.

Sheriff Barton, prodded by a growling stomach, turned and melted into the night and moments later came through the back door of the eatery like he came through life – slow, quiet, and alert. Many a troublemaker had mistaken his deliberate caution for fear or weakness, realizing too late he was quick as a church gossip's tongue and tough as last year's hardtack.

When he moved into the lamplight, it winked off the sheriff badge and the well-worn ivory grips on a .44 Colt Dragoon. The rest seemed unworthy of attention, seldom rating a second look. He shoved his hat back and his restless blue eyes burned behind narrowed lids.

He studied the room with those eyes, and then moved slowly to a corner table that put his back to the wall and the rest of the room in easy view. A couple of ranch hands from a little spread in the hill country south of town worked on their meal in silence. A man, woman, and two young children sat at a table in the center of the room. The sheriff saw at first glance the man's sodbuster uniform and that the fare on the table was the cheapest in the house.

Satisfied, Sheriff Barton lowered his six-foot-two frame of two hundred and twenty pounds into the battered chair behind the table. The chair groaned in protest until it recognized an old comrade and then stoically accepted the burden.

The eatery was run by a large, jovial widow who had taken no sides in the town social structure. Over the years the sheriff had found that most towns had such an establishment. He always took his meals there if they were at all decent.

He did his drinking at the bars of common folks and his gambling in the rich men's saloons. This, and his practiced manner of listening everywhere and talking only occasionally, kept him aware of all that was afoot in the community. He had thought with amusement many times that if he went into the gossip and rumor business he'd get shot much quicker than as a lawman. Even jovial, likable Mrs. Sutton, waddling toward him between the tables, had her interesting little secrets.

She puffed up to his table, round checks flushed and blue eyes dancing. "Evening, Mr. Sheriff. I done saved you the best steak I've ever seen."

He nodded solemnly, thinking, for the last four years every steak was the best she'd ever seen. He finally allowed a measured smile. "I declare, Mrs. Sutton, you've sure got me spoiled. If I ever hear you giving anyone else your best steak, I reckon I'll have to throw you in my jail."

The apron around her ample girth bobbed up and down as she chuckled. Her cheeks flushed a bit more. "You do and who'd fix your steaks like you like 'em?" She jerked her head and rolled her eyes across the street. "You'd be lucky to get sow belly from that place across the street."

They enjoyed the daily flirting sessions. Each knowing it was just that, but relishing the personal attention that two plain souls, past their prime of life, got little of elsewhere. She blushed and shook at his little jokes and compliments; he gleaned information from her comments about the endless stream of customers who ate and visited in her neat dinning room with the faded checkered tablecloths.

While he sipped his coffee and waited for the meal, another family came in and joined the nester, his wife, and their two sniffling children across the room. He'd seen neither family before. The two men shook hands and soon the families were talking freely, obviously relieved to be in company of their own kind.

The lawman watched the suppertime customers file in and listened as best he could to the nesters' conversation. Nothing new, just more talk about the prairie fire that had swept for miles north of Elk Springs. The man with the dumpy wife and runny-nosed kids hadn't suffered from the fire, but came to town because of Indians.

On the other hand, the second family had lost everything except wagon, team, and the clothes on their backs. They had sold the team to eat and get a hotel room for a week. That, the sheriff thought, is proof enough there is no God, or if there is, he isn't interested in people. If he were God, he'd burn out the first family of loud, dirty, ill-mannered trash and leave the second alone. They were worth twice the first.

Sheriff Barton finished his meal and paid his tab before stepping through the door and quickly into the shadows to let his eyes adjust to the dark. He probed every shadow and watched every figure on the street until he was sure of their identity or their intent. He didn't expect trouble, but there were a lot of dead lawmen who hadn't expected trouble. He was still alive. He figured that was good reward for small habits.

He started up the walk, nodding and speaking to those he met. On the corner of the main intersection stood the bank, the newspaper office, land office, and mercantile establishment. He left the sidewalk, striding between the bank and hotel. In the alley he turned south and walked until he passed the rear door of the War Bonnet saloon and stepped into the darkness between it and the general store. He could hear the out-of-tune piano and men's voices through the thin walls.

Stopping at the street, he remained in the shadows and watched full darkness settle on the town. He flexed his right arm, clenched and unclenched his fingers. Not bad, he thought and hoped the warmer spring days would ease the ache and stiffness that plagued him during the winter days and nights. He stepped onto the walk, sought the shadows in front of the saloon, and again watched and waited while he studied the horses at the hitch rail, not moving until he had recognized each and every one. Most of the people on the sidewalks were recognizable to him either by their clothes or their walk. Occasionally, a voice or laughter was enough for an identity.

Two men approached from the south, talking excitedly. The sheriff knew them before they walked through the yellow squares of lamplight spilling from the general store windows. The short, long, short, long singing of large spur rowels was the way Johnny Silven always walked, the result of a small injury and a large vanity. It was a limp and swagger that the young rancher had developed. His friend was another would-be rancher from the borders of the Guidon K. They were hard workers but stupid. The captain had 'em by the short hairs and they didn't even know it. He stepped out and greeted them as they were about to enter the saloon.

"Evening, fellas," he said.

His appearance startled the two until they recognized the sheriff. "Howdy, Sheriff." Johnny found his voice first. "We was just talking about you. Injuns is getting thick around my place. Any chance of getting the army in to whip their ass?"

"Don't hold much hope. Let's talk over a drink," the sheriff said, waiting to step in behind the two ranchers. Wanting to be polite to the law, they waited for him. The sheriff swept his hand toward the door. "Gentlemen, after you. I insist."

They pushed through the batwings grinning and yammering about Indians and prairie fires. The sheriff wondered to himself if chivalry had been born in the dark, dim past by wise lawmen or shrewd outlaws. Or perhaps a cautious lover. Getting someone else, even ladies, to walk through a door first put someone between you and whatever danger may be waiting on the other side.

Inside, he built a cigarette without taking his eyes from the small, smoky interior. Nesters and ne'er-do-well ranchers and a smattering of struggling merchants sat at tables and leaned on the bar. Nodding to men and calling them by name, he strolled slowly to the far end of the bar. It was understood by the regular crowd that this particular spot was the sheriff's. He could see the front door and the rest of the room in the mirror behind the bar. He fired a match with his thumbnail, lit his smoke, and called for the barkeep to bring his whisky.

Most of the talk was of Indians and the prairie fire. A couple of cowhands next to him were comparing details of dead beeves found on their spreads. "Damn strange," one said, "shot right between the eyes." They shook their heads and had another drink. The sheriff had sent his deputy out on the same kind of incident a few days back, but he had come back without any evidence or any answers.

The sheriff nursed his drink, speaking when spoken to, and listening to the talk that ebbed and flowed like the lazy, blue smoke. In the mirror he watched two young cowboys lose a month's wages at a card game. He heard the doors swing and the room suddenly go quiet. Captain Keeferly stood just inside.

No one could remember when, or if, the captain had ever been in the War Bonnet. Men at the bar, fear or hate in their eyes, gave ground to the captain and a space cleared next to the sheriff. Keeferly walked straight to the lawman.

"Sheriff, you've got one of my men in your two-bit jail. I want him out now," he said.

"Afraid I can't do that. Judge Harkin won't be in until tomorrow. Besides, Jake doesn't have bail money," the sheriff answered.

The captain slammed his fist on the bar. Bottles and glasses did a brief dance before settling down to listen. "What you should be afraid of is your job come election time. You just might be getting a bit old and slow for the job."

The remark bit the sheriff's pride. His eyes blazed and he pushed away from the bar aware of the hush that had fallen upon the room. The men were waiting to see how the law would buck up to Captain Keeferly. "Captain, I arrested Jake for disorderly conduct, destruction of property, and resisting arrest. Also, assault and battery if the girl presses charges. He stays in until the judge gets back. I'm sworn to uphold the law. That's what I'm doing, election be damned."

There were a few quick whispers in the room, a few exchanges of glances, and nods of approval at the sheriff's remark.

Jabbing his finger at the sheriff's chest, the captain said, "I'll by god talk to you again. I don't like the smell in here. The law's getting a little too big for its britches when a decent man can't come to town and have a little fun. I'll remember that next election."

The captain spun on his heel and left the bar. The sheriff watched him leave and then picked up his drink as the room exploded with voices. Men crowded back to the bar and one stepped up next to the sheriff. "Heard about that whore thing. That Jake and his blade are a handful I'd bet. The girl going to be all right?"

"I think so, just a hazard of the trade. Damn drunk barber sure ain't no doctor but he got the bleeding stopped and bandaged so-so."

Sheriff Barton finished his drink and left by the back door of the War Bonnet. He cut his rounds short and headed back to the jail. The captain was acting mighty strange lately, and damned if he knew why. Whatever caused the captain to come looking for him in the War Bonnet meant something very big was afoot.

– 23 –

THE SHERIFF COULDN'T REMEMBER THE WHOREHOUSES causing a single problem during his four years in Elk Springs until lately. The trouble always involved the new help the ranchers were hiring. Especially the Guidon K hands. Damn how he wished he were thirty years younger. He clenched and unclenched his fist; the arm was not too bad tonight – yet. Damn people had no respect for anyone or anything any more. With bitterness he knew that included Sheriff Barton and his mood turned as black as the alley he stepped into. He made his way silently around back of the jail. He moved down the outside wall until he was beneath the barred cell window. Inside, heavy footsteps paced back and forth, back and forth.

"God bless, will you sit down and quit that damn pacing." It was the captain's voice. The sheriff wasn't surprised.

The pacing paused. "Get me out. I ain't sitting no more."

The pacing resumed along with the captain's voice. "You weren't sitting all that time. I've told you not to cause trouble in town. I don't mind your drinking and your whores, but no trouble in town. Especially cutting up a woman, even if she is a whore. I've a half a mind not to bail you out this time."

The sheriff wondered if the captain was serious. It was a sweet thought. He would welcome the opportunity to keep the big bastard locked up. The son of a bitch should be locked up permanently.

Jake's nasal twang chased the echo of his footsteps out the small window. "By damn, Captain, I thought I had them. The fire was going good, and then the wind shifted and the flames damn near got me."

"You didn't do a bit of damage to any of the nesters except one and he wasn't the one you were supposed to burn out. It was a hell of a prairie fire and you're lucky the folks are blaming the Indians, but it didn't do a bit of good."

With that bit of information filed away, the sheriff quietly left the jail window and moved to the front door. It stood open. The room was dark. Damn, he thought, the captain is definitely riled and careless. Hell, anybody could have come in here and overheard the same conversation I just did.

The sheriff slammed the door and the voices stopped. The battered regulator clock on the west wall sounded like a hammer on anvil for a half-dozen ticks, then came the verbal charge that the sheriff had expected. "That you, Bart? Speak up and be identified. Rank and serial number."

Bartholomew Barton felt the annoyance anew as he did every time the captain called him by his first name. He didn't like the name his parents had given him and he didn't like anyone overlooking his official capacity. And, he especially hated it when the captain started playing military.

"You best be damn glad it's me," the sheriff answered, lighting the lamp on his desk and sinking into the desk chair. He knew the captain would be here tonight and he knew why. Suddenly he felt tired, like a wind-broke pony, just wanting unsaddled and left to roll in the dirt and graze quietly the rest of his worthless life. The dull ache that was starting in his shoulder and elbow reminded him why he didn't throw the captain into a cell with Jake and be a real lawman just one more time.

He was mad. Mad at himself, mad at fate, and mad at God, he guessed, for making people so stupid. And right now he was mad as hell at the figure that stood in front of his desk. Big, powerful, arrogant, and phony from the top of his blue cavalry hat to the heels of his polished cavalry boots.

"Sit down, Captain. We've got some talking to do."

"I don't want to sit down. I want you to let Jake out."

The sheriff flushed and rose slowly, leaned on the desk with both hands, face thrust toward a startled Captain Keeferly. The pain in his arm made the muscles stand out on his jaw. "Sit down. That son of a bitch will walk when the judge says he can."

Captain Keeferly lowered his eyes, then lowered his butt into the battle-scarred chair in front of the desk. Sheriff Barton sat down, took off his new John B. and set it carefully on the desk. He ran his hand over his bald head and knuckled back his mustache. He seldom sampled the bottle that he kept in the left-hand drawer of his desk, but tonight he pulled it open, reached past the big knife he had taken off Jake, and handed the bottle to the captain. The captain waved it off. The sheriff drank and tossed the bottle back in the drawer.

"Captain, your men are getting damn careless. If you can't keep them in line, I will. Need I remind you where you would spend the rest of your life if there is a serious slip-up?"

Ramrod straight on the edge of the chair, the captain grinned at the challenge. "And may I remind the esteemed lawman where he would spend the rest of his life if the good citizens knew the truth? We both know why we're working together. Anyway, nice show at the War Bonnet."

"Captain, we can't have Jake screwing things up. You need to hobble and muzzle that bastard. I know he can handle more liquor than ten average men and never show he's even had a drink. But this is the second time something has set him off. You and I don't need that."

The captain leaned back in the chair and crossed his legs. He silently studied the polished boot and brushed off a bit of dust before answering. "You're right. We don't need a mistake, but we do need Jake. You and I can't take a chance being involved in the rough, dirty stuff he does for us."

"Hey, when the hell you fixing to get me out of here?" Jake yelled from the cell. "Captain, how about rustling up a bottle? Damn flask is dryer than a busted rain barrel."

Captain Keeferly rose and pointed to the drawer. "Let me give him that bottle; it'll keep him quiet so we can do business."

The sheriff handed over the bottle trying to guess what was so urgent that he had come looking for him in the War Bonnet. The prairie fire was no big deal. It just didn't get the job done. The Indians couldn't be that big a concern to the Guidon K. Besides, as far as he knew there weren't that many new squatters moving in yet.

A brisk night wind moaned through the open window, rustling the papers on his desk and teasing the lamp flame. The shadows in the room moved across the wall and floor with nervous animation until the sheriff got up and closed the window and lowered the brittle blind. He also threw the bolt on the door. Relieved, the shadows returned to their familiar space, quiet now as if they, too, awaited the captain's message.

The captain didn't sit but paced the well-worn floorboards, hands clasped behind his back. "I was up on Vine River today and we got a hell of a bunch of nesters dug in up there. Nine of the bastards and they aren't the usual sniveling dirt grubbers."

He stopped pacing and faced the desk and chair. The sheriff showed surprise. "I knew a fella by the name of McGregor had staked a quarter section up that way. Figured I'd give him a little time so it wouldn't be too obvious when his luck started running bad."

"He's had enough time. Enough time to bring in eight of his kin and put up eight cabins down the river."

The sheriff let the swivel chair drop forward. "Nine cabins, you sure? Damn, they did that in a hurry."

"I'm sure. Saw every one of 'em. They all got a strip of sod plowed under too; they're working fools."

The sheriff was figuring in his head: nine squatters to get rid of at ten head of breeding stock per comes to ninety head. He knuckled back his mustache and looked up at the captain. "You're right. Probably do need Jake, but you get it through his head that we work a plan together so's not to leave any loose ends that get tied around our necks."

"I'll stay in town tonight and take him back to the ranch in the morning. When you're ready to move on them squatters, come out to the ranch and we'll lay out a battle plan."

The sheriff stood up and unbolted the door. "I'll come up with an excuse to ride out sometime next week."

The captain waited for him to open the door. "I had Todd and some of the hands push a couple hundred head of yearlings up that way yesterday. They should drift over to the good river-bottom grass before too long. Maybe we can use the cattle rustling game again."

Sheriff Barton opened the door, but the captain pushed it closed. "One thing more. You can earn an extra twenty head of beef if you can run 'em out without any bloodshed. I especially don't want the family on the south claim hurt." Then the captain opened the door, stepped outside, and pushed the door closed.

Bewildered, the sheriff stared at the closed door. Tight-fisted old Captain was getting mighty liberal with his stock, and he had never before shied away from violence. But the sheriff wasn't complaining. He locked the door, sat down, and fished a key from an inside vest pocket and unlocked the bottom drawer of the desk. From under a three-inch stack of old wanted posters he pulled a well-worn ledger. With near reverence he leaned back in the chair and opened the book. His dream was written there in a crude, but well thought out, code.

He moved his finger slowly down the column of letters and numbers. Most of the lettered entries had a ten beside them. Occasionally a fifteen and a few fives. After the last entry he penciled in a combination of letters and the number ninety. Below it was another entry after which he placed a twenty. There was only one other entry with the number twenty.

Twenty head was the reward for persuading Dr. Walters to leave the territory after Captain Keeferly's second wife had died in childbirth. It was something very personal and important with the captain. If making sure no harm came to a family of squatters was worth twenty head, then it must be very important and very personal to the captain. That would be worth a ride to Vine River soon to see just what was so special about the McGregors.

The wind played mournfully in alleys between the town buildings, now and then rattling the glass in the window and causing the dirty shade to ripple and wave. Jake was silent, lost and secure within the confines of a whisky bottle. Elk Springs, comfortable in its rut of routine, quietly endured the human opera of men afloat in a sea of green prairie.

The sheriff closed the ledger and returned it to the bottom of the wanted posters. Then he locked the drawer and leaned back with his boots on the desk. He rolled a smoke and let memories of Captain Keeferly parade through his mind. The big man was hard, tough, even ruthless in building his ranching empire, but never careless. Smart? No question about that. Like a sleek fox in an unguarded chicken coop. And, among the townsfolk, when it served his purpose, he could be as charming as a vote-hungry politician.

Sheriff Barton adjusted his bulk in the chair before continuing the mental parade. He understood from the old-timers that the captain had been here in the vanguard of westward migration. For reasons known only to the captain, he had stayed and fought the Indians, the droughts, the fires, and the paralyzing blizzards of winter. He had survived the early years as a road rancher, trading with the wagon trains that followed the sun and dreams of gold.

Keeferly was a shrewd trader, many times getting three worn out, sore-footed oxen, mules, or horses for one sound, strong, and rested animal. The weary travelers would curse and protest but, having no choice, traded on his terms. Then, about five years ago, the ranch had grown remarkably fast. The Guidon K laid claim to, and held against all comers, thousands of acres of graze. The sheriff knew what gave the Guidon K the capital for this vast and rapid growth. That bit of knowledge was the glue that held the captain and the sheriff together.

The chair groaned and squeaked as he again shifted his body to ease the pain in his shoulder. Only a little longer as a lawman. No more long lonesome nights drifting in and out of the shadows and being disillusioned with humans. No more feeling flesh and bone give under a big fist. No more swift death when men refused to listen to reason. The sheriff got up and walked to the back. He absentmindedly checked the cell door, a habit from the days when the only deals he made with men were the letter of the law and a deadly Colt Dragoon.

He dropped the bar in place across the back door and stood for a moment with ghosts of the past when Sheriff Bartholomew Barton couldn't be beaten and couldn't be bought. With a sad shake of his head he went back to the office. Idealistic and ambitious in his youth, he had dreamed of respect and reward from a grateful mankind.

Idealism was the first casualty. Ambition had taken a different path and self-respect was replaced by cynicism tinted with bitterness. He'd had all of mankind he wanted. All of the conniving town fathers and moneyed patrons who didn't want law, but a law for everyone else. Now he wanted his payoff any way he could get it.

Deputy Martin's approaching footsteps jolted him out of his memories with just enough time to beat the deputy to the door by a slim margin and unbolt it before stepping out and almost running into the startled man.

The men went through the routine of exchanging information while the sheriff berated himself for forgetting to unbolt the door after looking at the journal. It was a small thing, but he didn't want to explain anything out of the ordinary.

"Jake stays in no matter what," the sheriff said as he fetched his Stetson. "I'll be in early, because Captain Keeferly will be raising hell about Jake. Keep a lid on things."

Sheriff Barton worked his way through town to the livery stable. He was surprised to find the night hostler rubbing down two lathered mounts. Neither the bay nor the roan was branded, and he'd never seen either one before. He managed to slip past the talkative old-timer to the box stall where he rubbed liniment on his shoulder and arm, then splashed some on the sorry old mare's fore leg. With the liniment soaking fire into his arm, he went up front and watched the hostler work a minute before asking about the two horses.

"Couple of strangers rode in about an hour after sundown. Weren't no tenderfoots, but was real spooked and the little one sure enough appeared puny. Said they'd be looking for you as soon as they had a drink." The hostler talked around a wad of tobacco and answered the sheriff's question without stopping his work.

The sheriff interrupted, "Say where they was doing their drinking?"

"Just asked where the closest saloon was. I told them the Bear Skin. You reckon they's running from the law?"

That's the first assumption, the sheriff thought, as he built a smoke and watched the man work. "Say anything else?"

"Said plenty. Only thing that perked up these ol' ears was them carrying on about the Grand Forks cutoff. That there shortcut is a peck of trouble for any poor sons a bitches that tries it. Always has been."

Sheriff Barton sensed the old fellow had some exciting gossip. "Anything special about the cutoff just now?"

The old-timer stopped work, spat, and came around under the mount's neck, his eyes shining. "Gad damnedest story that's tickled these ol' ears in a spell."

Sheriff Barton wanted to choke the old bastard, but with a patience born of a lifetime of sucking information from people, he bridled himself and played the game. "The hell you say? Reckon I've heard and seen most everything, but unload it if you want to."

"Hoss turds against double eagles, ya ain't heard one like this." He stopped and fished in a baggy pocket and pulled out a plug and pocketknife. With deliberate concentration he whittled off a new chaw that replaced the one that plopped in the dust at the sheriff's feet.

"Now, there was this here train of eastern folks back in '63, or was it '64?" the sheriff began, only to be cut short by the hostler, new cud worked up and stored in a bewhiskered cheek.

"These fellers, at least the one that didn't have the runs, allowed they come across a huge pile of rocks out about three, four days ride north of here."

"Rocks? What's so special about a pile of rocks?" the sheriff asked, knowing damn well there weren't enough rocks in that area to circle a camp fire.

"Special? I allow they's special. Said all big ones, cut and piled up higher than your head. Most like some heathen altars is what he said. More than that, they sweared there was broken glass and blood on them stones."

"Interesting," the sheriff said, stringing him along. "Anything else?"

"According to them, two burned wagons, some dead horses, dead vultures, and a whole slew of Sioux and Cheyenne arrows. Spooked 'em enough to damn near killed these two horses. They said they didn't even stick to the wagon trail but cut across county to git here faster."

Sheriff Barton said "so long" to the hostler and by back street and alley headed for the Bear Skin. Inside the saloon he made his way to the corner table, studying the crowd. He sat and waited for one of the girls to bring his drink. It was understood that if the sheriff didn't stop at the bar, someone would bring a drink. It was a small ego luxury he allowed himself and it gave him the opportunity to look over the crowd with his back covered.

Captain Keeferly was playing poker with some of the local merchants and was losing heavily and he wasn't happy. He had lost fortunes and won fortunes at the table, but always, until lately, with good grace.

The sheriff gave the card game a rest and let his eyes and mind roam the room. This far west it was a showpiece with actual paneling on the walls, an honest-to-god wooden floor, and a real mahogany bar that ran fifty feet along the south side of the room. Three chandeliers shone like lighthouses anchored in a sea of swirling smoke. At the rear of the room an open staircase led to a mezzanine.

For those citizens who were accepted, it was like an elite social club. Membership was always some dealing with Captain Keeferly. Herman Maxwell, arrogant and abrasive, functioned as owner. Sheriff Barton knew it was Captain Keeferly who put up the saving capital when Maxwell was in trouble. It was the captain who had put up the grizzly-bear skins that flanked the back bar. Rumor had it that he killed both of them on the same day up in high country.

The sheriff looked around the room and wondered if the men realized that the one common bond they had was their indebtedness to the captain. That was the membership dues at the Bear Skin.

A brunette stopped at his table with a swish of silk and perfume. She smiled, wrinkled up her nose and patted his arm. "You still doctoring that poor horse? You're right kind. Bring you another drink?" she asked.

He smiled. "Nope, Maxwell's got a tad too much water in it to suit my taste."

Her eyes went wide. "You got regular? I'm going to kill the barkeep. Sheriff, the captain asked if you'd like to join the game? I'll bring you a good drink."

"That's right neighborly. Tell him I'll be over later."

She gave his arm another pat and moved away through the crowd laughing and teasing with the customers. Watching her, the sheriff wondered how many other Captain Keeferlys and how many dark-eyed brunettes there were in the world. As the men fell for the captain's grandiose ideas, the women simply fell on their backs. As the captain grazed his cattle on the helpless rancher's range and ravaged the merchant's tills, he grazed and ravaged the hapless womenfolk.

With a sad shake of his head he rose and made his way to the poker table. "Captain Keeferly, I appreciate the invite."

Keeferly motioned the players to give the sheriff a chair on his right. "Always glad to have the law around. Makes for a good clean game."

– 24 –

DEPUTY MARTIN PUSHED THROUGH THE BATWINGS and hoofed
it straight for the sheriff seated at the poker table. "Hell, Jake's
probably trying to tear the jail down with his bare hands," the
sheriff swore to the captain.

"Hating to bother you, but I'm thinking you'd want to have
a look at this yourself," the deputy said.

"Gentlemen, will you excuse me?" Sheriff Barton picked up
his cards and showed them to the deputy.

"Damn, sorry, but you need to see this."

"I'll be back," the sheriff said as he left the table. This had
better be important, he thought. I just left a full house back
there. Aces over eights.

Outside the sheriff asked, "What the hell's so damn important it can't wait until morning?"

"Couple of fellas showed up at the office. Asking about the
wagon trail cutoff, Indians, and military escorts. Before I knew
it, one of 'em keeled over."

"Must be the gents Roy told me about. Any idea what's
wrong with the sick one?"

"The other one said he'd had the runs since about noon.
Pitched his meal too." The deputy opened the law office door.
The odor was rank.

Inside the office a tall buckskin-clad figure stood quietly
leaning against the wall, arms folded. A man lay on the floor
by the desk. The sheriff knelt by the man on the floor a mo-

ment, then stood and turned to the buckskin against the wall. "I'm Sheriff Barton. Any idea what's wrong with your friend?" Then he turned to his deputy. "Best go find Curt and drag him over here."

"I'm Hank Brown, guide for a wagon train back at Grand Forks." He pointed to the floor. "That's Lem. Kind of likes to think he's in charge of the train. Don't rightly know what's ailing him. First thing after we stopped for coffee and biscuits about noon he got the runs. Biscuits didn't stay down long neither. Got a doctor here abouts?"

"Not a real one. Just a barber that works at it about half as hard as he works at barbering and that's about half as hard as he works at drinking."

The sheriff had wondered if or when the first of the trains would reach Elk Springs this season. Trains meant trouble, but mostly trains meant dollars. "How far out's the train now?" he asked.

Hank stepped to the office door and threw it open, breathing deep of the cool night air. "Train's still in Grand Forks. So many rumors of Indians that the wagon folk refused to go further until we scouted the cutoff."

The sheriff stood up, motioned to the chair in front of the desk, and sat down in his swivel chair. "May as well sit. Don't like the looks of your friend, but nothing to do but wait for Curt. The damn wagons ought to stick to the main trail."

The man on the floor groaned, rolled onto his back, and then was quiet. The guide shifted his Hawken into the crook of his arm, studied Lem for a moment, and then looked over the desk at the sheriff. "Lots of rumors coming back that some of the trains are getting caught in the mountain passes if snows come early. Everyone's pushing like hell to make as many miles as they can before we hit the humps."

The sheriff and Hank turned to the door as the deputy, holding up the drunk barber, entered the office. "Here he is, for all the good it'll do anyone, least of all that poor fellow on the floor," the deputy said.

He let go of the barber, and the little man, disheveled and bleary eyed, swayed like a sapling in a stiff wind for a second and then steadied himself as the deputy's remark registered. "Curtis DuPree at your service, gentlemen," he slurred. "I'll have you to know I've doctored more humans and animals than most saw-bones strutting around in them big cities."

He ran a hand over his mouth, the effort causing him to waver and take a step forward. He righted himself with some effort. "Where, where's the patient?"

"You about stepped on him," Hank snapped and pointed to Lem near the barber's feet.

The barber looked down and swayed forward, righted himself again, and toed the figure on the floor. Lem didn't move. Those in the room watched Curt plunge a claw-like hand into his coat pocket as he questioned, "When'd he take sick?"

The scout told him what he'd told the others. Curt knelt down and produced a downy feather from his pocket and held it over Lem's open mouth. The feather moved ever so slightly, first one way and then another. "I guess he ain't dead," Curt said. Thin, blue-veined hands found the man's wrist after some effort, placed fingers for a pulse, and fumbled a pocket watch from his vest pocket. After the pulse check he lifted the man's eyelids. Appearing soberer by the minute, he rolled the sick man over and recoiled from the soiled trousers, the soiled floor, and the stink.

When the barber stood up, his stance was strong and his face sober. The effects of drink stilled by a stronger stimulant. "Where'd you come from and how long you been in town?"

Riveted by the barber's changed demeanor, Hank told him everything. The sheriff was also caught up in the transformation of the town drunk. "What's a matter Curt? What's he ailing from?" the sheriff asked as he rolled his chair back.

Taking a step backwards and rubbing his hands vigorously on a soiled handkerchief Curt exploded. "God a' mighty, I believe he's got the cholera."

The impact was physical. Each man present had heard stories of cholera devastating whole trains or communities, stories that drew the hair to attention along one's spine.

The sheriff let his old swivel chair bang down as he jumped to his feet, "Hank, you been anywhere else except the livery and here?"

"Nope, it's a piece of luck we didn't make it to a saloon."

The sheriff took quick steps and pulled shut the door, then turned to those in the small, closed office. "Not one goddamn word of this to anyone. We don't need a panic on our hands."

Those in the room shook their heads in agreement as the sheriff stared at each one. Then he addressed the barber, "Anything you can do for Lem?"

Curt was licking dry lips. "Nothing much, except I'll see if I can find some camphor and cayenne pepper, but I doubt he'll last long enough fer it to do any good."

The sheriff stepped over and glared at the little man. "Remember, not one word to anyone and keep your damn head out of the jug."

Once the barber was gone the sheriff turned to the deputy. "Get these gentlemen's horses. Better yet, Hank, you'd better go get your own mounts."

Hank dropped the butt of the Hawken to the floor with a thud, his right hand brushing the Navy Colt at his belt. "Don't reckon Lem is up to any riding tonight. Don't see no reason why we can't make him comfortable in one of the cell bunks."

Sheriff Barton was carefully measuring the man. "Good Lord, Hank, cholera can wipe out a whole community. You two will have to camp outside of town and stay outside. We'll help any way we can, but I can't let the good people of Elk Springs be exposed to the cholera."

The fighting tension drained out of Hank and he sighed the sigh of one weary of responsibility. "You spoke a truth. Best get out as soon as possible. Any chance we can get a spring wagon or buggy for Lem?"

The deputy quickly procured a buckboard and a half hour later Lem was loaded into it behind the jail. The sheriff moved close to the buckboard seat and spoke to Hank, "You should take the turnoff just past Shoemaker Hill and hit the creek about a half mile below. Good water and camp site. One of us will be out with supplies and more medicine."

"Thanks, Sheriff," Hank said.

"One thing I'd like to know," the sheriff said. "Is it true what you told the livery man about a pile of rocks on the cutoff?"

"Damn straight. Strangest sight I've seen in twenty-odd years out here in God's big pasture. I'd like to know the story behind them rocks."

This is one hell of a note, the sheriff thought as he watched the buckboard move off into the night. He didn't necessarily like to see people suffer, but Elk Springs sure didn't need the cholera. What if the captain caught it and died before he got his payoff? Son of a bitch, he thought, wouldn't it be just my luck to die of the running scours just when I was about to be rich.

Jake hadn't moved during the whole ordeal. The sheriff looked at the snoring bulk. Funny how everyone is needed someplace in this old world. Now Jake – such as he was – was needed by the area's most influential citizen and by the law. He couldn't see any other way.

He instructed the deputy to scrub the floor good and open the windows before walking over to the Bear Skin where the captain was taking a last drink at the bar. Sheriff Barton slid up to the bar next to the big man. "Captain, could you stop by the jail?" he asked politely.

The captain finished his drink and turned to leave. "Whatever it is can wait until morning."

The sheriff stepped in front of him. "I think it'd be a good idea to stop by the jail."

Keeferly stomped out cussing Jake.

The sheriff waved to the barkeep, tossed off two quick drinks, and left the saloon. It was going to be a long night. His arm was beginning to hurt and he didn't want to dance anymore with the captain. When he got to the jail, Captain Keeferly pointed down at the wet floor and asked, "What'd you spill in here? This place stinks like hell."

Sheriff Barton passed by and dropped into his chair. Wearily, he waited until the captain shut up and then said, "Cholera. We've got a wagon train coming that's most likely infected with cholera."

"What the hell you talking about?"

Sheriff Barton laid out the story while the captain listened. He added, "I've taken care that few people know about this, and the deputy's out checking on any other strangers that might be in town. Only one to worry about is Curt. Thought maybe we ought to let Jake have a few words with him tonight."

"Good, good," the captain mused. "Suppose we can divert the train around Elk Springs?"

"Don't know. Only place for supplies, you know that."

The sheriff woke Jake and a plan of action was put to him by the captain. "Look up Curt and make damn sure he understands the consequences of talking about the cholera. Scare the hell out of the rummy little bastard."

Jake looked like a boy promised a handful of candy at the general store. He was so intent on scaring Curt that the mention of cholera didn't register. He felt under his left arm, then pointed at the desk drawer. The sheriff handed him his knife.

"Be back here by six in the morning," the sheriff said as Jake headed out. "Don't make me come looking for you, and use the back door."

25

SHERIFF BARTON SLUMPED INTO HIS CHAIR after Jake left. The captain sat straight and stiff across the desk. The clock, like a watching cyclops, said it was three in the morning. The sheriff lit a cigarette before speaking. "Captain, you think it's cholera like Curt says?"

"From what you told me, I'd say chances are damn good. I recall back in the '40s, the first infantry took down with scours. Mighty near wiped out the unit. Appears the same to me – running scours, vomit, weak as a lamb before they go down. Comes on real sudden. I'd say we don't want to take any chances."

"Any treatment that you know of?"

"None that worked worth a damn. Medics gave them plenty of medicine but they died just the same."

They sat in silence thinking their own selfish thoughts, personally afraid of a killer they couldn't see and fight. At length the sheriff gave voice to what they both were thinking. "Don't see no way we should let that train get anywhere near Elk Springs."

The captain nodded his agreement.

"Say," the sheriff said, "why don't we direct the train to follow the Vine River? That'll bring 'em to the McGregor claims. Might just solve that little problem."

"No!" the captain barked. "No," he repeated normally. "I mean I was thinking it would be better to send them the south way. Much farther from us and they would hit several of the small ranchers over that way that's been running stock on Guidon K grass."

"I suppose you're right, one's as good as the other," the sheriff answered. "Though, it'll be a chore convincing the wagon trains to avoid Elk Springs," he added.

"That can be arranged," the captain said carefully adjusting his hat. "I'll be back here before sunup and we can work out all the details."

The sheriff got up and headed for the door. "I'd better make a round or two. Wouldn't want the citizens feeling neglected."

Elk Springs lay quiet beneath a canopy of stars, the deserted streets were wide ribbons of dust and only two squares of lamplight winked back at the stars. The captain headed for the hotel while the sheriff dissolved into shadows, reappearing at the livery a few minutes later.

He was back at the office before five, built a small fire in the stove, and started a pot of coffee. In a few minutes the aroma of strong brew wafted through the office mingling among the layers of cigarette smoke. The sheriff had only a short time to enjoy the coffee and silence before Jake entered at the back. Jake poured a cup of coffee and then, smiling contentedly, walked back to the cell to wait for his boss.

At six-thirty, the cell door again swung open for Jake. The sheriff handed him a deputy badge and letter. "Make sure they understand that no wagon train will be allowed in Elk Springs. Tell them to turn off at Shoemaker Hill and head south."

Jake took the badge and letter. "Want I should scare 'em like I did Curt?" he asked.

The sheriff drained the tin coffee cup and set it on the corner of his desk before answering, "Just make it look official and professional. The letter explains Elk Springs is quarantined. Nobody in or out. They'll just have to go around the south way. Under no circumstances will any wagon train be allowed in town or anywhere near town."

Jake looked disappointed as he pinned the badge on with blunt fingers. "Can I just go on to the ranch once I give 'em the message?"

"Hell no," the sheriff snapped. "You're coming back here to answer to the judge. Don't want townsfolk talking."

Jake's stubble-covered face reminded the sheriff of a school-boy who'd been told to stay after school. He tapped the star on Jake's vest. "Take it off until you're out of town."

At Shoemaker Hill Jake stopped to pin the badge back on and check the percussion caps of the sawed-off scattergun before heading for the campsite. The sun balanced on the eastern horizon as he approached the dying campfire. That's the sick'n, he thought. "Here's some grub and medicine," he said dropping a sack of supplies next to a blanket-wrapped figure, but the man in the blanket didn't stir. Jake hello'd the camp without dismounting. Hank came silently from the creek, saw the sack of supplies next to Lem, the badge on Jake's vest, and relaxed the Hawken back into the crook of his arm. "Don't reckon Lem gives a damn, but I appreciate the supplies."

Jake gave him the letter. Hank read it slowly and then looked up. "Says we've got to go around Elk Springs. Where in the hell we supposed to get supplies?"

Jake touched the badge with his finger. "Letter's direct from the law, suppose you'll have to make do somehow."

"For all I know the train people may've come on ahead. They're a bunch of hardheaded Dutchmen. If they get here and need supplies or medicine, reckon we'll be in, law or no. There's women and children on that train."

"Sheriff said, 'No exceptions.'" Jake's lips parted, showing more snarl than grin. Hank recognized the difference too late. The scattergun's load of buckshot grabbed him in the chest and he stumbled backwards over the campfire, dropping in a shuddering heap. As he fell, he tried to bring the Hawken up but it was no use.

Teeth still bared, Jake discharged the second barrel at the blankets. He took a pull from the flask and wiped his hand over his mouth. "Reckon that'll keep you and your sick ones away from here."

Morning shadows were long when he pulled up behind the jail and entered. "Morning, Jake," sheriff said, looking up from the papers on his desk. "Did you find their camp?"

"Yea," Jake said tersely. "Captain been in yet?"

"In and gone."

Jake stopped. "Gone where? He'll be back to get me out, won't he?"

"Don't rightly know," the sheriff said. "Something about Todd and a big bay stallion up on Wild Horse Flats."

"Son of a bitch, he promised he'd get me out this morning."

The sheriff pointed to the cell. "Right now you need to get in there before someone walks in and starts asking questions."

"I ain't sitting in there no more," Jake said through clenched teeth, emotion and anger shoving his nasal words to a higher octave. His hand flicked across his chest, emerging with a fistful of gleaming steel.

"Damn, Jake, ease off." The sheriff held his left hand out toward Jake in a gesture of peace. His right hand, unbidden by conscious thought, dropped to his side.

"I ain't going back in there behind a damn locked door." Jake was standing on the balls of his feet tossing the big knife from hand to hand.

Outwardly the sheriff was easy and slow; inside he went taut as a catch rope on a big steer. "Jake, you'll get out, I promise. But right now we've got to keep everything looking normal. I'll bring you a bottle soon as the deputy gets in. What do you say?"

Jake's reasoning was simple. If the captain wasn't here, he'd go find him and bring him back. The captain always fixed things for Jake. He'd fix this. He lunged at the sheriff, more to knock him out of the way than cut him. When his fist got to where the sheriff had been, he became aware of the big Colt just before it met the side of his skull. Utter disbelief was his last thought before blackness settled around his slow, simple mind.

"You big dumb bastard," the sheriff said as Jake hit the floor. He kicked the knife toward the office and dropped the Dragoon back into leather. Only a mild stab of pain accompanied the move. Damn that felt good, he thought, as he grabbed Jake and pulled him into the cell, grunting as he wrestled him onto the cot. It had been a long time since Sheriff Barton had put his speed and skill to a real test. By god, he still had it, he thought as he fished the deputy badge from Jake's vest pocket. He locked the door and went back to the office, picking up the big knife and dropping it into the desk drawer.

Everything had gone so smoothly for years; now the captain and Jake were touchy as a bear with a sore ass. And, if that damn wagon train did have cholera and brought it to Elk Springs, the whole blessed thing could come unraveled. Still, that was the second time in forty-eight hours he had beat Jake. He could still sheriff, but for how long and what would that get him other than forty dollars a month and found?

26

THE LAST NOTE OF "AMAZING GRACE" faded with the twilight and nature wrapped Ben's wagons and men in a soft garment of quiet. For the men the release of long hours of tension and doubt was like a rebirth.

Isaiah's victory song slid unobtrusively into the silence, age-less prairie and sky being long accustomed to the ways of its native sons. To the whites the haunting song, understood only through its feeling and sincerity, compelled a tide of emotion among the men. Bewhiskered, dirty, and tired, the men shouted, wept, prayed, and cursed. Backs were slapped and hands grasped, even bare feet shuffled in spontaneous dance, and in so doing, they realized they were just as they had entered this world at another birth. Only Isaiah moved among the camp completely at ease and without embarrassment. He went about rekindling the campfire without so much as a second glance at the pale bodies around him.

Ben, leaning heavily on his cane, made his way slowly down the stone steps to Isaiah's side. After a brief exchange of words he called the men to the fire.

He spoke very formally. "It appears that we have been deliv-ered from the jaws of the lion for now, but Isaiah says some of the Sioux may keep watch to see if we really are crazy. We can't put on any clothes just yet."

"Ah Jeez, we'll catch our damn death. Going to set on frost tonight feels like." It was Niles, covered with goose bumps and shivering in the firelight.

Ben was aware of the cool night air seeping into his old wound and stepped closer to the fire. "It's going to be at least one more long night, but we're alive."

Intoxicated by their bloodless victory over the Sioux, his mind filled again with his dream, Ben spoke on about the journey that lay before them. Nothing could stop them now. But he took greater personal elation in the fact that he had proved there was a peaceful alternative to violence.

He raised his cane above his head. "To a new life in the West."

"To a new life!" the men shouted back.

Leaving the men, Ben worked his way through the milling herd of thirsty, hungry horses and the piles of wagon contents. As he crawled up to check on Smith, he thought that it seemed like a another lifetime when Smith had been wounded, another lifetime that Ben had examined the Sioux arrows, and then later removed a iron arrowhead from Smith's leg.

He moved around the dark interior of the wagon, every cold encounter with an object reminding him of his undress. Funny, he thought, how he noticed little things that he'd never felt before. The cold metal of the lantern brushed his thigh and the small campaign chest gave him a chilly kiss as he sat down.

He arranged blankets over the sleeping form on the wagon floor, adjusted the lantern, found the big journal, pen, and ink. No one had died and there had been no literal birth, but he needed to write it all down. God, what he'd give to sit under the oaks with Adeline and tell her of his victory. Thinking back, he realized she had always listened restlessly, probably out of duty and propriety, but at least she listened and that made him feel good.

A horse whinnied close to the wagon bringing Ben instantly alert, trying to guess if it meant anything. Then he found himself trying to read the wind like Isaiah. It surprised him that so quickly he was thinking like Isaiah. He got no message, only a fleeting thought about Ol' Jeb and Mule. Mule missed out on a hell of a show, he thought as he closed the journal and found his bedroll.

He blew out the lantern and made his way to the campfire and some sleep.

Next morning under a cloudless blue dome of prairie sky the wagons were loaded and the horses were curried and brushed and made ready for harness. The men joked and cussed about the chafed skin, bruised shins, and other minor injuries inflicted on unprotected bodies. Ben had to bandage a couple of feet that had been stepped on by uncooperative horses, which was the only accident requiring his help.

By mid-afternoon the morning sun's warm smile had turned to a fiery leer. Tender skin flushed pink. The joking had been replaced by what now could be considered professional-level cussing.

Elmo made his way on tender feet to Ben's wagon. "We're about ready to pull out and I'll sure enough be glad to quit this place. Some of us is wondering if it would be good to leave now, go a spell, then let the horses graze and water."

Ben glanced at the sun. "We've got about two hours until sunset. Are the men up to it?"

"Telling you the truth, we're all about beat but sure would like to be gone from here. We've lost two wagons and two drivers so I reckon we'll have to take your driver for one of the wagons 'cause Niles can't drive with that busted arm. It looks like you'll have to drive your wagon," Elmo said.

"Fine. Let's move just far enough to get good grass. And, one thing I want to do before we leave," Ben said moving to the rear of the wagon. "Take one of the foundation stones and mark Sam's grave."

"Already done," Elmo said and hollered at the men, "Hitch 'em up men! We're moving out."

A shout went up and soon the circle of wagons unwound itself and snaked slowly across the black, burned prairie toward lush grass and fresh water. As the wagons crested the rise where the Indians had camped, each man looked back one last time at the burned wagon remains, the stone that marked the grave of a fallen comrade, and the large rock platform – a lonely sentinel in a vast expanse of prairie. Ben pulled up on the crest and gazed at the sight. He wanted to be gone but he also wanted to fix the sight forever in his memory, a reminder that peaceful ways could be found for all conflicts. He vowed anew he would never resort to violence against another human. With his body crying out for rest, but his mind renewed, he lifted the lines and spoke to the team. His journey to a new life seemed entirely possible.

The second day out, they camped at a small stream with a thin line of timber along its meandering banks. They camped early, giving the horses plenty of time to graze and rest. It had been slow going with many of the wagons pulled by a four-horse hitch instead of six horses.

As men unharnessed teams and settled into camp, Ben watched Isaiah rub down his little mustang. There was a bond between man and horse that Ben understood. He glanced out over the rolling grassland and wondered if Ol' Jeb would be waiting for him at the next town.

The wind teased the canvas into fits of animation and tugged at Ben's hair. The spirit of this land is weaving a spell on this old Georgia boy, he thought. The vastness was almost hypnotic. In any direction one's eyes could stretch to their limit and still come up short. And always the wind. It was a living, moving thing. What was it Isaiah said about the wind? Ben remembered his friend had said that four old men lived at the four points of the compass and breathed on the land. Ben allowed there was nothing wrong with the old men's lungs.

Isaiah stepped to his side and nodded to the sunset. "Sun Boy is wearing his best paint tonight. Maybe going to court the maidens, maybe going to war."

"Courting beats fighting. I hope he's going courting," Ben answered as he watched the western sky blaze with scarlet and gold. After he'd said it, he thought of the only girl he ever cared about and wondered if courting was so great. Fighting and courting had been his undoing.

27

BEN STARED AT THE FIRE, waiting for the poker to get red hot. Elmo handed him a saw which he wiped on his trouser leg before waving it through the fire a couple of times. It was a carpenter's six-point rip, damn coarse he thought, and set his jaw at the rush of hatred he felt for the Sioux who had plundered his surgical tools. It probably wouldn't make any difference since he didn't expect Mule to live through the amputation anyway, but he had to try.

"Keep that poker cherry red," he said to Niles. "I'll holler when I need it."

Niles nodded.

"You sure you can handle this? It's not going to be pretty," Ben asked.

Niles swallowed hard. Ben turned to the figure on the operating table that had once again been unloaded to serve a victim of Sioux arrows. Mule's arm was swollen twice normal size and angry purple veins ran upward toward his shoulder. The broken arrow shaft protruded from a pocket of rotting flesh just below the elbow. A maggot squirmed in the puss and then fell to the table. Flies swarmed thick and the stench was a familiar thing inviting him back to the battlefields of blue and gray.

He wouldn't go back, he told himself and looked at Mule's dirty, drawn face. It was miraculous he was still alive. Or maybe lucky. Or maybe Ol' Jeb had good medicine like Isaiah said. Thankfully the two bullets had passed clean through Mule's torso, hitting no vital organs. They weren't a big concern to Ben, but the arm was critical, deadly. Unless he could perform a miracle, Mule was beyond help.

Ben put the saw on Mule's arm; Elmo and Isaiah tightened their grip although Mule probably couldn't and wouldn't move. Ben felt a bond with the old veteran, sympathizing with his desire to see his grandson. He'd given him Ol' Jeb to ride that night secretly envying the man at least some family to return to. If Adeline had been waiting for him, especially with his child, he'd have been the first to leave, asking no one's permission.

It was impossible. He couldn't keep back the rush of memories brought on by Mule's wound. It was the smell that kept reminding him of the many times he'd endured it. And of the time it was coming from his own body.

He'd been told it was two days before the medics found him under his dead mount at Shiloh. He'd first heard the medic's voices like a dream. "Don't see no use messing with this one until last. Lord he's ripe." He could see a pair of blue trousers and black boots but couldn't raise his head to see the rest of the men who belonged to the voices. He realized they were discussing him, and then he smelt the unforgettable odor of the battlefield – rotting flesh, this time his own.

"Poor bastard's going to lose his leg clear to the hip. Not much chance he'll make it," one observed.

"Yea," the second replied. "And damned if he ain't lost at least one nut. I'd rather be dead than like that poor son of a bitch."

The crude joke that followed had actually been a blessing. It shocked and angered him, making him resolve that he wasn't going to die and that no flippant Yankee sawbones was going to cut off his leg.

When they were gone, he gathered his little strength and managed to reach a derringer holstered in his boot. It was one of a brace his father had given him as a gift, and who insisted he carry at least one at all times. A gentleman should always be well groomed and well armed, his father had said.

Hours later when he was dumped onto the operating table, he silently called upon God and on the last of his strength. He grabbed the old surgeon by the beard and shoved the derringer against his throat.

"Nobody is going to cut off my leg," he said through the pain. "I'd rather die whole, but by god I'm not going to die just to spite you bastards."

Looking at Ben with steady eyes, the tired, old gray-bearded surgeon replied, "I think I understand. In your place I'd probably feel the same. But, son, shooting me isn't going to save your leg."

Ben's pain was getting unbearable again, his hand trembled and shook as he cocked the hammer. "Promise me you'll not let them take my leg, or I'll take one more blue belly with me."

"Son, we've got to—"

Fighting off the wave of blackness that he knew would take him in a minute, Ben jerked the bearded face closer. "Look me in the eye, damn it, and promise."

The medics finally overcame their surprise and moved toward the table. The old surgeon waved them off. He'd made a decision and it satisfied Ben when their eyes met. "Okay, Johnny Reb, I promise I won't let anyone take your leg. Good luck."

"Thank you sir," was all Ben could say before the blackness took him again.

"She's sure enough getting red." Niles's words, spoken against the quiet that had fallen on the camp, brought Ben back. He was aware that all the men were watching and waiting.

He lifted the saw from Mule's arm. "I can't do it."

"If you don't take that arm off he'll sure die. Even I can see that," Elmo said.

"True enough," Ben said. "But, it's also true that he'll die if I take it off. Lost so much blood, he's so weak his system won't stand the shock."

"We don't know that for sure."

Ben dropped the saw. "I know that for sure. Besides, I don't think Mule was the kind that would want to die cut all to hell."

"Ho, Little Knife speaks good words. A warrior should spend the next life with a whole body," Isaiah agreed.

Picking up his scalpel Ben motioned the men to hold Mule. "I'm going after that arrow and clean up his arm. Least he won't go to the hereafter packing a damn Sioux arrowhead lodged in his bone."

In his own mind Ben was wondering if he could do for Mule what the old surgeon had done for him. Just maybe, if Mule was strong enough and recalled that Isaiah had said he had sand.

While he worked, he thought about the morning and how they'd found Mule and Ol' Jeb. Three-days' travel away from the rock pile dawned gray and bleak, sucking away a big portion of the men's bright, optimistic outlook. As they ate an early breakfast, several men questioned Isaiah about the distance to the next town and what the town was like. He said they were still at least two days out of Elk Springs.

An early start and easy trail gave them a good six miles by noon when they stopped to rest the teams and rustle up some food. The leaden sky seemed to be held up only by the canvas top of Ben's wagon.

As the afternoon wore on, a brisk south wind rose and began to roll the overcast up like an old carpet. Sunshine broke through and poured bright golden pools onto the greening prairie, and the wind brought welcome relief from the swarming flies. Here and there a smile was seen and off-key tunes tumbled forth to join the creak of harness leather and the rumble of iron-rimmed wheels.

Late in the afternoon Isaiah loped back to the wagons and swung in beside Ben. "Got a strange looking horse about three miles east. Best hold up here and circle 'em until I get back."

"How strange?" Ben asked, feeling a sudden evil premonition.

Isaiah checked the Henry, shoved it back into the boot, and strung his bow. "Moving real slow toward us and carrying an odd pack or rider. I didn't get close enough to know for sure. Figured it could be a decoy."

Ben's confidence, gained from the previous Indian encounter, evaporated like the morning mists. "Tell Elmo to bring the wagons around. And, Isaiah, you be careful. We outfoxed them once. We can do it again if it's Sioux." He said it with a certainty he didn't really feel.

Elmo led the wagons to a small rise and circled them like he'd been guiding trains all his life. Teams were unhitched and unharnessed. As each man finished, he drifted toward Ben's canvas-topped wagon.

A tall teamster, a Spencer in the crook of his arm, a knife and revolver in his belt, glared down at his smaller friend. "I tell you it ain't going to work twice in a row. This time we'll have to fight."

"You Tennessee hill people always was slow," the little man shot back. "Hell, any dummy knows you can use the same trap and bait it the same. If you do it right, you'll always ketch 'em. Hell, Injuns ain't no different than animals."

"Let's ask Ben. Whatever he says goes with me."

Ben was always last to get unharnessed. His leg made it frightfully slow but he guessed it was his pride that insisted he do his own work. Hell, he'd best get used to it because there weren't any more slaves.

He leaned against the nearside horse working his arm under the harness wondering if Lincoln had harnessed his own teams. And now that the slaves were free, was President Johnson doing his own chores?

He arranged the harness on the wagon tongue, grabbed a square of burlap, and began rubbing down his team. He hollered to Elmo, "Any sign of Isaiah?"

"Not a damn thing. Only thing I see is some vultures circling way yonder." He swept his arm to the east and then climbed down from the wagon seat. A holler and banging from inside the wagon drew everyone's attention, "Ben, hey Ben! Somebody! How about something to drink?"

It was Smith. Ben grinned. "That's sure good news," he said to the group. "Roll up that canvas and give him some sun and fresh air."

Ben had little time to tend to Smith before Isaiah led Ol' Jeb into camp carrying a grisly burden.

28

BEN REMOVED THE ARROWHEAD and bandaged Mule's arm. It was the best he could do under the circumstances, but wondered if it would be good enough. He was cleaning his instruments when Elmo walked up and handed Ben Ol' Jeb's lead rope.

"Knowed you place a lot a store by this old fella. Thought you might like to say hello."

"Indeed I would," Ben said laying aside his makeshift surgical instruments. "Really kind of figured I'd lost him."

Ol' Jeb nuzzled Ben's dirty shirt while Ben gently stroked his blaze face and then ran his hands over every inch of the horse before loosing the girth and pulling off the saddle. He immediately dropped the saddle and studied a dark spot on Ol' Jeb's back. "Hey, Elmo bring me a piece of clean blanket and some clean water, Ol' Jeb's been wounded."

Elmo watched as Ben gently washed the dried blood away with a piece of wet blanket. "Is it bad?"

"It isn't too deep, but he can't be ridden until it heals. Since I don't have any medicine I'll put a little axle grease on it to keep the flies away."

Ben handed the lead rope to Elmo who said, "I run across a couple sacks of oats while we was unloading the wagons. With your permission I'd think Ol' Jeb deserves it more than any of the others."

"By all means and thanks, but what about Isaiah? What'd he find?" Ben asked.

"Wasn't wanting to have to tell you, besides Isaiah said it wasn't something you'd need to be fretting about."

He'd been so intent on Mule that he didn't notice until now that one of the wagons was missing. He pointed to the gap. "Burial detail?"

Elmo fidgeted with the lead rope. "Yes, sir. Isaiah believes the Sioux have likely moved on, but a good detail of armed men won't hurt none."

"How come nobody said anything to me until now?"

"Figured you was too busy with Mule."

The sun drew the shadows longer while the wind, tired of its constant tugging at all in its path, chose to gently caress the prairie instead. Ben felt the quiet before he became aware that the men were watching and waiting. "Elmo, why didn't you tell me about the other two men?" he asked.

"Isaiah wasn't wanting you to know just now."

"Why not? Why all of a sudden shouldn't I know about the death of those men?" He glanced at the watching men and rushed on. "How come all of a sudden you don't want me to know what's going on with my own wagon train?"

The big blacksmith looked like a schoolboy come late to class. He motioned a man over to take Ol' Jeb before lifting two chests from a wagon and setting them near the operating table.

Ben slumped down on one. "Thanks. Now what the hell is going on around here?"

Elmo took a seat. "Hoping I'd not be the one to tell ya, but guess you got a right to know."

"Know what?"

"Those other two were tortured real bad. Least ways Isaiah said about the best, or worst, job he'd ever seen."

"So?" Ben put a bite in the word. "I've seen everything that one human can do to another. There's something else that you're not telling me."

"When you didn't cut off Mule's arm, Isaiah talked to some of us." Elmo was speaking slowly, choosing words carefully.

"The whole group? When?"

"While you was working on Mule. Hell, you was so taken with fixing that arm the world could have come to an end and you'd not known."

"And?"

"Isaiah believes two spirits are at war in your head. He's not sure which will win. Thinks maybe the bad spirit is stronger, drawing its strength from things like war, killing, and torture. That's why we didn't want to tell you."

Ben was stunned. Was Isaiah calling him crazy? He swept his eyes around the wagons and men. Did they think he was crazy? It was a familiar question he'd asked himself many times since the war and not once had he received a definitive answer.

He got up and walked toward the wagons and squeezed through to stand outside the circle of men, horses, and wagons. He wanted to be alone. His eyes focused on the distant horizon where the glowing red sky melted into the swaying grass. The empty expanse, its enormity, was difficult to grasp. The night sounds floating on the wind were not sounds he recognized. This was not his land, not his country of slaves, industry, and wealth.

He was fleeing from that life, but there must be many more miles of this damn land between him and his dream. And Indians. And God himself probably didn't know what else.

Maybe the spirits had gone mad in his head. Here he was on the edge of the world, running around naked, falling under the spell of a half-breed who sniffs the wind like a dog, appears and disappears like an apparition, and kills without compunction.

Mother of god. I am crazy.

Sky of blood, he thought staring at the sunset. Hell, he was even thinking like Isaiah. Or was he thinking of Mule and how much blood he'd lost? Blood that was all over his saddle and Ol' Jeb. Damn smart of Mule to lash himself to the saddle. Must have figured that Ol' Jeb was his only hope. Had figured right. That was real. Real blood, real flesh and bone. A real human being wanting to see another human being.

Ben turned back to the wagons. If he was crazy, so was the rest of the world. Weary with fatigue, he forced himself to walk with determination and purpose. He knew what had to be done. He would not abandon Mule.

At sunup the next morning the wagons unwound themselves from the little rise and snaked their way southwest. Ben watched them go with little emotion.

All his feelings had been spent the night before around the campfire when he announced that the rest were going ahead while he stayed with Mule.

"You can't stay out here by yourself," Elmo protested heatedly, followed by equally passionate arguments from about everyone else.

Ben was deaf to their reason. "You all work for me. You've taken my money to drive those wagons. If you don't get to the next town, resupply, and find a guide within the next week, we'll have lost our chance to get over the passes before snowfall."

Isaiah, black hair braided and tied with red trade cloth and clad only in breechclout didn't give in easily. "I will stay with you and Mule. You do not yet know the ways of this land."

"True," Ben said, "but you have agreed to guide this train. Unless you quit, your job is to get these wagons to Elk Springs."

It was said with some anger and absolute finality. Isaiah argued no more.

Then Niles came around the campfire and again held out the Ballard. "At least keep this. Only a crazy man would stay alone, unarmed out here. Isaiah says there'll be lots of Indian hunting parties roaming this area."

Ben watched the wagons grow smaller in the distance and regretted being so angry with the men. Especially Niles. The young man had no idea of the two spirits that warred in his head. He hated to admit it, but Isaiah was right.

The camp was sparse. Only his wagon, the operating table, and a fire pit. What medical supplies he had were contained in his black leather bag. On a whim, he'd had the harpsichord set out by the front wheel of his wagon. It would help pass the hours.

Mule showed little change, hanging to life only by the thinnest thread. Ben checked the angry purple streaks anxiously. They hadn't progressed any further up the shoulder, and for that he was thankful. The odor was less pungent when he changed the dressing. Maybe, just maybe, he thought, then wondered if he also harbored the same doubts the old gray-bearded Yankee doctor had concerning his leg.

The sun gained strength as it rose in a sky cluttered with lazy, white fluffy clouds that occasionally made the bright orb wink. Isaiah, Ben thought, would say Old Man Wind was resting, his breath easy and rhythmic.

Ben checked Mule's arm again and then looked southwest. The wagons were gone. The dew was still clinging to the grass, sparkling as the light touched the clinging droplets. The air was clean, and one's eyes could walk unfettered in any direction of the compass. Almost at once two feelings overwhelmed him: he was very alone and very dirty.

His trousers were mud-caked and his shirt was stained with blood. He didn't waste water on the trousers but beat them like he'd seen servants beat rugs. He washed his shirt and draped it over a wagon wheel. His boots were in deplorable condition so he climbed up to the wagon seat and began to pick dried mud from the welt, wishing he had boot polish. Hell, he thought, he wasn't even sure how you polished boots since the black servants had always kept his boots immaculate. He guessed he'd have to learn, and figured that over half a million men lost their lives deciding who would polish boots.

After cleaning the boots, he cleaned and rearranged the wagon and its contents. When he'd finished, he felt much better.

29

CAPTAIN KEEFERLY REINED IN BENEATH a huge oak and looked down on Elk Springs as it stirred to meet the morning. First light was changing the sky from deep velvet blue-black to hints of soft, pale amber along the earth's eastern rim.

The beauty was lost on the lone rider. He used sunrise only as a time reference. If he rode hard, he could be at Wild Horse Flats by noon.

He wondered if Jake had convinced the scout and his sick friend to stay the hell out of Elk Springs. He imagined Jake had because the big man could be right forceful when necessary. He hated to lose the train's business, but he now had the luxury of money and power. He could do without the business and cholera scared him more than Indians. He shuddered at the memory of 1840. Men dropping suddenly and dying within hours. Doctors and their medicine were powerless once cholera took a body. Brave men who wouldn't hesitate in hand-to-hand combat defected and fled. Some never returned. Either way, a court martial was preferable to the cholera.

Perhaps he should send some of the Guidon K crew out to intercept and destroy all infected wagon trains. He'd kill every man, woman, and child before he allowed them into Elk Springs.

Jake would love the work, he thought, and suddenly remembered he hadn't made arrangements to free him. That stubborn old badge toter wouldn't let Jake out until it was all proper; Jake would be crazy. But, he was worried about Todd and curious about the McGregors. He asked himself why it was becoming so difficult to plan and execute maneuvers.

He needed a second in command who saw things like he did. It had been his dream that his son would fill those boots. Right now, Todd was too soft and too weak for a man's job in this country. But, he'd try to make a man out of him.

First sunlight was busy fighting with any sign of night that still lingered in the oak grove. Birds were singing encouragement to the sun and Captain Keeferly's horse pawed the dew-covered grass, insisting they be about the day's business.

The captain studied the town below him. Right here, he told himself, right here is where I will build the house. My office with a veranda to catch the rising sun and where I can look down on Elk Springs. He could visualize entertaining senators, business leaders, and their wives in his new mansion with his town, Elk Springs, sprawled at his feet.

Old Angelo would run the house of course, but he'd hire, or marry, a pretty young woman to tease lustful old men's eyes. He'd need to find a suitable woman to marry. A stunning, bright young thing would be a credit at his side when he courted the powerful lawmakers. The right woman could be the deciding influence.

Promising himself a new lady, perhaps the redhead, he'd purchase the land and start building the house even if he had to pay Lester's unreasonable price. With good planning it could be finished by the time he began campaigning for governor.

Spurring his mount, he reined it through the timber and out onto the rolling prairie. Todd had ridden out to Wild Horse Flats unaware of the recent Sioux activity in the area. When he struck the river, memories of the McGregors' string of claims, their cabins, the ugly fields of freshly turned sod, and a haunting redhead overpowered his concerns about Todd.

He crossed at the ford and swung parallel to the river on his left and let the big gelding settle into a ground-covering lope. He wished the whole lot of bearded clodhoppers would pack and leave because of the Indians. Or, that the Indians would scalp the hairy lot. One way or another, they would have to be driven off his grassland, but he hoped the redhead was still at the cabin. She'd made his blood run hot, stirred him with memories of youthful conquests.

The first homestead was alive with activity when the captain arrived. He steeled himself and put on his best manners. The corral fence was almost rebuilt by the hoard of bearded men sweating in the bright sunshine. He should have burned the damn place.

He rode up to Will. "Seen any more Indians here abouts?"

Will took off his slouch hat and wiped a sleeve across his sweaty forehead. "Morning, Captain. Ain't seen any, but they messed up Josh's place here right bad."

"Sorry to hear that," he said thinking how easy it was to fool the dumb bastards. "Anybody hurt?"

"Not a soul." Will pointed to the cabin where women and children gathered to stare. "Funny damn thing though, herded the stock inside. Don't know much about Indians, but can't quite reason why they didn't steal 'em."

The captain touched his hat brim to the ladies. "Indians can be mighty strange. Can't always figure 'em. Mostly do what you don't expect." He said, looking for the redhead.

It was exactly like his first meeting at the main claim up river. Smiling men and boys gathered around, women and a variety of girls watching from the porch. It galled him that they showed no fear. He got a tight rein on his emotions and addressed Will. "Any of the other places hit?" The redhead wasn't in sight.

Will leaned on the shovel, powerful muscles showing through a too-small faded green shirt. "They didn't bother a single thing on my brothers' claims and that's one more thing I can't figure."

"I'm mighty thankful to hear that. How's the missus?" The captain was taking a mental tally. A few of the clan were missing. He tried to look concerned as he met Will's eyes.

Will's smile widened and his eyes glowed with pride. "Why right well, thanks for asking. Her and a couple the other womenfolk are in Elk Springs."

He touched his hat again toward the house. "Pleasure to see you again, ladies." Then turning to the men, "I must push on. You keep a sharp eye for redskins."

"One thing more, Captain. You know Indians better than us. Just what would they do with a plow?" Will asked.

"They use iron to make arrow heads and spear points," he answered and spurred out of the yard.

Will leaned on the shovel and watched the horse and rider disappear around the tree line. The wind was picking up strength and the cottonwood leaves flashed silver in the bright sunlight. The squatter removed his hat and held it in his hand letting the breeze work through his thatch of graying black hair.

He had survived and prospered in his native land because he could read people. He'd never learned to read and write his own language, but he could read people like a scholar reads the written page.

The brothers, taking their cue from Will, removed their hats and stared after the disappearing rider. The only other man with gray showing in his beard stepped to Will's side. "You don't like the man, do you?"

Will turned to his kinsmen. "Lads, I reckon that man is going to cause us more trouble than the Indians. I think that someday either he will kill us, or we will have to kill him. Tell none of this to the lasses." No one questioned his announcement. Will had spoken and it was gospel. They returned to work, confident that it would come to pass.

Behind the tree line, out of sight of the cabin the captain dismounted, relieved himself, and adjusted the bedroll behind the cantle. He wanted to ride back to town but knew he should go on to Wild Horse Flats. He built a smoke and saw a mane of red hair in the match flame. Maybe she'd be at the cabin by the time he returned from the Flats.

It would have saved time to go directly to the Flats, but he chose to ride past the McGregors' claims which all held a strange fascination for him. At Will's claim, he drew up and stared at the cabin for long minutes before dismounting and stepping up to the closed door. No one answered his knock and the door swung open at his boot's impact. Inside he waited a moment for his eyes to adjust to the dimness, then looked until he saw a water pail and crude dipper that would provide an excuse in case someone happened along – he was just after a drink of water.

The cabin was big, well built, and well kept. A large plank table with chairs sat in front of the fireplace in the main room. He saw the ladder to a loft and a kitchen and pantry on the east, but the feature that intrigued him was a door at the west end of the main room. A sleeping room he guessed. Hers and Will's. He threw open the leather-hinged door knowing it was against all propriety, but then they were on his land, Guidon K land, and he was the master of it all. By damn, if he wanted to look inside a dirt grubber's bedroom, propriety could go to hell.

The room was frontier crude but unmistakably feminine. A fragrance lingered in the warm still air. In the southwest corner, where the sun slanted on a newly-made table, was a silver hand mirror, a brush, and a small round container. The bed was spread with a handmade quilt and on the wall were pegs where clothes hung awaiting their owner's choosing. Above the bed's headboard hung bagpipes, kilt, and sword.

He fondled the dresses that hung on one of the pegs, groping until his fingers touched an obvious nightgown. He held it to his nose. The fragrance he smelled earlier lingered faintly. His thoughts were wild and many faceted. Hate. Lust. Envy. Jealousy. Burning desire and burning rage.

The big man moved to the table in the corner, lifted the lid from the small container, and stood transfixed as the fragrance enveloped him along with images of red hair, green eyes, and smooth creamy skin. He set it back down, replaced the lid, and slowly picked up the hair brush. As it passed through the sunshine, the strands of red hair glowed like copper and brass. He chose one long strand and pulled it free.

His big hands trembled as he returned the brush to the table. Visions real and imagined crawled over his mind like swarming bees. He licked dry lips. Never in the last forty years had he felt this way. "By god," he said to the silent room, "I will have this woman."

He finally went back outside and gathered the reins. How long he'd been inside, he didn't know. It could have been minutes, it could have been hours. He didn't care. He pulled out his watch to confirm the low angle of the sun. Before he pocketed the watch, he wound the red hair around the stem and tied it off in a square knot.

Too late to head for the Flats now, he thought. Todd would have to be a man and look to his own welfare. A little scare with some Indians might just toughen him up, he reasoned as he swung astride the gray.

He crossed the river, put the sun at his back, and spurred toward Guidon K headquarters. He was going to push harder at those who opposed him. As governor he could enact and enforce laws – laws that could remove homesteaders and create widows.

30

ISAIAH LOOKED BACK OVER the winding column of wagons and felt a sense of pride and knew it would have made his mother proud. Then a sad moment galloped through his mind. What if Ben didn't want or need him after they reached Elk Springs? He would surely miss the crippled medicine man with the strange spirit.

Isaiah swung in beside Elmo's wagon and pointed west. "Elmo, see that rise? That's Shoemaker Hill. We'll strike the main trail there and Elk Springs is just beyond."

A grin got snagged on Elmo's big, bearded face. "Isaiah, you know, you're all right. At first I had my doubts about you. Now I don't question for a minute there's a town there just as you say."

Isaiah sat his pony loosely, his clothes clean and neat. He wanted to blend in with the whites and avoid trouble at Elk Springs. He grinned back at Elmo. "You're all right for a white man. I, too, had my doubts."

Elmo flicked a horsefly from the back of the off-wheeler. "Doubts about me?"

"You see," Isaiah said gravely, "to Indians, a great bear is strong medicine."

Elmo laughed. "A great bear, eh? Well, I'll tell you this bear ain't as great as he used to be."

Isaiah laughed with him. "You are like a great bear just out of winter's sleep, thin and grouchy. You need to fatten up on many berries and roots."

"Berries and roots, my ass. You know the first thing I'm going to do when we reach town?"

"Hit a saloon and get drunk like all white men?"

"Hell no, I'm going to find me a good mess of grits and a steak as big as a wagon wheel. Then I'm going to wallow in a bathtub until the sun goes down."

Isaiah studied the man out of the corner of his eye. The good humor still clung to the big man, so he asked, "Tell me, Elmo, do the women in your tribe have hair all over their body like you?"

Elmo laughed until tears ran down into his beard. "They ain't got no hair at all. They all mate with a giant black bear that lives atop the Smoky Mountains," he said. "That's where we men folk get all our hair."

"If that's so, who do the men mate with?"

"Don't." Elmo tried to sound serious. "That's what makes us such big'uns. Nothing to wear us down and take our strength."

Isaiah recognized a good story when he heard one, and thought it isn't much different than the stories around a Crow lodge fire. His mother had told him all people were pretty much the same, and now he saw her wisdom. He wondered if Ben had stories to tell around a campfire. Many, many, sad, true stories he guessed.

Isaiah finally grinned. "It is a good story. I'll remember it to tell around the fire on a night when Cold Man roars down from the north."

They rode in silence for a while, savoring the clear air and endless expanse of blue sky and prairie. After some time of quiet travel, Elmo's expression changed, bringing lines of concentration to his forehead. "Isaiah, ya reckon we can find a guide in this here town? And, how many days we got to spare before it's too late to get through the mountain passes?"

Isaiah's thoughts were on the same thing. "I don't know for sure how much time you have, but from what I've heard, I wouldn't want to start later than twenty suns from now. After that it won't make any difference about a guide."

Elmo asked Isaiah, "When we hit town I guess your job is officially finished, but I was wondering if you'd go back and help Ben? Mule ain't here and I got to stay with the wagons. How about it?"

"I'd always planned to go back."

– 31 –

CURTIS JAMESON DUPREE III WAS A LONG WAY from Boston and even further from the man his family had hoped he would become. The first casualty of his westward move had been his name. Only one person had used his full name, carefully pronouncing each syllable and drawing out the "third." It was a good laugh for the saloon customers. Now he was just Curt. Or the drunk barber. Or just the drunk.

He closed the door and drew the shades on the slovenly little shop. If he was lucky, later tonight he would lock the door and draw the shades on his mind.

I should sweep, he told himself. Looking behind the dirty curtain into the back room, he sighed at the scummy, week-old bath water in the copper tub. He hadn't had a bath customer for days. He'd clean it tomorrow. Tonight he possessed some choice information. Worth, he hoped, a bottle because he needed a bottle of the amber liquid that could dilute the image of Jake's graphic threat.

Business had not been good. He counted his meager earnings and panicked when he realized he couldn't buy his ticket to oblivion. That meant he'd have to work old Fats real good and make the story worth a bottle.

He pushed through the War Bonnet's batwings, bellied to the bar, and shoved his few coins across the wet bar top. The barkeep, Fats Mahoney, looked bored but less disgusted than usual at his arrival. Curt pointed to the money. "Keep 'em coming as long as the coin holds out."

The barkeep eyed the few coins and reached under the bar for the establishment's worst, not knowing if he hated the little man or felt sorry for him. "How's business, Curt?"

Curt drained his glass and slid it for a refill. "Business is suffering greatly. Matter of fact, most near dead."

The barkeep indicated the empty tables with a wide gesture. "That's damn sure right. Should be getting wagon trains soon if the damn Indians leave them alone. Elk Springs could use the business."

Curt watched his coins disappear beneath the bar followed by the bottle. He set his glass down carefully on the bartender's side of the bar. "Injuns ain't the only thing that we got to worry about," he said casually, watching the fat man behind the bar. The negotiations had commenced; both men knew the game from many previous sessions. Curt sensed his advantage – there were few customers, and the bartender was bored.

The bottle clicked on the edge of the glass as Fats poured. "One on the house for good luck this season. I can't rightly see what else except the Injuns that we got to worry about. Ain't near as many wagons as once was, but it still could be a good year."

Curt tossed off the drink and carefully set the glass on the bar in front of his opponent. "True enough, could be a good year if we don't have a streak of bad luck."

The barkeep set the bottle next to the glass and gently tapped in the cork. Taking the soiled towel from his shoulder, he began to wipe the bar. "Got some rain lately, grass should be good along the trail. No, sir, I think it's going to be a good year."

Curt felt the whisky seep through his body and deliberately changed the subject. Nodding to the card game at the far end of the room, he said, "Old man Shoemaker was in my place this morning. Wife's feeling poorly."

Two customers pushed through the batwings and ordered drinks. The barkeep left Curt, poured their drinks, and then worked his way with the towel back to Curt. Most of the time Curt's gossip was not worth the cheap whisky, but occasionally it was entertaining, and just once in a while he came up with a juicy morsel. It was clear that tonight something big was lodged in his whisky-soaked brain.

Fats picked up the glass and bottle, wiped the bar, and replaced them a bit further from Curt. "Heard anymore about the railroad that you said was fixing to come through town?"

Curt fondled the whisky bottle with his watery eyes. "Naw, ain't heard nothing, but, mark my word, I had that information from a good source." He wiped his mouth with a dirty shirt-sleeve and plunged on. "Did see a couple of strangers in town last night. Never can tell, could be someone with the railroad, but don't think so."

The two small ranchers picked up their bottle and moved down the bar closer to Curt. They wanted to hear about the strangers and they wanted to be entertained by the town drunk who also doubled as town jester.

One toyed with his bottle, slipping the cork in and out with great, exaggerated motions. "Say a couple of strangers here abouts last night?"

One of the ranchers poured and slid the glass to Curt. "Was they more hired killers like the others Keeferly is bringing in?"

"Nope, not so." He drank. Setting the glass down, he added, "But they sure enough could kill more of us than any gunfighters."

The two customers and the barkeep exchanged glances and the bartender slid the bottle to Curt. "How the hell can that be, my friend, if they ain't hired killers?"

Curt knew he had won, but if he wanted to win again in the future he needed to make the information worthy of a bottle. "Worst damn plague can come upon the human being, no cure, no hope once it lays its hands on a body."

A tall redheaded young man with an easy smile, turned to Fats. "How many has ol' Curt had already? He's not talking as much sense as usual."

"Unless he was drinking before he came in here, he ain't had but three, maybe four."

The evening customers were drifting in by ones and twos. The attention Curt was getting drew several of the curious regulars over to join the group. The down-at-the-heels barber and would-be physician reveled in the attention. He'd hooked them, and he had a bottle firmly clutched in his hand. Another drink passed over his thin, blue lips and suddenly the faces around him made him angry. They were waiting to poke fun and laugh at his expense. Damn you all, he thought. Damn you with a wretched death. Then he remembered. Perhaps a wretched death wasn't far away.

Fats waddled back. "Curt, what the hell's this about strangers and killings?"

Curt studied the line of light that the setting sun pushed between a crack and threw against the far wall. The line divided the smoky room in half – the living and the dead, he thought. "I was called to the sheriff's office to examine one of the strangers who'd fallen sick. In a bad way he was."

The group was anxious for the few laughs Curt usually provided. "Did you cure him like you did my toothache?"

Curt ignored the insult. "Ain't no cure I know of for cholera."

The half-dozen men around Curt fell silent. Curt turned back to the bar satisfied with the impact he'd made on the men. Visions of Jake flashed through his mind and he splashed some whisky in his glass spilling most on the bar.

"Damn," someone said. "Curt, cholera ain't nothing to joke about."

Curt turned and downed the drink, terror in his eyes. Half from the memories of cholera and half from Jake's threat. "I ain't joking. Everything about him said it was cholera." He pushed his way through the men and made for the door. Halfway there, he turned and retrieved the bottle off the bar.

The batwings banged open and a tow-headed kid with a string of catfish rushed inside.

Fats stared at the kid and growled, "What the heck you doing in here, Freddy?"

Freddy Shoemaker spotted his dad at the card table. "Pa, I was fishing down below the hill and on the way home I saw 'em. Wagon train coming about two miles north of the hill. Must of come through the cutoff."

Curt froze in mid stride. "You sure, kid? Damn, he said they was still at Grand Forks. Lord have mercy on us all."

BEN STIRRED FITFULLY IN HIS BEDROLL, groping in a haunted world somewhere between sleep and waking. He pushed himself to a sitting position and leaned back against the front wagon wheel. For long moments he rubbed the circulation back into his bad leg, then pulled the blanket up around his shoulders and stared at the morning glow touching the eastern sky.

His unkempt hair and a heavy stubble of beard framed listless eyes. How many days, he wondered, has it been since the train left for Elk Springs? Three, four, five? How many days since Mule died? Two, three?

His only answer was the wind dancing back and forth on the wagon canvas and moaning through the wheel spokes and running gear. It was daybreak and the wind was already bending the prairie grass low. Was it two days, or three? He couldn't remember but he knew that today he had to bury Mule. Yesterday afternoon he had seen vultures circling, effortlessly riding the air currents high above. Their presence ran cold claws over his mind and body.

Now, tipping his head slightly, he looked up into the overcast sky. Nothing, only low scurrying clouds, but suddenly he regretted not having accepted Niles's Ballard. Last night the coyotes had set up their lonesome chorus much closer than before.

Still sitting by the wheel, he shifted his trance-like gaze to the operating table. The wind teased and tugged at the blanket covering Mule's body. It gave the impression of life and Ben cursed the wind.

He couldn't face the thought of burying Mule. That would be the final confirmation that he'd failed. Failed to save Mule like the old Union doctor had saved him. Failed as a physician, failed as a healer. Failed in his new life. What tormented him most was his failure to give Mule a chance to see his grandson. That thought held him motionless.

How many days since he'd seen his team? They'd come back to the wagon the first morning looking for a ration of oats, but he couldn't remember after that. He had been so busy with Mule that he'd not even looked for them, and he couldn't remember seeing them since.

His thoughts roamed aimlessly, finally focusing on a memory of Ol' Jeb. Then on Isaiah, who openly admired the powerful stallion, and then on Elmo and the rest of the train. Had they reached Elk Springs? Had they found a guide? Was someone on the way back to help him? He really didn't care anymore.

He stared at the faint, pink glow above the trees' silhouettes along the creek. A new day was struggling to life. He wasn't interested in life and shifted his gaze to the operating table. "Damn it, Mule, I guess mortal man can't cheat fate after all. My time came during the war. I should have accepted it then."

He paused, drew a deep breath, and opened his mouth to continue. Instead he froze and held his breath as his eyes probed the morning. Something or someone is near, he thought. How he knew, he couldn't explain, but he knew that a living being was close. He remembered Isaiah's admonition about listening to the wind. Was he getting a message from the wind? Maybe fate had been listening and came to claim him. He would go now without a struggle. He was of no use in this world anymore.

Ben closed his eyes and leaned his head against the wagon wheel and waited. The sense of someone near, even death, was strangely comforting.

— ❖ —

Isaiah reined in at the twin cottonwoods that he'd picked as a landmark for Ben and his wagon. He sat for long moments in their deep shadows and studied the prairie. It was a good mile to the canvas-topped wagon but there was no sign of life. No campfire, no horses, no movement. He didn't like what he saw and felt.

He moved upstream, riding slowly and quietly, paying as much attention to his war pony's behavior as he did to the surroundings. The mustang gave no indication of trouble.

At a slough he swung west and rode until he was downwind of Ben's camp. Here the horse threw up its head, ears forward. Isaiah leaned down, speaking softly in Crow, reminding the pony that silence was needed. He checked the Henry and rode straight into camp.

His nose told him Mule was dead. In the pale dawn he saw Ben hunched against the wagon wheel. His first thought was that his crippled friend was also dead. Ben's eyes opened and stared blankly up at him.

Isaiah waited for Ben to speak or move. When he didn't, he said, "I am sorry about Mule, but we must bury him and get to Elk Springs quickly."

Ben just stared. Isaiah stepped off the little pony and squatted in front of Ben. He could sense the struggle between the spirits. The sunken, dull eyes wouldn't meet his. Isaiah feared he'd lost his crippled friend as well as Mule.

Isaiah reasoned that perhaps this was the white man's way of mourning the dead. He would leave him to mourn while he buried Mule, but a search of the wagon yielded no tool to dig a grave.

He spoke to Ben, "Take a long time to dig a grave with a knife. If you can tell me where the team is, we'll haul your friend to the trees and give him an Indian burial."

No response. "I'll find the horses and be back." Then bending over and laying a hand on Ben's shoulder added, "I, too, have mourned the death of a comrade. It is bitter for the spirit, but we will send Mule on his crossing-over journey and then continue our walk with the living."

Ben gave no indication that he had heard. Isaiah gathered the team's bridles from the wagon, mounted, and set off in search of the horses. When he returned with the team, the sun was two hours high in a leaden, gray sky. Ben was still slumped at the wagon wheel, the blanket at his waist, his black medical bag at his side.

Isaiah tied the horses, gathered his pipe bag and tobacco pouch, then sat cross legged before Ben. Slowly, Ben raised his eyes and looked at Isaiah. "I couldn't do it. I wanted to, but I couldn't."

Isaiah's hands untied the pipe bag while his eyes studied Ben. The anguish he read there was clear and deep. "What couldn't my friend do?"

Ben pulled his hands from beneath the blanket and held out two small derringers. "End it all."

Isaiah's hands paused only for a heartbeat, betraying the surprise and shock he felt. "Little Knife wanted to keep his friend company on the crossing-over journey?"

"No," Ben said, laying the derringers on the blanket. "I don't think I can live with the memories anymore and I failed Mule when he needed my help."

Isaiah was about to tell Ben that many more were sure to need his help when the cholera train reached Elk Springs but something bid him to wait. He sat, listening to the wind growing stronger. The grass rolled like waves on big water; yellow and purple flowers bobbing like small craft adrift in a tempest.

The horses were restless, testing the wind with flared nostrils and stamping nervous hooves. Isaiah felt again the strange feeling when close to this troubled white eyes. Little Knife's spirits were strong, his medicine great, but he feared for his friend's life. He was also filled with a great desire to know what was in this strange white man's mind.

His white mother's mind was open to him but he'd never met another white man that held his mind like this one. He lit the pipe, handed it to Ben, and picked up one of the derringers. "From the first day we met at the prairie fire, I believed that you were a strong man who could do anything you wanted. If you wanted to take your life, what stopped you?"

"I don't expect you to understand because no one else has, but I promised myself I would never do harm to another human life. I guess that includes my own. What good is a conviction if you don't live by it?"

Isaiah glanced at the sky and then swept the circling horizons with eyes squinted against the wind. He could sense no danger. "That is why you tried so hard to avoid a fight with the Sioux?"

"Yes."

"But you carry these," Isaiah said, turning the small gun in his hand.

Ben picked up the matching piece from the blanket and read aloud the tiny, delicate engraving: *To my son Benjamin Frederick Kelley. Your most loving father. The year of our Lord 1861.*

Isaiah turned the gun, touching the engraving and gold inlay with his finger. Then he spoke softly, "They are beautiful guns, a good gift to give a son."

Ben held out his hand for the other piece. "My father made these for me just before I went off to war."

"Does your father know of your feelings about fighting?"

Ben picked up his medical bag and stowed the brace of derringers beneath the false bottom. "My father died before I started this journey. He knew, but he thought it was foolish and believed I'd change my mind."

Isaiah watched Ben carefully close the black medical bag. "I believe your father was very wise. You will change your mind."

Ben's head snapped up, some of the old fire burning in his eyes. "Never. I have seen enough fighting and killing to know it doesn't solve a damn thing. It's insanity. I will not change my mind."

"It is not yet a part of your heart or else you would throw away the small guns."

"Those were a gift my father gave me. I keep them only as a memory of him. I loaded them before I left home to join the war and after this long they probably wouldn't even fire."

Inwardly Isaiah smiled. Anger was a powerful motivation; it would keep his friend among the living for now. Yet, he was sure Ben was still divided between the spirits.

Ben set the bag aside and looked at the blanket-covered operating table. Isaiah spoke after a long silence. "I do not doubt that you have seen much war and much wrong. But it puzzles me that you do not understand."

"Understand?" Ben almost shouted. "How can one understand severed arms and legs? Holes in a young man's belly that you can stick your fist through? Festering wounds and mutilated bodies that defy identification? All for what? To determine who will polish whose boots or hoe whose cotton?"

Ben paused and lowered his voice. "Do you have an explanation for such madness? If so, I would like to hear it."

Isaiah looked upward, reached down to touch the earth, and then swept his hand to the four winds. "This I know. The Great Spirit gave us all things to teach us, if we are willing to learn. He has taught me that even the small mouse, when he sees the shadow of the hawk approaching, doesn't sit quietly and offer himself to the hawk. He rushes to save his life, and if caught in the hawk's talons, fights with all his strength to live. It is the Great Spirit's will for all his creatures."

The wind had paused as if to listen. Ben didn't stir or speak. Isaiah picked up his pipe, and while putting it into the bag spoke again, "I have one more thing to say to my friend before we send Mule on his journey. You have seen the hawk's shadow from afar but someday the shadow will fall on you alone. Then you will know if you truly believe as you say, or if you will live."

Ben felt the old frustration. Everyone telling him he was wrong because he'd been changed, but Isaiah's simple reasoning had a core of truth that he couldn't refute. He was alive; he'd leave it at that for now. Struggling to his feet, he watched

Isaiah tie the pipe bag. "Do all Crows argue with their friends at such length?"

Isaiah rose. "No. It was enough words for many campfires. After we tend to Mule, I'd like to smoke with you and only speak enough words to fill a child's hand."

"Good, a lot of smoke and few words. But first a favor from you. Last night I was angry with many things. I threw my cane away and told God he could have it because I wouldn't need it anymore." He pointed. "It's somewhere in that direction."

Isaiah searched the area for several minutes before bending over and retrieving the cane. He examined it on the walk back and handed it to Ben. "I guess God didn't want your cane. But it's too heavy, probably the reason God didn't want it." Isaiah smiled, Ben didn't.

"It is heavy because it is also a weapon, but God let me have it back because he knows that I will only use it for walking."

"It is very beautiful like the pistols," Isaiah said. "Your father had great skill."

"Yes, my father was an artist, but also a practical man. He made this for me because after I was wounded he knew I'd never be able to fight like I used to. He thought I needed it for self-defense." Ben took the cane and then motioned Isaiah to sit. Once he was settled, Ben pointed to the overlay on the top half the cane's shaft. "As you can see, the engravings are leaves and acorns like the oak tree which is the tree that our plantation was named after. Oak is strong, enduring, and useful for many things."

"Oak isn't good for making bows and arrows. It isn't good for lodge poles. But, in the fall the deer do grow fat on the acorn."

Ben turned the cane around and held the knob end to Isaiah. "See this oak leaf and this acorn that are just a bit different than the others? Press the leaf down and then slide the acorn up. Now pull on the bottom."

Isaiah did and the lower half of the shaft came free. "Ho! A cane for a very short man or a child. But it still too heavy."

Ben took the cane, twisted and pulled on the knob handle. A small piece of branch fell down from the carvings. "It is now a shotgun ready to fire. By turning the knob and pulling it cocks the piece, and the small piece of leaf that falls down is the trigger."

Isaiah looked at the piece and then at Ben. "Your father had great medicine, but does it really shoot?"

"Of course it shoots, my father made it. It's loaded with buck and ball and would be very lethal at close range."

"I want to shoot it," Isaiah said holding out his hand.

"No, for two reasons. We need to bury Mule and we need to move as soon as we can. The second reason is that I don't have anymore power and shot."

"But, you said you'd never use it against another human, so it won't matter."

"No," Ben said as he uncocked and reassembled the cane.

By late afternoon Isaiah had fashioned a crude platform in the low branches of a big cottonwood. Ben helped when he could and the two found that they worked well together, each understanding the other without spoken words. When Mule at last was lashed to the platform, they stood side by side silently saying their goodbyes. Then wanting to leave Mule to his peace, Isaiah mounted his pony and Ben climbed to the wagon seat. They moved out traveling southwest through the windy, gray evening. The two rode in silence until Isaiah picked a campsite for the night. They cared for the horses and then built a small fire. The meal was hardtack, jerky, and weak coffee.

Isaiah sat by the fire braiding his hair while Ben wrote in his journal. It was a grisly account that Ben entered in the journal and he dreaded the task of writing the men's kinfolk. But he had promised. He would only tell them that the men had been killed by Indians. No further details were necessary. Remembering, he shuddered at the description Isaiah had reluctantly given about the men's death. Not able to deal with the memory at the present, he would put off writing the letters until they reached Elk Springs.

When Isaiah finished and tied off the braid, he uncased his pipe and filled the bowl with tobacco. He broke the long silence. "Shall we smoke and speak a handful of words?"

Ben finished what he was writing before answering, "Yes, I was about to ask you about the train and Elk Springs. Has Elmo found a guide?"

Using two twigs, Isaiah carried a small, glowing ember from the fire to light the long-stemmed pipe. He ignored the question while he drew life into the tobacco and solemnly offered it to the four winds before handing it across the fire to Ben.

Ben smoked and handed it back, seemingly to forget his own question. "Next time we will smoke the pipe you have given me, and you can teach me the proper way if you will."

"Sure," Isaiah answered. "It will make the Great Spirit happy if you learn the Crow way."

Ben blew out the lantern and placed the journal onto the crate. "Now, about Elk Springs and the wagons?"

"I was afraid you weren't going to ask again and afraid you were."

Ben frowned. "What's that mean?"

"It will take more than a handful of words to explain."

"Use two handfuls. Hell, use a whole damn armful. What's happening with the wagons and Elk Springs?"

Isaiah handed the pipe back to Ben. "By asking, it means the old spirit is back, ready to go on to your new life. That's good. On the other hand, if you hadn't asked I wouldn't have to tell you bad news."

Ben leaned further forward, ignoring the pipe. "Out with it! What's going on?"

Isaiah gave a complete report of all that happened from the time the train left Ben and Mule until he started back to Ben's camp. As the story progressed Ben leaned back against the trunk only to lean quickly forward at the mention of cholera.

Noticing Ben's reaction, Isaiah asked, "You know about cholera?"

Somewhere a coyote howled long and mournful in the quiet that had come with darkness. Ben turned and looked in the direction of the howling and then back at Isaiah, "It's worse than anything I could ever say about it."

– 33 –

ISAIAH'S STEADY BREATHING INDICATED he was sleeping, but Ben's sleep was interrupted by dreams of dying men, women, and children. In his waking moments he tried desperately to recall every detail he had read and heard about cholera. Although he'd never encountered cholera himself, he did know that many doctors themselves had fallen victim to its deadly cramps.

He arose well before first light, rekindled the campfire, and brewed the last of the coffee. He was just pouring the first cup when Isaiah sat up. "Ho, Little Knife is waking the birds."

Ben poured another cup of coffee and handed it to Isaiah. "Those people are going to need medical help and the sooner the better."

Isaiah took a sip, set it down, and disappeared into the trees. He relieved himself, knelt by the clear running stream where he drank and splashed water over his face and upper body. Returning, he sat by the fire and looked across the fire at Ben. "You're not planning to wait around and see whether that train carries cholera?"

Ben, gnawing on a strip of jerky, replied without hesitation. "I will if there is such a train."

Isaiah sat cross-legged by the fire, tin cup wrapped in both hands. "You haven't many days to waste if you want to get over the mountains this season. Besides, cholera would be a good thing to avoid."

"You say that like you've heard of cholera before," Ben said.

"It took a lot of my people many seasons ago."

Ben got to his feet and began to break camp. "I'm a physician. Treating sick people is what my life is about now. If there is cholera, I must do what I can to help."

Isaiah rolled his bedroll and was tying it behind the saddle when he asked, "Do physicians get cholera?"

"As easily as anyone else."

"How about half-breeds?"

"Same thing," Ben answered stowing his bedroll, lantern, and cooking utensils in the wagon. "But you got the train to Elk Springs, which was our agreement. Soon as we get there, I'll pay you and you can go your way if you choose."

Isaiah checked the Henry and slid it back into the scabbard. "Wasn't thinking of quitting or my money. I just want to live long enough to find out if I'm red or white."

The stars were beginning to fade before the first light of dawn. The wind lay calm and dew was heavy on Mother Earth. The smells were fresh and sweet. Isaiah noticed Ben was too preoccupied to appreciate the new day. Another beautiful gift from the Great Spirit lost to the eyes and mind of a white man, he thought.

He moved to the wagon and helped Ben harness and hitch. When the neck yoke was in place and the last tug hooked, Ben hurried over and stomped out the fire. Isaiah watched and saw a man driven by something he couldn't quite understand. He asked Ben, "Are you not afraid of cholera?"

Ben adjusted one of the lines and turned to Isaiah before crawling to the wagon seat. "Scared to death. Twice as afraid as I was of the Sioux."

It was too dark to read expressions on either face, but Isaiah knew Ben's mind was made up. He had to respect his friend's dedication and courage. "It is good that your medicine is strong. I hope it is stronger than this sickness. Can I do anything to help?"

"I want the quickest way to Elk Springs, and help me unload this harpsichord. It'll lighten the load because we need to reach Elk Springs as fast as possible. That would be a great help."

Minutes later Isaiah swung into the saddle, and without looking back, headed across the awakening prairie. Ben crawled up and slapped the lines hard across the bays' backs. The team lunged forward and Ben whipped them into a lope. The wagon rattled and lurched over the sod, the trunks and gear doing a shuffle dance from side to side within the small confines. Behind them, the harpsichord squatted like a lonesome stray dog beside the dead campfire.

Hour after hour Ben pushed the team until their bay coats were dark with lather. Several times Isaiah rode beside the wagon and shot Ben a questioning look. Ben had a cigar clenched in his teeth and he didn't answer or slacken his pace.

The overcast of yesterday was gone and the sun burned hot. When it was directly overhead, they came to a small stream where Isaiah pulled up in the shade of a spreading cottonwood. "We'd best let the horses blow and take some water after they've cooled down," Isaiah said.

He slipped from the saddle and began unhitching the team. Their flanks heaved and ribbons of froth hung from the bridle bits. His own mount showed fewer signs of the hard, steady travel.

Ben climbed slowly down, his leg stiff and sore, his face grim and lined. He'd been trying again to remember every word he'd read about cholera, trying to remember every story he'd heard from other doctors. Without his medical supplies he felt helpless. But, if he could save just one life, help someone to live through this, it would justify his still being alive.

They unharnessed and rubbed down the team without a word. Isaiah's face wore a mask of concern as he ran his hands over the four bays. They smelled the water and strained to move to the creek, but he tied them to the wagon while promising them a cool drink later.

Ben dropped the bridles on the ground and asked, "How much longer to Elk Springs?"

Isaiah tied his own horse to a sapling and then said, "I'd say it'd take you about two weeks to walk it."

"What's that supposed to mean?"

Isaiah fished out two pieces of hardtack from his war bag and offered one to Ben. "You keep pushing that team the way you are and you'll damn sure be walking."

Ben drew a deep breath and let it slowly out. His body relaxed and he stared at the horses for a long minute. He ran a hand over his face, then sat down at the base of the cottonwood tree and began rubbing his leg. "Guess I have been pushing too hard. How much longer if we go easy on the horses?"

"If we move out mid-afternoon, make camp at sundown, and pull out early in the morning, we should make town by tomorrow evening."

Ben bit off a piece of hardtack. "How far from Elk Springs to the nearest settlement with a telegraph and railroad?"

"It's a long ride to the talking wire and iron horse. I'd say five -days' ride over the long route."

"And if you don't take the long route?"

Isaiah had been leaning against a tree watching their back trail. Satisfied, he came over and squatted by Ben. "Maybe never. It goes through Sioux territory and some mighty rough terrain. If the rider had a couple good mounts and strong medicine, he might make it in half that time. Why?"

"If you remember, I lost all my medical supplies in the prairie fire. Just wondering how close supplies and information were."

"You aren't thinking of trying that kind of ride are you?"

Ben tossed the last crumb of his hardtack away and watched as a noisy jay flew down and claimed it. "Wasn't thinking of me," Ben said starting to get up. "Let's water the—" He stopped as a small pebble struck his chest. He looked up and saw Isaiah pointing across the stream.

Picking up the Henry, Isaiah moved quickly to Ben's side. "How would you like some buffalo steaks?"

Ben spotted the herd moving slowly in their direction. "I'd rather be hungry than announce our presence with a rifle shot. As I recall, you're not the only Indian in these parts."

"Ho, you're thinking like a Crow." Isaiah exchanged the rifle for his bow. Quickly he stripped to a breechclout and saddled his pony.

Ben watched, fascinated again by the bronze body with its smooth, fluid movements. Well-defined muscles rippled as Isaiah cinched the saddle and strung his bow. Ben thought it would be a perfect specimen for anatomy study.

Since the first time he saw the half-breed in a breechclout, he wondered about the several scars that marred the smooth skin. He wanted to ask, but was afraid Isaiah would then ask about his leg.

Isaiah led his mount over to Ben's side and waited, explaining that the animals had very poor eyesight.

"Won't they smell us?" Ben questioned.

"Little Knife is not listening to the wind. It is blowing from them to us. They will probably walk right down to water before they know we're here. But that would take all the fun out of the hunt."

He mounted and waited until the big shaggy creatures were a hundred yards from the trees before he moved across the stream. There he waited as they plodded to within fifty paces. The chase and kill were quick. Ben was impressed. The horsemanship was as good as he'd ever seen.

Later, as they feasted on the fresh meat, Ben asked, "How old were you when you learned to hunt buffalo?"

Isaiah grinned. "All Crow youth learn at an early age to ride and hunt. It is essential for the survival of the tribe. Good hunters mean the tribe will live and prosper."

"How old?" Ben repeated.

"I think twelve winters."

Ben helped himself to more meat. "Are the buffalo always this easy to find and kill?"

Isaiah shook his head. "It's getting harder and harder for all tribes to find the herds. Since your people have been coming west, the buffalo are disappearing. Soon our people will have nothing to eat. No hides for tipis, no warm clothing. That's why my mother wants me to learn the white man's ways."

"Surely with all this grass and space out here the herds will never disappear."

Isaiah pointed his knife at Ben and then across the stream. "How many animals you think were in that herd?"

Ben took a moment before answering, comparing the herd to the horse herds he remembered back home. "It was big, maybe a thousand head."

"Small herd," Isaiah said between bites. "There are still a few big herds left but nothing like when I was a boy."

Ben checked the sun. "Let's water the horses and move out. I promise I'll take it easy."

"In a minute," Isaiah said leaning back. "But first I want to tell you what a big buffalo herd is like. It is one of my sharpest memories as a child. In a way it is the reason I'm here now."

Ben stood up. "Let's water the horses and get them harnessed and move out. We'll go slow and you can tell me your story while we travel."

After watering the horses and hitching the wagon, they forded the stream and headed south. Isaiah scouted the countryside from a rise, then rode back and fell in beside the wagon.

"It was my tenth Moon of Fattening, and my father and most of the men were hunting. I begged to go but they said I must wait.

"When they were gone, my mother took me away from camp to teach me your language. This day she was telling me about the many whites who lived across the great water. She said they were like the rabbits making many babies, and because their land was full, they were coming across the big water in big canoes, like floating tipis.

"I was only half listening, wishing I could be with the men hunting. After a time we could feel the earth talking to us and the wind brought us a message. I didn't know what they were saying but my mother looked north and smiled.

"Mother Earth began shaking like one does when very cold. Suddenly, I remembered stories the old men told about buffalo stampedes which made the tipis tremble and the noise was like mighty thunder.

"We had to shout to hear each other. The herd stretched so far you couldn't see the beginning or end. The buffalo were bunched so tightly together that we could have walked on their backs from our hill to the hill across the valley. Mother told me a hunter and his horse sometimes get trapped in a herd and that's how they escape.

"It seemed like hours before the herd began to thin. A cloud of dust hung in the valley like thick fog making the sun weak. As the herd disappeared my mother told me that there were more white men in one village called London than there were in that whole herd.

"For many moons after that, whenever I heard the thunder at night, I expected herds of white eyes to come stampeding across the sea of grass to kill us and destroy our village.

"Many times I questioned my mother about the numbers of whites and she always replied that your people are without number like the stars. That is why I promised to live with the whites for three snows. She has almost convinced me the way of the Indian is dying, that the Crows are as living ghosts, not yet able to find their way across to the other life."

Ben started to disagree, but in his heart he knew Isaiah's mother was probably right. He finally said, "I would like to meet your mother and your tribe."

"Ho," Isaiah replied. "It would be a great celebration. Eating, smoking, dancing, and many stories around the campfire. How we defeated the Sioux would make a good story. I would call it the story of naked men who sing and carry rocks. It would be told around Crow campfires for many generations."

Ben wrapped the lines loosely around the wagon break and held out both hands, palms up. "It might make a good story but my hands are full of words, my arms are full of words, even my wagon is full of words! Go find us a place to camp. I've got to think."

The sun paused momentarily on the western horizon, then slid to rest, signaling the stars to take up their heavenly posts as watchmen over the resting earth. A gentle, southerly breeze tiptoed across the grassland carrying the sweet nocturnal fragrance of blossoming springtime.

Isaiah heard and sensed all around him, identifying all the night sounds that belonged, hearing none that didn't. Ben was lost in another frantic search through his memory for medical knowledge about cholera.

At midnight they stopped but didn't make camp, only rolled in their blankets for a few hours of sleep. Ben awoke before the first light teased at the eastern sky. Isaiah's bedroll was empty and his little war pony gone. Ben was backing the harnessed team on either side of the wagon tongue when Isaiah stepped silently beside him to help. Without a word they moved out.

The sun was the height of a tall man above the horizon when Isaiah rode alongside the wagon and offered Ben a small piece of jerky. He accepted it with a simple thanks.

At midday they stopped at a stream only long enough to water the horses and slake their own thirst. Ben's mind held no more room for worry. He'd rethought all his knowledge of cholera and resigned himself to deal with it as best he could.

Isaiah sensed the change. "You are ready to battle the sickness?"

"Not ready, but willing." Ben reached under the seat and retrieved the cigar box. "Only two of these left." He handed one to Isaiah. "We going to make it to town by sundown?"

They shared a sulfur match and when both had the cigars lit, Isaiah answered, "Before sundown. Another hour and we'll see Shoemaker Hill. Only two miles then."

"That's good, I'd sure like to be there before dark."

34

THE CRIPPLED DOCTOR AND HALF-BREED INDIAN passed Shoe-maker Hill an hour before sundown. The grassy knoll stood like a patient sentinel above the empty, rolling prairie. Elk Creek flowed in directly from the north, then looped around the eastern base and followed a snake-like course southwestward.

Rider and wagon swung onto the wide road which ran parallel to the tree-lined creek for half a mile. Then, as if tired of each other's company, the creek veered south, and the road continued due west. Another mile brought them to the crest of a low rise and Elk Springs lay dead ahead, skewed on the end of a long, hard trail.

Ben took it all in with a glance, surprised to find the settlement much larger than he'd imagined. At the edge of town the road turned sharply south and ran between rows of false-fronted buildings. Clapboard houses, log cabins, and a variety of canvas dwellings spread out from the main street. A church steeple poked up from the cluster of rooftops and reflected the setting sun's scarlet rays.

A rise almost as high as Shoemaker Hill dominated the landscape to the north of town, but instead of a smooth, grassy dome, its flat top was crowned with a grove of large oak trees.

Ben saw his wagon train was circled below the trees on the north edge of town. Between the wagons and town, a line of armed Guidon K ranch hands and townsfolk stood grim-faced in the fading light. A mounted rider and a teamster confronted each other halfway between.

Ben saw Isaiah jerk the Henry from the rifle boot. "Put it back," Ben ordered. "We'll work this out peacefully."

Isaiah hesitated, then slid the rifle back, saying, "Most of those are Guidon K hands. Not a peaceable one among the lot."

"You know these men?" Ben asked, reining the team toward the two men.

"Yes, I left – they would say ran yellow – because of my promise to Mother I decided not to kill the big one arguing with Elmo. Name's Jake and if ever a man needed killing, he does."

Ben saw armed teamsters behind every wagon. The Guidon K riders were either damn sure of themselves or damn stupid, he thought. They've not a bit of cover and they don't outnumber us.

Lights began to wink on in the town's streets and then Ben saw armed men at every corner and doorway. Isaiah nodded when Ben looked his way and said, "They're serious. The whole community's out and armed."

Ben was suddenly very angry. Surely the townsfolk could see the teamsters weren't sick. Just once he wished grown men would reason things out with their heads instead of following their emotions.

He checked his own anger and pulled the team to a walk, still heading for Elmo and the big man on the dun. "Isaiah," he said, "ride over and tell the men there'll be no shooting. Weapons down and out of sight."

Isaiah, eyes never leaving the armed men, stayed close to Ben's wagon. "You can fire me later, but I'm staying with you. Jake likes knives and loves to cut people. Besides, he works for the man that runs the town. He could slice you into jerky and get paid extra for the job."

Ben drove his team and wagon between Jake and Elmo, making both give ground. Just enough light remained for him to see Jake's angry face as he reined around to face Ben.

Elmo appeared in front of the wagon with a double-barreled shotgun in his hands. Isaiah pulled up near the rear of the wagon, the Henry now resting in the crook of his arm.

Ben extended his right hand toward Jake. "I'm Dr. Ben Kelley. No need for force or fighting."

Jake spit and ignored Ben's hand. "Before we can talk, you got to get rid of that damn breed. We ran him off once and he still ain't welcome. Besides, the filthy bastards carry disease like dogs carry ticks and we ain't wanting cholera hereabouts."

Ben stiffened. He'd only hated one other man so quickly and intently in his life. If he could have reached Jake, he'd have slapped him like he had Thomas Griswold years ago. A vivid image of the big, arrogant slave trader overran his mind, taking him back eight years to a social occasion in Atlanta.

He was home from Mercer College in the summer of '58 at an urgent request from his father. The letter didn't give a reason for his return, but to Ben it was a welcome excuse to see Adeline.

At Oak Grove his father had come straight to the point, as he always did when business was at hand. "Ben, what's your position on the slave issue?"

"I guess I don't really have a strong position either way, except our economy would suffer greatly without them." He then realized that every student at Mercer had an almost radical opinion about the slave issue except himself.

Sunlight streamed through the window of his dad's study and washed over the rich oak paneling. Cigar smoke mingled in the patina of the wood and leather.

Shoving a ledger book across the desk, his dad spoke as he selected a cigar from the humidor. "Then this decision won't cause you any lost sleep. You're right about the economy and that's why I've contracted to sell all the slaves and all the plantations except five hundred acres where this house and the buildings sit. And, we'll keep a hundred head of the best horses."

Ben sat bolt upright. "Why – when – what are you going to do without the plantations?"

"I believe war is inevitable," the elder Kelley said as he shoved the ledger book at Ben. "That's why I've made these arrangements now." William rose and closed the door and returned to his chair. "There are very few men that know about this so for right now just don't say anything to anyone. I didn't want you to hear it from anyone but me. When this war is fought, the South is foredoomed to fail."

"How can you be so sure?"

"It's really very simple. The South has a population of about eight million with about three million of those being slaves. The North has a population base of some twenty million from which to draw soldiers and support personnel. The South has no army, no navy, no treasury, and very few manufacturing firms capable of producing military hardware. And, it's certain that the South will be cut off from the rest of the world by a blockade."

"That may be so but I'd bet that a good old Southern fighter could whip at least three or four city boys from the North. Maybe even more like a half dozen." Ben argued.

His father leaned back and grinned. "That may be so in the beginning but time will prove otherwise. Those Yankees will learn soon enough. Besides, I imagine you'll be treating the sick and wounded so you'll not be part of the fighting and dying."

"If it comes to war, I'll fight. I like things the way they are," Ben snapped.

William continued. "If we fight and lose, it follows that we'll be in no position to hold our property or work it without slaves. I'm a businessman and I'm protecting my holdings so you and my grandchildren can survive better than the others."

Ben ran a finger down a column of figures, stopped at the bottom, raised his eyes and whistled. "Two million three hundred thousand!"

A smile softened the corners of his father's eyes. "Not bad for an old horse trader, eh? I've invested the three hundred thousand to build a weapons manufacturing plant in Atlanta. The South will need arms and a hell of a lot of 'em. Should be profitable in the beginning anyway."

The young man tossed the ledger on the desk, rose, and began pacing. "So we've got money. What good will that be if we lose as you say we will? And, I'm not so sure we would. What will people say? They'll think we're siding with the North."

The senior Kelley relaxed in his chair and watched his son pace for a moment. "They might say that, but I can do more for the South's cause by furnishing weapons, not slaves. In any event, gold along with the rest of my assets will buy whatever we want or need later, regardless how the slave issue is resolved."

Ben's head was spinning with thoughts of gold, war, fighting, and decisions he'd have to make. How would Adeline take the news? What would his friends say? He heard his father explain that there was physical gold on the property and half of the gold was to be his.

He sat down across from his father, "You said there were other assets. Just what are they?"

"Well, I guess it's time you knew because they are in both our names and if anything happens to me you'll need to manage them. I, rather we, own part of a gold mine, a wagon works, and all of a steamboat company. And we have a small number of shares in a bank in London."

"My god, Dad, I had no idea. When did you have time to manage all this?"

"I made sure that I hired good men to manage my investments. That way I was free to concentrate on what might be another good opportunity. I'm not a planter in the sense of working with crops. I don't know how to work the land, but I do know how to work the system. Oh, and we have a nice amount of railroad stock."

Ben sank back in the chair and tried to grasp what he'd just been told. "Dad, I don't know the first thing about business. I wouldn't know what to do with all your investments if something should happen to you."

"I'm counting on you to learn once the time comes. In the meantime I've listed all the managers in this ledger." He pulled open a desk drawer and handed the book to Ben. "All the information is there, and you'll find they are all Northern men so the investments and managers should, hopefully, be in place when it's over."

Suddenly Ben needed to be alone to think, to see Adeline. He excused himself and prepared for the dance in Atlanta, promising he'd talk more with his father the next day.

The social and Adeline's intoxicating presence made him forget the conversation with his father until Thomas Griswold asked Adeline to dance. She accepted and, while she was waltzing, Ben engaged in idle talk with his friends.

Returning Adeline to Ben's side, Thomas said, "Perhaps, my dear, you would like me to escort you home?"

Ben flushed, Adeline giggled and fluttered her eyes at Thomas. "Whatever for? I'm with Ben. He knows the way to my house." Then added coyly, "When he's here."

Thomas grinned. "I'm always here, but I've heard rumors that Ben and his pa may be moving north. Reckon they don't believe in slaves no more. Guess he don't need no slaves seeing they ain't going to have no land to work. Only thing I'm wondering is—" He paused. "What's the old man going to do when he wants some of that fresh, young, black she-stuff?"

Ben slapped the man hard across the face and demanded satisfaction for the slur on his father's honor. He wanted to settle it then and there with fists but protocol demanded that he give Thomas choice of weapons, time, and place.

He didn't return home that night, but prodded awake Mule Anderson, at the new gun shop in Atlanta. It was two o'clock in the morning when Mule let Ben into the shop to select a brace of dueling pistols.

Mule served as his second, and when the twenty paces separated both men, Thomas's hurried shot grazed Ben's arm. Ben slowly sighted over the barrel at Thomas's colorless face, lowered his pistol, and hollered at Mule. "Get his weapon and reload it. I'll shoot the first man who moves except Mule."

Mule protested and a whisper ran among the select few spectators.

Mule didn't move and Ben snapped, "Mule, do it now, or by damn, I'll shoot you in the knee."

Thomas's weapon was quickly reloaded and as they again stood back-to-back, Ben said to Thomas, "You were stupid to duel with me and you were stupid to miss the first shot. Now I'm going to put a ball right between your eyes unless you make a public apology."

Griswold answered with an oath and ten paces later died with a leer on his face and a .50 caliber ball between his eyes.

A booming cry of "Wagon yonder!" interrupted Ben's memory of hate. All eyes turned toward the road where the dying sun colored the wagon's canvas blood red as it crested the rise east of Elk Springs.

35

GRAND FORKS WAS GRAND ONLY in the mind of the town's oldest resident, an ancient, grizzled road rancher. But forks it was to all travelers, for here they either clung to the wide, well-worn road leading mostly west, or if they were adventurous or hurried, they could choose a lesser-traveled route bearing west by north. Known as the Forks Cutoff, it could save travelers one hundred seventy miles of hard, slow, but safe travel. Or, it could take your life.

The cutoff traversed miles of prairie as unmarked as the trackless ocean. It was a harsh land swept in winter by raging blizzards and in summer by blistering south winds, and any time by the Sioux, Cheyenne, and Arapaho.

At the height of the travel season during the '49 gold rush to California, Grand Forks boasted a population greater than Westport, Missouri. Of an evening, a thousand wagons could crowd the flat plain in a horseshoe bend of the Platte River.

Most travelers, after hearing truth and legend about the cutoff, swung their teams west along the main route. Occasionally there would come the Ben Kelleys and the Samuel Dawsons. Men who by their nature couldn't, or wouldn't, fall in step with the masses.

Samuel Dawson's intense blue eyes scanned the group of men. He was six-feet-two of lean, hard muscle with long blond hair spilling from under a worn Jeff Davis hat. Never still or at ease, his energy sucked up patience like a dry field did the spring rains. Men grew restless in his presence.

He looked once more around the circle of men. "We ain't waiting. Don't know what happened to our guides Hank and Lem, but the only way we'll get to Oregon is to head west – now."

It was settled with little argument, the only question being whether or not to include the group of wagons that had just arrived last night.

A slight, middle-aged man protested. "They're a damn sorry lot. Be slowing us down I reckon. Stock's plumb used up and wagons will be busting down regular like."

"I'm thinking the extra numbers is worth the risk. We can help each other. The old man allows a group of freighters took the cutoff less than a week ago, and we ain't heard of no problem and their tracks should be fresh enough to follow."

No one argued.

"We shove off at high noon. Form up the wagons over by that lone cottonwood."

There were forty-three families and wagons along with the livestock. Enough, they agreed, to make their way safely over the shortcut.

Samuel walked back toward his wagon and family. Before he reached the wagon, eight-year-old Timothy ran to meet him. "We going ahead this morning, Pa?"

Timothy's father reached out a big hand and pushed back the boy's unruly cowlick. "You bet. Pulling out at noon."

The boy whooped with delight as Carolyn watched the two from across the campfire. She wasn't sure if she liked the new Samuel. She loved him – always had, always would – but since the war he'd been very different from the shy, reserved surveyor she married. Two short days after their wedding she'd watched him march off to war with the 20th Ohio. Not to complain, she'd prayed daily for his safety while he fought; she'd thanked God daily since his return.

For some reason known only to him, Samuel had kept his real feelings buried before he became a soldier. She guessed the war had removed any need for pretense. He was what he was.

Sometimes she, too, felt that she lived beneath many layers of deception. She pushed back the strands of hair that had been teased loose by the wind and, using a corner of her apron to protect her hand, pulled a tin of biscuits from the Dutch oven.

She watched the exchange between Samuel and Timothy and knew they were going ahead, guides or no guides. She frowned. She didn't feel that they should leave without hearing from the guides and they sure shouldn't allow the train of Missouri ruffians to travel with them. She wanted to protest, but she smoothed over the ruffled layers of doubt and smiled as Samuel walked up.

He stepped to her side and hugged her close, the top of her head coming only to the middle of his wide chest. Looking down at her he said. "Mrs. Dawson, you're as pretty as the first apple blossom of spring."

She blushed, eyes soft and liquid brown, as she pushed him gently away. "Shame on you. What'll folks think, you being so forward right out in front of everyone?"

He laughed an easy laugh, grabbed her arm, and whispered something in her ear. Her eyes grew wide and the color deepened on her neck and face.

"Samuel Dawson, you're just awful," she said, handing him a plate of biscuits and fried ham. After she fixed plates for Timothy and herself, she moved to the log and sat close to her husband. "Mr. Dawson, when we get to Oregon, I just may see if you can live up to such bragging."

One week later Carolyn Dawson was very afraid. Praying-and-trembling afraid she admitted to herself, but she mustn't let on in front of Samuel and Timothy. Her father and seven brothers had taught her that you can't get nothing done when you're bawling and sniffling. Figure what you gotta do and get to work. Leave the crying and carrying on to the weak ones.

She'd hated to leave the other wagons behind with the sick folk, but getting on and finding help for Samuel was more important. She hadn't even stopped at the last burying, urgently prodding the span of tired oxen past the grim family of mourners. The Missourians had brought a sickness.

Her swelling tide of fear had begun two days earlier when she realized Samuel's symptoms were that of cholera. It clutched at her belly like the icy jaws of a beaver trap. The grip tightened when her husband started retching during the night. By sunup, he was too weak to yoke the oxen. It took Timothy's help before she finally got the oxen teamed up and headed down the faint trail of some previous travelers.

Samuel, wracked by stomach cramps, vomiting, and diarrhea, just lay in the wagon all day. Pray to God he'd survive until they reached the next settlement. Pray to God there'd be a doctor there.

Holding her son's hand and carrying Samuel's rifle, she pressed onward, constantly searching the horizon for a landmark to steer by. Now, at last, the prairie was green again. She shuddered when she recalled the blackened burn they had traveled through earlier. A shiver went up her spine and her neck hair bristled when she remembered the huge pile of cut stone that hinted at ancient rituals and unknown gods. What could it be? Some place of worship for the bloodthirsty savages who roamed the plains?

She scanned the landscape, half expecting to see hordes of painted savages racing toward them. But there was nothing but rolling prairie, a cloudless sky, and the wind. She was weary of the constant wind snapping the wagon canvas, pulling at her long skirt, and forever whipping strands of hair loose from her bonnet and into her eyes. She stopped the oxen, and tucked the hair back in place. "Timothy, I think that's it," she said, pointing into the gathering dusk.

Timothy squinted hard. "Don't see nothing." He dug in his trousers pocket and brought out a rumpled and soiled map. She took the map and handed her son the Sharps rifle, a war trophy that her husband had managed to bring home. She studied the crude map for the thousandth time. "That's got to be Shoemaker Hill," she said, pointing to the map and then back southwest.

"There," he said pointing, "I think I see it. Will there be a doctor there for Pa?"

"Not at the Hill, but the map says it's just a couple miles to a town called Elk Springs."

"If there isn't a doc there, will Pa die like the others? He don't say nothing to me when I talk to him."

Prodding the oxen into motion, Carolyn took Timothy's hand in hers, fear constricting her throat as they walked silently amid the creak of the wagon, the muffled sound of the oxen's hooves in the grass, and the call of night creatures stirring to life.

Timothy tugged at his mother's hand. "Will Pa die?"

She put her arm around the youth, fighting to keep her voice even and calm. "I don't honestly know. He's very sick, but he's also very strong and he loves us very much." They trudged past Shoemaker Hill in silence, mother and son bone weary, lost in their thoughts, fears, and prayers.

Carolyn checked in on Samuel for the hundredth time. The close confines of the wagon were rancid with the vomit and diarrhea that was now uncontrollable. Like Timothy had said, he didn't respond, not even to her promises of help nearby.

She climbed out of the wagon and fell in step with her son. She didn't dare risk speaking, and thankfully Timothy was too exhausted to ask about his father.

Night was spreading a gray-black velvet quilt over the land, the time of day when shadows become nothing and nothing becomes shadows. Carolyn tried to measure distance. How long could it be to the town and how long could they keep going?

Step after weary step. Prod the oxen. Help Timothy struggle one more step. Prod the oxen. Don't think about cholera. Step after exhausting step. Prod the oxen. Look for landmarks. Help Timothy. Pray. Prod the oxen. Step after step after step until at last they crested the rise that revealed the beckoning, twinkling lights of Elk Springs.

"There it is, Timothy. Praise the Lord, just like the map said!" She shoved the Sharps into the wagon, grabbed her son and held him tight, thankful for the gathering darkness; it hid the tears that streaked down her checks.

The oxen sensed the end of an arduous journey and quickened their step. Carolyn released her son, pointed with a sweeping gesture that included Ben's wagons, the town, and the townsfolk. "That must be the train that was ahead of us. Look, the townsfolk are out welcoming them."

Timothy ran and jumped on the wagon, hollering inside, "Pa, Pa, hang on. We're just about to town and a sawbones."

Carolyn gathered her skirts and hurried to the oxen, urging them on. "Come on, Sam and Joe! Grain and rest just yonder."

The rolling boom of a big bore rifle came a heartbeat behind the unmistakable sound of lead impacting living flesh. The big ox shuddered under Carolyn's hand, stumbled, and then collapsed.

She gasped and looked up as the meaning registered. Two armed riders were bearing down hard. The Dawson wagon lurched to a stop. Timothy ran to his mother, "Ma, what's—?"

"Timothy, quick, fetch me the Sharps. My gosh, they've shot poor Sam."

As the two riders galloped closer she grabbed the rifle from her son. "Quick, Timothy, find more cartridges."

Raising the rifle she fired at the nearest horseman, now less than fifty yards away. The recoil forced her back a step. Timothy, mouth open and eyes wide, watched as she levered open the breech. "Hurry, Ma, hurry!"

Her first shot had put down one horse. Its rider, thrown from the saddle, was rising to one knee, pawing for his belt gun. The second rider, sliding to a stop beside his companion, shouldered his rifle. She closed the loading lever on another round, thumbed back the hammer, and raised the Sharps. "We got sick folk here and need a doctor. Go away, leave us be or, so help me, I'll kill you."

Her voice was strained but determined, her focus so intent on the two men that she failed to see the plunging team and wagon until it burst into her view. One moment the teams strained into their collars, the next slid hard on their haunches, halting the rig between her and the ox killers.

Silhouetted against the last glow of sunset, the driver played the lines deftly and rode the plunging wagon like a ship's captain leaning into a rough sea. Sounds of a struggle came from the far side of the wagon and Timothy crowded close to his mother. "Are they helping us?"

"Don't know, but I think so. I pray so." She leveled the gun over the front wagon wheel. "Stay close, and if anything happens to me, try to care for your father best you can."

She watched the driver wrap the lines around the brake handle and speak to someone on the far side of the wagon. His voice was heavy with fatigue and brittle with aggravation. "Don't kill 'em, Isaiah. Just get their weapons and hold them until we sort this all out."

She aimed the Sharps at the driver as he climbed from the wagon and, with the aid of a cane, limped stiffly toward her. If he saw the rifle leveled at his chest, he gave no indication.

He was not quite as tall as Sam and not quite as wide through the shoulders. Several-days' growth of beard blended into unkempt hair, but by his actions and bearing she judged his ragged appearance was not by choice but the result of a long, hard trail.

He stopped with the muzzle of her gun not an arm's length from the top button on his shirt. He ignored the weapon and said, "I'm Dr. Ben Kelley. You all right, ma'am?"

"Yes. No – I mean I'm all right, but my husband's lying terrible sick inside the wagon."

"Townsfolk suspect cholera on a train headed this way. Reckon that's why they shot your ox. Cholera's right terrifying to some people."

Carolyn began to relax her grip on the rifle. "They're right to be so. I lost a passel of kinfolk to it back in '48." Her hands began to tremble and her voice broke.

Ben reached out and took the Sharps and handed it to the boy. "Son, you can put this away now and you best get that yoke off the live ox or it'll get tangled something bad. But first, if you have a lantern, I'll look at your father."

The boy took the gun and climbed into the wagon returning immediately with a lantern.

Carolyn turned at the sound of footsteps and harsh language. "Breed, you'd better kill me now or I'll sure as hell slice you to dog meat the next time we meet."

A long-haired man who moved like a cat shoved two men ahead of his rifle barrel. "And, I should have scalped you a long time ago, Jake. The spirits would rejoice to see your hair dangling from my lodge pole."

The blaze of the safety match nibbled at the lantern wick for a second and then bit brightly. Ben dropped the globe into place and set the lantern on the wagon seat. Carolyn stepped to his side, then whirled, fear back on her face as teams and wagons emerged from the night and circled on all sides.

Ben laid a hand on her shoulder and spoke. "Not to worry. Those are my wagons and men. You're safe now."

In the lantern light, Carolyn turned to face the stranger who seemed too calm, too unafraid. "Are you really a physician?"

"Yes ma'am, educated at Mercer College and got a lifetime's experience during the war. Now, let's hope this isn't cholera, but just some bad food."

Elmo, Frenchie, and Niles had joined Isaiah and at the mention of cholera they exchanged nervous glances through the lantern light. Jake broke the silence. "Knew all along it was cholera. Should have turned you away at Shoemaker Hill. Should have killed every damn one of you."

The men looked her way, some with concern, others with fear. Except for Isaiah, they all drifted away, too afraid or too embarrassed to come near. Carolyn stood by the wagon awaiting word from the crippled doctor, who had appeared like an angel on a chariot, like an answer to prayer.

Gathering Timothy under her arm, she reached in her mind for the dream that had held Samuel and her together. She couldn't find it. It was gone like an apparition scattered by the wind and swallowed by the vast emptiness which seemed without beginning, without end. Out here there was no reassuring wall of cabin or forest to hold dreams and memories together. The hungry wind snatched them away, flung them beyond reach amidst the borderless sky in a country that made dreams disappear like the morning mists that laced the lowlands, beautiful for an instant and then devoured by the burning sun, forever wind, and immense sky. They were gone as if they never existed, and even with her son held close, alone and afraid described her universe.

Looking about at the circled wagons, she was confronted by the long-haired man who had accompanied the doctor. In one hand hung a rifle with a brass receiver that winked back at the lantern as he moved. His other arm carried a bundle which he extended. "Nights get chilly out here when the sun goes down. Thought you might like a coat and blanket."

The concern in his voice didn't match the ferocious countenance. She took the coat and blanket. "Thank you; there is a chill about."

She slipped into the long field coat and draped the blanket around Timothy as Ben climbed down beside them. The kindness of the stranger and the warmth of the coat restored her courage and directness. "Was I right about cholera?"

Ben set down his medical bag and drew a deep breath. "Yes. I'm sorry, but it does appear it is. I've given him some camphor and brandy. He's obviously a very strong man so there's a good chance he'll make it."

"I'm very grateful for your help. Is there anything I should do?"

She was surprised when the doctor reached out and took her hand. His hand was small, almost like a child's compared to Samuel's. But, it was strong and gentle. He turned her hand palm up and then he closed her fingers around a small bottle. "Every fifteen minutes give your husband one drop of this in a half cup of water that has been boiled. Please don't lose or waste any, it's the last I have."

"I'm afraid I can't pay you just now, but—"

She stopped when he held up his hand. "Don't worry about that. You traveling alone or are there other wagons?"

"Forty-two more just behind us."

"Any sick ones that you know of?"

"Been burying them regular since yesterday sunup and someone lying sick in most every wagon."

36

THE SUMMER OF 1867 WAS SPECTACULAR in its beauty and epic in its tragedy. The spring rains had been generous, flooding the prairie with a rainbow-colored carpet of flowers.

The wind blew.

Animals grew fat.

People died.

Residents of Elks Springs found sleep almost impossible. Grim-faced survivors hammered together coffins in the light of day or the dark of night. Heedless of the hours mortals set for work and rest, noisy wagons crawled up and down the streets carrying cholera victims to their final rest.

The Lutheran cemetery gorged itself, overflowing the crude fence which enclosed the hallowed burial ground. Those who found their way inside were the people of means. The poor, the transients, and the ungodly were unceremoniously buried outside of town, their graves marked only by a bare rise of earth among the carpet of grass or occasionally graced with a wooden cross or some personal belonging.

The threat of cholera exposed men's souls, laid bare each citizen's moral fiber. Longtime friends and neighbors were unwelcome and uninvited inside the doorway of their closest friends' homes. Some simply fled Elk Springs, leaving house and home, traveling light, trying to outdistance death. "Avoid Elk Springs" was a byword that passed up and down the trail. Westward travelers sought circumventing routes across unfamiliar, hostile country. Before the moon of gathering, Sioux, Cheyenne, and Arapahoe lodge poles hung heavy with fresh scalps.

Then, seemingly bored with destroying white flesh, cholera turned its morbid attention to the red man. The wail of mourning echoed from lodge to lodge and swept the hunting grounds like a raging blizzard.

Dying and burying were the main event of '67. Whites hacked dark chambers in the sod, lowering the dead down closer to the netherworld, while the Indians lifted their dead up into trees or on scaffolds, nearer the unfettered sky and soaring spirits.

The prairie grieved.

In Elk Springs Ben enforced a strict quarantine of the sick, and ordered the burning of soiled clothing and even some wagons and their entire contents. He insisted that camps of the sick were moved daily. And, he dispensed the vital medication that Isaiah brought by riding two hundred miles in two days to bring back the latest medicine.

Some people ignored Ben's unbending rules and unconventional treatment of the disease, clinging to the belief that it was caused by atmospheric conditions. Those who chose to ignore, died.

Ben pondered often about his newfound knowledge of cholera. Through the long hours of waiting and caring for the sick, he searched for a reasonable explanation. He found none. Someday he would speak to Isaiah about the vision that came to him on the wind. Isaiah would understand, but for the present he kept it within himself.

Sitting with Samuel Dawson, waiting for him to die, and listening to the south wind tear at the canvas of the big Conestoga, Ben remembered an army bulletin issued after the cholera outbreak of '48. Or had he really remembered? Had he even read the bulletin? He couldn't remember seeing it, what it looked like, or who had written it.

Had the wind spoken to him as it did to Isaiah? He felt that he had breached the world of the spirits, yet he knew the information was true. His regret was that it came too late to save Samuel and Timothy Dawson.

Dr. Benjamin Kelley saw the epidemic through to the last sick patient, saving those he could and comforting the dying and the living. He won the hearts and respect of the people not by miracle treatment and cures, but by concern. He pushed himself through the days and nights until exhaustion forced him to sleep for an hour or two. Then he would be about his rounds again. To the grateful community he was no longer Ben, but affectionately called "Doc."

By the time the epidemic was over, there was no chance of continuing west with the wagons for it was too late to make the passes safely. For Doc and his men, the survivors of the ill-fated Dawson train, and the others who had felt the sting of cholera, it was a question of remaining in Elk Springs until next year, or turn around and head back east, abandoning their dreams of a new start in the Willamette Valley of Oregon.

As the leaves of the willows and cottonwoods changed into their fall colors, Elk Springs had gained in population. Isaiah moved freely about the town, accepted because of his heroic ride for medicine and because he worked for Doc Kelley.

As humans are wont to do in good times or bad, the people of Elk Springs made love and fought. Doc was busy, and he hadn't had his nightmare in months.

37

ELK SPRINGS, NEBRASKA, FALL 1868

Carolyn Dawson stepped through the gate and closed it softly behind her as she'd done every Sunday morning for the past year. A weathered sign proclaimed the fenced area as the Elk Springs Lutheran Cemetery.

Carolyn stopped just inside the fence and let the morning settle over her. A calm that came only occasionally to the prairie was pristine this morning. Not a leaf rustled on the cottonwood trees, and soft, first light caressed the polished headstones conspicuous among many crude and primitive markers. The clear song of the meadowlark drifted like a melodic mist over the land. She felt it was a fitting day to deliver her decision to Samuel and Timothy.

The morning was already warm as she placed a small bouquet of flowers on her husband's and son's graves. She took the shawl from her shoulders and spread it between the graves and then knelt. She read a passage from Matthew, said a short prayer, and then sat down.

So quiet and peaceful, so hauntingly beautiful this land could be, she thought, but I must tell them. In a voice respectful of the hushed daybreak she began, "Samuel and Timothy, I know I promised never to leave you alone here, but I must go. God knows I have grown to love this land, but I don't have a choice. I hope you can understand."

She sat with legs drawn up under her chin, her yellow dress starched and pressed, a red ribbon tied in her hair – a rare flower gracing the grassland. She stared eastward, not seeing the red-tailed hawks circling above Shoemaker Hill and a pair of prong-horn antelope gliding gracefully along Elk Creek.

"You both know I'm no quitter," she began, then paused to check the anger that she heard in her own voice. She didn't, no, couldn't blame them. At first, she'd blamed God, she'd blamed the Missouri ne'er-do-wells, and she'd even blamed Doc Kelley. Now, all but a hint of bitterness was gone from her heart.

She began again, "Times are hard here now and I've been un-able to find work since Mrs. Sutton had to let me go. After the chol-era epidemic the trail shifted south. To the north the mines have played out and the railroad is going to miss Elk Springs. I think it best if I go back to Ohio and start following another dream."

She closed her eyes against the tears that threatened. "There will never be another dream like ours. It was good but now I must let it go. And you must let me go. Please, please understand if I don't return."

Without more words or a backward glance she gathered her shawl and Bible and walked slowly to the cemetery gate. There arose no words from hell to condemn her, no overpowering guilt from within. She knew her goodbye was accepted, her soul free to live and dream again.

As she closed the gate behind her and walked slowly toward town, she saw objects clearer and more distinct than ever before, as if seeing them for the first time. Oak Grove was startling in its beauty. She stopped and pondered the white mansion as it basked in the rays of the awaking sun. The stately old oak trees stood behind and on each wing, like protective and loving arms enfolding a child. She finally understood why it had caused so much talk in town last summer. She remembered hearing the comments in the eatery, but at the time she was too filled with grief to pay attention. Now in the early morning light, she un-derstood why people had exclaimed, "Damn miracle, that's what it is. He hauled that big house all the way from Georgia and put it up in one summer."

She did remember Doc's men and local carpenters working on the house almost around the clock that summer. They'd come in for the evening meal and to talk about the house. Now, realizing how big it was, she too thought it a miracle.

She wondered if Doc really was richer than Captain Keeferly. Had Doc bought the hill just to spite the captain as some folks said? What happened to his leg, really? Was he ever married? She'd heard whispers about a dark-haired Southern belle. Were they true?

More than once she'd wanted to go to Oak Grove and thank him for trying to save her family. She had never offered to pay him even though she always intended to. Maybe she should go right now and thank him, and offer to pay. But she realized she was almost penniless.

The sun broke over Shoemaker Hill striking the steeple on the church and the huge mansion. The town still lay in the shadows giving the appearance that the house floated in the heavens. The many windows of glass and the fresh white paint glinted with a fiery glow. It was haunting and beautiful to Carolyn.

38

DOC HAD BEEN UP MOST OF THE NIGHT and now, just before sun-up, he sat at his desk and recorded the events of the last twenty-four hours. Finished, he closed the journal and slid it back on the shelf thinking it was sure a pleasure to record births instead of deaths. And, it had been a long time since he felt so useful and needed. Perhaps getting stranded in Elk Springs was a blessing. Maybe this was the place out west where he was meant to start anew. He realized it had been months since the nightmare had ridden through his dreams.

Elmo and Niles had done well, laying out the house to take advantage of nature's finest assets. Sitting at his desk he could see the first rays of sunlight striking the chandelier, sending blue fire racing through the crystals. He scrawled a note reminding him-self to try again to order replacements for the crystals destroyed by the Sioux rifle ball.

Doc got up from his desk and closed the study door. Then, drawn by feelings he lacked the courage to explore, he moved to the east window like he'd done every Sunday morning for months. Standing to the side of the window he peered across the top of the town and toward the cemetery where he saw Carolyn Dawson as he'd seen her every Sunday morning.

He'd discovered her visits by chance. Last fall, after being up all night with a patient, he'd stood by the window to watch the sunrise, much as he was doing now. Some slight movement along Elk Creek had captured his attention.

Indians had scalped young Freddy Shoemaker some weeks ago and he thought perhaps they were back. He used the officer's field glass to scan the prairie, finding only deer moving along the tree line. Then, sweeping the glass over the town, he'd discovered Carolyn Dawson kneeling by her loved ones' graves. From that day until now he couldn't help himself from viewing her Sunday morning visits.

He'd wondered and thought about her, but never had the courage to seek her out. He'd been out on social occasions with a few of the town's eligible ladies but they were like the whore in Atlanta. They didn't count. The ones whom he thought he could care about were threatening. Adeline's rejection was still an open wound, one he was powerless to treat.

Watching Carolyn, lost in his thoughts, the opening door made him jump. Guilty like a damn spying kid, he chastised himself and laid the glass on the Victorian table. What the hell? It was his house and his window. He'd damn well watch what, or whom, he wanted.

"Come, Isaiah, since you're already in," he said.

Doc made his way to his chair, leaned his cane against the desk, and once seated, selected two cigars from the humidor and tossed one toward Isaiah who had moved to the window. "She is pretty like the flowers, right?"

Doc stopped in the middle of lighting his cigar. "Who's pretty? Did that black mare foal?"

Isaiah turned from the window, sat in one of the red leather chairs that faced the desk, and fired his cigar. "You were not looking at horses." He grinned and pointed to the glass on the table.

"You appear to know a lot about what I do. You been sneaking around and spying on me? And, don't give me that stuff about listening to the wind. There's no wind this morning."

"Widow Dawson could ask you the same question about spying. And, from your training as a Crow you should realize that Old Man Wind doesn't always run. Sometimes he walks quietly, but he is always there if you listen. This morning he told me two things."

Isaiah had become a part of the Elk Springs community, and he'd even cut his hair short and went to church with Doc from time to time. He always wore a brightly colored flannel shirt, a leather vest, and faded trousers. Except for the bandanna he occasionally wore tied around his black hair, he looked like the average working hand. A belt knife instead of revolver was always on his hip.

Doc had learned a wealth of knowledge about this land from his friend. "Did the wind tell you when that black mare is going to foal?"

"Nope, wind don't have to tell me that. She'll foal tomorrow."

Doc leaned back and blew smoke toward the ceiling. "That'll make sixty-three colts so far. By the time they've all foaled your half's going to be about a hundred head. What's a civilized Crow going to do with that many horses?"

Isaiah ran a hand through his hair. "Maybe I'll take them back to my people. I'd like to see my mother again and show her how I've done in the white-eyes' world. It's been almost three snows now, but I'm not sure I'm civilized yet."

They both thought on that in silence, cigar smoke moving about the room, touching the big grandfather clock, kissing the rich oak woodwork, and drifting around the books and bookshelves, then hung like a soft blue curtain in the sun's shafts.

Isaiah grinned and said, "Or maybe I'll just buy a squaw." He pointed his cigar at Doc. "You should buy a squaw too. Hell, you should buy three or four to help around this big lodge."

The only thing that the two had never discussed was the opposite sex. As the smile left Doc's face, Isaiah knew that he'd touched pain within his friend.

"No," Isaiah said. "You don't need to buy a squaw. You just need to listen to the wind."

"All right, what two things did the wind tell you this morning?"

"Carolyn Dawson is going to leave Elk Springs."

"And?"

"She will visit the graves no more. Her time of singing the song of mourning is finished."

Doc glanced at the window. "I'm glad her grief has passed, and I hope she finds happiness wherever she goes. She was a tremendous help during the cholera, strong as any woman I've seen."

"Ho," Isaiah snorted. "My friend doesn't hear and doesn't see much either."

"Meaning?"

"Meaning you don't see what you have, and what you could have."

"I know I have a house full of patients that I need to check on. Saturday nights are crazy. Damn sheriff must leave town every Saturday. Had two broken arms, a knife wound, and one bullet wound last night, plus a birth."

Isaiah stood and moved to the window. "Fighting and making babies is what it's all about." Without turning, he held up his hands. "I know how you feel about fighting, but nothing a man can do makes the blood run so hot."

"I can certainly attest that fighting makes the blood run and I personally have seen enough."

Isaiah turned from the window. "The graceful lady with the palomino hair is gone. You won't be able to watch her from here anymore."

"If I really want to, I can see everyone from up here." He rose, gathered his medical bag and cane. "If I can get away from here this afternoon, I'd like to ride out and look over the horses."

As they left the study, the faint rhythm of hammer on anvil reached through the open windows of Oak Grove.

Carolyn walked toward the small house she rented but suddenly turned toward Elmo's blacksmith shop. She had heard the sound of his hammer and knew he was at the shop even though it

was Sunday morning. She would ask him if he'd buy her belongings. They weren't much, but maybe enough for fare back home.

The cook stove needed repair and she feared the small parlor
stove had a cracked fire pot, but maybe he could find some use
for them. Her pride wilted like a drought-stricken sunflower and
she almost retraced her steps as she neared the smithy lean-to,
but she steeled herself for the necessary task and stepped around
the opening into the shadows, then froze at the scene before her.

Elmo reached out a huge hand and took the horse's reins. "I
don't care if the last smithy gave you credit. I deal in cash. That's
six bits or this horse ain't going nowhere. Especially when you
roust a man out early on the Lord's day."

Captain Keeferly and Jake had been at his door the very day
he'd taken over the business after the former owner had died of
cholera. The two, using veiled threats, explained how they expected Elmo to run his business when it came to doing work for
the Guidon K.

Why in the hell have I put up with the sons of bitches this
long he asked himself, then realized it wasn't proper thoughts for
a Sunday morning before church, but every time I think on the
captain I get unholy angry.

Elmo knew it was not right to hold a man's horse, but looking up at the sneering, arrogant ranch hand, he tightened his
grip. Jenny was here now and you couldn't take care of a family
with promises and threats.

"Let go, you big hairy bastard before I gut shoot you," the
ranch hand swore.

The veins swelled along Elmo's neck, muscles bunched and
corded. "You can tell the captain I'm not doing no more work on
credit. You cough up six bits or I pull that shoe right now."

The man's draw was almost too quick for Elmo. But anticipating the move, Elmo yanked hard on the bridle bit, stepped
under the horse's neck as it reared, and tore the man from the
saddle like a child's doll. His hand closed over the gunman's
hand and revolver. He squeezed.

Carolyn winced as bone snapped, dropped her Bible, and clasped a hand over her mouth.

Tearing the weapon from the man's hand, Elmo flung him against the smithy wall. Tools rattled against one another and then swayed silently like dozens of pendulums without clocks. Elmo deftly removed the .44 Remington's cylinder, tossed it into the water cask, and chucked the gun into the forge.

The Guidon K rider pulled himself to his feet and stood like a rodent paralyzed by the unblinking eyes of a snake. Elmo moved quickly, at home in the smithy like a cook in a familiar kitchen. He pumped the forge billows, once, twice, three times. The coke went white hot. He spoke softly to the horse and picked up the forefoot that he'd just shoed. In a few seconds the clinched nails released their grip and he pried off the shoe. Elmo pitched it at the scrap pile.

He grabbed tongs, fished the Remington from the bed of coals, laid it on the anvil, and the echo of a half-dozen hammer strokes still sounded when the weapon hissed into a water cask. Steam was rising from the water as Elmo fished the gun out, its grips charred black and the barrel hammered flat. He thrust the gun at its owner. "Now get the hell out and don't come back."

The man threw the gun down and gathered the horse's reins. "I'll be back, and I promise we'll run you out of town." Horse and owner limped off down the street.

Elmo watched him go and drew a great breath. He exhaled and shuddered, then shook his shaggy head and looked around as if getting his bearings in an unfamiliar place. Carolyn was still glued to the patch of shadows just inside the corner. "I've come at a bad time," she finally stammered.

Elmo's face lifted and he smiled. "Sorry, I didn't see you come in. What can I do for you, Mrs. Dawson?"

Carolyn glanced down the street after the departed horse and man. "That was a Guidon K hand, wasn't he?"

"Yep, despicable lot far as I'm concerned."

"Aren't you afraid Captain Keeferly will do something awful to you? He isn't a man who likes his things to be broken."

"Didn't come out here to work without pay." He retrieved her Bible, dusted it with his shirtsleeve, and handed it to her. "Looks like you're early for services this morning."

"Well, actually I've come to talk business, if you don't mind being it's the Sabbath."

His eyes twinkled. "Business with a lovely lady is a pleasure any day of the week as long as she doesn't wear the Guidon K brand."

Instead of smiling back, a cloud crossed over Carolyn's face. "Not yet anyway."

"Now what on earth you meaning by a statement like that?"

"Jobs are right hard to come by for a widow woman, and the captain has been after me to come and be house servant in his new house."

"You don't say. Thought an old Mexican had that job."

Carolyn watched as Elmo went to the scrap pile where he retrieved the shoe and put it in a bin. "Ever since Doc Kelley put up his house, people around town have said the captain is mad with jealousy. Built that new house on the ranch to outdo Doc and wants a woman around the house to impress his important friends."

Elmo believed the captain was crazy for power and money, and the thought of him taking advantage of Carolyn, or any woman, rekindled his anger anew. He decided to bend his rule of not interfering in another's personal life. "Mrs. Dawson, if you're looking for work why don't you go talk to Doc?"

He believed he saw a hint of blush at the ruffle collar about her slim neck. I'll be damned, he thought.

"Why should I talk to Doc Kelley about a job?"

"You must not be keeping up your end of the gossip mill. Just the other night at the War Bonnet he was saying how busy he was and could use a nurse. Babies, bar fights, Indians, and the such."

"That's nice, but I'm no nurse."

Elmo banked the forge fire and put away his tools before turning to Carolyn. "Not wanting to bring back painful memories, but

I'm remembering how you pitched in and helped with the sick when the cholera hit us. And that after you'd lost your own. Heard more than one survivor say you was an angel right enough."

Carolyn dropped her eyes and was silent. Elmo fidgeted with his heavy leather apron, and finally broke the uncomfortable silence. "Sorry, Mrs. Dawson. Hoping you'll forgive me, but it's the honest-to-god truth. People love you almost as much as they do Doc."

"I've always liked people, but if they like me so much, how come I can't get any work?"

"Got to understand this here town. Sickness was hard on people. Trains didn't come. Less money. And, if people don't work for the captain, he can make it mighty rough."

"I'm beginning to see that. This country kind of grows on a person, but I've decided to move back to Ohio as soon as I can save enough money. I do hate to run because of the likes of Captain Keeferly."

"Mrs. Dawson, promise me you'll go see Doc about that job?"

Carolyn stood with her back to Elmo staring toward Oak Grove. "Thanks, Elmo, your concern is appreciated. Life is so strange isn't it?"

Elmo followed her gaze to Oak Grove, where the morning sun struck the white columns and winked off the many glass windowpanes. In a way it looked out of place. Yet it fit, as if the hill and grove of oaks had been planned with the house in mind. Elmo spoke as he and Carolyn gazed up at the house. "I reckon life is strange for sure, but what'd you mean in particular?"

"There sits Oak Grove, a Southern mansion in Yankee land. I used to pray that my husband would be spared from you dastardly rebels. Now you all are some of my best friends. And the captain, a Union man, is despicable. Kind of makes all the killing and fighting seem worthless."

"You're beginning to sound like Doc. By the way, would be beholden to you if you didn't mention this little ruckus to him. He kinda doesn't like fighting much any more."

She turned to him and said. "Thanks, Elmo, you're a good and true friend."

"Seeing how you're ready for services, have some breakfast with Jenny and me and then we'll go to church. We can talk business over the noon meal. I won't take no for an answer."

– 39 –

"IS HE STILL ALIVE?" Captain Keeferly asked as he reined in beside the wagon. The riders and mounts wore the fatigue of battle and hard travel like a heavy mantle. The horses were caked with dried lather and trail dust, the men were red eyed, dust covered, and grim faced. A stiff drink and a full night's sleep were foremost in all their minds, but the unrelenting discipline of Captain Keeferly kept each rider alert in the moonlit night.

After a hard-fought scrimmage with a band of Sioux two days ago, and being in the saddle since, the twenty-man escort still maintained a textbook diamond escort of the team and wagon. Jake Smith rode point while Shorty Auld rode drag, the rest of the crew fanned out to form the flanks.

The Guidon K wagon carrying young Todd Keeferly lumbered slowly along in the protective center. Angelo Duarte, the loyal ranch house servant, rode in the wagon and watched over the still form resting on a bed of hay and blankets. The young man had not moved for some time and Angelo placed his hand to the boy's neck. "Yes, Captain, he's alive."

"Still have a fever?"

"Yes sir, but it's not worse. I hope the doctor is home tonight because your son needs more than I can do for him."

"The bastard had better be home and best be good at keeping people alive," the captain growled.

They continued through the night. Jake pulled long and often at the flask he always carried; not much longer and we'll be in Elk

Springs, he thought. Checking the stars, he decided there would be time for drinks at the Bear Skin saloon and then he'd spend the night at Madam Marie's place. He licked his lips before taking another pull at the flask, then corked it, and wiped his mouth with the back of his hand.

Riders and wagon splashed through the crossing on Elk Creek and rounded the cottonwood grove that formed the southern limits of the town. Main Street was alive with a Saturday night crowd of small ranchers and homesteaders driven by the Indian raids to the safety of the only large settlement within a hundred miles of open range.

Captain Keeferly left the wagon and rode ahead to Jake. "Nobody leaves this detail until I dismiss them."

"The boys are going to want a drink and some shuteye and I was hopin' to—"

The captain cut him short. "I don't give a damn what they want. I pay 'em and they stay until I say different. Understood?"

Jake nodded and reined around to pass the order to the others. The captain continued to lead the group down Main Street past late-night drinkers and gamblers who had quit the saloons to seek the cool night air. Sheriff Barton and his deputy were crossing the street and stopped to "howdy" the captain. They received a curt answer and had to move off the street to let the riders pass.

The deputy pushed back his soiled hat. "Wonder what's got a burr under his saddle?"

Sheriff Barton watched them move up the street toward Oak Grove. "Had someone in the back of the wagon, probably a run-in with the Injuns. Damn strange though; didn't think he'd ever bring anyone to Doc Kelley." The sheriff watched them pull up at Oak Grove, thinking the old bastard has been more unpredictable and stranger than usual lately. Must be something damn serious afoot.

Captain Keeferly drew rein and sat looking at the sprawling white house, hating it and hating Doc Kelley. If that goddamn sawbones lets Todd die, I'll kill the son of a bitch, he vowed to himself.

Jake nodded toward the house and the lamplight that shone from the windows. "Looks like he's here. You want me and Shorty to carry Todd inside?"

The captain sat the saddle as if in a trance. All his hate for Doc welling up like bile in his throat. Why the hell did it have to come to this? If Todd wasn't the only one to keep the Keeferly name alive, he'd let old Angelo do the best he could and just ride away. But, Angelo had begged him to get the boy to a doctor and he'd given in when Todd slipped into unconsciousness.

"Shall we take him in?" Jake repeated the question.

"God, I hate this. Having to ask that bastard for help is harder than fighting Indians."

Jake was not deep enough to understand just why the captain hated Doc, but he did understand hate. If the boss hated this man then he hated him also. It was the only way Jake knew. He waited for a word from the captain.

"Just keep 'em all here in the yard for a spell." Then he turned and rode to the wagon. "How is he, Angelo?"

"Not good, sir. His back is as rigid as a corral post. I've never seen this before."

The captain dismounted, climbed into the wagon, and knelt by his son.

Inside the house Doc finished checking Mrs. Avery and her newborn son. He turned to the father. "They'll both be fine, Red. You've got yourself a healthy son. The missus lost a great deal of blood, but with rest and good care she'll be fine, although I do want to keep her here for a few days."

The redheaded father, rolling and twisting the brim of his hat, looked from his wife to the baby. "I'm sure beholden to you, Doc. We don't have much money, but the next time we butcher a beef, I'll bring you a hindquarter."

Doc snapped his medical bag shut. "Don't worry about it. If you like, you can sleep in one of the other rooms tonight."

Red broke into a grin and stretched. "Well, I kind of thought I'd go down to the saloon and brag to the boys."

Carolyn Dawson came into the room and tucked the quilt around the sleeping baby. Her bright green dress set off her rich blond hair that shone in the lamp light. A few strands had fallen over her forehead and she brushed them back with a slim hand before removing her shoes to ease tired feet. It made her seem even smaller than her petite five-feet-three inches.

But even the tired feet and late hour didn't dim the light in her brown eyes. She smiled at Doc as Red bent over the crib. "Young feller, you're about the best dang thing ever happened on the Rocking A spread. Going to make a good hand I'm betting."

Doc smiled back at Carolyn, thinking how rewarding it was to help bring a new life into the world, especially to a fine young couple like the Averys.

Back in his study, Doc sat down and recorded the Avery birth in his journal. With satisfaction he noticed it had been several pages since he'd recorded a death. He appreciated how good it felt and how good life had become.

Carolyn stepped through the door. "Mrs. Avery would like something to drink and maybe something to eat. Should I make some tea and gruel?"

"That's just what she needs. As soon as you finish, you can go for the night. When that big, proud redhead leaves, maybe I can get some rest too."

Carolyn smiled. "I don't think he can decide whether to stay with the boy or go brag about him."

Doc watched her leave the room and realized he looked forward to her arrival at the house every morning and to her warm smile. She was becoming a good nurse and if she wanted, she had a job for as long as she liked.

His thoughts were interrupted by footsteps on the front porch. He laid aside his pen and headed for the door, knowing that callers at this hour usually meant sickness or injury. He'd hoped for a few hours of sleep, but he'd never turned away a patient.

40

DOC WAS HALFWAY ACROSS THE PARLOR when the door flew open and Captain Keeferly stepped through and held it as Jake and Shorty carried Todd inside. Noticing the trail-worn condition of the men, Doc figured they'd had a run-in with some Indians.

He pointed to the sofa. "Put him down there until I have a look. How bad is he wounded?"

Captain Keeferly crossed the room until he stood directly in front of Doc. "He ain't hurt, he's sick. I don't like doctors and I especially don't like you. But you're going to help my son and if you don't put him on his feet again, I'll run you out of the country, or worse."

Taken aback by the outburst, Doc met the man's glare. "I'll do all I can for your boy but there's no need for threats," he said, stepping around the man to check Todd's pulse.

Shorty went back outside as Jake leaned against a hallway doorjamb and helped himself to another nip on the flask before unsheathing his large Bowie knife and began picking at the dirt under his fingernails.

Without looking up, Doc asked, "How long has he been unconscious?"

"Don't know."

"When did he first feel sick?"

"Don't know that either."

"Well, what can you tell me about this that might be helpful?"

When Doc straightened up, the captain grabbed his arm

with such force it threatened his balance. "You son of a bitch, you're supposed to be the great healer. You tell me what's wrong with my boy."

Doc struggled to retain his calm, but his voice was loud when he answered, "Captain, I'll do the best I can, but anything you can tell me about your boy would be helpful."

Across the room, Jake watched and waited as he drew a small whetstone from his vest pocket and began to strop the knife blade.

Doc shook off the captain's hand and turned to leave. "I want to examine your boy before we move him. I'll be back in a minute."

When he returned with his medical bag, Jake was still playing with his knife and the captain was pacing back and forth by the sofa. He whirled on Doc. "I swear by god, you'd better not let my boy die."

"I will do the best I can for your son," Doc repeated.

Down the hall in the Averys' room, Carolyn gathered up the dishes on a tray, checked the sleeping baby, and said, "You two sure do have a handsome boy. I don't know when I've seen a young one with so much hair."

Mrs. Avery looked at her husband, "Yeah, he sure does have his daddy's red hair. But I just hope and pray he doesn't have his daddy's temper."

Red Avery tried hard to keep a solemn face. "Ah, honey, you know it was that fire in me that made you want to marry me."

Carolyn picked up the tray and moved to the door. "I'll leave you two to argue by yourselves. Good night."

Carrying the tray down the long hall, she heard angry voices from the parlor. She immediately recognized Captain Keeferly's belligerence. "I'll tell you one last time, I don't know when he got sick or what he's eaten lately. From now on I'll ask the questions unless you want another bad leg."

Doc removed the stethoscope from Todd's chest and snapped, "Perhaps you two should wait outside, or better yet, come back in the morning."

Carolyn had never heard Doc raise his voice. She quickened her pace.

Jake pushed himself away from the doorjamb as the captain shouted, "We're staying here with Todd and you're going to shut up and get to work. Where's this exam room?"

Carolyn was almost running as she rounded the door to the parlor and slammed into Jake. A teacup crashed to the floor. Jake whirled and lashed out with the knife and the blade drew a crimson line across Carolyn's breasts.

Captain Keeferly spun at the sound of the cup hitting the floor, saw Jake react, and grabbed him before the knife slashed again. "Goddamn it, Jake!" he bellowed.

Jake stood on the balls of his feet, tense, eyes glittering with high emotion.

"Captain, get that son of a bitch out of my house! You're both crazy!" Doc shouted.

Carolyn stood with her hands over the wounds, blood making a dark stain on her dress. She sagged against the wall as Doc reached her. "Come on, Carolyn. Let's get you down to the examination room. I'll have to stop that bleeding."

Keeferly grabbed him and shoved him toward the sofa. "You're not going anywhere. She's just cut some. My boy may be dying."

Jake stood by the front door turning the knife, studying it in the lamplight. Carolyn opened her mouth, and Jake waved the knife at her. "Woman, you sit down and shut up." Carolyn backed up and sank down on a Victorian settee.

Red Avery entered the parlor and stopped short as the scene unfolded before him. "What the hell's going on here?"

The captain faced the small-time rancher. "You best give me that six-gun."

The redhead's hand dropped to the Colt at his hip. "Carolyn, who did this to you?"

She pointed out Jake with her eyes as Doc spoke to Red. "We've a sick man here and don't need trouble. Do as he says."

Red clawed at his holster. Jake's arm moved and the knife rode a quick, golden thread of lamplight to Red's shoulder and buried its long blade deep. It beat the Colt by a fraction of time causing the slug to plow into the floor at Jake's feet. Red tried to change the gun to his left hand but it tumbled to the floor.

The old fighting spirit overcame Doc. He braced his bad leg against the sofa and swung his cane at Keeferly. It caught the captain a glancing blow which he warded off before driving a right fist into Doc's chin sending him sprawling onto the floor.

Red had scooped up the fallen Colt with his left hand but Jake kicked him in the head before he could get off a shot. The big man then reached down and jerked the knife from Red's shoulder, wiped it on the redhead's shirt, and returned it to his sheath.

Shorty burst through the door, gun in hand. "We heard a shot, are—"

The captain cut him short. "We're fine. I want you and the boys to spread out around the house. Secure the perimeter. Nobody comes or goes unless I give the word. Now get going, soldier."

Shorty looked confused and shot a glance at Jake who also looked surprised. "Go ahead, Shorty. I'll be out and talk to you later."

Doc pulled Red's gun across the floor with his cane.

"Put it down, or die." Doc looked up into the barrel of the captain's revolver. Slowly, reason prevailed and he placed the gun back on the floor and struggled to his feet, a trickle of blood showing at the corner of his mouth.

"You win for now. Let me attend to these people."

"First, my boy," he said to Doc before turning to Jake. "You take the redheaded son of a bitch and throw him out."

"He needs medical attention," Doc protested.

"I said he goes. Have two of the boys haul him down to the War Bonnet. Old Curt can patch him up if he isn't too drunk to stand. It'll serve notice for folks to stay away from here." Jake grabbed the redhead under the arms and dragged him out the door.

Captain Keeferly pushed the door shut. "Now get busy with my boy."

Doc tried to focus his thoughts. He'd hit the captain and if he could have gotten Red's gun he would have shot Jake and killed Keeferly. The realization shook him. That wasn't what he came west for. Could it be that he really hadn't changed at all?

"Damn it, Doc, move!" The captain's voice, closer now, jolted him back to reality. So far, he had no idea what was wrong with Todd. Carolyn sat rigid, her brown eyes smoldering, her face white and drawn. She needed care, yet so did the boy. "Can you carry your son to the examination room?" he addressed the captain, who nodded. "I'll go get things ready and be right back," Doc said.

"Carolyn, you come with me," Doc added and led the way down the hall and into the exam room. "I won't have time to look at you until I can pacify the captain. Do you think you can hold up for just a little longer?"

"Yes. I'll be all right if the bleeding will stop."

He went to the row of shelved bottles and took down a large brown container, grabbed some bandages, and handed them to Carolyn. "Put some of this on the cuts and bandage it the best you can. I'll have a look at you just as soon as Todd's taken care of. You can use the study."

She paused before leaving the room. "What's wrong with the captain? He's acting crazy."

"Damned if I understand it either. One thing's for sure – his boy is very ill and it sure seems to have him on a short fuse. Now, go before he gets here."

Doc went back and led Captain Keeferly, carrying his son as easily as if he were a doll, to the examination room. Doc pointed to the table. "Put him down there."

Doc looked at the boy's father after he'd completed a quick exam. "Captain Keeferly, can you have one of your men draw a bucket of fresh well water? I'll also need some water heated in the big boiler from the back porch. And have one of your men go to the barn and bring a couple dozen ears of corn to kitchen." He braced himself for another outburst. It never came, and the captain obeyed without question.

The pail of water arrived within minutes and Doc instruct-ed the captain how to bathe the boy's head, cautioning him not to allow any of the water to enter the boy's mouth. "That's just the ticket," Doc commented as he watched the big, rough hands dampen the towels and apply them to Todd's face and forehead. "Just keep the towels cool, I'll be back shortly."

"Where do you think you're going?"

"To the kitchen," he answered, thinking he sure as hell couldn't go far with the place surrounded with men who are or-dered to shoot to kill. In the kitchen he gathered the ears of corn and dropped them into the boiler.

"Captain," Doc said, "I don't know what's wrong with your son but he is gravely ill. In fact, the outlook is not good." He braced for an outburst; this time it came.

The captain dropped the wet towel and charged around the ta-ble. "What the hell do you mean the outlook isn't good? I brought my son to the almighty Dr. Kelley. Don't tell me the outlook's not good. And just what does that mean in doctor language?"

"It means I will use every bit of medical training and experi-ence I possess, but your son may die."

Captain Keeferly turned away abruptly and began to pace the room. "He can't die. They're all dead except Todd."

Doc wrung out a towel and bathed Todd's forehead, waiting and hoping the old man would come back and tend to his son. He didn't and Doc feared he didn't have one sick patient, but two, and he didn't know how to help either one.

He searched his mind for everything he knew about Captain Keeferly. He was over sixty but appeared physically sound, habitu-ally leaning forward as if in a rush to meet the world's challenges. From what he'd just witnessed in the parlor, he knew Keeferly was a man willing to use violence to get what he wanted.

Trail dust clung to the range clothes he wore, but beneath the dust his high-topped cavalry boots showed signs of a recent polishing. The silver spurs were expensive pieces of art which sang on the hardwood floor as he paced.

A black leather vest hung loosely on wide, powerful shoulders. Around his neck a white silk scarf accented the weathered face. Crows feet at the corners of his eyes were deep and long, reaching down to join the heavy furrows that cut along the corners of a wide mouth.

The pacing stopped abruptly. Slowly he lifted an arm and then stabbed a finger in Doc's direction. "Whatever hurt is done, you shall give life for life, eye for eye, tooth for tooth, hand for hand, foot for foot, burn for burn, bruise for bruise, wound for wound. A righteous man shall leave an inheritance to his children and his children's children. So it is written."

Jake entered the room and stood riveted by the sight of his boss reciting Scripture. The captain raised both arms upward and continued, "The miserable have no other medicine but only hope: I have hope to live, and am prepared to die. Be absolute for death; either death or life—"

The spell was interrupted when a Guidon K hand stepped through the door. "Water and corn is a cooking real good. Anything else?"

"No, go outside and man the barricades," Jake answered.

For a moment the captain seemed bewildered. Finally, he stepped to his son's side and asked, "What do we do now?"

Doc was unbuttoning Todd's shirt. "We need to get him out of these clothes and into a bed."

Gently, the captain pushed Doc aside and began to remove his son's garments. As he worked, he spoke to Jake, "I think it best you go out and check the troops."

Jake shifted from foot to foot. "Sir, the troops are plumb played out. Can't they go to the hotel and get some shut-eye?"

The captain didn't look up, but his voice was crisp and hard. "Absolutely not. What's the matter with you, Sergeant? Have half of them sleep and half stand guard. Change the watch every two hours. Now go."

The captain picked up Todd. "Where to?"

Doc led the way down the hall. "Put him in the bedroom on the left."

They had just settled Todd into the bed when Jake was back. "Sheriff's outside and wants to talk to you and Doc."

"I'll talk to him in the parlor," the captain said, tucking a blanket around his son's shoulders. "And Jake, make damn sure he's not armed."

Doc sank into the bedside chair and checked Todd's pulse. Snapping the watch case closed, he prayed the young man would regain consciousness long enough to find out how he'd taken sick.

He finally rose, took a straight-backed chair and turned it over so the crest of the chair back and the front of the seat were on the mattress and then slid it under Todd's back until he had the patient in a half-sitting position. The boy's shallow breathing immediately became somewhat easier.

Now he could help Carolyn, but before he reached the study, the sheriff and Captain Keeferly intercepted him. "Got any idea what's wrong with Todd?" the sheriff asked.

Doc noticed the empty holster on the sheriff's hip. "Not for sure." He won't be a hell of a lot of help, Doc thought, and remembered some rumors that the captain owned the law. But, to his credit, he insisted that he and Doc talk alone. Finally, the captain consented and the two moved to the parlor. The sheriff sat in a chair and motioned Doc to sit. "What's going on here? Red Avery says the captain and Jake are holding you prisoners. Said Jake knifed him and Carolyn."

"You're damn right. Look around you. Over there's Red's blood on the floor and Carolyn is down in my study with a nasty cut that I haven't had time to treat."

"Is she going to be all right?"

"Yes, I think so. How's Red? Did he get the shoulder patched up?"

"He'll be okay. Did the captain say you're his prisoners?"

"He said nobody could come or go. And I heard him tell Jake to have the boys shoot to kill. Are they outside?"

"Yes," the sheriff admitted.

"I want you to get the captain and Jake out of this house. That son of a bitch Jake is as dangerous as a rattlesnake and the captain is going insane."

"I talked to Jake and he said the thing with Carolyn was plain accidental. Says he's sorry. Now, what do you mean the captain's going crazy?"

"That's the only way I can call it. He's unreasonable, irrational, and has threatened to kill me if the boy dies."

Sheriff Barton knuckled back his mustache. "Is his son going to die?"

"I don't know for sure, but it doesn't look good."

"Do you think what he has is contagious?"

The sheriff was only half listening to Doc's answer. "Well," he said, "I had a talk with the captain and he swears everything will be fine. I'll check back in the morning."

"You're going to leave them here?" Doc asked in disbelief.

"The captain wants to be with his son and I can't arrest him or run him off for that."

"What about Jake? Can't you arrest him for attacking Carolyn?"

"I'll talk with the judge on Monday morning and maybe we can hit him with a fine. The captain wants him here and promised to keep him out of trouble." With that he rose and headed for the door. "I expect you need to get back to your patients. Good night, Doc."

Sheriff Barton retrieved his six-gun from one of the guards and jammed it into the empty holster thinking bitterly how little good it was to him. Hell, couldn't outdraw a schoolboy with this shoulder tonight. Next to his deal with the captain, his bum arm was his most closely guarded secret. His pace quickened once he was down on the town's sidewalk and a plan begin to fall in place. He cut across the street toward the newspaper editor's house and imagined he could almost hear him squawking like a hooked chicken – but this was an emergency and warranted waking someone at two-thirty in the morning. Hopefully Jenkins could have the signs printed by breakfast time and the story ready for the Monday paper. Things were going to work out just fine, he thought.

Worthless coward, Doc thought as the sheriff closed the door. How could he give up his gun at a time like this? He then realized he was wanting someone else to do what he had sworn he would never do again – use a gun to right a wrong, or an imagined wrong. He leaned on his cane and shook his head to clear the conflicting thoughts. Sort it out later, he told himself, and headed for the bedroom and one of his two immediate concerns.

Todd was as he had left him. "Captain, could you give me a hand in the kitchen?"

They went into the exam room where Doc handed the captain a half-dozen towels. Next Doc led him into the kitchen and instructed the captain to fish the scalding ears of corn out of the boiler and wrap them four to a towel. When the bundles were ready he told the Captain to take them to Todd's room.

"Damn, these are hot. What are you going to do with them?"

"Make a sweat tent for Todd. I hope it will relax his muscles and break the fever." The hot bundles were placed next to Todd's body and Doc piled on two more heavy quilts. Soon beads of perspiration glistened on Todd's forehead.

"Looks like it's working," the captain said, squeezing out a towel and applying it to his son's head.

"That's all I can do for him right now. If you want, you can go to the hotel and catch a couple hours' rest. I'll send word if there is a change in his condition."

"I'm staying put until Todd walks out of this house. Either that, or they carry both of you out feet first."

"Suit yourself." Doc took his cane from the foot of the bed and made his way down the hall to the study. Carolyn was relieved when she saw it was Doc, and asked, "Is that awful Jake still here? Have you heard anything of Red Avery? They can't hold us. The sheriff—"

"Let's don't worry about him right now. The Keeferlys are both down the hall and Jake is outside. How do you feel?"

"It's not the most desirable place to be cut, and it hurts."

"Having been treated in a military hospital and then serving in one, I can assure you there are less desirable places to be cut," he commented as they moved to the examination room.

She stopped just inside the exam room suddenly realizing she would have to disrobe. It would be different, she thought, if he were the elderly, white-haired doctor she knew back East, but Doc was not much older than she. Besides that, he was unmarried, very eligible, and quite handsome.

Doc cranked down the exam table and motioned her to sit. "Now you're going to have to get out of that dress," he said as he arranged medication and instruments.

Carolyn looked down at her dress. "I don't have anything else to put on."

"Cut off the top and leave the skirt," he said handing her a pair of scissors. "I'll get you one of my shirts to wear."

When he returned with the shirt, the top of her dress was on the floor and she had covered herself with a towel. The lamp-light was kind to her bare shoulders giving her flawless skin a lustrous patina.

"I'll be right back with some warm water," he said leaving the room. Carolyn looked at the gleaming instruments he had arranged on the table. Most of them she had seen him use on patients but never thought of them being used on her flesh. She shuddered.

Doc returned with a basin of warm water, fished in his vest pocket, and retrieved a pair of half-rim spectacles. "Let's have a look." She let the towel fall to her lap.

"Do you want some whisky or morphine? This is going to hurt some."

"No."

He sprinkled a few grams of disinfectant into the water, squeezed out a towel, and began cleaning the wounds. She shrank back at his touch and couldn't suppress a shudder that ran through her body.

"Sure you don't want something to take the edge off the pain?" he asked without looking up. "These are going to need some stitches."

"No, I don't want to dull my senses as long as they're in this house. What do you think is wrong with Captain Keeferly?"

"Can't rightly say, but I'm hoping that after he gets some rest he'll settle down."

"Do you know what's wrong with Todd?"

"No, but he's bad off. Hope he lasts long enough to give me a chance to help him."

The cuts were an inch above the nipples, two to three inches long, and deep enough to require stitches. He picked up a curved suture needle and began to thread it with catgut. "I'll try to be as quick as possible but it will be painful."

She watched him thread the needle. His hands were small, almost delicate, but steady and sure as he adjusted the length of catgut and turned to face her. She gripped the edge of the table, bit her lip, and nodded. She sat rigid as stone while Doc closed the first cut. She finally looked down and saw the evenly spaced stitches and his intense focus on his work. His head was quite close and she noticed that a little bit of gray was beginning to show in his black hair. The tired lines about his eyes and the spectacles made him look older. There was dried blood at the corner of his mouth, a heavy stubble of beard, and he smelled of medicine and cigar smoke.

Doc finished and turned to the table for more catgut. Carolyn sighed and relaxed. "It will leave a scar won't it?"

"Yes, but not one too many people will see if you're a good girl."

She jerked back as he began on the other cut. "I'm sorry, but your hands are cold."

He knew his hands weren't cold, knew she'd been using all her willpower to stay calm, but now shock was about to set in. He looked up. Tears puddled in her brown eyes and threatened to make their way down her cheeks. "Carolyn, I'm very sorry this had to happen, and I don't mean to make light of it."

She still had a white-knuckle grip on the edge of the exam table, so Doc reached up and gently brushed the tears away. His voice was gentle as he said, "The doctor insists that the patient take some proper medication. Will she do that?"

"Yes."

Doc retrieved a small apothecary jar from a cabinet, measured out a small amount of powder, mixed it with water, and handed it to Carolyn. After a second's hesitation, she downed it and then made a face. "That's awful."

Doc waited a moment and then wiped another tear from her cheek. "Now what do you say we get this over with before one of our unwanted guests interrupts?"

She nodded and steeled herself as Doc began to stitch and talk. "Reminds me of a situation old Doc Jacobson once told me about. Seems that over the years one of his patients gave birth to nine children. All were big, ornery, healthy kids. The problem was that the first boy bit one of the woman's nipples clean off."

"Oh, how dreadful."

Another tear had rolled down Carolyn's cheek and dropped to her chest. Doc wiped it away before it got to the cut. "Almost finished," he assured her.

"Was the woman able to nurse her children?"

"According to old Doc Jacobson she was a large woman and an excellent milker. Able to provide enough with just the one breast. Understood she did become a little lopsided."

"This won't interfere with my ability to nurse children will it?"

"Not in the least."

41

ISAIAH SADDLED HIS WAR PONY in the cool predawn and then stood savoring the gentle wind that caressed his body. He tried to remember how long it had been since he'd worn only his breechclout and paint. Standing and listening to the wind and feeling the touch of Mother Earth through his moccasins, he knew it had been too long.

A large Sioux war party roaming the sand hills had scared the residents of the surrounding countryside of Elk Springs and sent them behind locked doors and closed shutters. Isaiah, enticed by the thrill of counting coup on his old enemy, slipped out of town and followed their trail to Wild Horse Flats. Here, shod tracks over Sioux sign told him the Guidon K crew had picked up the trail. Isaiah knew the Guidon K hands didn't know a half-breed Crow from a Sioux – and didn't care which they shot as long as it looked Indian. He dropped off the trail and swung wide to the west end of Wild Horse Flats where he spent days watching the wild horses.

Now he was back at the edge of Elk Springs, needing to wash off his paint and put on his store-bought clothes. He stood like a bronze statue and watched the dawn, admitting to himself that the only thing that drew him back was Doc and his horses.

How many more mares have foal, he wondered as he rolled up his war bag with his breechclout, moccasins, and pipe bag. Maybe Doc will let the black mare's colt go with my half of the bunch. Not likely, he realized, knowing Doc had a special affinity for the black mare which he had never explained.

Filling his lungs with clean prairie air, he mounted and rode toward town. He rounded the west end of the oak grove and reined in sharply. The hair bristled on the back of his neck as he noticed the barn doors open, the gate poles down, and not a single horse in the corral. Riding quickly into the trees he jerked the Henry from the rifle boot before sliding from the saddle and making his way soundlessly to a point opposite the south barn door. Squatting in the shadows he watched and wondered.

What the hell was happening? Did some of the Sioux double back? He didn't see how. Maybe another small band of warriors had followed the main party?

He sprinted silently to the open door and stepped into the shadows. The familiar smells of newly-sawn lumber and horse manure greeted him. But no sound of stomping hooves or metal snaps jingling on halter rings. Cautiously he worked his way through the building. Nothing.

He stopped again to listen. His ears caught faint, rhythmic snoring coming from above. With his blood pounding and his senses alert, he crawled up the hand-hewn ladder to the loft. When his eyes were just above the floor of the loft, he hung on the ladder letting his eyes adjust to the dim light. He could make out bedrolls scattered about on the loft floor. Two showed the bulk of sleeping men.

Patiently, he carefully checked the loft a second time. Nothing, or no one, but the two sleeping forms. Slowly, he inched his way up into the loft, keeping his back to the wall and his eyes on the men in the bedrolls. His nose sorted out the sweet smell of turkey track hay from the sour stench of unwashed white men.

He wondered if these could be some new hands that Doc had hired? He dismissed the thought. Where were the horses? What was happening at the house? Was Doc in trouble? The patients? Carolyn?

Carolyn had started to work for Doc some weeks ago, which Isaiah considered as a gift of the Great Spirit to his crippled friend who was too blind or too stubborn to see.

He counted the bedrolls. Sixteen. Where were the other fourteen? Had they ridden away with the horses? Since their bedrolls were here it wasn't likely. They had to be close.

Silently, he moved to the sleeping figures and prodded one with the barrel of the Henry. Only the breathing changed. He gave the man a kick. Shorty sat up with a start. "Damn, it can't be time—" His eyes opened wide and focused on the rifle muzzle and then moved up the gleaming barrel. He made a slight move for his gun belt.

"You touch it, you die," Isaiah said, motioning for the man to stand.

He kicked the other man. "I want answers," he said. "Where are the horses?"

They looked at each other. A silent understanding passed between the two and Shorty said, "Go to hell, breed."

Easing the hammer down, he raised the rifle barrel slowly back over his shoulder. "Last chance, where are the horses?"

There was no answer but Isaiah knew Shorty was judging his options. The other man was too frightened to concern him just now.

Keeping his eyes on Shorty, he asked, "I know the captain's been interested in buying some of Doc's stock. Did they finally make a deal?"

Shorty grinned, "Yeah, we made a deal. We take the horses and you die."

Here it comes, Isaiah thought as Shorty lunged. The heavy octagon barrel arched down on Shorty's head and dropped him in mid stride. Isaiah stepped over the downed man and thumbed back the hammer before placing the muzzle against the second man's throat. "What are you bastards doing here?"

"Honest to god, I just got here a couple of hours ago. We was out looking for the kid. When I stopped at the captain's new house, I was told to hotfoot it up here."

Isaiah knew the man was too scared to lie. "To do what?"

The man's eyes darted from side to side; he hesitated. Isaiah lowered the rifle and drew his knife. The man's eyes followed the knife as Isaiah flipped it from handle to blade and back again.

"What?" Isaiah snapped, and thrust the knife quickly at the man's belly.

"Oh god, don't," the man stammered. "The captain and Jake's holed up in Doc's house. I heard Todd's damn near dead. We ain't supposed to let nobody in or out."

"Why?" Isaiah's blade flashed just below the trembling chin.

The man drew back, face colorless. "Oh, mother of god, something about if Todd died he'd kill Doc and everybody. Then we was to get some of the horses for ourselves."

Isaiah tied and gagged the two men before slipping out of the barn and into the trees. Deep in the shadows of the towering oaks he stopped and considered his chances of fighting the whole Guidon K crew. Better if he could get inside the house.

A giant oak overspread the roof at the back window of Doc's bedroom. It kept the room cool during the hot days of summer. It was his best chance, and before it got full daylight. Minutes later Isaiah stood inside the bedroom. Ho, he thought, not a challenge for a Crow. The hall door was open, the hallway dark. The familiar smell of medicine and cigar smoke came to him along with distant voices.

The big, mahogany four-poster bed hadn't been slept in; a pair of Doc's riding boots sat by a chair. He stood the Henry carefully in the corner and drew his knife. He'd stalk them one at a time. Jake first.

He wished he was in his breechclout and paint. Just maybe, he thought, and moved quickly to the dresser. In the faint first light filtering through the window he found the bootblack. He stripped off his shirt, tied his hair with his bandanna and in the dresser mirror applied the black to one side of his face. He was Two Suns now, a Crow warrior. He'd waited a long time for an excuse to gut and scalp Jake Smith.

42

IT WAS STILL TWO HOURS BEFORE FIRST LIGHT when Sheriff Barton got the newspaper editor awake, down to the newspaper office, and instructed him what to print on the fliers.

"How soon?" the sheriff asked as he reached for the doorknob.

Jenkins, eyes still foggy with sleep, looked around the small print shop. Cases of type, cans of ink, and random stacks of yellowed newspapers floated like jetsam in the dull lamplight. With a hopeless shrug he said, "With a little luck, about noon."

"Noon, my ass." The sheriff spun around. "I want something by nine o'clock latest."

Jenkins's brows shot up, and he looked like a surprised basset hound. "Better go wake up Harley and bring him down. Ain't no way I can do 'em myself by nine."

Sheriff Barton turned and hurried through the door almost running into Red Avery. Both were surprised, but the sheriff recovered first. He saw a revolver in Red's holster and the sawed-off scattergun clutched in his left hand.

"Son of a bitch, Red, I thought I told you to stay put. I was just on my way to see how you were."

"Did you see my missus and baby?"

"Not exactly, but I did talk to Doc. Everything's fine up at Oak Grove."

"Can I go up and see her?"

The sheriff glanced up and down the street. Lights were coming on all over town, folks were on the walks, and he could see a knot of citizens in front of the jail. News spreads fast, the sheriff mused, and hoped to hell the captain wasn't doing something stupid to give the folks a reason to poke their noses where they didn't belong. Red paled and staggered a little as he moved to lean against a porch post.

"Red, you're lookin' a bit wobbly. Best get you over to the jail and down on a bunk. Where's Curt?"

Red and the sheriff moved across the street. "Curt left with a bottle. Probably passed out in some alley," Red said.

"My deputy?"

"I kind of tied him up in the back room."

"How in the hell?"

"I kind of tapped him on the head so as he'd hold still."

"Damn it, Red, you keep this up and I'll have to lock you up for your own good."

"Can I go see my wife?"

The sheriff had expected the crowd at the jail to be listening to his deputy, but since he was tied up, the sheriff wondered who it was. They stepped into the crowd and heard Curt's slurred words, "Cut her tits plumb off, that's what he done. Yes sir, I say it's time we protect the fair sex, our wives, and the mothers of our children."

Sheriff Barton lunged through the crowd and grabbed Curt. "Easy ol' son. You've got quite a load. Best let me help you to one of the taxpayers' bunks so you can sleep it off."

He shoved Curt through the jailhouse door and into a cell. "Now this is getting serious, you little bastard. Next thing you know, I'll have a war on my hands."

He took the bottle from Curt and pushed him hard at one of the bunks. "Now flop your ass down and go to sleep. If I catch you out and about again this morning, I'll lock you up instead of giving you a place to sleep it off."

The town drunk crashed onto the bunk, grunted, rolled over onto his back, then bobbed up like a cork on a cane pole line. "Say, Sheriff, did you know that smartass Reb Doc Kelley's got a million in gold over at the bank?"

"Sure, Curt, and my mother's the Queen of England."

The barber was struggling to free himself from the sagging bunk. "Yes sir, it's true. Heard it from the captain himself."

About to dismiss it as whisky talk, the sheriff paused at the door and came back to look down on the pathetic little man. He'd never known Curt's gossip to be totally fabricated. Usually it was based on some truth which got scrambled in the whisky.

"When'd he tell you that?"

Satisfied with the reaction he'd gotten from the law, Curt was now ready to sleep. He sagged back on the lumpy mattress. "Didn't exactly, but I heard it from Angelo."

Sheriff Barton wanted more information but the town drunk had gone to whisky land, so the lawman walked out the door thinking this put a different light on the whole matter. Oh, how a man could live in Mexico with a million in gold. Sure as hell beat five hundred head of longhorns. He needed time. He looked at the clock, only five-thirty. He'd have to stall 'em until the printing was finished.

Out on the porch Red Avery had taken over where Curt left off. Everyone agreed that the captain and Jake had gone too far this time and it was time for the law to act, or they would.

The sheriff faced them and held up his hand for quiet. When the muttering stopped, he said, "I've been up to Oak Grove and talked with Doc, the captain, and Jake. I'll be going back up about eight this morning. Todd Keeferly is gravely ill. Naturally, his father and Jake want to be near him."

Red Avery, holding onto the porch post, cut in on the sheriff, "Todd's sure enough sick, but I tell you the captain's gone crazy and Jake's mad as a rabid cur. Look at my arm and think on poor Mrs. Dawson. To hear Curt tell it—"

The sheriff interrupted, "True, Mrs. Dawson was accidentally cut, but Doc assured me she's all right. Red, you need to give that shoulder a rest."

Elmo elbowed his way through the crowd. Sheriff Barton watched him and thought that son of a bitch will cause more trouble than two Red Averys and a half-dozen Curts. Elmo came straight to the point. "If everything is like you say, how come the place is surrounded by armed Guidon K men who refuse to let me see my friends?"

"Todd's illness seems to be of such a nature that any undue noise could be very bad for his recovery. The doctor asked that for the time being no one should come or go."

Elmo snorted like a horse catching wolf on the wind. "Sheriff, meaning no disrespect, but I think that's a crock of road apples."

"Gentlemen, I've been up all night," the sheriff said, pulling out his pocket watch and ignoring Elmo's comment. "As sheriff I call a town meeting at nine o'clock in the War Bonnet. I'll have some critical news at that time."

43

ISAIAH MOVED TO THE HALL DOOR and listened. Voices were coming from the medicine room. He listened hard – this is why I don't like houses, you couldn't hear the wind, he thought – and put all the other noises into a small bag and tied it tight.

Listen. Heavy footsteps in the parlor. Jake is in the parlor.

Listen again. The captain is silent.

Listen. Carolyn's voice. She is in the medicine room with Doc.

Where the hell is Keeferly? I've got to know where the bastard is, so I'll have to listen at every door, he thought. He started down the hall and paused at a door. Silence. Then Doc's uneven steps and thump of his cane coming toward him. A second set of footfalls. Not Jake's. Not Carolyn's. Captain Keeferly was coming too.

Turning the knob with his left hand, knife in his right hand, Isaiah backed into the room. The scream was unexpected. Isaiah whirled and put his finger to his lips. "I'm Doc's friend, Isaiah. I won't hurt you." He spoke soft English to the terrified woman in the bed.

She screamed again.

Isaiah heard footsteps racing toward the room. He leapt behind the door a heartbeat before the captain burst into the room and stopped at the sight of Mrs. Avery, wide eyed, lips moving silently, and finger pointing behind the door. It was all the time Isaiah needed to thrust his knife at the captain's throat, his left hand over the big man's mouth. "Drop the gun."

Doc took it in at a glance. "Isaiah, don't—" The rest of his words were halted by Jake's knife at his throat, a hand in his hair pulling his head back. Jake kicked Doc's cane across the room.

"Should I kill him, Captain?" Jake asked.

Isaiah put more pressure on the blade and took his hand from the captain's mouth. The room froze at the sound of a gun being cocked. Carolyn had drawn Jake's Colt and had it pressed into his back. "Turn Doc loose, or I'll kill you right here."

"You little bitch, shoot me and I'll cut his damn head off on my way down."

Doc had difficulty speaking around the knife at his throat, but said, "Captain Keeferly, your son needs me and I need Isaiah. You can kill us all later, but at least let's talk about helping your son."

The infant wailed. "My baby, my baby," Mrs. Avery cried.

Doc spoke around the blade. "Carolyn, put the gun down and tend the baby. Isaiah, can you make another ride like you did two years ago?"

"Why should I? These men need killing."

"Isaiah, you rode two days and nights to save people from the cholera. You didn't know them and no doubt some of them were not good people. Think of your mother and your decision."

"Could this damn breed get help for Todd?" the captain asked.

"I've been thinking that if someone could get to a telegraph and army post they might could bring me the information and medicine I need to save your son. Violence won't help anyone. We can talk in the study."

The child's crying picked at raw nerves like a hungry bird. Blood oozed along Jake's blade at Doc's throat. He felt Jake's muscles tensing. "Captain, for god sakes, Todd needs your help. Carolyn, your job is helping my patients. Put the gun down and help Mrs. Avery and her little one."

The sound of doors opening and more running footsteps told everyone that the Guidon K crew was in the house. Carolyn eased down the hammer and dropped the Colt back into Jake's holster.

"Let me go, you goddamn stinking breed. Turn over your knife and any other weapons and tell us how you got in this house. Then we'll talk about Todd," Captain Keeferly demanded.

"Do it, Isaiah," Doc said.

Isaiah hesitated. "It is not the way of a warrior."

"Think of your new life and your promise to your mother."

Isaiah reluctantly released the captain who, with Jake, quickly escorted Doc and Isaiah to the study at gunpoint. Doc sat down and began writing, Isaiah motionless and expressionless waiting by his side. The captain covered them with his Colt while Jake sat in the corner and examined the Henry he'd found in Doc's bedroom.

Doc blotted and folded a letter. "Bring this medicine and any other which the medic may suggest." He stood and handed the letter and a small leather bundle to Isaiah. "Take Ol' Jeb along with your pony."

Jake grinned as Isaiah took the paper. "Ol' Jeb's gone. So are all the others."

"What do you mean gone?" Doc asked.

"I have them," the captain said. "Another reason to make sure my boy lives."

"Captain," Doc said, "give Isaiah his knife and rifle. It may make the difference between bringing help or being scalped."

The captain consented and Jake sent the knife flashing across the room to bury itself into the wall by Isaiah's head. Unloading the Henry, he threw it after the knife. Isaiah caught the gun and pulled the knife from the wall. "Jake will give you all the cartridges for the Henry when you're ready to ride," Keeferly said.

Doc gave Isaiah a half-dozen cigars and offered his hand. "Good luck, and remember what an ol' friend once said about listening to the wind."

Isaiah took his hand and replied, "Little Knife should listen too, and watch carefully for hawks and shadows."

44

WILL McGREGOR SAT ON A ROUGH-HEWN ASH STOOL mending a harness tug and watching Anna. The children had kissed them both good night before climbing the ladder into the loft. A gentle south breeze played with the lamp's flame and cooled the evening air.

A week had passed since the recent Indian scare, and his brothers and their families had returned to their cabins. It had been a hard week of rebuilding; muscles were weary, but spirits were high for everyone except Anna.

They had every reason to rejoice; the season had yielded bountiful crops beyond their expectations. Occasionally, the Guidon K would push a herd of cattle across the river and into their fields, but unlike the other homesteaders, they'd been left alone to prosper. From time to time this was a subject of speculation along the bar in the War Bonnet. What kind of a deal did Will have with Keeferly? Will would smile wider and guess it was just meeting the captain halfway. That, and not being intimidated by the man.

But Will had known for some time now that Anna was not herself, something was bothering her, but he didn't know what. He watched her knit for several seconds and then pull out the stitches and begin again. Finally, she laid the knitting beside her rocker and went to the bedroom.

Will picked up his rifle that was always within arm's reach since the Sioux scare. He blew out the lamp, opened the door, and stepped outside where he stood quietly in the shadows. He listened for several minutes until a small collie came from the barn and stood at his feet. He squatted down, and they grinned at each other while he rubbed its ears. Satisfied that all was right with his world, he went back inside the cabin and latched the door. All's right except Anna, he thought as he entered the bedroom.

He could hear her soft sobs as he stepped into the dark room. Moving to a nightstand he lit a candle and then sat down beside her on the bed, his rough and calloused hands gently stroking her hair. Tears pooled and flooded down her checks. He looked deep into her eyes and saw more hurt there than at any time since he'd known her.

"Doll, I've known for some time that you've been troubled. Is it the Indians?"

She shook her head.

"Is it the loneliness and missing some of your kinfolk?"

She shook her head.

"Ah, have I not been paying you enough attention? You know the kids are fast asleep now."

Anna turned and buried her face in Will's chest clinging desperately to his body.

"Anna, you've got to be telling me now what it is that's bothering you. You know I'll be doing all I can to set it right."

She quieted and looked at her husband. "That's what scares me, Will. If you kill him it could ruin everything all over again."

"Kill who?"

"Promise me that you won't kill him. Just make him stay away."

Will pushed Anna to arm's length. "Damn it, say it plain. Kill who and why? What's happened to you?"

She told him of Captain Keeferly's visit, knowing it was useless to drag it out, and welcoming the relief that unburdening herself would bring.

"Did he—?"

She nodded. Told me he'd kill all of us if I said anything."

She looked at Will, searching his dark eyes. He pulled her close, held her gently. "It's not your fault. I'm still loving you like before. Always will no matter what." He brushed the hair back from her face and wiped away the tears.

She grabbed him as he moved to leave. "Will, please don't do this."

"It has to be done, Anna."

"Will, please," she begged, watching him move to the chest at the foot of the bed. "I hate him more than you'll know, but I also love what we've built here. It's a wonderful place to raise our family, and we have the independence we've always wanted."

"I like it too, but as long as he's alive, it will be threatened."

She stood watching him change into his kilt and hose before reaching up and taking the sword and pipes off the wall. "Will, the last time you wore those we had to flee three thousand miles to have any peace of mind. Don't make us flee again, for the children's sake."

"I would rather be on the run than living with something like this and I did nothing. I can't let it pass."

His gentleness was gone now, his face set. She knew it was useless and when he said to wake the children, she obeyed, but knew it would be fighting and killing all over again. Where would they go? Where were the dreams bigger and better than in America?

As prearranged for emergencies, Will's sixteen-year-old son saddled and rode to gather the clan. It was a fast, silent ride to the next McGregor's cabin and by the time Will's wagon rolled into the yard at Jacob's place the other families were arriving. This was the midway claim, remodeled after the Sioux raids to serve as a gathering point. Built like a fort, it provided protection and supplies for emergencies.

Will stood by the fireplace clad in his kilt and hose, the big claymore at his side, a pistol and dirk in his belt. He wore no smile tonight. He sent the women and children to another room before speaking to the men. "Lads, I'm going to kill Captain Keeferly. It's not proper for a man to force himself on another's wife. I'll go alone or you can come with me."

He questioned the brothers one by one. Then the young men. No one disagreed or argued.

"Get your gear into the wagons, and don't be forgettin' the pipes and drum. We hit Keeferly at dawn."

– 45 –

THE SWISH, SWISH OF STEEL ON STONE made Carolyn's breath catch and her pulse race. She willed herself not to show any surprise or emotion. But, she knew Jake was in the kitchen. How could he move so quietly? And, why did they insist she make pies at a time like this?

She finished putting the freshly baked pies in the pie safe and turned back to the stove and closed the damper before cleaning up the cooking utensils. Finished, she took off the apron, gathered her courage, and turned to leave. The object of her hate stood leaning against the wall just inside the door, his hands thoughtlessly stropping his knife against the whetstone, his dark, hooded eyes following her every move.

Back straight and head high, she walked past him through the door straight down the hall into Doc's study. Please, God, don't let him come in here, she prayed. She stepped inside and to the left of the door, waiting to see if he would follow. She gave a weary sigh of relief when she heard him talking with the captain in the sitting room.

Carolyn was disappointed that Doc wasn't in the study because she'd resolved to talk to him tonight about what he planned to do if Todd should die. For a moment she looked at row after row of books and journals on the bookshelves. They stared back defiantly. Is the answer hidden somewhere in those thousands of pages? God, she was weary, and it was stuffy in the house since Captain Keeferly had the windows and all but one door nailed shut.

She walked to the fireplace and stared at the Indian pipe on the mantel. She never had understood the bond between Doc and Isaiah, but now she hoped the strange half-breed was safely on his way back from the fort with saving information and medicine. Would he make it back in time?

She focused on the ornate grandfather clock that stood on the south wall, and like the rest of her world, tonight it was transformed. Instead of a handwrought work of art, all she could see was a device slowly measuring her life and reminding her of a horrible death near at hand.

The eleven-thirty chimes brought a gasp and sent a hand to her bloodstained shirt. You've got to get hold, she warned herself. Weakness in anything wasn't attractive to her, which made her wonder if Doc was weak because he didn't believe in violence? Or was he stronger than most? Would he do anything to prevent being killed?

If Todd died, and Captain Keeferly made good on his threat, how would Jake kill them? Would he just shoot them, or use that damn knife? She'd fight, she vowed, but with what? Jake had removed all the knives from the kitchen and everything else that could possibly be used as a weapon. He'd even taken the medical instruments – scalpels, scissors, and probes – to the back porch.

Her rush of thought was interrupted by the unsteady step and thump, thump of Doc coming down the hall. She inquired about Todd as he dropped into his chair. "I don't see how he stays alive," he answered.

He set his medical bag on the desk, slumped down in his chair, and rubbed his bloodshot eyes. His shirt was stained with sweat beneath the arms and at his collar, his trousers were wrinkled, and a three-days' growth of beard shadowed his haggard face.

"I'd give anything to sit at old Doc Jacobson's feet for a long stretch and try to figure out what's ailing Todd," he said at length.

"I was wanting to talk with someone too," Carolyn said. Watching his face closely, she asked, "How much time do you believe we have?"

"Barring miracles, I don't think he can last more than twenty-four hours at the most."

"Dr. Kelley, can I talk with you?" she asked.

"Of course, I've been meaning to talk with you about something that's weighing heavy on my mind. But first, what's it you want to talk about?"

"I've heard that you don't believe in fighting or killing. If the worst happens, will you just let them kill us without a struggle?"

His eyes met hers briefly, then looked away. He got up and moved to the window where he stared at the town below. How very much he wanted to sleep. Even the captain had given in to fatigue and was dozing in a chair. How was he to answer her without discouraging her, or worse, frightening her into some unwise attempt to escape or fight?

Impatient for his answer, she moved to his side at the window. She could almost feel his fatigue, even his mental weariness was almost tangible. She suddenly felt sorry for him. "Now isn't a good time. We can talk about it later."

He caught her hand as she began to turn away. "Now is the time. You have a right to know."

In as few words as possible he told her of the war and his vow to avoid violence at any cost, that he believed that mankind should be able to reason out its differences without bloodshed. Finished, he realized he was still holding her hand and she made no attempt to withdraw it from his grasp. "I've made it this far, and since my vow there has always been a nonviolent way."

She looked up, her eyes soft. "Unless you can cure Todd, I don't see how it will work this time. I've said goodbye to Samuel and Timothy and am going to go back to Ohio. I'm ready to start a new life."

"I know."

"How could you possibly know?"

"Isaiah told me about your decision."

"How – how could Isaiah have known?"

"I've stopped trying to figure out how he knows what he knows."

"I guess it doesn't matter; it's just that I don't want to die before I have another chance at life," she said.

"Nor I. The worst part is I do have a way to stop them, but I can't deal with it in my mind."

It took a moment for the words to register. She squeezed his hand hard and grasped his other arm. "How, my god, how?"

"Perhaps I shouldn't have mentioned it to you. I'm struggling with it something fierce in my mind. Maybe I don't have the right to endanger those I care about just to keep my convictions."

She grabbed both arms and shook him. "How? Tell me."

He told her he had three concealed firearms. A light of hope came to her eyes and she drew him to her and laid her head on his shoulder and wept. "Thank God, thank God. Tell me where they are. I'll get them for us. We'll be safe."

He couldn't answer. The softness of her body, the smell of her hair, all the things feminine that had been missing in his life for so long rushed in to confuse his thinking about guns, powder that may not ignite, and percussion caps that may not fire – and a vow.

She seemed reluctant to leave, clinging to him. The thought struck him like a blow. Could this be what Isaiah had meant? Was he not seeing? Was he not listening? If it were true, if it could possibly be true, how could he stand by and watch it end without fighting?

But, could he live with the nightmares if they started returning again? It was no longer black and white but a murky gray that swirled around his world. Her nearness sent old, almost forgotten yearnings coursing through his body, only to collide with his mind and his reason.

"My god," he spoke softly. "Could it be Isaiah was right after all?"

She looked up. "Right about what?"

"Another of his mysterious feelings which the wind told him, but it's something we'll have to discuss later."

She stepped back, tucking her hair behind her ears. "What are you going to do? If you won't do it, then give me the guns and I will."

Why not, he thought. Kill two people, who like Isaiah had said needed killing, and it would be over and maybe Carolyn would – he cut the thought short. She wouldn't want a man who let a woman do his fighting, and more important, he would then be like all the rest, resorting to violence to get what he wanted.

He shook his head. "I'll have to think on it some more. Right now what we both really need is some rest. I promise you in the morning there will be an answer."

A sadness crossed Carolyn's face. "I'll go sit with Mrs. Avery and the baby. Isaiah gave her quite a scare and she's been asking that I sit and talk with her. What should I tell her when she asks what's going to happen?"

"Tell her that Isaiah may make it back. Tell her that a miracle may happen, tell her to have faith."

Carolyn took a step back. "I was taught that God helps those who help themselves. How can you be so selfish, so stubborn as to have your principles at the cost of innocent people's lives?"

She didn't wait for an answer but turned and walked away. Doc watched her back until she faded into the hall shadows.

ISAIAH KNEW BY THE SUN that he'd been running beside his pony for almost three hours. He was deep in Sioux country and he wanted his mount rested. He'd not touched the canteen that hung on his saddle; water could be vital in a run for his life. At the next stream they would stop and drink.

He'd had no trouble at the military post and the information and medicine Doc requested were safely in his war bag. He wondered how Little Knife was doing with those sons of bitches. "If anything happens to my friend I will let my knife drink deeply of those two's blood. It's almost as thirsty as I am," he promised his pony.

Two more miles of easy jogging across the hot grassland brought horse and man to a clear stream shaded by a sparse growth of trees lining the waterway. As he knelt to drink, the reflection of his naked torso showed a familiar medicine bundle around his neck. The memories it brought were bitter and sweet.

He'd made his way in the white-eyes' world for almost three snows now. If he got his share of the horse herd, he'd be a rich Crow and an almost-rich white. He grinned and patted his horse's neck. "You'll like being a rich man's horse because there are some mighty pretty fillies in that herd."

More important, he had a white brother. Doc was a little strange when it came to certain things, but his heart was good. Very few white hearts were good for even their holy men had called Indians and breeds heathen. The memory of that Sunday morning was foul as spoiled meat on a hungry belly. He'd gone to services to learn more about the white man's god his mother had told him about. She said he was a strong god who fought for his people, yet was kind enough to love all races.

Isaiah had cut his hair a little shorter at the admonition of the holy man who talked long on Sunday mornings. He'd even left his medicine bundle on the altar, a sacrifice he was sure would please their god. Instead, the holy man had ranted and raved the next week, throwing the bundle out the open window and denouncing all pagan items as a stench in god's nostrils.

Isaiah remembered how the whites stared at him as he got up and left the church. He never went back, except for that night to look for his medicine bundle but it was gone. Later he learned that Doc had retrieved it for him, so maybe, he wondered, did Doc have two gods, one Indian and one white? He wondered if maybe the Indian god and the white man's god were the same.

He crossed the stream, still leading his pony, and started trotting across the prairie. He was making good time which pleased him because at first he'd worried what living with the whites had done to his lungs and his strength. Thankfully, he still felt no fatigue and decided that toward evening he'd ride when it was cooler for his mount.

About two hours before sunset he topped a low rise, the prairie spilling out before him in endless waves. He rested for a moment drinking in the wind and savoring the feeling of freedom that he could only feel away from the white settlements. He'd almost forgotten how natural it felt, like coming home.

The prairie looked like an empty lodge to unfamiliar eyes, but Isaiah saw and heard all the sounds he'd grown up with. A red-tailed hawk's shrill whistle blended with the warnings of prairie dog lookouts and the rustle of field mice at his feet.

He'd not gone more than a mile when he stopped short at seeing fresh horse droppings. These were unshod horses that carried riders. It was obvious that he was not the only Indian close by, so he changed his direction west away from their trail.

Instead of riding as he'd intended, he continued to jog beside his mount.

Even though he saw more signs before sundown, he wasn't worried and was confident that by sundown tomorrow he'd be in Elk Springs. He stopped once during the night, drinking at a stream, eating some jerky, and letting his horse graze. Then before continuing, he listened long and carefully to the wind.

He rode the last three or four hours before sunup, traveling slowly, dozing briefly, trusting his war pony to warn him of danger. At sunup he dismounted and again trotted beside his horse. Huge white clouds billowed up from the west and floated lazily across the sun, giving them a few moments of welcome shade from time to time. He guessed it would be a long stretch before another stream.

An hour later he knew he was being followed. Four, maybe five riders. They didn't worry him too much as long as they didn't have friends on his flanks. Those following him were moving up fast but he kept moving without changing pace as he gradually angled almost due north.

It has to be a Sioux or Cheyenne hunting party, he thought, even though they were too far away to identify. He could still not see any of their party ahead or to the side, only behind; pressing closer. The change of direction put the south wind at his back. He knew if Sioux were back there his pony would let him know.

They were Sioux, fanned out five abreast and soon one rider pushed far ahead of the others. Going to wear us down in relays, he thought. He swung astride and loped toward high ground to check his flanks, all the time matching the lone rider's speed to keep the distance between them from dwindling. His horse was still fresh and he was in little danger, but it did make the blood run hot.

He checked the Henry and his belt knife, twisted in the saddle, and untied his war bag. He found his tomahawk, stuck it in his belt, and tied his hair with a strip of red trade cloth.

He heard the crack of a rifle and smiled. Damn dumb Sioux wasting powder and shot. They would have to be a lot closer and a lot luckier before he worried about a long shot like that. But it did make the hairs prick on the back of his neck. A good feeling after so long.

The first rider dropped back and another took his place on a leggy bay. This brave pushed harder, but it took him an hour to work the distance down to five hundred yards. Isaiah touched heels to his pony and began pulling away. As Isaiah hoped, it angered the rider into a long shot. Isaiah laughed and reined in a bit. Most of them probably didn't have but a half-dozen shot's worth of powder and ball. He had a full magazine in the Henry and an extra box of cartridges in his war bag.

The country was new to him, but he knew he'd have to swing west before long which was perfect because his pursuers would be facing the sun – not good for shooting – and the Sioux didn't like to fight at night.

The fourth rider came up fast, dismounted, and shot from a kneeling position. Isaiah heard the ball pass very close. He turned in the saddle and held up a fist. "Ho, you shoot like a small child!" he yelled back in Sioux.

He topped a line of low hills that fell away to a flat narrow floor between another ridge of hills running almost directly west. It was a perfect place to let a horse run. And it was headed west into the sun. He didn't want to risk a fall or to lame his horse, so he let the pony pick its own way down. The riders were at the top before he reached the level floor. A volley of shots sent a few balls close enough for him to hear them hit the ground. He slid to the other side of his mount and spoke a command. He let the horse gallop until it put enough distance between them and his pursuers to ride at an easy lope across the valley floor.

Once the Sioux were down into the valley a warrior on the big paint pushed hard and was closing the distance. Isaiah talked to his pony saying, "I think it's time to let them know I have a Henry. If I snap off three quick shots, it'll probably discourage them. Not many warriors, no matter how brave, liked to ride down the barrel of a repeating rifle."

Isaiah heard the ball strike flesh before he heard the rifle report. His mount stumbled. He tried to kick free but his pony went down too fast. The earth rushed at his face as he cursed the white man's god for making his medicine weak. Then blackness.

47

SHERIFF BARTON SELECTED A GREENER SHOTGUN from the gun rack and checked the loads in both barrels. "It's about nine o'clock," he said to the deputy. "Looks like most of the town's already at the War Bonnet."

The deputy looked up from the stack of posters on the desk. "Don't envy your job none this time. Everybody's nervous as hell and Red's as dangerous as a cornered cougar. You want I should go along?"

"Nope. I want you to take those posters and put 'em up at the edge of town same places as we did during the cholera. Don't nobody comes in or go out. Understood?"

The deputy gathered the posters. "If we end up with a bunch of sick ones, is Doc going be able to help us again?"

"Ain't your job to be worrying about that. We'll deal with it if it happens." He jammed his hat on against the wind and said over his shoulder, "Meet me back here in about an hour."

The wind teased a tumbleweed down the middle of the dusty street where horses lined the hitch racks in front of the saloons. He nodded to banker Peterson as he angled toward the War Bonnet. A cloud passed overhead and its shadow crawled momentarily over the town. He looked up at Oak Grove as the shadow slid off the white edifice and he wondered how long before people began dying up there.

The War Bonnet was thick with the odor of sweaty bodies, cheap whisky, and heavy tension. A few Guidon K hands and local merchants whom the captain owned lounged at tables along the south wall while Elmo, Red, and the rest of the community stood at the bar.

The sheriff banged on the bar with the butt of his shotgun. He waited until it was quiet, then spoke, "This town is under quarantine." He held up a poster. "All you merchants are to post one of these on your doors. All of you should take one to your home so everyone will know what we're dealing with here."

Silently, the men passed the posters. A chair scraped, a glass clinked, but mostly the men were reliving the memory of cholera and wondering if they'd be burying loved ones soon.

Red pushed his way to the bar. "How's my wife and child? I've already been up there. Seems it wouldn't matter none if I went back."

"Your wife and child are fine, but nobody goes to Oak Grove. Doc said he'd know something more soon as the breed gets back. In the meantime all we can do is tend to our business best we can – and wait."

The men started drifting outside to talk, but once outside stared silently at the sight of the McGregors coming up the street from the ford at Elk Creek. The two wagons drew up in front of the crowd as the sheriff pushed through the saloon doors. The McGregors, all clad like Will, spilled out of the wagons and formed up behind Will as he started toward the sheriff.

Someone snickered. "Look here boys, got some new women-folk around town. Can I have this dance?"

Hardly breaking stride, Will hit the man sending him reeling into the crowd. The unfortunate fellow had misread Will's face. He should have looked in his eyes. The rest of the McGregors stood with rifles and shotguns at the ready. The crowd parted as Will made his way to the sheriff. "Where's Captain Keeferly?"

Sheriff Barton wondered what the captain had done now. In a way he wasn't surprised. The old bastard had been making a lot of mistakes lately.

He handed Will a poster. "The captain is at Doc Kelley's with his sick son. As you can see, he can't be visited now."

Will crumpled the paper and let it drop. "Ain't wanting to visit. I'm wanting you to go bring him out, or I go up and get him myself."

"Why don't you come to the sheriff's office and tell me what your trouble is with the captain? We don't need another epidemic on our hands. A lot of people could die. I'm sure it can wait."

"It won't wait, and you're right, lad, some people are going to die." Will turned to the crowd. "This business is just between us and Captain Keeferly. If you try to stop us, you'll get hurt sure."

Sheriff Barton watched the crowd. He believed some would fear another plague more than they'd fear Will and his skirted bunch. He opened his mouth to speak, then thought better. What more could he ask? It'd keep the whole town busy. Damn, what a break.

The sheriff spoke to Will. "Don't make it tough for both of us. I'd hate to have to arrest you and your kin."

Will ignored the sheriff and spoke to his men. "Lads, we'll be going up afoot so bring the pipes and drum." He faced the crowd of townsfolk. "I've no fight with any of you. I'm only wanting Keeferly, so don't be getting in my way."

48

THE SIOUX TONGUE CAME TO ISAIAH like the spirits that walk in the early morning mist. Slowly, he remembered. He'd traveled all day and night to reach the military post and the telegraph line and was on his way back to Doc Kelley with the lifesaving medicine. A small band of Sioux had been shadowing his trail since early morning. For hours they were content to follow at a distance until one pressed ahead and got off a lucky shot that hit his pony. The horse went down hard, and because he was turned in the saddle to snap off some rounds, he hadn't been able to jump free. He hadn't remembered anything until now.

His first impulse was to fight, to die like a Crow warrior, but the Sioux words made him wait. He would be like brother opossum – remain still and listen.

An authoritative voice said, "You each had your chance, but it was my shot that the Great Spirit guided. Do not kill him."

A different voice argued, "He's a Crow, a long way from his people, perhaps scouting for a raiding party or for the whites. He must die."

Isaiah wished he could see them. From the voices he judged the first to be old, the other young. Why was the old one hesitating? If he just had his knife or tomahawk he'd show them how a real warrior dies.

Angry words came from the old one. "All these items belong to the tribe because I declare it. We will put his gear and extra meat on a travois. I will keep the paper that speaks words."

Then it registered. The damn Sioux are eating my war pony. That pony had been with him since he left the Crow camp. It was like family. The toe of a moccasin interrupted his thoughts and rolled Isaiah onto his back. A voice growled, "I want to kill him and hang his hair in my lodge."

The old voice, weary but firm, replied, "Did not my lance tell me we would find a warrior and many buffalo in a valley between the small hills? You can see he is a warrior."

"True," a voice agreed. "But, we've not seen a single buffalo. We are alive, but our lodges are empty of meat and the people are hungry."

"The sun is still high. There may yet be buffalo," the old one said.

Their argument told Isaiah that they were more interested in meat than fighting. Maybe he had a chance. Ho, he thought, now I'm like Doc, trying to decide if I will fight or not. Maybe it's time to try his ways.

Without moving he spoke Sioux. "Old one, what else has your lance told you?"

He slowly opened his eyes. The old one stood at his feet calmly studying him. "You speak our tongue well," the old one said. "My lance has mentioned only a special warrior alone between two hills. Who are you?"

"I am Two Suns, a Crow warrior."

The old Sioux looked into Isaiah's eyes. "You are a breed?"

"Yes," Isaiah answered.

"Why are you so far south? Are you a scout for the soldiers?"

"No, I'm returning from a visit to an old Kiowa who is my father's uncle," Isaiah answered, thinking the old warrior looked familiar. Perhaps he had been in a dream or vision.

The old one held the prescription paper toward Isaiah. "You came from the fort. You must be with the soldiers?"

"No, I am taking the paper that talks to my friend, a white medicine man."

The old one listened calmly while Isaiah studied the Sioux. Their horses were fine animals, sleek from the plentiful grass, but the warriors were thin and their clothes worn. Hard times showed.

Suddenly Isaiah knew where he'd seen the old one. His remembering was interrupted by hateful words. "Enough talk, let's kill this breed and hunt for buffalo."

Isaiah spoke to the old one, "Do you remember a wagon train caught in a sea of mud after a great prairie fire?"

The old man's eyes brightened. "You know about the naked men who sing and carry rocks? Their medicine was great."

"The wagons belonged to my friend, Doc Kelley, a white medicine man."

"You have learned this medicine?" the old warrior asked.

Isaiah stood up, started to say no, then answered, "He is my brother and his medicine is mine."

The four young Sioux grew weary of the talk and argued long and heatedly to kill their prisoner. For a while it seemed that the old Sioux would give in to their arguments, but he stubbornly refused.

With one last, bitter statement the young Sioux grew silent and began examining Isaiah's belongings.

The old one turned back to Isaiah. "I am Talking Lance and I am weary of arguing. I am old and know that sometimes it is good not to kill. We will let your medicine decide your fate."

"Give me a weapon; let me die like a warrior," Isaiah answered.

Talking Lance shook his head, "Anyone can fight if his heart is strong, but I would see if you have medicine and my lance would see. Then we will know if the spirits sent you to this valley."

One of the young men snorted. "How will we know?"

"We will give him the talking paper and this," Talking Lance said as he held out the paper and the vial with the medicine. "If he can reach his friend, then his medicine is great and to kill him would displease the Great Spirit."

A young warrior stepped forward. "You're going to let him go?"

Talking Lance nodded and pointed west down the valley and then to the warrior. "We will continue the chase on foot. You,

Red Wolf, will challenge him first. If you can catch the Crow, you can kill him."

I'll be damned, Isaiah thought, a wise old man. It was the Indian way, whether he be Sioux or Crow. He liked the old one even though he was a Sioux.

"You can go. We will start the chase when you are a long bow shot away."

Isaiah touched his empty knife sheath and held out his hand. The old one shook his head and pointed west.

Isaiah trotted off slowly, his right leg stiff but otherwise he felt fine. He chuckled to himself. If the old one could keep the boys in line, he was safe. What the old one's lance hadn't told the Sioux was that Two Suns had never, not once, lost a footrace. He touched his medicine bundle and thanked the Great Spirit and Doc.

Red Wolf was a good runner and Isaiah had to push harder than he wanted to at the beginning but soon they both settled into a steady pace.

The valley narrowed and widened again, the hills low in one place, sheer and high in another. Isaiah splashed across a small stream, scooped up a handful of clear, cool water, drank it and then splashed some on his glistening body before resuming his run.

They pressed on hour after hour, first one Sioux dogging his heels, then a fresh warrior would take his place. The mounted Sioux rode the high ground, watching the race from the hills that bordered the valley. They shouted encouragement to their runner and occasionally hurled taunts at Isaiah. It began as a game to the young Sioux, but when they realized they couldn't easily overtake him, it settled into a long, grueling trial under the burning sun.

Isaiah hardly noticed the shaking of the ground at first, but when it made the ground pitch and roll, he knew it was a great buffalo herd on the run. Maybe Talking Lance had more medicine than he thought. Then he saw them, coming fast, a wide brown ribbon stretching across the valley. He slowed to a walk and considered his chances. He had no choice but to turn and run toward the Sioux. The Sioux runner also stopped, uncertain what to do. The earth trembled wildly, the roar of hooves like thunder between the hills.

The herd was closing fast. He ran toward a low cut in the hills to the north. The valley was beginning to narrow and the banks became sheerer. The ground moved beneath his feet as he ran harder.

His pursuer stood rooted to the sod, terror on his face and lips moving in his death song. Isaiah didn't slacken, just yelled above the thunder, "Run or die – that cut in the hills." Even as he said it, he knew they couldn't reach it before the buffalo would overtake them. He glanced back. The Sioux was a few paces behind him chest heaving and legs pumping, all thought of combat gone, fleeing for his life.

In the backward glance Isaiah saw the herd squeeze in between the rising banks, and suddenly he remembered his talk with his mother long ago – you could walk across to the other side.

He slackened his pace until the Sioux was at his side. "Follow me. If your heart is strong and your medicine good, we will walk across their backs. It's our only chance."

The buffalo were a scant fifty yards behind them when Isaiah stopped and faced the onrushing mass. He touched his medicine bundle and shouted to the youth, "It is a good day to die," then sprinted toward the herd.

He studied the animals as they ran with shaggy heads bobbing, mouths open, tongues lulling out, and unblinking eyes rolled back in their heads.

Isaiah picked an animal, ran toward it, and measured his leap carefully. He knew he'd get but one chance. His right foot landed between the sharp horns, his left foot touched lightly on the hump, and then he settled astride the shaggy beast. Out of the corner of his eye he saw the young Sioux atop another animal.

Isaiah paused only a second then stood on the swaying animal and began picking his way from animal to animal. The roiling dust stung his eyes and throat as he leapt from animal to animal. After what seemed like hours, the herd thinned and it became difficult to jump from one animal to another. He selected a small critter and settled down behind its hump.

As the herd ran on he lost sight of the young Sioux and wondered if he had made it? He was supposed to hate them, but for some reason he hoped the young brave was still alive.

His extra weight caused the beast to drop further and further back in the herd so, choosing his timing carefully, Isaiah picked an opening and jumped. He lit on his feet and dodged a few old cows and some young calves as they lumbered past.

The earth was churned brown by thousands of hooves and the dust hung like a heavy blanket, but there were no more buffalo to avoid. He had survived. His medicine was strong. He was a Crow warrior. What a story it would make to tell in the lodges.

The wind swept the dust away enough for Isaiah to see the mounted Sioux riding toward him. While he was deciding to run or stand and fight to the death, he heard the old one singing a victory song. It took Isaiah a moment to realize it was for him.

The Sioux rode up with awe on their painted faces and their eyes glittered with excitement. Talking Lance led Red Wolf's war pony and handed the reins to Isaiah. "Your medicine is great. This horse is our gift to you; his owner won't need him anymore. You have brought the buffalo. Here are your weapons."

"You will smoke the pipe with me?" Isaiah asked.

"Our people are hungry. We must go kill the buffalo. Another time we can smoke. Even though you are a Crow with white blood, you are welcome in my lodge anytime. You can even ride with us now."

"It is a great honor," Isaiah said. "It is good to be an Indian again. I will remember Talking Lance and his friends. If I were to be Indian, I would go back to my people. It has been a long time."

"Who was your band's leader?"

Isaiah answered, swinging up on the Sioux pony.

Talking Lance's face grew long and a sadness clouded his eyes. "You have been in the white man's world for a long time. Your people are no more. The white sickness took them."

Isaiah stared at the old man, seeing in his eyes that he spoke the truth. "All?" he asked.

"There is only a shadow left, a few living on a reservation."

Silence, then Talking Lance spoke again, "Perhaps after you take the medicine and the talking paper to your friend you can look for your people at the reservation."

Isaiah fumbled for the paper, it was gone. He frantically opened his war bag. The glass vial was broken. Were there any ties to the white world now? He looked at the hungry Sioux. Reaching down he picked up the Henry and handed it to Talking Lance. He then handed him the box of cartridges. "A gift for you. It can put many buffalo robes in your lodges and meat in your belly. Go. My heart is sick and my mind walks in two paths; I need to let the wind speak to me."

The old Sioux's eyes gleamed as he accepted the gifts. He only nodded toward Isaiah, turned his mount, and loped after the buffalo.

Isaiah sat motionless for many minutes. The wind brought him many familiar smells and sounds. His spirit savored them all, like returning to an old friend's lodge.

He looked up when he heard the shrill cry of a red-tailed hawk that was circling directly above. It dipped in the air current, its shadow passing directly in front of Isaiah as it raced across the prairie toward the setting sun.

He said a Crow prayer for Little Knife, asking the wind to warn his friend that the shadow was falling. His friend would soon know if he would fight or die. Isaiah spoke to the pony, reined around, and rode after the Sioux.

DOC'S MIND WAS EXPLORING feelings long suppressed. Was this lovely woman what Isaiah said he could have if he'd only listen to the wind? Reality, not the wind, told him that unless he could keep Todd Keeferly alive, it didn't much matter.

He returned to his desk, put on his half-rim glasses, and forced his mind to rethink Todd's symptoms. For two hours he again searched through medical books and journals only to admit he had no idea what sickness Todd had, much less how to treat the boy.

He slumped back in his chair, flung his glasses on the desk, and mopped the sweat from his face. Discouraged and bone weary, he caught himself thinking the same thought he had battled during his recovery after the war – would death bring relief?

But, like he always did, he found a reason, a purpose to wait one more day. Maybe Carolyn's warm embrace, which still lingered on his mind and body, was a good reason to wait. And after all, he could always get killed tomorrow. He pushed himself out of the chair, grabbed his medical bag, and made his way down the hall to check on Todd.

The room was stuffy and oppressive with the odor of sweat-soaked bedclothes, urine, and foul breath. He checked Todd's pulse and listened to his heart. Young Keeferly was alive, barely alive. Where was Isaiah Benteen? Doc wet a towel and bathed the young man's fevered face.

While he worked, his mind was bedeviled by thoughts of Carolyn Dawson. Suddenly he wanted to talk to her, wanted to be near her, wanted to hold her close. The need was an ache, but she couldn't want him, couldn't want a man some people considered a coward. Still, there was that damn thing Isaiah had said about listening to the wind, and Isaiah was always right about the wind.

He sat down in the chair beside the bed and picked up his medical bag, his mind screaming that he should not, but his hands ignored his mind. Piece by piece, he took the medical instruments from the bag and laid them on the bed beside Todd. He slowly lifted the bag's false bottom and let his eyes run over the brace of ivory-handled weapons.

He couldn't stop the thoughts marching through his head so he just gave up and let them run their course. It would be so easy, he told himself, and no one on this earth would blame him. He knew if he chose to, his mind and body would make the deadly weapons an extension of his will. In his mind's eye he saw the captain's head over the barrel of the derringer. He visualized the dark hole that would appear between the shaggy brows and shuddered at his medical knowledge of what the .40 caliber ball would do to a man's brain.

His inner eyes switched from the captain to big, crass, and contemptible Jake. Jake would almost be a pleasure, if the derringers would fire after years in the bottom of his medical case. Lost in his thoughts and mental struggle, Doc didn't hear Captain Keeferly enter the doorway. "How's my son?"

Doc grabbed the stethoscope from the bed and managed an even reply. "Alive, but the fever is still raging."

He exhaled a shaky breath and leaned back in the leather chair. Doc noticed that the big man's shirt was soiled and his vest rumpled, but his face was relaxed, less hard than before. He couldn't tear his eyes from the shaggy brows of the man until Keeferly turned to pick up a chair.

Doc glanced again at the guns while the captain's back was turned and saw the engraving dedicated to William Kelley's son – a son who had argued long and hard against any more violence in his life; something he also saw in his mind's eye.

He closed but didn't latch the bag as Keeferly set the chair down in front of Doc, straddled it, and spoke in a low, determined voice, "I've never told anyone this before but I'm going to tell you."

Puzzled, Doc replied, "You don't have to tell me anything unless it pertains to Todd."

The captain glanced at Todd and then back to Doc. "It's got to do with me and Jake. You see we was both with the Massachusetts Regulars back in '40. I'd been made a captain and Jake was a raw recruit. Cholera hit the post and men were dying faster than we could bury them. When things was the worst, the medics skipped out leaving all them sick ones. That's when I begun hating doctors."

Doc started to speak, but the captain leaned forward and talked over his reply. "I made up my mind right then to leave before someone buried me. I was about clear of camp when a sentry stopped me. Jake was also trying to desert that same night and was also challenged by a sentry. We made our escape but we both had to kill the sentries. There's been a price on our heads since."

The captain leaned back and there was a calm about him that was foreign to his rugged features. He reached out and took Todd's hand. "He's going to die, isn't he?"

"I don't know."

Letting go of his son's hand, the captain slowly stood up, set the chair carefully by the nightstand, and moved to the door. He turned, the gentleness gone. "The Good Book still says 'an eye for an eye.'" Then he vanished.

I wonder why the hell he told me this now, Doc thought, then answered his own question by realizing that the captain had no intention of letting them live even if Todd recovers. He tried to sort it all out in his mind until he became unclear and confused. His military experience shouted for him to make a decision, to take command, to attack while he still had the advantage of surprise. He peeked again at the derringers, but he didn't trust his hands to touch them. Instead he relived his encounter with Carolyn until a crushing fatigue overcame him and he fell asleep.

Down the hall in Mrs. Avery's room, Carolyn rocked the baby and prayed Mrs. Avery would fall asleep. It had taken all her patience to quiet Mrs. Avery after the scare Isaiah had given her. Finally, she convinced the new mother that Isaiah was on his way bringing help at this very moment. They'd talked on for almost an hour before Mrs. Avery relaxed.

In fact, Mrs. Avery was now much calmer than Carolyn was. She'd barely been able to talk logically with the mother because her mind kept returning to Doc's statement that he had three firearms. Where could they be hidden? In one of the rooms with the doors nailed shut? Somehow, she had to find them.

Mrs. Avery stirred, "I hate to bother you, but I'd sure like some more tea, if it ain't too much trouble."

Carolyn managed a tired smile. "No trouble at all, but it will take a minute for the water to boil. I'll be back soon as I can." She gently laid the sleeping baby at his mother's side and then made her way to the kitchen.

She stood by the kitchen door fanning herself with a folded newspaper while waiting for the water to boil. The heat was oppressive, making her stitches itch like sin. Her hair hung limp and she felt unclean. So very badly she wanted to take off her clothes and bathe in cool water. She wasn't paying any attention to the captain's and Jake's words that drifted from the sitting room until she heard her name. She tiptoed down the hall and listened.

Jake was pacing like a tethered dog and growled, "I tell you the breed ain't coming back. Todd's as good as dead and it's hotter than hell in this damn house. Let's just kill 'em and be done with it. Anyway, the doctor said he can't do no more for the boy."

Captain Keeferly's voice was detached, monotone. "Justice must be done. They should die, but let's wait another hour. Maybe Todd—"

Jake stopped pacing, his voice now high with emotion. "Can I have the Dawson woman before we kill 'em? I haven't been to Madame Marie's for over two weeks."

Carolyn's mind screamed no, oh please, God, no. She waited for a reply. Surely the captain wouldn't allow such a thing.

The captain's answer stunned her. "She is a pretty thing, a shame for it to go to waste. Serve her right for refusing to come work for me."

Boiling water and tea forgotten, Carolyn fled to the apothecary room. Shaking with fear and anger she began going through the drawers.

Nothing.

The shelves, even the big medicine jars.

No guns.

She listened. Quiet, except for the captain's and Jake's voices in the sitting room. She ran to the kitchen.

Cabinets, drawers, flower bin, pantry.

No weapons.

She hurried back to the study. At the door she stopped and surveyed the room inch by inch. Be calm, she told herself. They have to be here some place. She wished Doc were here. Surely if he knew what Jake was going to do, he'd get the guns and drive them out. But sadly she realized Doc may not be of any help so she began searching for the guns and vowed she'd kill them herself; she'd always had to do things herself. But, the study yielded not a single firearm. Defeated and almost in tears, she sagged into Doc's desk chair.

"About chow time." She jumped. Jake stood in the doorway. "I said the captain and I is hungry. Fetch us some grub, little lady."

He eyed the open drawers and disturbed room. "What you looking for?"

"Something Doc needs for Todd," she lied.

"Don't be taking too long. We're hungry. And I'm especially hungry," he said.

She almost collapsed as he turned and left. A desperate new thought jumped in her mind. She'd say she needed to go to the privy and, when she was outside, she'd make a run for it. Anything was better than waiting like a dumb butcher hog in a pen. She took off her shoes and then removed her petticoat to give her more freedom to run. Upstairs, she thought, I haven't looked upstairs. I have to find a way to get past the captain and Jake so I can search upstairs. If I can't find them upstairs, I'll run. Her mind told her running was useless, but she couldn't endure this any longer.

50

ELMO NIEMECHEK STOPPED AT THE DOOR of their house and turned to his wife. "Jenny, if the worst was to befall me, you know what to do." It was more a statement than question.

She looked up at her husband. "Don't see why you got to go up there. We got a proper sheriff here abouts. It's his job, not yours."

Elmo put a huge arm around Jenny's shoulder. "Ain't right sure the sheriff's proper. Doc's helped us aplenty and now he needs our help. Besides, I've got something to settle with the captain and his crew." He reached up and took a double-barreled shotgun from pegs over the door. He kissed Jenny and then stepped outside.

He walked the alley until he came to a side street that intersected Main at the Mercantile Bank building. Somewhere two cats fought and a dog sat scratching itself in front of the general store, but otherwise Elk Springs was as quiet as a Sunday morning. Quarantine posters fluttered at every building making Elmo wonder just how many more people were about to die. Only this time he suspected the sickness wasn't cholera or any other disease. It was humans preying on other humans. Doc had fought Yankees, he'd fought the Indians, he'd fought cholera, but Elmo didn't think Doc could fight this without violence.

The big blacksmith slowed his stride as he came to Main Street. Wouldn't be no good to walk into the middle of something, he thought, glancing through the bank window and waving to the banker, Jonathan Peterson.

Isaiah should be back most any time now, he thought and hoped to see the breed's pony in front of the sheriff's office. It wasn't. Well, maybe he went directly to Oak Grove. There wasn't a single Guidon K mount on the street. However, at the north end of Main Street a crowd of townsfolk were arguing with the McGregor clan. Elmo guessed that hell would start popping if those boys got involved.

Looking up at Oak Grove he could see wagons and buggies turned over in the yard plus firewood and logs arranged to make a bulwark of defense. Where in the hell was the sheriff he wondered? Elmo started toward the crowd, then stopped. Something was wrong at the bank. Banker Peterson had moved his mouth wide when he look at Elmo through the window. He'd first thought Peterson was saying "hello." Now he was sure the banker was saying "help."

Elmo hurried to the back of the bank and tried the door. Locked. He shrugged his shoulders and guessed it'd have to be through the front. When he stepped softly to the front door, he found the shade was drawn and the "closed" sign stared at him through the window. He stepped back and with a kick sent the door crashing open. The sheriff, on his knees in front of the open safe, dropped the gold bars and clawed at his belt gun. Elmo vaulted over the dividing panel and slammed a big fist into the lawman's chest. Sheriff Barton bounced off the safe while still struggling to draw his Colt Dragoon. Elmo slapped the gun from his hand, laid his shotgun aside, and shook the lawman like a dog shaking an opossum. "There ain't no contagious sickness at Doc's, is there?"

No answer.

"He was robbing the bank, but I think you've killed him," the banker stammered.

Elmo held the sheriff at arm's length with one hand and drew back his fist. "You were lying about things at Doc's, right?"

The sheriff looked at the fist, then at Elmo. "I was lying. Captain and Jake will kill 'em anyway. What difference does it make? There's plenty of gold here for us both." Elmo hit the sheriff square in the chest and the lawman's eyes rolled back and his body went limp.

Elmo untied the banker and then helped stack the gold back into the safe. The banker locked the safe door while Elmo grabbed his shotgun, and then they both hustled up the street toward the crowd. Shoving their way into the middle of the men Elmo shouted for quiet. "I've just had a talk with the sheriff and he's admitted there is no need for the town to be quarantined. Tell 'em, Peterson."

"That's right," the banker said, then added, "the sheriff tried to rob the bank, but Elmo stopped him – I think he killed him."

There was a silence, then a babble of voices. Elmo shouted for quiet again. "I'm going up to Oak Grove. Those who think we owe Doc some help can come with me. The rest get out of the way."

Half the men followed the banker toward the bank while those remaining crowded around the big blacksmith. Will pushed his way through the group and faced Elmo. "I ain't got nothing against helping Doc, but I'll be wanting Keeferly."

Elmo took a quick count of the men standing with him before he answered, "Since we're all going up there, let's divide up and get a battle plan."

Will interrupted, "Don't need no plan. The McGregors are going straight through the buggers. The boys'll keep 'em busy while I go through the front door."

Elmo knew by the look on the bearded faces that the front of the house was spoken for. "Well then, I reckon we'll be coming through the back door. Let's go!" He led his small group of citizens to flank the house through the oak grove.

Will McGregor formed up his small command and stepped out to the cadence of pipes and drum.

51

DOC'S BODY SLEPT THE SLEEP of exhaustion while his mind hurried through corridors of remembrance. It deftly sidestepped present happenings and people, like Todd Keeferly, Isaiah Benteen, and Carolyn Dawson, to grope its way back to Shiloh.

When his mind grew tired of stumbling over the memories of dying men in blue and gray uniforms, it switched to painted Sioux warriors riding war ponies around naked men beside a rock platform. It stopped to poke at images of cholera, death, and a beautiful lady. The dreaming continued on to include old Doc Jacobson, his worn volume of Sun Tzu's wisdom, and solemn nonviolence vows. The nocturnal return of exploding melons and eternal buzzards brought Doc awake, wide-eyed and sweating.

He came slowly to the present. I don't know which is worse, then or now, he thought. He knew Todd was dead as soon as he touched the boy's wrist. He started to draw the covers over the corpse, then decided against it. A little deception wouldn't matter now since he'd reached a decision on how to deal with the captain and Jake.

He quickly shoved his instruments back into his medical bag, left the room, and went directly to his study. As soon as he stepped through the door he knew that Carolyn had been searching for the guns. He had to find her alone before the captain discovered Todd.

Outside he could hear voices much nearer now, so he went to the study window where he'd watched Carolyn visit the graves on Sunday mornings. He saw Elmo talking with Will McGregor and his brothers. Was help on the way?

It didn't matter now; he was ready, but he must find Carolyn. She wasn't in Mrs. Avery's room, nor Todd's room, nor the exam room. He could tell she'd searched the kitchen. Stepping into the hall he nearly collided with Carolyn.

"Shh," he whispered. "Quick, to the study."

She tried to shove past him saying, "Todd's—"

He put his hand over her mouth and pressed her against the wall. "Come with me. It's your only chance," he said softly, almost intoxicated by the closeness of her.

Slowly she calmed and Doc removed his hand. "But," she said quietly, trying to push him away. "Todd's dead. I heard the captain tell Jake he could rape me before they kill us. I'm making a run for it."

He drew her close, whispering, "The guns are in the study."

She pulled back and studied his face. "But, I searched—"

Doc interrupted. "I know. Come with me and I'll show you the guns."

"Thank you, dear God, thank you." She clung to him a moment and asked, "How many? And, will you help me kill them?"

"I'll try to reason with them first," he said as they stepped into the study. He closed and locked the door.

"Where are they?" Carolyn asked. "Hurry, sooner or later the captain will check on Todd and discover he's dead."

Doc emptied his medical bag onto the desk, pulled out the false bottom, and set the bag before Carolyn. "I recall you know how to use a rifle. Do you know how to use these?"

"Yes," she said reaching for the derringers.

Doc took her hand before she could grab the guns. She didn't pull away but leaned against him and put her head on his chest. Her nearness overwhelmed; outside gunfire erupted and shouting grew nearer, but he couldn't push her away. Instead he pulled her close, thinking of Isaiah's lectures about listening to the wind and what he could have if he'd only listen. "Carolyn,

Isaiah was right. I should have listened to the wind. Now, it may be too late."

"Too late for what?"

"Too late to—"

A bullet shattered a window glass, and Captain Keeferly's voice came from behind the study's door. "Kick the son of a bitch in."

"It's Jake and the captain," Carolyn said looking into Doc's eyes. She saw no fear there, only a quiet resolve. She reached again for the derringers.

"No," he said picking up the guns and placing them on the corner of his desk.

The banging at the door grew louder. Carolyn glanced at the door and then at Doc. "You said you didn't want to fight or kill anymore so give me the guns."

"I realize now that Isaiah was right about another thing. Carolyn, please promise me you won't interfere. I will protect you, I promise."

Doc leaned against the desk and removed the lower half of the cane's shaft.

"What are you doing? Just give me the guns."

"Remember I said I had three guns? This is a 12-gauge loaded with buck and ball. If it fires, it will eliminate our problem. And, I think Elmo and others are on their way to help."

"Please, can I just have one of the derringers?" Carolyn pleaded.

"Only if they kill me. Then you can defend yourself. But now please get behind me."

A heavy crash announced the entrance of Jake and the captain. Jake's knife flashed from its sheath as Captain Keeferly drew his Colt and leveled it at Doc. "My son is dead. As I promised, an eye for an eye."

Holding the cane in both hands, Doc leveled it at the pair. "I don't want to kill you, but I will. Now get the hell out of my house."

The captain and Jake paused at his change of demeanor. "Kill him! His own crew says he's a coward and won't fight," the captain yelled at Jake.

Doc didn't waver. He just rested against the desk holding his cane with the derringers beside him on the desk. "Don't be fooled," Doc said. "Sometimes things ain't what they seem." He was aware that Carolyn's hand was on his shoulder and he could feel her body against his.

"Go ahead, Jake, carve up that damn cripple, and then you can have that stubborn woman. Maybe she won't act so high and mighty afterwards."

"Captain, I don't want to kill you, but I will. Anyway, if I don't, you'll never leave this house alive unless you surrender," Doc said.

Jake lunged; the roar of Doc's firearm was deafening. Jake staggered back with the slug in his chest. Surprise registered on his face as he dropped his knife and stumbled backwards into the captain.

Doc exchanged the cane for a derringer. Through the smoke he saw the captain drop his six-gun and saw the dark spot on his forehead that meant one buckshot had found its mark. Doc had one of the derringers leveled at the pair when Will McGregor burst through the doorway with his sword at the ready.

He jabbed the captain's chest with the point of the claymore. "I don't reckon you'll be bother'n any more women and lasses now." Will turned to Doc. "I was hoping to kill him myself, but he's dead and I'm satisfied."

Doc lowered the derringer as Carolyn put her arms around him. "I didn't want to kill him, but Isaiah was right."

Will looked at the two. "You and your woman, being alright?"

"She's not—I think we're going to be fine."

Epilogue

IN THE YEAR OF OUR LORD 1868 Dr. Benjamin Fredrick Kelley found his way out of the valley of the shadow of death and stood at last on the sun-swept plains of peace.

Listen.

Doc's ledger entries of September 22, 1868:

Isaiah Benteen never returned.

Todd Keeferly died of an unknown illness. I failed him.

Should I not survive, I, Benjamin Fredrick Kelley, make this last will and testament: Half of the horse herd belongs to Isaiah Benteen or his kin. Five thousand dollars goes to Elmo Niemechek to be used to help any men of the wagon train to move on west if they so wish. The remainder of my earthly goods shall go to Carolyn Dawson, with the sincerest of wishes that she maintain Oak Grove as a residence for herself as well as an establishment to succor the sick and infirm.

The final entry read:

I finally realized my father was right about my vow. As a result I killed Captain Keeferly and Jake. I have no regrets. I also realized that I should have listened to the wind sooner.

Listen.

"Being deeply loved by someone gives you strength, while loving someone deeply gives you courage."

— LAO TZU

KANSAS NOTABLE BOOK AWARD AUTHOR and state native Rod Beemer is a writer, researcher, and speaker who has authored and co-authored twelve nonfiction books, a novel, numerous magazine and newspaper articles, as well as inclusion in several anthologies. He is a member of the Kansas State Historical Society, West Texas Historical Association, Smoky Hill Trail Association, Westerners International, Fort Larned Old Guard, and the Custer Battlefield Historical & Museum Association. Rod lives in Minneapolis, Kansas, with his wife of forty-nine years.

Visit the author's site at **rodbeemer.com**.

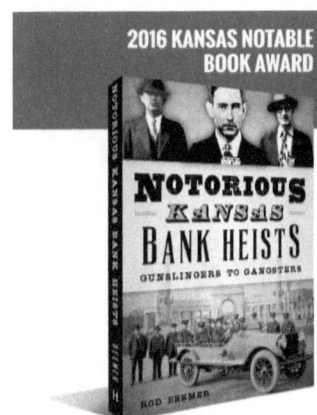